PRAISE FOR THE NOVELS OF JACK DU BRUL

"ACTION-PACKED."
—*Publishers Weekly*

"A MASTER STORYTELLER."
—Clive Cussler

"STRONG, FRESH WRITING."
—*Kirkus Reviews*

"MERCER [IS] A COMBINATION OF DIRK PITT
AND JAMES BOND."
—*The Sunday Oklahoman*

The adventure novels of Jack Du Brul

Pandora's Curse

"A rare treat—a thriller that blends some of modern history's most vexing enigmas with a hostile, perfectly realized setting. This is one thriller that really delivers: great characters combined with a breakneck pace and almost unbearable suspense."
— Douglas Preston and Lincoln Child, coauthors of *The Ice Limit* and *Relic*

The Medusa Stone

"[*The Medusa Stone*'s] nearly 500 pages of fast-paced prose propel DuBrul closer to the front ranks of thriller authors." —*Publishers Weekly*

"**Jack Du Brul is one of the leaders of adventurous intrigue novels.** The story line of his latest thriller continually ebbs and flows, but each new spurt builds the tension even further until the audience realizes that this is a one-sitting novel in spite of its size. Philip Mercer is a fabulous lead character and the support cast brings to life Eritrea and some questionable activities in the Mediterranean area. However, in hindsight, what makes Mr. DuBrul's novel a strong candidate for adventure book of the year is the brilliant fusion of Eritrea, its people and customs woven into a dramatic plot." —*The Midwest Book Review*

Vulcan's Forge

"An exciting, well-honed thriller that will have Clive Cussler fans taking note of the new kid on the block."
— William Heffernan, author of *The Dinosaur Club*

"DuBrul's well-calculated debts to Fleming, Cussler, Easterman, and Lustbader, his technological, political, and ecological research, and **his natural gift for storytelling bode well.**" —*Publishers Weekly*

ALSO BY JACK DU BRUL

*The Medusa Stone**
Charon's Landing
Vulcan's Forge

*Published by Onyx

PANDORA'S CURSE

Jack Du Brul

AN ONYX BOOK

ONYX
Published by New American Library, a division of
Penguin Putnam Inc., 375 Hudson Street,
New York, New York 10014, U.S.A.
Penguin Books Ltd, 27 Wrights Lane,
London W8 5TZ, England
Penguin Books Australia Ltd, Ringwood,
Victoria, Australia
Penguin Books Canada Ltd, 10 Alcorn Avenue,
Toronto, Ontario, Canada M4V 3B2
Penguin Books (N.Z.) Ltd, 182–190 Wairau Road,
Auckland 10, New Zealand

Penguin Books Ltd, Registered Offices:
Harmondsworth, Middlesex, England

First published by Onyx, an imprint of New American Library,
a division of Penguin Putnam Inc.

First Printing, September 2001
10 9 8 7 6 5 4 3 2 1

*Published in the year of our wedding,
this book is for Debbie, with all my love.*

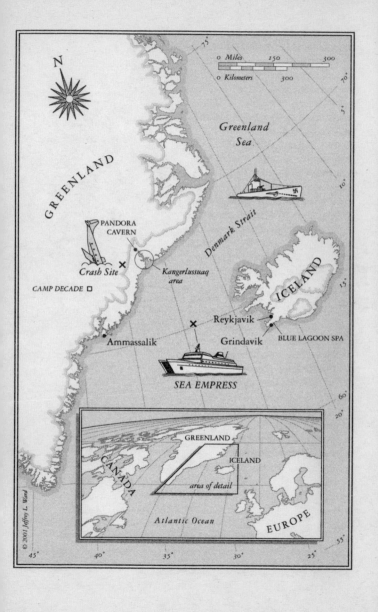

The entire length of the Air Force C-97 Stratofreighter shuddered as the port-side outboard engine began misfiring again. This time was much worse
than before and rather than risk his plane becoming
too unstable, Major Jack Delaney shut down the
twenty-eight-cylinder Pratt and Whitney Wasp. He reduced the drag by feathering the prop so the blades
cut the slipstream edgewise, but the plane still felt
sluggish in his hands.

"We're in a world of hurt, aren't we, Major?" asked
his copilot, Lieutenant Jerry Winger.

Delaney didn't respond as he studied the gauges for
the three working engines. Every instinct told him that
they hadn't seen the last of whatever had affected the
power plant. The remaining engines were running hot,
making him think that the problem wasn't with the
plane, but with the fuel they'd taken on in England.
Most likely poorly maintained tanker trucks had contaminated the fuel. He looked out the windshield,
known as the "greenhouse" throughout the Air Force
because it was made up of nineteen individual panes
of Plexiglas. It resembled the cockpit of the venerable
B-29, on which the Stratofreighter was based.

Eighteen thousand feet below the Military Air
Transport Service cargo plane, the desolate north Atlantic was as dark as the slag heaps in Delaney's native
West Virginia. The sky was thankfully clear. Only a
few stringers of high cirrus clouds smeared the air high
above the plane, but Delaney didn't know how much
longer his aircraft would remain aloft.

"Yeah, Jer, we might just be," Delaney finally replied. Glancing at Winger, he saw his own concern reflected in the younger man's eyes. Despite the heat blasting into the pressurized cabin, the major felt a chill race across his skin like sheet lightning. "Tom, where the hell are we?"

Tom Sanders, the navigator, was seated at his tiny desk behind the cockpit, a chart spread before him and a worried frown on his face. "Closer to Greenland than Iceland if that's what you're wondering."

"That's what I was afraid of," the pilot grunted.

"I'd say we're about forty miles from the Greenland coast."

Delaney's experience was that it took a series of small mishaps to lead to the catastrophe of a crash. Except, he thought darkly, during the war when flak or a Japanese Zero came out of nowhere. He'd had a few close scrapes during his command of a B-29, but Delaney had never lost a man. Now, however, his luck might have finally run out. This time fate was dealing him one problem after another, and there wasn't much the major could do.

It had started an hour out of England when they were rocked by a sudden wind gust that shifted an improperly secured cargo pallet in the hold of the giant aircraft. It was not a mortal problem; it merely caused the C-97 to fly out of trim. Delaney was forced to keep firm pressure on the wheel so the plane maintained an even keel. He had reported the incident back to the controllers and had them inform the isolated Air Force base at Thule, Greenland, that their supply plane would be coming in late. He also said he wanted the head of whoever was responsible for tying down cargo when he returned. The crew then had several trouble-free hours until an electrical fault had sparked in the radios, shorting out the entire system. They were one hundred miles past Iceland, flying northwest, and suddenly the plane was without communications. Tom Sanders had tried to fix the set but got nothing for his troubles except some singed fingertips. Delaney had considered turning back, except problems at Dover Air Force Base, where normal cargo flights to Thule originated, had hampered three recent attempts to resupply the base above the Arctic Circle. He also knew the narrow weather window they were enjoying would close before another mission could take off. He now considered his decision to press on as another of the small mishaps befalling the crew of the Stratofreighter.

Then, just half an hour ago, Lieutenant Winger had noticed the engines were running hot. Delaney had opened the cowls around the four Pratt and Whitneys in an effort to cool them, adding more drag to the aircraft and slowing them further. The tactic had worked for a while but the temperatures began creeping inexorably back toward the red. That was when the number one engine began to misfire. It cleared itself for a few minutes and then started sputtering again, vibrating the airframe until her aluminum ribs creaked. Delaney had no choice but to shut it down.

"When the temp drops enough, we'll try to restart the engine," he told Winger. "Tom, are there any landing strips on this side of Greenland?"

"No, sir. Chart shows nothing except mountains and ice. There is a place called Camp Decade about a hundred and fifty miles south of where we're going to cross the coast, but its strip's designed for planes with skis."

"Damn." Delaney paused, his mind working out distances and odds. "All right. If the engine doesn't refire smoothly, we'll swing around and try for Iceland."

"Major, that's about two hundred and thirty miles behind us." There was a tight edge in Sanders's voice. He was too young to have seen combat during the war, and Delaney suspected that this was the first time the young officer had tasted true fear.

During the five minutes the pilot waited for the number one engine to cool, the flight deck was quiet, even when the towering ramparts and dark fjords that protected eastern Greenland came into view. Delaney had never seen such a forlorn place. The mountains were all snowcapped, and behind them, the relentless Greenland ice shelf pressed against their landward side so that great glaciers spilled between the valleys, tumbling to the ocean like frozen waterfalls. Delaney knew that, beyond the small strip of coast, there was a sea of ice about eight hundred and fifty thousand miles square and as thick as any ocean was deep.

"Okay, Major, temp is down in number one. In fact, it looks like all the horses are running in a row now."

Delaney scanned the gauges and saw that the open cowlings had worked in cooling the engines again. He restarted number one and it began purring sedately, as though there had never been a problem. Working the prop controls, he felt the four blades bite into the air and the C-97 become more responsive.

"That's a little better," he breathed and Winger and Sanders exchanged grins. "Feet dry in about five minutes."

The plane cleared the mountains at one hundred and eighty knots, well below her optimum cruising speed and much lower than her most efficient altitude. Beyond the strip of ice-carved mountains, Delaney and Winger were faced with an expanse of ice that stretched far beyond the horizon. Under the immense weight of new snow dropping in the interior, the billions of tons of ice were slowly moving toward the coast like an endless conveyor belt. As the ice moved, it scraped against the underlying rock so that any irregularities under the mile-thick mantle appeared on the surface as huge fractured ridges. The cap was so riven that to Delaney it looked like a hurricane sea had been flash frozen, every wave rendered in razor-sharp crests that sometimes reached a hundred feet into the air.

"Jesus," he said under his breath.

Lieutenant Winger was just turning to say something to Delaney when engine number one exploded. The double banks of cylinders came apart like a bomb, shrapnel and oil and burning fuel blasting apart the nacelle like it had been hit by antiaircraft artillery. In seconds, the wing around the burning engine was blackened by flame, and soon it began to come apart as the wind ripped at the tears in the aluminum caused by red-hot debris.

The C-97 winged over as she lost lift on her left side. Delaney fought the plane, taking just an instant to see the altimeter spinning backward in a blur. He noted that Winger was already shutting off fuel to the wrecked power plant. Good man.

"Tom, what do you see?" the pilot shouted, his lips pulled back around his teeth from the exertion of keeping his crippled plane in the air.

The navigator looked out the tiny window next to his station. His training had taken over, and rather than give in to the fear that cramped his stomach, he spoke calmly. "The engine's gone and the wing looks like it's about to let go too. She's still burning. Wait. She's going out."

"Fuel's off," Winger said as he straightened back to the controls and added his strength to Delaney's on the wheel.

"Son of a bitch, we've lost most of the aileron on the port side. Jerry, feather the number four prop. We've got to level her out. She's pulling too hard on the starboard side."

Winger did as ordered, and since the crew halved the thrust on her one side, the Stratofreighter slowly began to straighten, but still she was losing altitude. In the thirty seconds since the explosion, they had dropped to ten thousand feet and continued to plummet. The two pilots held on grimly, teasing the weakened controls so the plane stayed level. There was nothing they could do about holding her in the sky. It was just a matter of how gently they could put her on the ice.

"Start looking for a smooth area we can set this crate." Delaney had recovered from his initial terror and his voice was crisp and commanding once again.

"I'm looking, but the ice is just too broken up." Winger glanced at the altimeter. "Five thousand feet."

In the denser atmosphere, there was a little more lift under the wings and her descent became easier. Delaney tried to raise her nose slightly, hoping to regain some altitude, but the C-97 dipped to port again. For a panicked second he fought to level her. "What do you see out there?"

Before Winger could respond, the cockpit was suddenly filled with smoke, a noxious mixture of burning oil and hydraulic fluid that cut visibility down to zero. The thick pall made all three men gag as petrochemicals scoured their throats and burned into their eyes like acid. Sanders screamed that he had a fire right behind him. Groping blindly, Delaney reached forward to shut off the cabin pressure and vent the cockpit's air. In an instant the smoke cleared, leaving the men choking to draw in the fresh, yet frigid, air.

"Get that fire out," Delaney rasped. In the moments between the time the fire ignited and the time he'd cleared the cockpit, the plane had lost another thousand feet. It was now dipping in a dangerous, lazy spiral. "Talk to me, Jerry. What's out there?"

"Nothing." Winger coughed, one hand on his chest as if the gesture would extinguish the pain from his scalded lungs. "Hold on a second!" He studied an area of clear ice. It was under the shadow of a black granite mountain.

"I got it," Delaney said at the same instant Winger pointed it out to him.

"Fire's out, Major, but I can't promise for how long." Sanders had been hardest hit by the smoke and his voice sounded like he was drawing his last breath.

Banking the lumbering cargo plane as gently as he could, Major Delaney brought them around, lining up the C-97's bulbous nose with the patch of smooth ice with as much care as he'd ever shown in his life. They were at two thousand feet, and the airspeed was down to one hundred and ten knots. He judged that his landing site was about four miles away and began to reduce their altitude. This was a one-shot attempt and his knuckles were white on the control wheel. He barely noticed that the cockpit temperature was thirty degrees below zero and ice was forming on the inside of the windows.

"She's feeling a little more responsive," Winger said as he helped turn the C-97 into the prevailing northward wind for her final approach. "Must be the thicker air."

"Yeah," Delaney agreed, feeling just a touch of optimism for the first time since the explosion. Every second he had the plane under control meant their chances were that tiny bit better.

"Should we try flaps?"

"No. If they don't deploy on the port side, the plane'll flip."

At two miles out, the pilots could see that the area they intended to use as a landing strip wasn't nearly as smooth as they'd first thought. It was ravaged by the high winds, and the layer of new snow that would have cushioned the plane had been torn away, leaving grotesquely shaped daggers of ice that could tear through the Boeing's thin skin and slice open her fuel tanks. Delaney ordered Winger to dump their remaining fuel, then prepared himself for the inevitable lift as the plane became lighter. He calculated that there would be just enough Avgas in the lines for him to maintain power until the plane was safely down. He feared fire more than he feared the upcoming landing. He'd seen too many comrades returning from bombing missions in crippled planes make a safe touchdown only to have their B-29s burst into flames on the runway.

"What about the landing gear?" Winger's hand was poised over the switches.

"I'd rather flop her in on her belly. We can't risk a landing strut hitting one of those ice ridges."

Had they lost their instruments, there would have been no way to tell their proximity to the ground. It was one of the bewildering aspects of flying in Arctic conditions: the absolute sameness wherever you looked. It was mostly the trees Delaney missed. He could determine altitude by gauging their height. His only visual reference here was the barren mountains looming out the starboard windows. Experience said they were about three thousand feet high, but they could easily be just three hundred. His hands tightened even further on the yoke. The cold was affecting him now. His eyes felt dried out though tears streamed down his cheeks. He could barely feel the rudder pedals. The altimeter spun through five hundred feet.

The Stratofreighter droned in, her two working engines maintaining a steady descent. Details of the ice field became crisper the closer they got and what Delaney and Winger saw was not good. This would be a rough landing even if the ice were smooth. But it wasn't. The veil of snow blowing off the ice swirled and eddied against countless concrete-hard ridges.

Delaney bumped the throttles, feeling he needed a bit more altitude before flaring the crippled plane. She came in level despite the wind's desire to slew her around. The closest mountain was only a quarter mile off the right wing, yet it offered little protection from deadly wind shears. He sensed a gust coming up and reacted accordingly, fighting the spongy controls to keep the wings of the artificial horizon indicator balanced. "Call the altitude."

"One hundred feet," Winger replied at once. "Tom, you strapped in tight?"

Sanders's answer was a pained moan. Delaney had the plane, so Winger twisted around to check on the radioman. He gasped. Tom Sanders's face was coated with blood that ran from his nose in twin jets and steamed in the flight deck's freezing air. Most of the blood had solidified into a crusty sheet covering the lower half of his face. He cradled his head in his mittened hands, pressing against his skull with so much force his upper body trembled. His eyes bulged as though they were on stalks, and more blood leaked from around them.

"Tom, what happened?" Winger assumed their radioman had hit his face against the navigation table.

Sanders moaned again, louder, and began clawing at his chest, smearing blood on his leather jacket like paint strokes.

"Jerry, I need you," Jack Delaney called. They were fifty feet above the ice.

Winger turned back to the controls. "Something's wrong with Tom. He's hurt."

A gust took the C-97, pushing it to the left. Winger and Delaney responded in concert, easing the plane back on course. They brought the nose up ever so slightly. Air beneath the wings was forced against the ice, providing a cushion called ground effect that the plane gently sank through.

"Speed's one hundred knots."

Delaney's concentration was total. This was nothing like the countless flights he'd done for the Berlin Airlift, where planes were stacked up four and five high waiting for landing instructions. This was a one-time thing: land her safely or crash. There was no third option.

In the clear air, the ground came up deceptively fast. He held her aloft for a moment longer, then felt pressure against the yoke as though a weight had been forced against Winger's column. He turned and saw his copilot slumped forward in his seat, his stiffened arms pushing on his wheel. Winger spasmed, throwing himself back again. Droplets of blood from his nose and eyes splattered the inside of the cockpit. A scream came out as a gurgling cry. More blood fountained from his lips. Delaney guessed that it was the effects of the smoke inhalation. Fortunately he hadn't gotten it as strongly as his two crewmen.

There was no time to help. Delaney focused his vision on the landing just as the fully loaded plane hit the ice. With a rending scrape, her belly smashed into the ground. Delaney was instantly blinded by a fury of ice particles and snow. He felt the props on the two working engines tear into the surface and then shatter, the huge blades breaking off, one sounding like it had scythed through the aluminum skin of the payload area.

The engine drone was replaced by the sound of the plane being ripped apart by the ice. Every jarring crash into a ridge slammed Delaney against his seat restraints until his shoulders felt broken. It went on and on. The airspeed indicator had barely dipped below one hundred knots. It wasn't possible, Delaney thought. They should have been slowing.

His view was completely whited out. He had no references, nothing to judge their position or progress. But it seemed that the plane was turning to the right, toward the mountains. The shaking vibrations continued unabated, the airframe shuddering. Delaney's head pounded with the strain of trying to see what was happening. He kept his hands away from the control yoke, but his feet remained on the rudder pedals. Now he was sure the plane was turning to the right, so he applied left rudder, hoping to straighten them out to avoid the rocky projections that fronted the mountains. When he felt he had corrected the skid, he released the rudder and prayed he was right.

Blinded by the maelstrom of snow blowing around the hurtling aircraft, Delaney couldn't have known how wrong his perception had been. The plane had been following a straight line until he hit the rudder pedal. The pilot's actions turned the Stratofreighter, and now she was traveling toward a gentle hill that rose out of the ice. The plane hit it and climbed up to its crest. The low friction between aircraft and ice had not reduced her speed enough and for a moment they became airborne again.

Lifting off the surface, the plane flew out of the snow it had kicked up. Delaney screamed, seeing they were headed for the rocks. The C-97 hit the ground a second time, more violently than the first. The ice here wasn't level. It sloped down toward the mountains, riding up and over hills that aeons of glaciation had worn down. Incredibly, the plane picked up speed like a toboggan. Delaney's vision was obscured once again, and for this, he was thankful. There was nothing he could do.

The aircraft hit an outcrop of rock. The crash twisted it on its axis so that the port wing led its headlong rush. Momentum tilted the plane until the wing hit the ice and gouged a furrow into it, throwing off tons of material like a snowplow. This was the drag the plane needed to slow, and when the wing finally snapped near its tip, it was moving at no more than thirty knots. Another impact with a rock scrubbed off more speed and Delaney felt that they would make it.

Several windows had shattered and snow blew into the cockpit on a shrieking wind. Delaney's face was scoured as though hit by a sandblaster. Even numbed, he knew he was bleeding. The C-97 stopped suddenly when her nose dug into a snowbank on the leeward edge of a foothill. Avalanches of snow poured through the broken windows, piling into the cockpit until Delaney's legs were buried. But he was alive.

At first everything felt silent and still. He sat there, his labored breathing producing billows of condensation like cigarette smoke. But he could not hear it or feel it. Everything just felt calm as his terror subsided into immeasurable relief. And with relief came pride. Not one in twenty pilots could have pulled that off. Not one in fifty.

Only then did he become aware of the wind howling outside and the volleys of ice that raked the fuselage like machine gun fire. He wiped his cheeks, and his hands came away covered with blood. He felt no pain—he was too numb for that—but it reminded him of Winger. In his seat, the copilot was dead, his eyes wide and sightless. The blood on his face had turned into a frozen mask.

"Tom?" Delaney called to the navigator behind him. "Tom, are you okay?"

There was no response. His crew was dead. The veteran pilot couldn't allow himself grief just yet. He knew that if he didn't act soon, he'd be joining his

men. First, he had to dig himself out of the cockpit.
So much snow had blown through the windows that
he couldn't move his legs more than a fraction of an
inch, and even that took all his strength. He felt weak,
weaker than he should have. Delaney wanted to close
his eyes and rest for just a minute.

A particularly loud fusillade of ice pummeling the
aircraft roused him even as his eyelids drooped. Once
he was free of the flight deck, Delaney was sure he'd
be all right. Loaded onto the Stratofreighter were
thirty tons of supplies destined for Thule, including
fuel, food, survival clothing, and other Arctic gear—
everything he would need to survive on the ice until
rescue came.

Of that he was supremely confident. They would be
searching for him within hours of his overdue arrival
at the base. He could use the plane as a base until
then, warm and with his belly full. It was only a matter
of time, a few days, maybe a week at the most. But
they would find him.

If only his head didn't ache so much. If only he
could stop the nosebleed that continued to pour cop-
pery fluid into his mouth . . .

When the weather was nice, the old man and his little dachshund were a fixture along Karntnerstrasse. The trendy shopping street that passed next to the inner city's celebrated Opera House was regularly jammed with gaping tourists and hustling locals, yet many of the shop owners recognized the shuffling man and his sausage-shaped dog. He had walked this route for years. Many called him Herr Doktor, though no one knew he truly deserved such a title. It did fit him, however. His eyes were bright despite his years and his voice was captivating and learned.

It was late July, and the air was warm and filled with the smells of pastry and traffic. The Doktor was affected by the pains of age, so he wore a thin jacket over his buttoned shirt and cardigan and a homburg on his head. In winter, Handel, his dachshund, sported a tartan sweater that made her look like a small piece of luggage, but today her sleek black fur glistened like anthracite.

He strode with a special purpose this morning and many who recognized him were surprised to see him walking so early. Usually he wouldn't pass the wedding cake–like Baroque Staatsoper until ten or ten thirty. Handel seemed to sense his urgency and she trotted at his side obediently. Beyond the looming Finance Ministry building, the 444-foot spire of Stephansdom Cathedral shot into the air. The massive Gothic church with its mosaic-tiled roof was the symbol for Vienna the way Paris was defined by the Eiffel Tower.

Before reaching Johannesgasse, the old man guided

his dog to the right, waiting at the curb for several red trams and a string of cars and trucks to thunder past. The exhaust of so many vehicles had darkened the lower floors of many of the buildings so that architectural details were lost under countless years of grime. In the warren of small streets near St. Anne's Church, Handel began to get excited. She knew they were approaching their destination.

The house, like all the others on the narrow lane, was two stories tall and fronted with white stucco. There was a tiny courtyard garden behind it and decorative wrought ironwork over the windows and at the eave of the steep roof. Affixed next to the heavy door was a discreet bronze plaque that read INSTITUTE FOR APPLIED RESEARCH.

The men who ran the Institute allowed their caretaker, Frau Goetz, to live in the two-room apartment tucked into the back corner of the house. Though it was only nine, she already had the front door unlocked, and when the Doktor stepped into the entry, he could smell coffee and a freshly made torte. He reached down to unclip Handel's leash, and she ran off to her favorite spot in the back of the house, where the morning sun had warmed her blankets.

"Guten Morgen, Herr Doktor," Frau Goetz said, coming out of the kitchen to help the elderly history professor off with his jacket.

"Guten Morgen, Frau Goetz," replied Doktor Jacob Eisenstadt.

The two had known each other for forty years, and yet they had never uttered the other's given name. Only a few years junior to her employer, Frau Goetz shared his deep respect for the more formal traditions from before the war. He was no more likely to call her Ingrid than she was to wear slacks. This in no way diminished the care she showed Eisenstadt and his partner in the Institute, Professor Theodor Weitzmann. Both men had been widowers for so long that without her influence they would have reverted to a bachelor's slovenliness. She made sure the clothes they

wore had the proper number of buttons and the lunch
she prepared for them would be at least one whole-
some meal they ate each day.

"Professor Weitzmann is already upstairs," Frau
Goetz informed him. "He beat you here by an hour."

"We agreed not to come in before ten. The old fool
couldn't wait, eh?"

"Apparently not, Herr Doktor." The housekeeper
knew what these men did and believed strongly in
their cause, but she just couldn't get caught up in one
more batch of musty papers the way they did. At times
they were like young boys. "I will bring aspirin for his
eyestrain when I bring up your lunch."

"Danke," Eisenstadt said absently. He had already
turned toward the stairs.

The Institute was cluttered beyond reason, and no
amount of straightening by Frau Goetz could help.
She dusted regularly but so many old books and papers arrived at the quiet house that she could never
seem to keep up. Bookcases lined every wall in the
front rooms, stacked floor to ceiling and interrupted
only by the small windows that overlooked the street.
There were even shelves above the doors for little-
used manuscripts and documents. There were books
in the bathroom, piles of loose papers atop the toilet
tank, and since Frau Goetz had her own shower in
the apartment, the claw-footed tub was also mounded
with binders of material. The stairs to the second floor
were narrow and made more so by piles of books on
one side of each tread.

Every book and binder and loose file of documents
ran to a single theme and Doktor Eisenstadt had read
all of it. This had been his life for forty years: accumu-
lating information, sifting through it carefully to find
the one thread he could pull to get answers and
retribution.

On the wall at the top of the stairs was a narrow
space between two more bookcases. In a simple frame
was a picture of Eisenstadt's inspiration, Simon
Weisenthal, and below it was a epitaph etched in a

piece of wood and signed by the great man himself:
NEVER AGAIN. Eisenstadt didn't need to see the en-
graving as a reminder. His own memories and the
numbers tattooed on his forearm would never let
him forget.

Like Weisenthal, Eisenstadt and Weitzmann were
Camp survivors turned Nazi hunters. More accurately,
these two were hunters for the gold and other precious
commodities stolen from the Jews by the Nazi regime.

At the head of the stairs, Eisenstadt turned to his
left and stepped into the office. "Theodor, we promised not to come in early today," he said, though he
wasn't really upset.

"You are here an hour before your normal arrival
too." Theodor Weitzmann was shorter than his partner and not as round in the middle. His hair was a
wild mane of white, and his eyebrows were huge
bushes above his dark eyes.

The office overlooked the garden and smelled of
pipe tobacco, for both men indulged despite doctor's
warnings. Two desks butted against each other in the
center of the room, their scarred tops littered with
papers and pipe ash. Each man had several framed
photographs on his desk, the two largest being their
long-dead wives.

"Have you started going through the new material?" Eisenstadt eased himself into his antique chair,
the wood creaking as loudly as his joints.

"Of course. Why do you think I got here two hours
before I promised I would?"

"And what have you learned?"

"Jacob, I won't draw your conclusions for you." The
two had the abrasive relationship of friends who knew
they could never hurt the other.

Jacob took the mild rebuke in silence and lit his
first bowl of the day. Finally he had to say some sort
of rejoinder. "Stop overfeeding Handel. I think she
is constipated."

"Who isn't?"

Frau Goetz came up with a silver tray laden with

coffee and two slices of Sacher torte. As was a Viennese tradition dating back centuries, she also brought two small glasses of water. Theo had told her countless times to dispense with the water since neither man drank it, but she continued the custom.

"So tell me, what has you two so excited this morning?" She placed the coffee service on the only open area of the joined desks. "I assume it has to do with the courier delivery just before you left yesterday."

"You know we have been cultivating a source in Stalingrad," Weitzmann said. Like Jacob, he used the wartime names for many of the cities in the former USSR.

"Yes, he started sending you recently declassified archive material."

"Rather mysteriously too. We don't know who this man is or how he's getting the documents, but we are more than grateful for them. Aren't we, Jacob?"

"Highly irregular," Eisenstadt said from around a mouthful of cake. "But it is first-rate material, mostly originals of German documents captured by the Soviet Army when they took Berlin in 1945. The Soviets have held on to this information for decades."

"And now someone is sending it to *you*?" Frau Goetz asked with a trace of mockery.

"The Institute has a good reputation," Theo defended automatically but he knew what the housekeeper meant. They were not as well known or as well funded as other organizations involved in the same work. "Two months ago it started, just a trickle if you recall: two small envelopes in a week and then nothing for another ten days and then that large parcel that the deliveryman had to help us drag up here. For the past three weeks we've been receiving more small envelopes through the regular mail. They tell an amazing story, one we hope will conclude with the special delivery we received yesterday."

"I see." Frau Goetz knew enough not to ask the men to divulge their tale until they were ready. "Then I shall leave you to your work. Lunch will be promptly at twelve. Herr Doktor, I will walk Handel for you at eleven if you wish."

"Thank you, Frau Goetz." Eisenstadt was already absorbed in a loose collection of papers emblazoned with the Wehrmacht eagle that Theo had passed across to him.

At noon, Frau Goetz brought their lunch but the two hardly noticed. They were lost in another world, one of evil and corruption where the existence of men and women had been reduced to numbers on bills of lading: six thousand to Dachau on November 10, two hundred for labor use at Peenemunde. Such was their preoccupation, Theo Weitzmann didn't bother with the aspirin she had brought, though his weak eyes watered painfully.

The delivery yesterday consisted of five hundred pages of documents, and they scoured each one, talking only when they had a question about a specific reference. Much of this was not new to them. They knew the names of many of the SS officers and guards mentioned within the material. By four in the afternoon, they had each read everything word for word. Not one detail had been overlooked. They sat in silence, lighting their pipes to distract them from the inevitable conclusion.

"Nothing new," Theo said sadly. "We still don't know the shipment's final destination."

"Have patience, my friend. The Nazis were fanatical record keepers. They tracked everything. We could follow the life of one particular paper clip if we wanted. Do you seriously think that they didn't maintain detailed reports on the transport of twenty-eight tons of gold looted from Russia?"

"I know the records exist. I just wonder if our enigmatic benefactor has them and if he will send them to us."

"He's sent us everything else to this point. Remember, until he first contacted us, we didn't even know this consignment existed. I'm sure he will tell us every-

thing when it becomes available to him." Eisenstadt's
eyes narrowed in the particular scowl that had terrified
hundreds of students he had taught at the University.
"Besides which, there was something new here that
you overlooked."

"Where?" Theodor leaned forward, offended.

"Look here." Eisenstadt leafed through papers until
he found the one and handed it to Professor Weitzmann. "At the bottom, see it? The name?"

"Ah, I am sorry, old friend, you are right. A Major
Otto Schroeder was present when the gold arrived in
Hamburg on 29 June 1943. This is the first time I've
seen his name."

"At least connected to the gold," Jacob agreed.
"We need to check our files to see if he's in anything
else we have. I must say, though, I don't recognize his
name at all."

Weitzmann was thoughtful. "No, neither do I. It
doesn't appear he was with the SS or with an Unter-
seeboot squadron. Major is an army rank, not naval."

The biggest fear they shared was that, since Hamburg was a port city, the gold had been loaded onto
a U-boat and spirited out of Europe. If that was the
case, they doubted they would be able to track it
themselves. They would have no choice but to turn
over their findings to a larger and better endowed
agency.

"We have a new lead, it seems. We need to learn
about this Major Schroeder. It is possible he's still
alive and can tell us what happened once the gold
reached Hamburg. Or maybe one of his children
knows something."

"Are you suggesting that we will not receive more
documents from Russia?"

"I am making sure," Eisenstadt snapped, "that we
are pursuing every possible avenue. We know the gold
was stolen from Russian Jews by the German Army
as they rolled into the country. We also know that it
has never been recovered. This represents almost a

billion U.S. dollars. I will not rest until that money is returned to its rightful owners!''

"Calmly, Jacob," Theodor soothed his agitated friend. "Neither of us will rest."

Eisenstadt looked contrite but he did not apologize for his outburst. His passion to restore stolen property was something for which he would never apologize. With his head wreathed in aromatic smoke he added conspiratorially, "If we are lucky, we will find Schroeder alive and we can send our top operative to interview him."

Frau Goetz had come into the room and stood in front of the closed window, her broad body all but blocking the light streaming through. She had heard this last comment, and on this one subject, she would voice her concerns. "You two should leave her alone. You pressure her too much. She has her own life to live."

"Frau Goetz, Anika is my granddaughter and she helps us because she wants to, not because of any pressure." Eisenstadt and Frau Goetz had had this debate every time he'd asked his granddaughter to assist them. He would never set foot in his native Germany again. Austria's complicity in the Holocaust was almost as reprehensible, but in his line of work, he needed to be in the center of things. Anika, who lived in Munich, had become an unpaid assistant whenever they needed something from there. Deep down, he knew her aid was more out of loyalty than conviction but he took help wherever he could get it.

"She would be married with children by now if she wasn't helping you two every time you wanted something."

"There is where you are wrong," Theodor said quickly, for he loved Anika as much as her grandfather. "Anika would be climbing every mountain between Antarctica and Spitzbergen if it wasn't for us. We are helping her find her focus."

"You are helping her find *your* focus, not hers," Frau Goetz stated and crossed her arms over her breasts. She would say no more. "Herr Doktor, you must go walk Handel. It will be past her suppertime by the time you get home."

Eisenstadt fumbled a pocket watch from his cardigan sweater and noted the time. "Yes, thank you. Theo, I will see you tomorrow and maybe we'll get something new from the mail."

"I am going to work late tonight. Maybe we already have something on Major Schroeder in our files."

"Very well. I will see you tomorrow."

A few blocks from the Institute was a high-rise building that rose from the heart of a quaint neighborhood. It was an eyesore of modern architecture filled with subsidized apartments for low-income families. From the top two floors, there was an unobstructed view into the walled yard behind the Institute. At that height and distance, the garden was a small grassy speck amid the city's asphalt and stone. In one apartment on the very top floor, a remote recording device that used a laser to measure sound vibrations against glass had been installed, its beam fired at the window in Jacob and Theodor's office. Unknown to the two Nazi hunters, an enemy they thought vanquished sixty years before was recording every word they said.

The Klinikum Rechts der Isar, Munich's largest hospital, was also the city's chief trauma center. No matter how often the roof was swept, grit blew into an eye-closing maelstrom whenever a rescue chopper landed on the designated helipad. Dr. Anika Klein shielded her face from the blast as the white MBB helicopter swooped over the building's edge and settled on its skids. Her cotton scrubs rippled in the wind, flattening against her lean body as she fought her way toward the craft.

Okay, AK, let's do it, Anika thought and ducked under the blur of blades. Two orderlies guiding an unwieldy gurney raced in her wake.

The helicopter's side door crashed open and the life-flight paramedic jumped out holding an IV bag over his head, a thin coil of tubing trailing back to the patient's arm.

"He went asystolic about thirty seconds ago," he shouted over the turbine's din. "This is the second liter of Ringer's since the first ambulance reached the accident."

Anika wasn't listening. All she heard was that the patient's heart had stopped. Right now everything else was details. Without waiting for the orderlies to transfer the stretcher to the gurney, she hopped up and straddled the accident victim, keeping her knees away from the blood saturating the sheets under his body. Pulling away the blankets, she noted his skin across his torso was deeply bruised, his ribs probably broken. She began CPR anyway, compressing his chest to keep his heart forcing blood through his body. Only when she had her rhythm did she once again pay attention to the paramedic.

"He was unconscious even while they pulled him from the car. Blood pressure's too low to measure. His pulse has been thready since we took off."

"What about his injuries?" she asked as the stretcher was maneuvered out of the chopper's cargo area and onto the gurney.

"Both feet crushed, multiple tib-fib fractures in both legs. Right arm nearly severed, right clavicle fractures, lacerations to face, legs, and back. Pupils are nonreactive. Likely closed head injury."

"Was he wearing a seat belt?"

"No."

Anika finally looked at the face of her patient. He couldn't have been more than twenty years old. "Asshole."

She knew the driver would be coming to the hospital too. He'd be wheeled straight to the morgue, where his parents could claim him. He had been the same age as the man whose life Anika now held in her hands. An hour ago, they'd been playing Formula One driver on the Autobahn in a stolen Porsche. Now both were dead, though one had a slim chance of coming back.

Astride her patient like a jockey, Anika rode the gurney toward the waiting elevator, her upper body sawing with the beat of the CPR. An orderly had a ventilation bag over the patient's face and forced air into his lungs in time with her movements. Once the elevator doors closed, she felt a sudden calm overcome her. It was always like this. For the first frantic moments she worked without thought, her training guiding her hands and her body. And now came the descent to the emergency room. She had forty seconds before the door opened again and until that time there was nothing she could do except maintain the CPR's steady cadence. Her mind was freed.

It was the gift that kept her sane amid the carnage of negligence, stupidity, and increasingly, violence.

Her eyes were on her hands, but her consciousness was focused on nothing at all. She was completely detached now, actually as calm as though she were in a trance. It was the same when she ran marathons. The last quarter of the distance was not run with the body but with the mind.

She became aware that her heartbeat was synchronized with her CPR.

The doors opened, and just as quickly the chaos returned. The orderlies wheeled the gurney down a bright hallway toward an open trauma bay. The life-flight helicopter had radioed information about the car crash victim during their inbound journey so nurses and another doctor were waiting. A portable defibrillator was standing by, and a nurse was poised with jelly and the electrodes for the heart monitor. Voices crashed above the sounds of electronics. Amid the pandemonium, Anika continued massaging the patient's chest until everyone was ready to take over.

She shifted her weight so the heart monitor could be attached to his bare torso, its green line showing activity only when she compressed his body. When she stopped, he'd flatline once again. The gurney wheels were locked down, and an orderly stood to help Anika from the table, but she vaulted off like a longtime horsewoman, landing lightly on her rubber-soled shoes.

A nurse intubated him, running a direct oxygen hose into his mouth to keep his lungs working. The second doctor, Petr Heimann, had the defib's paddles positioned in an instant. "Clear!"

The young man convulsed as electricity jolted his body. The heart monitor gave a matched spike but returned to a steady whine.

"Again," Anika called.

The defibrillator charged and Heimann sent another blast through the dead man. This time a slow beat followed the spike.

Come on, come on, Anika silently prayed as she looked at his ruined legs, already thinking what would need to be done if they could get his heart beating normally. His pants had been cut away at the accident site, and even without X rays, she knew he'd lose both legs below the knees. One leg was held on by only a few ribbons of flesh. Tourniquets around his lower thighs were keeping back the blood and turning his skin a deathly gray. She imagined the gushes of blood that would pour from the ragged limbs when they'd release the thick rubber bands.

"He's crashing again," a nurse said.

Anika didn't need to ask for epinephrine in a cardiac needle. Another nurse had it ready without being told.

The needle was long, an instrument better suited for a nightmare than a hospital, but Anika slid it between his ribs without pause, pressing it directly into the patient's heart muscle.

Once she'd injected the drug, she removed the needle. "Shock him again."

For the third time Heimann greased the paddles and applied them to the man's naked chest, upping to 360 joules. At this stage, the dangerously high current couldn't hurt him any longer.

"Clear," he said with less anxiety. They all knew the outcome of this battle.

The jolt of electricity arched the patient's back as though he was a bow being drawn taut. He fell back to the table, and somehow, miraculously, his heart began beating with an anemic rhythm. Anika and Petr began to work on the other injuries.

Checking his eyes, she discovered the pupils were pinpricks and did not respond to the penlight she flashed into them. He was in a deep coma. She ran her gloved hands through his hair and discovered a knot the size of an egg on the side of his skull. Closed head injury. They needed a CAT scan to determine the amount of brain damage. Judging by the other injuries, she believed it was safe to assume his head had taken a brutal pounding.

Anika crushed down her suspicions. Her job was to

keep the patient alive long enough for the surgeons to take over. Once he left the ER, the future of the young joyrider was out of her hands.

"Tell radiology we need full trauma series X rays and a CT," she told a nurse. "What do you think, Petr?"

"He'll lose the legs even if he has enough mind left to control them."

"The arm?"

Dr. Heimann glanced at the shattered limb. "Hamburger."

The two doctors looked at each other, both silently thinking that maybe they should have called the patient when they had the chance. Was the Hippocratic oath meant to cover saving the life of a brain-dead triple amputee?

"Surgery is ready anytime we are," a nurse announced.

"Okay, thanks." Anika opened the tourniquets to allow blood to seep to the open wounds, returning natural color to the skin. Before the flow turned into a torrent she retightened the bands.

The patient's heart rate was steady but shallow, and no matter how much saline they forced into him, his pressure remained low. He had internal injuries. Knowing the violence of the accident, Anika felt that some of his organs had likely detached, and that was where the bleeding was. A ruptured spleen was common with this type of crash. She sounded his abdomen and found it tight with the stress of blood filling the cavities.

She was about to confer with Heimann about a chest tube when the patient went into cardiac arrest for the third time. No matter how heroic the efforts, there was nothing they could do but watch him die. After a further ten minutes of frantic work Anika felt a touch on her shoulder. Petr's stern eyes said enough.

"Call him."

Angered, she looked at the wall clock, stunned to

see they'd been working for a half hour. "5:18 P.M."
Her shift had ended eighteen minutes ago.

Anika stripped off her latex gloves and yanked the
cloth cap from her head. More than anything she
wanted to wash the sweat from her spiky black hair
but there would be police outside the ER waiting to
speak with her. The patient had been a criminal,
after all.

As an emergency doctor, she knew the importance
of distancing herself from her patients, yet losing even
one pained her in a secret place she told no one about.
She had to force herself to push back those feelings
until she gained the perspective of time. Anika washed
her hands in the scrub sink outside the trauma bay
and changed into fresh scrubs in the doctors' lounge,
taking a moment to soothe her hair back against her
head. In the mirror, her eyes were surprisingly clear
considering what had just happened and that she'd
just finished a twelve-hour Saturday-night shift. Heimann met her on her way out.

"Go start your vacation. I'll handle the police and
the paperwork."

"Are you sure?" She was startled. Heimann wasn't
known for his bedside manner toward patients or
coworkers.

"*Ja.*"

"Thank you, Petr. I owe you one."

Anika decided to go to her apartment for her
shower rather than do it at the hospital. She wanted
to avoid Dr. Seecht, her boss, at all costs. She threw
the laundry that had accumulated in her locker into a
shoulder bag. Since her apartment was across the
street from the huge medical center, she'd wear
scrubs home.

Her mind was on the last-minute details she needed
to finish before leaving for her trip. She had to get a
key to her neighbor, a surgical nurse here at the Klinikum, so she could water the plants. She also needed
to clean a week's worth of leftovers out of her refrigerator. Then there was tomorrow's trip to the town of

Ismaning for her grandfather, and then on Monday it was time to leave for Greenland.

"Dr. Klein, just the person I wanted to see." Dr. Heinz Seecht had been waiting in ambush outside the women's changing room. "I was afraid you had already left."

Damn. Anika had been avoiding Seecht for weeks. She knew what he wanted to talk to her about, and she was hoping to delay it until after the Greenland expedition. If she could, she'd put off this conversation indefinitely. Seecht was about to box her into a decision she still wasn't ready to make.

"I was just leaving. My shift's been over for a while." A moment ago, she had been hyped up on adrenaline, but now she felt nothing but exhaustion. She crossed her arms over her small breasts.

"Yes, I just spoke with Petr. You lost the patient." It was said with condescension, as if the kid's death had been her fault.

Her body stiffened. "We did everything we could."

"I'm sure you did," Seecht said absently. "Petr's a good doctor."

By force of will, Anika remained silent. She and Seecht had been at odds since she first came to the hospital. He was nearly sixty and believed that only men made good doctors. His was an extreme form of sexism that was pervasive in Germany. However, now was not the time to lash out.

"I wish to be blunt with you, Anika," Seecht said as though he'd been any different with her in the past. "Your performance is not up to the Klinikum's standards and hasn't been since you first arrived."

Anika hadn't suspected he'd take this tack and she was thrown off for a moment. She quickly recovered. Rather than let him complete his thought, she went on the attack. "It isn't my skills as a doctor that are substandard," she stated. "Every review places me near the top of all the trauma teams. I have been honored by the medical boards and I have been singled out by the mayor when his daughter came in

with a ruptured appendix. I am more current on new
techniques than anyone on your staff, and I did a year
of ER work in Los Angeles before coming here. I saw
more trauma in a weekend there than doctors here
see in a month. So please tell me, in what way am I
not meeting your standards, Dr. Seecht?"

She took a deep breath.

"I don't question your surgical abilities."

You're goddamned right you won't, Anika wanted
to shout.

A pair of technicians approached from down the
hallway, and Seecht touched Anika on the elbow to
lead her away. She resented the touch. He wouldn't
have done it to a male doctor. He wouldn't even have
done it to a male janitor.

He continued when they were alone again. "There
is more to being on my staff than skills. I demand
dedication from my people, and that is something you
lack. In your year and a half here, you have taken
leaves of absence totaling six months. I encourage doctors to have interests outside their field, but not when
it interferes with their work. Your little adventures
have become such an interference, I'm afraid."

"My little adventures," Anika snapped acidly,
"have given me the research material for two published papers on the chemistry of stress."

Seecht was not impressed. "You were not hired to
be a research doctor. And even if you were, you didn't
need to go on a four-week climbing expedition to the
Himalayas to gather that information and you know
it. The papers you write are just your excuse, your
cover story."

He spoke as though on a telephone, looking at a
spot over her head so he didn't see the aggressive flare
in her eyes. It was at times like this she hated being
just over five feet tall. In a confrontation, being short
gave others a perceived advantage. Seecht needed
only glance over her head and he completely isolated
her from the conversation.

Anika wanted to deny his accusation, but she would

never outright lie to Seecht. He was right. Writing papers *was* her way of legitimizing the fact that she wanted to go away to climb mountains or trek through jungles.

Seecht finally looked her in the eye. "I wanted to catch you before you left for the Arctic or wherever it is you're heading and let you know that you have a decision to make. You will be gone for three weeks, and when you get back you will find that my patience has run out. There will be no more trips or expeditions or anything else. You will work every shift I assign to you without complaint or you will find yourself without a job. Do I make myself clear?"

She had long known that she had a decision to make, one that would doubtlessly affect the rest of her life. She didn't need this misogynist to point it out to her.

"Do you understand, Dr. Klein?" Seecht repeated more forcefully.

"I understand." No matter how bitter the words, she wouldn't turn away from him as she said it.

His voice softened. "You have the makings of a fine doctor, like your father. Don't throw it away because you want to go play in the mountains. It is time you grew up and faced the responsibilities of your profession."

To anyone overhearing the conversation it would have sounded as though Seecht was being understanding. In fact, evoking her father was an attempt to cut her as deeply as possible. Anyone who knew her understood how much her memories of her father meant to her. And how it was his footsteps as a doctor she now followed.

Without another word, Seecht retreated down the hall, leaving Anika amid a storm of emotions. Being fired wasn't what bothered her. With her credentials she could work anywhere in Germany or the rest of the world for that matter. It was the decision that upset her. Did she want to stay in medicine and honor her long-dead father or would she leave to pursue her own interests?

With an angry shake, Anika cleared her head, refusing to allow this to dampen her enthusiasm for the upcoming Greenland expedition. Although three weeks at a remote Arctic research station were far from the toughest challenge she'd faced, she felt the old stirrings of excitement already pushing aside Seecht's ultimatum. Something told her that the answer to her dilemma was waiting on the Arctic wastes and she was eager to see what it would be.

Having traveled to some of the worst hellholes on earth, Philip Mercer still had difficulty recalling a smell worse than a New York garbage truck in the summer. It was a rank odor that hit like a nuclear blast. The lumbering vehicles were making their pickups as he walked along Amsterdam Avenue, a steady stream of wet offal drizzling from their gaping tailgates. On one level, the scientist in him was morbidly curious to know exactly what had been discarded that could be so putrid, but his interest wasn't nearly strong enough to overcome the stench. Had he known the gauntlet he'd have to walk, he would have had the airport taxi drop him at his destination rather than embarking on this random stroll from Midtown.

Mercer abandoned Amsterdam, crossed Columbus, and began walking northward along the much better smelling Central Park West. The morning sun beat against the sidewalks and he shed his suit jacket, tucking it into the crook of his elbow. Doormen in uniforms paid him little heed as he passed their buildings, monoliths of granite and limestone containing some of the most expensive apartments in the world. Brass handrails and awning supports gleamed like gold.

Between 79th Street and 81st stood the massive American Museum of Natural History, his favorite spot in the city. If he had time later, he would come back to see the new Rose Center for Earth and Space. He paused, as he always did, to study the statue of Theodore Roosevelt at the museum's Central Park West entrance. Flanking the statue were two walls chiseled with one-word descriptions of arguably America's most dynamic president.

Making comparisons between T.R. and himself was humbling. Statesman. For a year, Mercer had had a pair of diplomatic plates for his Jaguar as a gift from the United Arab Emirates, but that didn't count. Author. Mercer's doctoral thesis from Penn State on mining and quarrying techniques had been used as a textbook for a short while. Soldier. Not with any army, but Mercer had seen more combat than even old T.R. Governor. Ah, no. President. Not on a million-dollar bet. Explorer. Mercer was on his way to a meeting at the Surveyor's Society, an exploration club of which even Roosevelt hadn't been a member. For the rest, he didn't come close. But then again, who could?

Along 81st Street were more Art Deco apartment buildings, fifteen stories tall, solid and opulent. A professional dog walker hurried by with a brace of stately Afghan hounds in a well-pampered pack. A block to the west, the neighborhood changed to nineteenth-century brownstones with facades much more ornate than the town house Mercer lived in just outside of Washington, D.C. He found the one he wanted: the Surveyor's Society standard of a compass face overlaid with a theodolite and a sextant had been carved into the wall next to the door. The three-story town house was built of reddish stone, with fluted railings flanking the wide steps leading to the front door. From the street, he couldn't see inside, but he felt a prick of excitement as he checked his watch. A mere invitation for lunch at the exclusive club was something to brag about and here Mercer was being made a formal proposal to join.

To his dismay, Mercer saw that he was half an hour early for his meeting with Charles Bryce, an old friend who had put Mercer's name up for consideration. Unconsciously, he'd pushed his pace to get here. Just as he turned to go, the wooden door swung open and an elderly steward in a black suit called to him. "Dr. Mercer?"

"Yes, that's right. I'm afraid I'm a bit early. I was just going to wait at the coffee shop down the street."

"That won't be necessary, sir. Mr. Bryce expected that you would arrive before your appointed time, and he asked me to keep a lookout for you." The servant opened the door wider. "Won't you please come inside?"

Mercer slipped on his jacket and mounted the stairs. "Thank you."

Passing the steward, Mercer stepped from the early twenty-first century to the late nineteenth. He had never seen so much woodwork in one place. The walls of the foyer were paneled mahogany, the stairs to the second level were of oak, age darkened to a smokey black. The parquet floors showed only around the perimeter of a stunning Oriental rug so tightly knotted that it shimmered. Adorning the walls were hunting trophies, antelope heads, a pair of boar tusks that looked like they came off a small elephant, and a rhinoceros that appeared as if it had just smashed its way through the paneling. Judging by the sizes, he was sure all would be listed in the Rholand's Guide. There were also dozens of old framed photographs of various expeditions carried out under the Society's banner. Mercer also recognized a couple of paintings by Joy Adamson, the celebrated author of *Born Free*. The furniture in the reception area just off the lobby was all heavy, leather covered, and well worn. On the floor under one window was a misshapen lump of iron about the size of a steamer trunk that could only be a meteorite. It sat next to a gold-leafed wooden mummy case leaning into one corner.

The steward cleared his throat delicately and Mercer saw that he was waiting with an arabesque silver plate in his hand. Realizing his gaffe, Mercer pulled a business card from his breast pocket and placed it on the plate. The servant returned the tarnished antique to a small entry table next to a golden figurine of the Hindu god Shiva. "Mr. Bryce will be right down. Won't you please be seated?"

Mercer chose instead to wander around the room. In glass-fronted display cases were exquisite collec-

tions of cultural and natural artifacts. One contained
scrimshaw carved on whale's teeth; another held ivory
Japanese Netsuke figurines. Above a shelf of delicate
butterflies lay cleaved geodes, their interior crystals
shimmering in rainbow hues. The display tags next to
them listed where each artifact had been collected, by
whom, and when. Without doubt this was the finest
private collection he'd ever seen, and this was only the
first room. Rumors surrounding the Surveyor's Society
claimed that they maintained a special vault in a
downtown bank containing items so precious, and
some too controversial, that they would never be put
on display. He was studying a flawless yellow diamond
still in its kimberlite matrix stone when the floor
creaked behind him.

"A gift to the Society from Barney Barnarto,"
Charles Bryce said, entering the reception room. "It
was his half of the New Rush claims that Cecil Rhodes
needed to cement his monopoly on the diamond trade,
one that exists to this day as the DeBeers Company.
Look at you, Mercer. Full head of hair, no gray I can
see, and in the same shape as when we first met."

Bryce was shorter than Mercer by several inches,
with a comfortable paunch pressing against his clothes.
His brown hair had retreated up his forehead and
looked like it wasn't going to stop until only a fringe
remained. His once strong jaw was starting to show a
little fleshiness underneath. He wore tortoiseshell
glasses that were too small for his face and made his
dark eyes appear narrower then they were. A banker
by profession, Bryce wore a discreetly striped blue suit
with a white shirt and club tie.

"Great to see you, Charlie," Mercer said, shaking
hands. "For a nine-to-fiver, you don't look too bad."

"That's the problem," Bryce said with a chuckle.
"Somewhere along the line, nine to five turned into
twenty-four/seven. I can't complain. Another ten years
I'll have a massive heart attack and leave Susan with
a couple million dollars."

Mercer laughed. "Always the optimist. How is Susan?"

"Good, thanks for asking. With the kids at prep school, she's had a lot of time to raise money for the city's animal shelters."

"What's the count these days?"

"We now have three dogs and six cats and every month she brings home a couple more for foster care. I feel like Noah," Bryce said as they began climbing the stairs. "Congratulations, by the way. I read the *Time* magazine article about you finding that diamond mine in Eritrea. I can't tell you how glad I was when you called back. This has all been rather short notice, and I didn't know if you were even in the country."

"I've been back from Africa for a while," Mercer explained. "After taking some time off to recover from that one, I had a contract to teach mine rescue in western Pennsylvania. That's where I was when I got your message."

"Who answered your home phone? He sounds like a real character."

"That's Harry White. He's a cantankerous old bastard who watches my place when I'm away. He tends to move in and make himself right at home." Mercer didn't need to add how much Harry meant to him. The affection was in his voice. "He and I have been friends since I moved to Arlington. He just turned eighty, and while he smokes and drinks like tomorrow's doomsday, he'll probably outlive us all."

On the second floor, Mercer glimpsed a large dining room with eight tables set for lunch. There was a fireplace at the far end of the room faced by an arc of overstuffed chairs. A couple of old men sat there either dozing or reading the paper. Bryce continued down a narrow hallway adorned with an assortment of weapons, big Holland and Holland nitro express rifles, swords from medieval Europe and Asia, spears from Africa and the South Sea islands, and blowguns from South America and Australia. They came to a closed office door that belonged to an assistant administrative director.

"Here we go," Bryce said.

The office was small, crammed with books and yet more artifacts. The single window behind the desk overlooked an airshaft between the club and the neighboring brownstone. Mercer noted the window was wired for a security system and he'd already spotted five roving cameras.

"I thought we would chat in private first," Bryce said, "though I'm not too sure of the protocol. You are the first invitee the Society's had since the *Titanic* was discovered."

Bryce took one of the seats in front of the desk and invited Mercer to sit in the other. From a pile of papers on the tooled desktop, Charles grabbed an issue of the Society's quarterly magazine, *Surveyor*. "This comes out next week. Thought you might want one early."

Called one of the finest magazines in the world, *Surveyor* had won every award it could. Its photographers were all the tops in their profession, and most of the articles were written by authors and journalists who'd at least been nominated for a Pulitzer. Its readership wasn't as large as the better-known *National Geographic*, but its followers were more fiercely devoted to collecting each one. Since the Society predated *Geographic* by fifteen years, some of the early editions went for tens of thousands of dollars at auction.

"I don't know much about publishing, but I can't imagine you make any money with this," Mercer said, holding up the two-hundred-page glossy magazine.

"Oh God, we lose thousands on each issue, I suspect. Subscription and circulation barely cover the printing costs. But the money's not important. I should explain a little about how the Society works. There are three types of people who belong: real explorers, like yourself, who are invited to join; those of us who wish we were real explorers, which is my category, I'm afraid; and those who are rich enough to pay others to explore for them. They pick up the tab for the expeditions we sponsor and the publishing of our magazine and video documentaries. Did you notice the gentleman in the dining room wearing the tan suit?"

Mercer nodded.

"His name is Jon Herriman. Back in the early 1970s he invented some little gadget that goes into automobiles, something about pollution control. That device was only recently replaced with something newer and better. He earned royalties for every car sold in this country until about five years ago." Charles noted Mercer's awed expression. "He's only one of eight billionaires on our board. That's why I say money isn't important. A few years ago, one member paid five million dollars to the Russian government so he could use their submersible *Mir* to visit his old ship, the USS *Yorktown,* which was sunk during the Battle of Midway.

"The Surveyor's Society is a labor of love to most of us. Of course we have paid staff to maintain our collections, produce the magazine, and all that, but the actual members are here because we have an interest in exploration and have the money or influence to buy our way in."

"No offense, Charlie, but I didn't think you fit into the billionaire category."

Bryce laughed. "Too true. Actually, Susan's grandfather spent his family's fortune tramping around South America looking for the *El Dorado* treasure before World War Two. He didn't find anything, of course, but his work garnered him an invitation to join. He brought me on board mostly because I'd begged him for years and also because of my banking connections." He leaned back in his chair. "I've recommended you because you actually are an explorer, something the club is sorely lacking."

"I want you to understand what this means to me. I know the caliber of people who've been members, and I never thought I would be considered. But I'm not an explorer. I'm a mining engineer."

"You're being modest, Mercer. That mine you discovered in Eritrea would be reason enough to bring you in, but your reputation has more than qualified you. I read in the *Time* profile on you that accompanied the story that the value of the minerals you've found since you became a prospector-for-hire is around four billion dollars and your fees total three percent of that number."

"Consulting geologist, please," Mercer laughed. Secretly, he admitted Charlie's description better defined what he did. "And both figures were grossly inflated."

"No matter. Your work has helped our understanding of the planet and our ability to use its resources more than any geologist since Alfred Wegener first proposed the continental drift theory."

"Does all this flattery mean I don't have to pony up membership dues?"

"Afraid not. However, your dues entitle you to a room here at the club five nights a year, use of our dining room for private functions, and of course a seat for our weekly lunches, provided you tell the staff a week before you come. Our new chef was stolen from the hotel Georges V in Paris and makes the best chateaubriand you will ever taste. I think, though, just being a member is what most interests you."

Mercer didn't respond. He didn't need to. The golden age of exploration and discovery was long gone. It was part of a bygone era, much like the Society itself. And yet to be invited to join, to be a part of the organization that had helped open up so many frontiers, was an honor that Mercer couldn't refuse. His education and work entitled him to a string of initials after his name if he so chose, but the prestigious MSS—Member Surveyor's Society—was a title he'd coveted since first reading their magazine as a boy. Much to his irritation, a great deal of his work now took place in front of a computer rather than in the field. The invitation was a way for him to reconnect with the pioneers of his profession. He broke himself from his silent musings. "There's that, and I want to find out if some of the rumors are true about parts of your collection."

"Ah, the rumors."

Speculation about the Society's secrets had run rampant for generations. Because of its private status and the powerful people who'd always run it, many believed it had become a repository for a great many unsettling discoveries. Some said they had a portion of Amelia Earhart's Lockheed Electra and others believed the Great Mogul Throne from India was here. He'd heard of a group who believed the Society's vault contained definitive proof of pre-Columbian exploration by Phoenician explorers. And another who said they owned a portion of the True Cross.

The Internet had served to accelerate the pace of conjecture. A year ago, a group on the Net learned that a farm in Roswell, New Mexico, near where a UFO had supposedly crashed in the 1940s had been owned by a member of the Surveyor's Society. The inference that the Society possessed hidden evidence of alien contact came immediately afterward and the furor had yet to die down.

"Even I don't know half of it," Bryce admitted. "Our ten-person executive council are the only people who know what's in the secret part of our vault."

There was a knock at the door, and the elderly steward entered holding a tray with two glasses on it. "It is noon, gentlemen. Lunch will be in thirty minutes in the dining room. May I offer you a cocktail?"

Bryce turned to Mercer. "It's still gimlets, isn't it?"

"Good memory." Mercer accepted the vodka and sweetened lime juice concoction from the butler. He'd recently switched to Gray Goose, a French vodka, and noted this drink was made with his old standard, Absolut.

Bryce took a tumbler of iced Macallan Scotch. "I seem to recall a night a few years back where you and I went through quite a few of these in very short order. The only thing I remember from then is the weeklong hangover afterward."

The air-conditioning kicked in. Mercer could feel cool air blowing from the brass grill recessed into the wall behind his back. It was as though the chill had changed the mood of the meeting. Bryce went silent for a moment, his eyes focusing on a middle distance only he could see. He almost appeared upset by something they had said or something he was about to say. Mercer braced himself.

"Our review committee," Bryce opened, "has already approved you for membership. That was taken care of a couple of weeks ago. As I understand it, this usually takes upward of a year. However, you are a special case."

"Why's that?"

"Well, people who are invited to join by virtue of their earlier exploits must participate in a Society-sponsored expedition before they can become members. It's an old bylaw of the club. About three months ago we were approached by the Danish government to see if we were interested in joining an expedition being planned by a German nonprofit group called Geo-Research."

"What's this have to do with Denmark?"

"The expedition is going to Greenland, which is still a Danish protectorate. I don't know if you're aware that Denmark has recently gotten very selective about who receives permits for scientific research on the Greenland ice sheet. During a Japanese expedition last year, a mishap killed eight people and left eleven thousand gallons of spilled fuel on the ice. The bodies were recovered, but no steps were taken to clean up the diesel. Just a month later, four American mountain climbers died in a plane crash. A search-and-rescue helicopter looking for the wreck also crashed, killing three more.

"Since then the Danes are demanding better oversight of what takes place on Greenland. They've closed several foreign-run meteorological stations they feel are unsafe and limited climbing parties to just a small region in the south, well away from the higher mountains as a way to discourage treks. They've even started rattling their sabers about closing Thule Air Force Base.

"Add to this the fact that Germany and Denmark are at odds over oil-exploration rights in the North Sea and it was surprising that Geo-Research didn't have their permits rescinded altogether. Their expedition is planned to gather global warming data and has been in the works for a year."

"Where does the Surveyor's Society fit in?" Mercer asked. He'd been to Greenland's tiny neighbor, Iceland, once before, but had never visited earth's second-largest island. He felt his interest rising.

"Back in the 1950s, there was an American base on Greenland's eastern coast called Camp Decade. It had to do with Project Iceworm, something about determining if permanent towns could be sustained under the ice sheet. One of our board members was assigned to Camp Decade when it closed in late 1953, and he wants a team sent there to see what the place looks like today. Bob Bishop's his name and he's unable to make the trip himself. He's been bound to a wheelchair for the past two years. What he's sponsoring is a small team to reopen the facility and videotape the interior, check what kind of damage has been done to it—that sort of thing."

"I'm not saying I'm not interested, but this Bishop is willing to pay for an entire expedition just for a tape of the base? Are you serious?"

"Money's meaningless to most members. I told you about the *Yorktown* expedition. This one's a bargain by comparison."

"I read about a group who recovered a P-38 Lightning from southern Greenland that had crashed during World War Two," Mercer said. "They found the plane in near perfect condition, but it was a couple of miles from where it crashed and buried under two hundred and fifty feet of ice. Camp Decade might be in good shape, but it could be almost as deep."

"You'd think, but it's not. Don't ask me to explain the phenomena—I'm no glaciologist—but the camp was anchored to a subice mountain of rock that cuts the natural flow of Greenland's glaciers, splitting the ice around it like an island in a stream. The base is actually only about thirty feet under the surface. New snow that falls on it gets carried away by the moving ice, but the base has stayed in just about the same place. I'm familiar with the search for the 'Lost Squadron' that you mentioned. It was actually a whole flight of planes that went down, six P-38s and two B-17s that hit a blizzard and were forced to land. There is a hell of a lot more snowfall where those planes went down than where our team's heading."

"So the catch to joining the Society is to lead your expedition?"

"Well"—Bryce drew out the word—"we already have someone to lead it: Bob Bishop's son, Martin." Charles waited for a reaction, but Mercer remained impassive. "This doesn't mean to say you can't handle it. I know you can. Even though the Danish government has pushed up our schedule, this has been in the works for a year, and Bob *is* footing the bill. That's why I said earlier that your application was rushed through the committee. We don't have any other trips planned until next year. If you want to wait until then, I certainly understand."

"What would my job be?"

"That's the other reason you'd be perfect for the trip. We can put you right on top of Camp Decade, but you'll need to pinpoint the main entrance before starting your tunnel down to it. You have experience with portable subsurface radar sets as well as ice tunneling."

"What are you planning on using to open the base?"

"Thermal chemicals that melt ice and snow. You are familiar with the technique?"

"We call them hotrocks. I can't remember the exact

chemical makeup, but yeah, I've worked with them before. They're tricky as hell to use and produce a god-awful stench but they can melt about a foot an hour, depending on the diameter of the hole. Problem is, you need powerful pumps for the water runoff or the chemicals become too diluted to melt the snow."

"Apart from you and Marty, there will be two others. One's an old friend of Marty's, an Army colonel with some Arctic experience and the other's a guy I recommended. He'll be responsible for the pumps and generators."

There was no doubt in Mercer's mind that he would go. Charles could have offered him the latrine digger's job and he would have done it. Still, he was curious how this would work. "That's an awfully small team to unbury an entire town."

"Camp Decade is actually a large H-shaped building. Everything's connected. All you need to do is dig your way to the main entrance and you should gain access to the whole facility."

"Four guys alone on the ice? I've done a lot of stupid things in my life, but this sounds like an invitation to a suicide party."

"You're forgetting how we got invited to go in the first place. The Danes want teams working in the same area rather than spread across the ice. Geo-Research is the umbrella organization for the entire trip. We are joining up with them, plus another group doing some sort of meteorological work. Everyone in one location, which reduces the chance of accidents."

"I get it now. We're piggybacking onto their expedition. How many people in total?"

"About forty, I think. Since Geo-Research is bringing a full support staff for their scientists, we'll pay them for your room, board, and any additional labor you need. The Germans are furious about the arrangement, by the way. Because our expedition is site specific, the Danes told them they had to work near Camp Decade to accommodate us. It shouldn't really matter to them. In terms of global warming research, one patch of Greenland is pretty much like all the others. But they wanted to work about a hundred miles north of our destination."

"And the other team you mentioned?"

"They couldn't care less just as long as they get their work done." Charles knocked back the last of his drink and set the Waterford tumbler on the desk. "We pulled a few strings to get the Danes to force Geo-Research to agree to our location."

Mercer cocked an eyebrow, inviting an explanation.

"One of the Society's armchair explorers like myself happens to be the U.S. ambassador to Denmark. Some members buy their way in with money and others with position." Bryce then added with a smile, "Because of his geology background, Herbert Hoover belonged to the Surveyor's Society long before he went into politics. You can imagine the bloody murder we got away with when he became president. For the club, Prohibition ended at his inauguration, not when Roosevelt repealed it in '33. Not that we took much notice anyway."

Mercer smiled with Bryce. "Any lingering problems with Geo-Research?"

"There shouldn't be any difficulties by the time you arrive. Geo-Research has had a couple of months to calm down about the change. Even if there are problems, our part of the expedition shouldn't last for more than a couple of weeks. After you leave, the Japanese who were kicked out last year are going to replace you."

"What do you know about Geo-Research? I've had a run-in with an environmental group before that I'd just as soon forget."

"They're not tree huggers, if that's what you're afraid of. Geo-Research is dedicated to hard science, not flavor-of-the-month crusades. They've been around for about six years, contracting their ship and services to various governments and universities." Charles looked at Mercer levelly. "Do you have any other questions? You haven't said even if you want to go."

Fighting to keep the grin off his face, Mercer set his empty glass next to Bryce's. His murky gray eyes were bright. "The only question I have is, when do I leave?"

"Congratulations and welcome to the Surveyor's Society." Charles pumped Mercer's hand vigorously. "I knew you'd do it. In fact, we've already submitted your name to Geo-Research and your participation was posted on our Web page a few weeks ago."

"Am I that easy?"

"You have a choice as to when you leave. You can join Geo-Research's ship, *Njoerd,* in Reykjavik in three days and sail with her to Ammassalik, Greenland, where she'll be offloaded for the trek to the camp. Or you can leave about a week later when the base camp has been established."

"When is the rest of our team leaving?" Mercer noted he was already using the possessive in reference to the expedition. He was truly excited about this. It was a tremendous opportunity on so many levels. The geologist in him wanted to explore one of the largest ice sheets on the planet and the romantic in him loved the idea of joining the Society.

"They're opting for the sea voyage."

"I'll bring my shuffleboard stick." Because he worked on a contractual basis, Mercer could easily shift his schedule to accommodate the trip.

It was nearing four in the afternoon by the time Mercer left the Society's headquarters. Lunch had ranked as one of the finest meals he'd ever eaten and the company around the table had been fantastic. They'd dined with the billionaire Herriman and several others who regaled Mercer with slightly embellished stories about expeditions they'd financed or been part of.

With a three-day window before the flight to Reykjavik, Mercer decided to spend the night in the city and visit the Natural History Museum the following day. Mercer explained his plans to Charles, and ten minutes later, Dobson, the steward who'd met Mercer at the door, had arranged for a Town Car to take him to the Carsyle, where a room was waiting. Dobson had also booked him on the following evening's shuttle to Washington.

Charles Bryce waved to Mercer from the stoop and went back inside. In the borrowed office of the assistant administrative director, he threw himself behind the desk and reached for the phone. He had the number memorized.

"Paul, it's Charlie Bryce," he said after getting past a legion of secretaries.

"How did it go?" asked the cultured voice from the other end of the line.

"Mercer's on board," Charles said with a trace of bitterness. "He'll meet the ship in Iceland and sail with them to Greenland."

"Good job. I told you recruiting him wouldn't be difficult."

"I don't like this. Mercer should know what he's getting into."

"Charles, *you* don't even know what Dr. Mercer is getting into."

"You know what I mean," Bryce snapped. "I don't have a lot of friends, and I hate using the few I have without at least warning them first."

"This operation is compartmentalized on a need-to-know basis, and at this point Mercer has no need. Besides, he's just a backup. Chances are, he won't even know what's happening in Greenland. He'll enjoy his stay there, open that base for Bishop, and that'll be the end of it."

"What happens if something does go wrong?"

"You might know the public side of Mercer, Charles, but there are things he hasn't told you. Like how he took time off during his doctoral studies to help the Defense Department by going into Iraq with a commando team prior to the Gulf War to see if Saddam Hussein had been mining uranium ore. Or how he had a hand in averting the terrorist attack against the Alaska Pipeline last year. If for some reason something happens that puts our mission in jeopardy, Philip Mercer is more than capable of looking after himself and our interests at the same time."

"I didn't know about that other stuff and it sounds impressive," Bryce persisted. "But he doesn't know the full story. He's going in blind."

"If the time comes, he will be informed. But that is my decision to make. Your part in this is over." The line clicked dead.

"I'm sorry, Mercer," Bryce whispered to the empty office. "I wish I hadn't gotten you involved."

It seemed to outsiders that the white smoke signifying the election of the first pope of the new millennium was barely out of the chimney of the Apostolic Palace when Leo XIV, the 263rd man to take the seat of St. Peter, began changing the Holy See. Those who worked within the Vatican knew this wasn't exactly true, but it was close enough. And many were stunned by what the former Cardinal Giuseppi Salvi was planning to do.

Salvi had been was seen as a temporary compromise between factions within the Curia. Politicking during the electoral conclave had been rampant, and the election dragged on for ballot after ballot with no end in sight. After five days, it became apparent that neither of the two principal contenders would ever receive the two-thirds needed, so each side began to play a waiting game, hoping that the final ballot on the twelfth day, when a simple majority would take the election, would see their man victorious.

The reasons for this loggerhead were varied, but the church was at a crossroads, changes in the world had to be addressed, issues that the Curia had put off for decades could no longer be ignored, and a leader for the twenty-first century was needed. Some cardinals felt it was time for Catholicism and the papacy to modernize while others believed a more conservative, and in some instances reactionary, hand was needed.

On the eighth day, several of the more diplomatic cardinals realized that the bitterness infecting the conclave would likely spill over and infect the new pope's reign. The church must show a united front, they felt. A compromise was needed. A third candidate was put forth, a man who could act as a temporary solution while the church decided its future. Cardinal Salvi was seventy-four years old and in poor heath. His reign as pope, they knew, would be a short one, giving each side time to further debate points of doctrine.

A week after Giuseppi Salvi became Leo XIV, he was in the hospital and the cardinals feared their solution had been too temporary, much like the first John Paul, who'd been pope for just over a month in 1978. However, tests confirmed that his ill health was not a grave concern. Instead, doctors found he suffered from gastric reflux, a condition he'd never discussed. Surgery for his malformed stomach valve was performed, and within a few weeks, he had made a near-miraculous recovery.

It was at this point that Leo XIV began to change the church, reshaping it into his vision of what it should be with a vigor that stunned the hard-liners who'd elected him. He appointed his closest friend, the liberal Cardinal Peretti, to the secretariat of state, the Vatican's number two position. Leo had always been considered a moderate but this crucial appointment loudly stated that the status quo was about to end. He made it clear that the topic closest to him, and thus all of the church, was raising religious tolerance around the world and stamping out fanaticism. Rather than issue papal decrees on the subject, he decided to go directly to the bishops who oversaw the dioceses.

He called for a special synod of bishops, and such was the importance he placed on this meeting, he made Peretti its president. In another unusual step, Leo XIV invited other religious leaders to attend. Though they would have no voting rights, he wanted them all to understand the Vatican's position on the subject of tolerance. Eastern Orthodox patriarchs and bishops were common at synods, but Leo also wanted Jewish leaders from Israel and the United States, prominent Buddhist monks including the Dalai Lama, influential Mullahs and Imams from both the Sunni and Shiite branches of Islam, Shinto priests from Japan, the Archbishop of Canterbury, who headed the Anglican church, and hundreds of others.

Gathering this great body fell on Cardinal Peretti, and the sheer logistics were staggering. An ordinary synod took a year to organize and the pope had given him only six months, not only to bring together one hundred and seventy bishops from the Catholic Church, but all the others as well.

Dominic Peretti was a native Roman, sixty-five years old and something of a Curia outsider because of his modernist views on artificial birth control. Like Leo, he believed that some form of population control was going to be crucial for the sustainability of civilization. As pope, Leo couldn't openly declare such a belief, but by giving Peretti power within the Vatican, his intentions were clear.

The Synod on Tolerance was a planned first step to bring the church closer to other religions so that, at some point, this other topic may be discussed. The Vatican was a two-thousand-year-old institution that moved at the ponderous pace of the world's largest bureaucracy. Incremental change was the only way to get the church to reform and even the synod was seen as a radical departure.

Peretti was sitting at his desk on the second floor of the Apostolic Palace when a priest knocked at his door. "Forgive me, Cardinal Peretti. His Holiness has finished with his lunch and will see you now."

"Grazie." Peretti removed his reading glasses and slipped on his all-purpose pair. He'd tried bifocals but they gave him a pounding headache.

He stood and stretched. At six foot five inches, he was the tallest person in the Vatican, excluding a few of the *corpo di vigilanza*, the Holy See's police force, and a couple of the ornamental Swiss Guards. As a boy, he'd been something of a basketball star and on rare occasions he would still shoot a few baskets with some of the Vatican's lay workers. His face was remarkably unlined except for a deep crease on each side of his large, hooked nose. Behind his steel-rimmed glasses, his eyes were dark and possessed captivating intelligence. He grabbed up two bundles of papers and left his spacious office.

Although the Palace was a place of opulence and quiet dignity, Peretti moved through it with a loose-limbed gait that was only now beginning to slow. He climbed the marble steps to the papal apartments and found the pontiff in the gilded library. With him already was Bishop Albani, relator for the Synod on Tolerance. He would act as a facilitator for the discussions and make sure that a consensus was reached at the event's close.

"You look tired," the pope greeted his secretary of state.

"I am," Peretti agreed and took a chair across the desk from Leo. "This has been a trial."

"Another week and we'll convene the synod, Dominic," the pontiff said with genuine sympathy. "Our relator here will take over and you can get some sleep. While I've limited the time allowed for opening remarks to quicken the pace, you'll have a few quiet days before anything of significance takes place."

Before Albani could mutter a protest that the opening discussions would be important, Leo XIV raised his hand, the sunlight streaming through the windows glinting off his fisherman's ring, one of the many symbols of his office. "I'm joking, of course. We've given ourselves only two weeks for the synod, half the normal time, and not a moment will be wasted. Have there been any last-minute delays?"

"Hundreds," Peretti sighed. "But I'm dealing with them. If I may speak frankly, many of the other religious leaders are acting like prima donnas on opening night. Some want more time to address the bishops. Others want better control over their meals. Still others resent the cabin assignments. For men and women who dedicate themselves to the spiritual salvation of others, they seem inordinately preoccupied with their own corporeal needs."

"There are many dietary and cultural customs we must be sensitive to," the pope reminded.

"Those I can understand. However my office has been deluged with other requests. Why an American minister needs to bring his wife with him, I'll never know, but he telephones me every day repeating his displeasure that she won't be allowed to join him. I finally relented and told him she could come."

"Who is it?"

"Tommy Joe Farquar. He's a former car salesman turned evangelist with a substantial television ministry."

"How America puts up with some of those charlatans I'll never understand," Albani said

"How about the ship?"

Because of the international scope of the Synod on Tolerance, the pope had wanted it in Rome, as was tradition. However several of the key invitees refused to come to Vatican City. Jerusalem would have been his second choice, but that turned out to be even more contentious than Rome. It was Peretti's suggestion to avoid the question of territory altogether. Rather than deal with political squabbling, he recommended that the synod be held at sea, on a cruise ship large enough to accommodate the two thousand people attending. The vessel they had leased, the *Sea Empress*, was one of the newest cruise liners in the world.

Having so many important people on one ship had created other sets of problems, not the least of which was security. The Swiss Guards were responsible for checking every member of the ship's crew and the attendees. They would work with the individual security specialists from dozens of countries. Getting the group safely on board was the biggest single concern. Once the ship was in international waters, she was well beyond the reach of all but the most sophisticated terrorists. Still, the pope procured the services of the Italian Navy to provide an escort for the modern

ocean liner—a destroyer that would follow behind the
Sea Empress on her voyage.

"The ship is ready. With one week to go before we
depart, the crew has been sequestered aboard her. No
one not already checked by Interpol and the Swiss
Guards is allowed anywhere near her."

"She's provisioned, then?" asked Albani.

"With everything from champagne to dog food for
the bomb-sniffing dogs that sail with us."

"Dominic, you've done a remarkable job. This
meeting is as much a testament to your organizational
skills as to the need for world understanding."

Peretti demurred. "I will gladly fade into the background if we can get just one person to stop killing in
the name of religion."

"We will, my friend," the pope said with unwavering faith. "How about the items we are returning to
the other faiths? Are they at the ship yet?"

"Everything has been put aboard the *Sea Empress*
already. The response we've gotten has been tremendous, I might add."

"I thought it would. John Paul's *Mea Culpa* in
March of 2000 was a first step. The church should
have made such a formal apology to the world decades
ago. Some of the atrocities carried out under our banner were unspeakable. The Inquisition, crusades, po-
groms, and our failure to counter fascism are just the
most notable. Saying we are sorry was not enough. I
thought it necessary to give back something tangible
and what better than the thousands of religious texts
and artifacts belonging to other faiths that the Vatican
has accumulated over the centuries? These items
should have been returned long ago."

"Has there been a final count of items we are returning?" Albani asked Peretti. "I need to know for
my speech to the assembly."

Cardinal Peretti rifled through one of the batches
of papers he'd brought to the meeting. "Seven thousand eight hundred books, mostly Jewish texts and
torahs that we hid during the war, Islamic writings

that were captured during the Crusades, and Eastern Orthodox material that we've held on to since the Council of Chalcedon in 451."

"That's it?" The pope's eyes widened at such a low figure.

"You gave us only six months to prepare." It was fact, not complaint. "There are two million books in the Vatican library as well as 150,000 manuscripts. This doesn't include the seventy-five *kilometers* of documents in the archives. We've only begun to comb through to find material that belongs to others."

"I'm sorry." Leo smiled. "Forgive me. What else is being given back to the proper owners?"

"Five hundred icons that belong to the Eastern Orthodox Church. They will decide what particular group gets what. There are also forty statues, about two hundred paintings and a great many religious pieces such as candlesticks, menorahs, ornamental crosses, and reliquaries. In all, we've shipped eleven containers to the docks in Belgium. I've already drawn up a manifest of what goes to whom, and we've kept some of the more symbolic pieces separate so you can give them out directly."

"And you say that the world's interest in this step is high?"

"Despite the best efforts of our press office, many journalists are focusing on the restoration more than the synod, which by the way we can't seem to dissuade them from calling the Universal Convocation."

"It is our synod, but it is also a universal gathering," the pope countered. "I actually prefer the title they've bestowed on the gathering. A synod smacks of secrecy. What we want is an openness that has never been seen before. This meeting is not about religion. It is about people and how to get them to improve relations with each other."

Albani, who would be leading the synod, picked up the thread. "Modernism is dividing the world into fanatics or secularists. Evangelism has become such a bitter battle that many religious leaders have lost sight of why we spread our various beliefs. Souls have become a commodity, no different from oil futures or stock shares."

Suddenly the pope laughed aloud, and it took him a moment to recover. "I'm sorry, Albani. In my head I heard a radio announcer quoting religions like a stock ticker." He deepened his voice. "In today's trading, Catholicism is up two points, Judaism up a quarter, and Buddhism down an eighth." He laughed again before the reality of his joke hit him. He became subdued once more. "We have to put an end to this way of thinking. I hate to think what will happen if we don't. Politics and race breed fanaticism on their own. The world does not need its religious leaders adding fuel to such an incendiary mixture."

Anika Klein spent her morning packing for her trip. She was leaving tomorrow, Monday, to spend a few days in Iceland before the rest of the team assembled for the ship to Greenland. Her domestic chores took her longer than expected but still she went for a run after lunch and returned to her apartment an hour and a half later.

After a long shower, she spent thirty grudging minutes in front of the mirror attending to beauty details she'd put off for too long. Her eyebrows were particularly bothersome since they hadn't been tweezed in three months. The ritual left her eyes swimming in tears. She purposely kept her glossy black hair trimmed almost like a man's, with short bangs and just a little length at her neck. A dollop of gel and a quick slash with a brush was all it took to tame it.

Her face was angular, with large, almond-shaped eyes, high cheekbones, and a sharp chin. Her mouth was wide, luxurious. Except on dates, she'd learned to not wear lipstick because of the distraction her pout caused. Her ears were tiny, with a total of nine rings, five in one, and four in the other. Anika was thirty-six years old but had the style of someone half that age. And she could get away with it. Studying her reflection closely, she decided she could maintain the ruse for a few more years. Because she'd rarely allowed herself to tan, her skin, which would eventually give her away, had yet to show lines.

She gave her reflection a smile. It was only then that her face lost the intensity she showed to the outside world. Her smile made Anika look like a teen-

ager. Her ex-husband had often compared her beauty
to Audrey Hepburn's. She'd done little to dissuade
him of that opinion.

Normally she wore all black in a pseudogothic look
that hadn't yet gone out of fashion in Europe. For
today, she was meeting someone for her grandfather,
so she threw on a bright but modest skirt, a creamy
silk blouse, and flats. She was comfortable enough
with her height to wear heels only when necessary.

In the kitchen on her way out of her apartment, she
grabbed a liter bottle of water from the fridge and a
container of oily kalamata olives. She had chewing
gum in her car for her breath later. Her purse was a
small leather backpack. Anika tossed the water inside,
fished the keys to her battered Volkswagen Golf from
the bottom, and popped a handful of the rich olives
into her mouth. Her car was in the garage under her
building; it started after a mere five attempts.

The town of Ismaning was only about a half hour
from her apartment, which worked well for her grandfather. Had this Otto Schroeder he'd asked her to
speak with lived any farther from Munich, she would
have postponed the interview until after her trip to
Greenland. *Opa* Jacob had insisted that she visit him
before heading north, but he treated everything about
his work as a matter of urgency.

Anika did what she could to help. He knew she
would never take up the crusade, but by assisting him
when she could, Anika hoped that *Opa* knew she
wouldn't forget either. He'd often said that people
aren't truly dead until they are forgotten. He'd told
her that the first time when her own father, *Opa* Jacob's son-in-law, died from a heart attack. As long as
she remembered her father, he was alive. That was
why Jacob worked so hard. As long as he remembered, the six million were still alive, and if Anika
could carry even a part of the memory, then the victims would not fade for another generation.

The traffic was heavier than she expected. She'd
forgotten that road repairs were under way even on

the weekend. The Volkswagen's air conditioner had not worked since she'd bought it thirdhand and heavy blasts of hot air percolated from the asphalt. Anika felt constricted, the seat belt like a band of iron across her chest. The back of her blouse was sticky. She tried to take a deep breath and managed to inhale a dose of diesel exhaust from the truck idling next to her.

The frustration pricking her skin was only partially due to the delay. She'd hoped the distraction of driving would banish thoughts of work but the constant starts and stops served as a reminder. Was her career going to go forward or end? The choice was hers.

She dug out her water bottle and took a gulp, forcing herself to calm down. Rather than deal with the decision, she fumbled through her bag for the directions to Otto Schroeder's farmhouse that *Opa* Jacob had dictated a few days ago from Vienna. She knew from the research she'd done for him in the past not to be surprised how he had tracked the former military officer. Jacob Eisenstadt could find anyone, it seemed, once he put his mind to it.

On the sheet of paper with the directions was a list of questions Jacob wanted answered. Anika had read through the list once after writing them down and found herself more intrigued with this interview than the previous ones she'd done. It appeared that Schroeder might know the whereabouts of a huge shipment of gold spirited out of Russia in 1943. According to Jacob, this wasn't one of the fabled "lost shipments" that had never been recovered. Until very recently neither he nor Theodor Weitzman had even known of its existence. They were convinced that they were on the trail of something completely new.

Anika doubted that anything would come of her interview. *Opa* had learned that Schroeder had been a career soldier from before Hitler came to power. He hadn't been part of the Nazi elite. In fact, he hadn't even been a member of the party. It wasn't very likely that he would be privy to secrets of stashed gold or anything else for that matter. She had said this to *Opa*

Jacob, and he had reminded her that, even if Otto Schroeder was simply another link in the chain, it put them one link closer to their goal. His absolute dedication and unshakable faith was something Anika knew she could learn from. She was sorely lacking in both.

In the center of Ismaning stood a tall stone tower, a medieval leftover whose original purpose was lost to time. She turned right and very quickly the urban congestion vanished. It was as if she'd traveled a hundred kilometers from the city. Plowed fields and dense forests flanked the narrow road, with farmhouses nestled at the end of long, crushed stone driveways.

She felt herself relaxing. Anika loved the country, the clean air, the open vistas, and especially the lack of people. She checked her directions again. She had to stay on this road for eight kilometers and then veer to the left for another three. There she would find Otto Schroeder's house. According to her grandfather's report, Schroeder owned the land but no longer worked it. That was leased to local farmers while he stayed on in the isolated house, living out the last of his years.

The sun dipped below the layer of smog covering Munich, and the reddened light made the fields of wheat look like sheets of dancing flame. Anika found her turn and popped a stick of gum in her mouth to mask the taste of the olives she'd been munching. The road this far from Ismaning was little used, and there was even grass growing across stretches of it. She noted a single set of tire tracks had cut grooves through the patches of green. She feared it meant that Otto Schroeder had just recently left his house. Possibly for a Sunday-night beer in town? Doubtful. He was near ninety years old.

She was just going to dig into her bag for her cell phone to call Schroeder's number when from around a copse of huge oaks she saw the house. A black Mercedes sedan was parked in the drive next to an ancient Opel. The house itself was unremarkable. One story and built of dressed and mortared stone, it looked in poor repair. Several of the porch roof's support columns had settled into the ground, giving the facade a wavy look. It was the incongruous presence of the Mercedes that gave her pause. Of course, they were common all over Germany. But out here? On the very night she was to interview an obscure ex-soldier who might know something about missing gold?

Anika was suddenly very alert. She eased her Volkswagen to a halt well short of the house. She slung her bag onto her back and in one arching bound was across the narrow irrigation ditch fronting Schroeder's property.

The air was still. The wind that had moved through the fields earlier was gone, and the night insects had yet to come out. She could hear the Mercedes's engine pinging in the silence as it cooled. She thought about the car. It was possible that it belonged to a well-off child out to visit his father. Yet would a child let an elderly parent live in such isolation? Something wasn't right here, but she couldn't place what. She kept to the lengthening shadows as she approached the house.

She reached the front door without spotting or hearing anything out of the ordinary. She chuckled silently. Her feeling of vague anxiety faded. So much for her sixth sense. It might work while climbing a sheer mountain face, but it was worthless on the ground.

She was about to knock when an agonized scream pierced the night, a high keen that rippled up her spine like static.

It came from the back of the house, not from within. As much as her training urged her to rush to its source, she held her ground. It wasn't a question of if she would back away. Rather, she had to determine the best way to proceed. Stepping off the porch, she peered around the corner of the house. A stone wall extended beyond the back of the building as part of an enclosed backyard. She heard a sharp moan and knew the cry had come from there.

The wall was four feet tall, capped with flat blocks of slate. Guessing there would be a gate at the back, she moved along the fence, keeping low. Her acute sense of balance more than made up for the poor traction of her shoes on the loamy soil. Halfway down, she heard voices, muted at first but clearing as she got to the far end. Around this corner she could see a rotted wooden gate hanging open on one hinge.

"It is a simple question, Mr. Schroeder," a man's voice snarled. "We know you were a combat engineer during the war, and we know that you were attached to the Pandora Project. What we don't know is who you've told. Who else knows about Pandora?"

After a moment's pause, the answer came in the form of another screeching wail, much louder than before.

Otto Schroeder was being tortured!

Anika felt paralyzed. She turned to look behind her. She couldn't see her car, but knew she could reach it in seconds. She even took her key ring out of her skirt pocket and got the ignition key centered between her fingers. But she could not move. The long-ago war that had claimed most of her family and drove her grandfather was continuing just a few feet away.

"I've told no one." This had to be Schroeder. The words came out between wheezes of pain. "The secret of what we did dies with me."

"You had better hope so," said a third voice, lower than even Schroeder's and menacing.

There were two of them, maybe more. Anika had only one option. Her cell phone was in her backpack. All she needed to do was move far enough away so her call to the police wouldn't be heard. She took a cautious step backward and then another.

The pain came suddenly and was unlike anything she'd ever felt. A hand had come over the top of the wall and buried itself in her hair, the thick fingers threading down to her scalp. She was nearly lifted off her feet. Her skin felt like it was about to be ripped from her head. She cried out, batting at the arm, but even a small movement made the agony even more unbearable.

"I've got someone." It was yet another male voice, one that sounded younger than the first two. "A woman."

The pain forced Anika onto her toes, and still the man pulled her higher. Held immobile, she began to scream. The gate was wrenched open, and a man approached her with an automatic pistol in his hand. He was tall and fit with blond hair and a dark expression.

Only when he was behind her with the pistol pressed against her back did he speak. "Okay, Karl, I've got her. Let her go."

The strain on her hair vanished, and Anika would have dropped to the ground had the gunman not propped her up with one hand while keeping the weapon screwed into her kidney. He forced her forward with a savage prod.

The walled garden was overrun with weeds and the uneven flagstones were slick with moss. There were a rusted iron table and a couple of mismatched chairs next to the door that led to the house. Otto Schroeder lay on a chipped concrete bench with two men standing over him. One of them must have been Karl, the one who'd grabbed her. A fourth figure stood back in the shadows. Anika guessed that he was the leader of the group. She couldn't see his features, but somehow he seemed older than the others.

She focused her attention on Schroeder, and when she realized what they had done to him, hot vomit shot into her mouth. Fear had stripped away her ability to remain clinical. One of Schroeder's legs had been flayed open, and a large slab of tissue had been carved away. Blood pooled in the gruesome wound and spilled over onto the patio. Anika looked into the old man's gray face and was amazed to see defiance in his watery eyes. At some point in his torture, he'd bitten into his lip or tongue because more blood dripped from his face.

"Who are you?" the man who had grabbed her, Karl, asked. He was a near copy of the one with the gun, big and blond with shoulders like an executioner's gallows. His partner was holding a long knife. In the fading light Anika saw crimson on the blade.

Her silence was from fright, not resistance. She knew that since she'd seen their faces, they would never let her live. The man with the knife had a container of salt in his free hand, and he poured a measure into the long gash in Schroeder's thigh. The old soldier tried to fight the pain and failed. His scream echoed in Anika's head. All the trauma experience in the world couldn't inure her to this kind of human suffering. She prayed unconsciousness would spare him the agony.

"Who are you? Or do I dump the rest of this into his leg?"

"It doesn't matter," the man in the shadows said so quietly that Anika almost didn't hear him. "Kill her."

Karl had taken one step toward her when suddenly he flew back as if jerked on a string. Fragments of gore exploded from the side of his head. The sound of a shot came at the same instant. The man holding Anika pushed her away and wheeled toward where he thought the gunfire had originated. She fell heavily and tried to scramble under the bench, Schroeder's blood smearing against her skin and clothes. Another shot rang out and a piece of stone above the bench exploded. The torturer who'd poured the salt into Schroeder's leg had been at that spot a fraction of a second earlier. He had drawn his own weapon, a small machine pistol that had been under his dark jacket. He fired a long burst over the wall, the gun buzzing like a saw. Hot brass arced from the weapon in a tight necklace.

Anika pressed her hands to her ears as more shots rang out: high whipcracks of rifles, the deeper boom of handguns, and the staccato ratchet of the machine pistol. Chips of stone filled the air, carving visible streaks through the thickening gunpowder smoke. A fresh spray of blood landed on her, and she knew Schroeder had just been hit. Yet the former soldier hadn't reacted. It was either a fatal shot or his body was now beyond pain. She peered into the smoky gloom and saw the leader of the torturers. He was backed against the house, a weapon in his hand. He spotted Anika and the pistol's aim dropped to her position. Closing her eyes was a reflex.

She never heard the shot. A frantic burst of rifle fire covered all other sounds. She did feel the impact, a razor slash of fire that tore along her outer thigh. The fusillade pouring into the garden had distracted the leader and thrown off his aim. Crying out and clamping a hand over the long wound, she wriggled deeper under the bench. Her body was drenched in sweat. She was sobbing and didn't care. A bullet ricocheted against a metal chair, and a burned ember of steel fell into the blood, sizzling obscenely as it cooled.

Out of the gloom, the torturer lurched toward her, his body spasming as the rifles found their mark. He took half a dozen hits before falling to his knees and then collapsing to the ground. His eyes were fixed in death. Anika noticed that his knife had fallen just out of her reach. She twisted to see if the leader was still there and saw two silhouettes running through the haze, racing toward the open farmhouse door. Bullets pounded into the building after them, sparking more shrapnel from the stone. An instant later, a car's engine rumbled to life and the big Mercedes pulled from the house.

Just as quickly as the firefight had started, it was over. The echoes of gunfire faded even as Anika's hearing returned.

She spat the taste of gunpowder from her mouth, not knowing if she should move from her hiding place. She wanted to lie there forever. Then she heard Schroeder moan above her and knew she had to tend to him. It was instinctive.

Okay, AK, move. Painfully, she rolled from under the bench, clutching at the oozing wound in her leg. Nothing happened when she raised her head, no gunfire, no shouts.

The bullet had caught Otto Schroeder in the lower

chest. The blood bubbling from the neat hole appeared carbonated. A lung shot. Fatal if he didn't get attention immediately. She looked into his face. Schroeder stared at her with the certainty of his own death.

"Help!" Anika shouted into the twilight, hoping to draw the attention of whoever had fired into the garden with rifles, the people who'd just saved her life. "Help us please!"

There was no response from beyond the garden walls. A minute might have passed—she didn't know. Whoever had just saved her by killing two of Schroeder's torturers and chasing off the others was not coming. Anika was on her own. Ignoring the throb radiating from the gash in her thigh, she turned to the old man. Schroeder's breathing became more shallow, and less blood was coming from his injuries. Even if she called an ambulance right now, she doubted it would arrive before he died.

She knelt gingerly next to his head, taking one of his big farmer's hands into hers. All she could offer was comfort.

"You'll be okay, Mr. Schroeder." Her sympathy felt flat. Both knew it was an empty platitude.

"I was told someone would come for me," Schroeder breathed through bleeding lips. "But I beat them. They didn't get what they wanted."

"Who were they?" Despite everything that happened, Anika wanted to know.

"I don't know. A call one week ago said people were coming to question me. It was a warning I ignored. Then I got two more calls, but nothing was ever said." Anika thought that one of those calls must have been *Opa* Jacob. It was a favorite trick of his to make sure his quarry was around: just ring and hang up at hello. The other call could have been the torturers doing the exact same thing.

"But who are they?" She pressed, fearful that he would die before she understood what had just happened.

"My past." Schroeder coughed up a clot of blood that Anika wiped away with her sleeve. "I was warned a week ago that it wouldn't end with me. I thought I was the last to know."

"Know what, Mr. Schroeder?"

"The truth." Even with death rapidly approaching, he wouldn't reveal why he had been tortured.

Inspiration struck her. "About the gold? They wanted to know about the gold, didn't they?"

Pain had pulled his face in on itself, but he managed to open his eyes wide and stare at her. His voice quavered. "How do you know about that? Are you with the people who warned me?"

Anika ignored his questions. "The men who did this to you knew about the gold and wanted to know what happened to it. Is that right?"

"The gold is only a small part of it," he dismissed and then fell silent. For a moment Anika thought he'd died, but then he squeezed her hand. "They wanted to know if I've told anyone about the rest of it."

"Have you?"

"I always knew the secret was worth killing for." He smiled a bloody smile. "I just never imagined I would have to die for it."

"What secret?" Anika asked frantically. He wasn't making sense. She had another minute or two before he was gone. "What secret, Mr. Schroeder?"

"Pandora's Curse. I have prayed my entire life that the nightmare would end with me. But now I know it won't. It's going to continue."

"What is Pandora's Curse?"

Schroeder closed his eyes tightly, fighting death by force of will. "They told me there is a man who can help. . . . "

"The people who warned you about these . . . torturers? They told you someone can help?" The old man nodded vaguely. "Who? Who can help?"

Schroeder's chest rattled and he coughed another, larger mass of blood. "An American. Philip Mercer," he wheezed, the words no more than a whisper. His grip on Anika's hand relaxed. His arm fell off the bench and into the pool of their mingled blood. He was dead.

Anika wasn't surprised to feel tears on her cheeks. Somehow this old soldier had kept a horrible secret, and at the end of his life, his silence had killed him. She slumped next to the body. The smoke had cleared, and the full horror of what had just happened was splashed against the garden walls and leached into the dirt between the flagstones.

With an effort, she firmed her jaw and forced herself to separate herself from what had just taken place. Anika had to think like a doctor and not a victim.

Okay, AK, get to work. There were three dead from multiple gunshot wounds and one injured. Her wounded leg was the first priority. The pain was something she could work through, but she would need stitches to close the gash. That meant a hospital. She knew that calling an ambulance would put her in the middle of a police investigation and that was out of the question. Once she explained her presence here, it was only a matter of time before Schroeder's torturers learned her identity, and judging by their savagery, she would be killed long before they were apprehended. The nurse with the apartment next to hers could suture the wound, and Anika herself could get the drugs she needed for infection and pain if necessary.

Using the rough stone wall as a crutch to gain her feet, Anika swayed until her head cleared. It wasn't blood loss accounting for the dizziness, she thought. It was the shock of Schroeder's death and the others. She had to get out of here. Pausing at the gate, she considered the possibility of driving all the way home and knew she wouldn't make it. Once she reached Ismaning, she would call her neighbor to come get her. She had to get her car away from the scene and knew that was something she could handle.

Anika was panting by the time she got to her car. She grabbed a towel from the backseat and tied a rough bandage around the foot-long slash with the strap from her backpack. The last of the water was like a flash flood on a dry desert when it reached her throat, cooling and nourishing and desperately needed. She used another towel to wipe the worst of the blood from her face, arms, and legs. In the rearview mirror, her eyes shone with equal measures of fear and resolve.

Anika took one last look at the house, a single lamp in a front room casting a feeble glow into the night. She was certain her being here at the same time as the torturers wasn't a coincidence. She dialed her *opa*'s number but cut the connection when she heard his gruff "Hello." Anika sagged. He was all right. She'd feared that the gunmen had learned about Schroeder through Jacob Eisenstadt, using the same techniques they'd employed against the former soldier.

If the information hadn't come from *Opa*, it had come from another source. When she was up to it, she'd talk to him about it. But not tonight. And that was only one of the mysteries that needed to be solved—that she needed to solve. Who had tipped off Schroeder's killers? Who had saved her life by chasing them away? She felt they had to be the same people who warned Schroeder a week ago but she didn't know how they knew to be here tonight. Who was this person he mentioned? Mercer? And how could he help? Finally and possibly most tantalizing, what was Pandora's Curse?

She put her car into gear and pulled away, needing all of her concentration to keep the vehicle on the narrow road. One other question worked into the back of her mind. What could possibly be so valuable that Schroeder had dismissed an enormous shipment of gold as only "a small part of it"?

Because his overnight stay in Manhattan wasn't really planned, the airline had held Mercer's luggage from Pennsylvania for him at Reagan National. He presented his identification and baggage claim checks when he deplaned from the New York flight, and a skycap retrieved his bags from storage. He had little trouble finding a cab to take him home. The flight to Washington had lasted an hour and it felt good to sit again. His legs were sore from hours of wandering the Natural History Museum.

It was nearing ten o'clock at night and traffic was light as the taxi threaded around Arlington Cemetery and hooked up with I-66. He'd lived in Arlington for a little over seven years, and the amount of growth near his neighborhood was astonishing. It was only a matter of time before the ten blocks of row houses around his brownstone were replaced with high-rises and strip malls.

From the outside, his building was similar to all the others on the quiet street. It stood three stories tall and was faced with ruddy stone that was corbeled over the windows and the front door. The entry steps were cement flanked by wrought iron railings.

Under the streetlights, he recognized two of the cars parked behind his black Jaguar. The battered Plymouth Fury belonged to Paul Gordon, a retired jockey and the owner of a neighborhood bar called Tiny's, and the Ford Taurus was Mike O'Reilly's, one of Tiny's regulars. Mercer left his bags on the sidewalk and fished his car keys from his pocket, chirping open the locks as he approached the sleek English convertible. He peered in to check the odometer. The last three numbers were 823, exactly as they should be, and the tenth's wheel was between the six and seven.

"I'll be damned," Mercer said aloud. He was certain Harry White would have taken the car for a spin while he was in Pennsylvania, which is why he'd memorized the mileage before leaving.

Then he noticed that the odometer had rolled over a complete thousand miles, right down to the last hundred yards. "Oh, you sneaky old bastard." He chuckled without malice.

Mercer grabbed up his matching bags and mounted the stairs. The front door was unlocked. While the outside of the brownstone was conventional, the inside was something else entirely. The whole structure had been gutted and rebuilt according to plans Mercer himself had drawn up. The front third of the building was a marble-floored atrium that soared up to the roof, with balconies overlooking it from the second-floor library and the third floor, where the master suite was located. Connecting the levels and partially blocking the view of the kitchen was a spiral staircase. The railings on the balconies had been custom made to match the antique stairs.

On the ground floor behind the kitchen and the laundry area were his home office and the dining room he used for a red-topped pool table. The unused dining table sat in a corner of the entry foyer in what should have been the living room. He heard a roar of laughter from the second floor. This was where he had his version of a family room. Only it was closer to an English pub with wainscoting on the walls, an oak wet bar fronted by six stools, a couple of couches and chairs, and his entertainment center.

He left his bags at the base of the spiral stairs and climbed up to the library. The cigar smoke wafting from the bar through the connecting French doors was as thick as a fire on a tobacco plantation. The couches had been pushed aside to make room for a folding table, and seated around it were Harry, Tiny, Mike O'Reilly and Mike's brother-in-law, John Pigeon. The table was littered with ashtrays, half-empty glasses, and poker chips. The forest-green carpet beneath the table looked pale from all the spilled ash. They'd been here for hours. Maybe days, for all Mercer knew.

"You're pushing it, Harry. You're really pushing it." Mercer tried to put some anger in his voice but failed. He didn't care that Harry had let someone chauffeur him around in the Jag or had the guys over for cards. He'd expected no less.

"Hey, Mercer, welcome back," Harry boomed. He might be eighty, but his voice carried the power of a train wreck, with half the charm. "Got any cash on you? Mike's cheating and I think I'll figure out how if you lend me a hundred."

"You mind telling me how you managed to put a thousand miles on my car in two weeks?" Mercer noticed that Paul "Tiny" Gordon had two encyclopedia volumes on his chair so he could sit at the same height as the others.

"Oh, that. Well, Tiny and I decided to go to Atlantic City for the weekend."

"That's only four hundred miles round-trip."

"Twice." Harry's attempt to look contrite appeared more self-satisfied than anything.

"And the other two hundred miles?"

"Errands."

Tiny cut in, shouldering some of the blame. "I wanted to catch a few races at Belmont," the former jockey said. "Besides, we needed to roll your car over to an even grand."

"I hope to God you drove, Paul."

When the diminutive Gordon laughed, he looked and sounded like a gnome. "I had blocks installed on the pedals of my car so I can drive it. To reach the gas in your Jag, I'd have to crawl on the floor and use my hands."

Mercer looked back to Harry, horrified that the octogenarian would drive that far. "You?"

"You need to have the tires rebalanced," Harry suggested mildly. "It started to shimmy at a hundred miles an hour."

"Oh, Christ." Mercer rubbed his forehead. He went behind the bar to get a beer from the rebuilt lock-lever refrigerator next to the ornate back bar.

"While you're back there," Harry called jovially, "mind making me another Jack and ginger?"

"Yeah, grab me another beer," Mike O'Reilly added.

"Might as well mix up another margarita." This from John Pigeon.

Before answering, Mercer slid his wallet from his pants pocket and counted his cash, which totaled nearly three hundred dollars. Despite the late hour and his exhaustion, his decision was an easy one. "Get an extra chair, Pidge, and I'll make it a pitcher."

On one corner of the bar, Mercer's mail lay stacked in a pile that was in imminent danger of spilling onto the floor. The deal with Harry was that he could stay at the house whenever Mercer was away as long as he got the mail and took care of phone messages. The deal didn't include opening the mail, however. Mercer shook his head in mock frustration. One item caught his eye—a long, skinny tube, like those used for shipping posters.

"The one thing that was for you," he said, holding it up for Harry to see. "And you didn't open it."

"I thought someone had mailed you a snake."

"Actually, it's your birthday present, only it's a couple months late." Mercer made the drinks, set them on the bar for John to dispense, and passed the tube to Harry.

"What is it?" he asked suspiciously.

"An anorexic anaconda. Just open the goddamned thing."

Not one to stand on ceremony, Harry crushed out his cigar and tore the tube apart like a kid. Inside was a walking stick, a custom-made cane of black walnut capped with an ornate silver grip. Harry White had only one leg; he'd lost the other during his years as a sea captain following World War II. He didn't have a noticeable limp, but Mercer had seen him wince a few times when he walked and knew it was time for his friend to bow to the inevitable.

"This ain't bad," Harry admitted.

Mercer took it from him, twisted part of the handle to release a secret catch, and pulled a gleaming thirty-inch sword blade from the cane.

Harry's face lit up. "All right!"

"And the best part," Mercer said, and twisted the sword near where the tang went into the handle. The blade came free, leaving a nine-inch-long wand with a screw cap set in the top end. Mercer opened it and gave it an appreciative sniff. The cane maker had gotten his final instructions before shipping his creation.

Harry took the handle, smelled its open end as Mercer had done, and laughed. The cane/sword was also a flask filled with Harry's version of mother's milk, Jack Daniel's.

Harry's eyes were bright blue and they were usually filled with mischievous sarcasm. Now they clouded over, unguarded, and showed how much Mercer's gift meant to him. He looked up. "Thanks, Mercer," he rasped quietly. "This is something else."

"Happy birthday." Mercer handed over five twenty-dollar bills and took a seat, muttering, "You still have to pay back the hundred."

They played poker until midnight, talking mostly about Mercer's upcoming trip. Mike was the only driver sober enough to get behind the wheel, so he said he'd give Tiny a ride back to his condo after dropping off Pidge. He offered the same service to Harry, but he'd already staked his claim to the couch. Harry lived only a dozen blocks away, yet he slept at Mercer's at least once a week and never used either of the small guest rooms at the back of the house.

Orphaned when he was twelve and raised by his grandparents who were now also dead, Mercer had no family, which made his friendships all the more precious. His father had been a mining engineer as well, and he and Mercer's mother, Siobhan, had died in one of the countless uprisings in central Africa. During his training for the Iraq mission, an Army shrink had told Mercer that his early loss had created in him an acute fear of abandonment and an overdeveloped sense of loyalty and responsibility. Mercer agreed and knew that, despite the more than four decades separating them, he valued Harry more than anything else in his life.

Mercer usually woke at dawn. However, he slept an hour later the following morning. He showered quickly, threw on a pair of shorts and a T-shirt, and went down to get the *Washington Post* from the stoop. He'd set the timer on the coffeemaker behind the bar last night. The brew was thick as tar, and the steam rising from it was strong enough to scald his eyes. He poured the pot into a carafe and made more coffee for Harry's less masochistic tastes.

"Do you mind not making those pounding noises over there?" Harry grumbled as he came awake.

"That's not me. It's your head."

Sitting up, Harry looked around the room, his mouth scrunched up as he tasted the aftereffects of a pack of cigarettes, a couple of cigars, and more whiskey than was strictly necessary. He coughed viciously. "Yeah, you might be right."

Before getting off the couch, Harry rolled up his pants leg and strapped on the flesh-colored prosthetic limb. He slid his thin arms into the sleeves of an over-laundered blue oxford, buttoning it over the undershirt he'd slept in.

"I've always wondered," Mercer said, pouring a cup of coffee for his friend and adding several spoons of sugar, "if you slept in your clothes at home."

"Only on those nights I pass out."

"Every night, huh?"

"Let's just say most nights and leave it at that." Harry went off to use the guest bathroom and Mercer scanned the newspaper.

A scandal involving Washington's school board

couldn't hold his interest for more than the headline. Because so much of his work took place overseas, Mercer was more interested in international news. He read about the upcoming Universal Convocation. The article had a photograph of the *Sea Empress*, the ship the pope was using for his meeting. Although the vessel was the largest cruise liner ever built, she was as sleek as a race yacht, with raked decks and funnels on each of her two hulls. Somewhere he'd read that a lap around the enormous catamaran was half a mile. Harry returned as Mercer was finishing another piece about a German company that had agreed to pay $1.2 billion in reparations to slave laborers they had used in their factories during the war.

"Hey, last night you never said when you were leaving for Greenland." Harry sat at the bar near Mercer. He'd taken the time to shave the silver stubble from his lantern jaw.

"Tomorrow afternoon," Mercer replied, sliding the crossword puzzle over to him.

Seated or standing, the two men were the same height, but this news made Harry slump in disappointment. He preferred Mercer's company more than the use of his house. He took a gulp of coffee and lit a cigarette.

"I know, the timing kind of sucks," Mercer added. "This is an opportunity I just couldn't pass up."

"I guess I can't blame you. Joining the Surveyor's Society must be a hell of a thing for you."

"How many childhood dreams really do come true?" The question was asked seriously.

"Besides losing your virginity? Not many." Harry's wrinkled face broke into a smile. "I'm glad for you, but I don't envy you. What's that place like this time of year?"

"Believe it or not, spring is just starting. July is when the ice packs that surround Greenland break up. We'll probably be one of the first ships over this year. The weather should be in the low twenties though I think storms can blow up at any time and the temperature can drop below zero in about five minutes."

"You're nuts."

Mercer laughed but didn't argue.

While Harry worked at the crossword, Mercer grabbed a sheet of paper and a pen from his office and began a list of things he wanted to bring. For a job, he usually knew exactly what items were needed. This was the first time in a while, however, that he would work in such harsh conditions and he wanted to be prepared.

"Ten down," Harry White interrupted. "A five-letter word for friend? Middle one's 'o.' "

Mercer looked at him pointedly. "Mooch."

"Bastard."

"Try crony."

An hour later, as Harry thumbed through the rest of the *Washington Post*, Mercer was getting together some of the equipment on his list. Later, he would need to go to a specialized outfitter's store for the things he'd need, but many of the small items he had lying around the house. Some were elusive though.

"Harry, have you seen my glacier glasses?"

Twisting on his bar stool, the octogenarian shot him a withering look and his voice dripped sarcasm. "Don't you remember? I borrowed them the last time I climbed Mount Everest."

"Just for that, I'm going to lock up my liquor when I'm gone and ban you from smoking in here." Such clean living would probably kill him in a week.

"Hey, I was kidding." Harry backpedaled quickly. "There's no need to get nasty. When you're done today, you going over to Tiny's? It's two-for-one night, which means double-fisted drinking."

"No. I want to do some research on the Internet. I'd like to find out more about Project Iceworm and this Camp Decade we're going to reopen."

During his lunch at the Society, Charles Bryce had also told Mercer about an Air Force plane that had crashed a few months before the base closed. The search for the wreckage had been extensive and it should have been easy to spot the plane on the ice, but no trace was ever found. He hoped to find something about that as well, just for curiosity's sake.

"Suit yourself," Harry said, grabbing his new cane for the walk home. "You leaving from Dulles or National?"

"Dulles. You mind giving me a ride?"

"That's why I asked."

"Thanks. Come by around noon."

Harry left, and a few minutes later Mercer went on his shopping trip. Considering the list of items and the work he had to do tonight, he realized that he shouldn't have stayed in New York for an extra day. However, anything he forgot here could most likely be purchased in Iceland before they boarded the *Njoerd* for the run to Ammassalik, Greenland. He also trusted Charlie Bryce about Geo-Research being a first-class outfit. Surely they'd take care of him.

Since Mercer was a geologist, this small island in the middle of the Atlantic fascinated him. Formed a mere eighteen million years ago by subsea volcanoes that were still active today, Iceland was living proof of the turbulent nature of our planet. Earthquakes were a daily occurrence, and one of the many volcanoes dotting the country erupted every couple of years. The landscape was littered with incredible geologic features—geothermal vents, ancient craters, and a mountain valley that was the only place where the mid-Atlantic ridge crossed dry land. By contrast, Greenland, its huge neighbor to the west, was once part of Pangea, the supercontinent that formed as the earth cooled. The rock there was upward of 3.5 billion years old and geologically dead.

That didn't mean that Mercer was too keen on the place as a tourist. Iceland was rather desolate. Half of the population of a quarter million lived in and around the capital, Reykjavik. If not for the geothermal plants that provided hot water for heat and electricity, the sustainable population would have been only a fraction of that number. Also, its isolation ensured that everything was sickeningly expensive.

Reykjavik's international airport sat on an open plain blistered by the radar domes of an adjacent American military base. As Mercer stepped through the revolving exit door of the futuristic terminal, he was hit by a blast of cold wind shrieking off the north Atlantic. The Gulf Stream, the river of warm water that flowed from Florida to Europe, passed along Iceland's south coast and warmed the island enough to make it habitable, but by no stretch was it comfortable, even in summer. The sky was leaden, with low tumbling clouds that seemed to hang just a few hundred feet off the ground. A distant beam of sunlight made a far-off mountain glow neon green.

Mercer zipped up his bomber jacket and donned a khaki baseball cap while he waited at the curb with his two large bags. The air smelled fresh, sharp with the scent of the sea, and it only added to the unreality of his position. Eight hours ago Harry had dropped him at Dulles with the promise that he wouldn't use the Jag, and now he was here. Though he traveled constantly, the thrill of being in a new place never wore off. It was like a flicker of lightness in his chest.

Mercer had also asked Harry to forward his mail to the satellite office Geo-Research would maintain in Reykjavik to transship mail and supplies to the team in Greenland once a week. While downloading the two hundred e-mail messages from his server, Mercer had come across a cryptic note from a lawyer in Munich about some documents being sent to him on behalf of an unnamed client. Mercer had no idea what it was about and had sent a query back. There hadn't been a reply by the time he and Harry left for the airport, so Mercer asked his old friend to keep an eye out for it and make sure it reached him.

Mercer had been waiting for five minutes when a Toyota van pulled up to the building. The burly passenger rolled down his window. "Dr. Mercer, *da*?" His accent was Russian.

"I'm Mercer."

The Russian threw open the door with a big grin. Even without the bright blue parka he was huge, taller than Mercer by at least a foot and broad across the shoulders and chest. To judge by his florid face, he appeared to be in his early fifties, but he looked like an outdoorsman and might have been younger. "Welcome to Iceland. I am Igor Bulgarin."

Mercer's hand vanished in his grip. "Thank you. Are you part of Geo-Research?"

"*Nyet*. They are all Germans. I am from Russian

Academy of Science. But I am lone Russian on expedition. All others from my group are from Western Europe." He spoke in a flood of words as if fearful they would dry up.

The driver got out of the Toyota. He was Mercer's age and about the same build. His sour expression seemed to be a permanent feature, and he had slow, watchful eyes. Mercer made the quick assumption that the two were not working together. Bulgarin had the jocularity of an excited puppy, while the blond-haired driver seemed overly taciturn.

"This is Ernst Neuhaus," Igor introduced. "He is head of Geo-Research support office here in Iceland."

"Oh, how do you do?" Mercer said.

"Good evening, Dr. Mercer," Neuhaus replied, briefly shaking hands without first removing his glove. His voice was sharp and lightly accented. "You're the last of the Society's people to arrive. In fact, everyone's here except for one person from Igor's group."

Mercer turned to the Russian. "Is there a problem?"

"We have medical doctor coming. She is German who studies stress but not part of Geo-Research. She had accident back home and will join us on Greenland."

"I thought your group were all meteorologists?"

"*Nyet*. Three of them investigate sunspots, I look for meteorite fragments, and Dr. Klein looks at us."

"I never asked you, Igor," Neuhaus interrupted. "Why go to Greenland to look for meteors?"

"Meteor doesn't hit ground. Meteorite does," Igor Bulgarin corrected. "We search on ice for same reason polar bear is white. White bear, white ice—no can see. Black meteorite on white ice, find easy. Meteorite in desert looks like all other rocks. Very hard to find."

Mercer decided quickly that he liked the animated Russian. His less than positive reaction to Neuhaus was irrelevant since the German wasn't going to Greenland. "Are you guys my ride to town?"

"*Da*. Others wait at hotel. Very boring. I volunteer to come with Ernst for something to do."

Mercer's luggage was tossed into the cargo section at the rear of the van, and he jumped into the seat behind Neuhaus's. "I'm surprised Marty Bishop didn't come to pick me up."

"He's getting drunk," Igor Bulgarin scoffed. "Last night he learn that friend of his not coming on trip. Last-minute crisis cause him to cancel."

"You mean there's only going to be three of us opening Camp Decade?" Mercer had thought that four was ludicrous but losing Marty's buddy meant they would be even more shorthanded.

"Mr. Bishop has already taken care of that," Neuhaus said. "Geo-Research is sending thirty people to the ice. He's made arrangements to use some of our workers as needed. Plus, we have enough equipment and provisions to last a couple of months for anything else you may need."

"*Da*, is true," Igor admitted with a grunt. "Four Sno-Cats with trailers, a Land Cruiser with special tires, and many, many preformed buildings that are supposed to go up like house of cards."

"How are we getting all that equipment to Camp Decade?" Mercer asked. "It's too much for choppers."

Bulgarin twisted in his seat so he could look at Mercer. Although his smile was missing a tooth, it conveyed his boundless energy. "From dock in Ammassalik, everything is transferred to ice by blimp."

Mercer must have made a surprised sound because Ernst Neuhaus elaborated. "It's a heavy-lift cargo airship that Geo-Research leased for the job. I guess it's only been flying a few months."

"Believe it or not I know something about it," Mercer said. "It's got a semirigid body that supports four engine pods with tilt-rotors that can pivot from horizontal like an airplane's to vertical like a helicopter's. It's similar to the system used in the Marines' V-22 Osprey."

"This type of dirigible's a modification of Frank Piasecki's ill-fated heli-stat. The owners call it a rotor-stat." Neuhaus steered the van off the airport grounds and on to Route 41 for the drive to Reykjavik. "It will ferry the vehicles to the ice directly inland of Ammassalik, where you then drive them to the camp. The heavier stores and prefab buildings will be flown to the site. By the time you arrive, an advance team will have one building ready for your use while you erect everything else."

"Sounds like this is going to be one hell of a trip." Mercer had always been fascinated by airships. They represented something special in the world of aviation, an evolutionary branch that was as elegant as it was short-lived. Modern materials and computer-aided design, as well as the use of nonflammable helium, were creating a minor resurgence in these flying behemoths. That flicker of anticipation he'd felt since arriving was burning a little brighter now.

"Look." Igor pointed to a road to their right, away from where the ocean was pounding Iceland's black volcanic coast. "That is way to Blue Lagoon. Geothermal hot spring used as natural spa. Water in huge outdoor pool like lake. Very curative. I went yesterday with a few of the Germans."

"The water's actually effluent from the adjoining thirty-two-megawatt Svartsengi power plant," Ernst explained. "They use volcanically heated water to produce electricity. It has the same salinity as seawater but it is high in silica, which helps people suffering from psoriasis."

"I've been to the old Blue Lagoon," Mercer said. Across the lichen-coated lava field, a white cloud clung to the ground just over the horizon. It was steam from the power plant. "A few years ago I came to Iceland for a conference. I understand they built a new spa about a quarter mile from the plant."

"Yes, yes. Very nice," Igor confirmed eagerly. "We must go tomorrow before ship leaves for Greenland."

Mercer shook his head. "Sorry. I've got a meeting

in the morning." He added nothing more and his two companions didn't pry.

They drove in silence, and eventually the rolling hills of lava gave way to urban sprawl. In Icelandic, Reykjavik means "smoking bay." It was named for the steam that rose from the geologically active vents nearby. The city's suburbs were newer, with a distinctive European flair. In the distance, dominating the skyline, sat the Hallgrimskirkja, a huge cement church topped by a 200-foot spire. Locals nicknamed it the "Concrete Cathedral" for obvious reasons.

The tidy old town abutting the harbor was a jumble of narrow streets laid down randomly, as though a giant had thrown a fistful of straws. The older buildings were rustic and the newer ones were given historic architectural touches. Ernst Neuhaus pulled up before the Hotel Borg, a white stone edifice across the street from a small public park.

"Home for the night," he announced and waited while Igor helped Mercer unload his bags. "I must return to Geo-Research's office. I can't see you off tomorrow, so have a great trip."

Again, Iceland's constant wind struck Mercer when he closed the van's side door. Igor Bulgarin didn't seem the slightest bit fazed by it and Mercer suspected he had spent a great deal of his time in climates much worse than this. "Is it this bad in Greenland?" he asked.

The big Russian laughed, hefting one bag over his shoulder for the short walk to the hotel entrance. "They have wind there called the *pitaraq*. Is gravity driven, like *katabatic* in Antarctica. It starts with small breeze from the south and then there is calm. You have about ten minutes to find shelter. Then *pitaraq* hits from north at about two hundred and forty kilometers per hour. Ten years ago a man I was working with was picked up by such wind. We find him twenty kilometers away. He looked like he was dragged by truck. Clothes and flesh stripped from his body by contact with ice."

"Jesus."

"*Da.*" Seeing Mercer's concern, Igor grinned again. "*Pitaraq* is mostly in winter. Not so common this time of year, but must always be prepared."

Although it was approaching ten o'clock at night, it was still light out because Reykjavik was only a hundred fifty miles south of the Arctic Circle. According to Mercer's internal clock it was four hours earlier, but he knew he had to acclimate himself to the time change. And the best way to do that was to force himself to sleep. He got his key in the retro-1930's lobby, thanked Igor for picking him up, and took the elevator to his room. He would meet with the Surveyor's Society team at breakfast.

The room was small but functional and overlooked the park. Hot water would be a precious luxury once in Greenland, so he took a long shower to wash the flight from his skin. He thought about his meeting in the morning.

While researching Camp Decade on the Internet, he had come across an old article about the downed C-97 cargo plane and the subsequent search for survivors. He read that Stefansson Rosmunder, the son of one of the first men to climb Mt. Everest, had been part of the search-and-rescue effort. Because Rosmunder had been so young at the time, Mercer figured he would still be alive and he wanted to talk with the Arctic specialist about his experiences. He spent the better part of the morning before his flight to Iceland on the telephone trying to track down Rosmunder and finally reached his elderly mother just a few minutes before Harry had come over.

Her son, she'd told him in a remarkably clear voice, had been dead for many years. When Mercer explained where he was going, Mrs. Rosmunder said that she would like to speak with him before they sailed to Greenland. She told him that she fed the ducks living in the small lake called the Pond in the middle of Reykjavik every morning at nine-thirty and asked if he would meet her there. Of course, Mercer agreed.

Just in case he overslept, Mercer put in one wake-up call for six and another for six-ten and fell into bed. He wasn't tired and the meal he'd had on the flight was churning in his stomach, so it was difficult to slow his mind and relax. Over and over his conversation with Elisebet Rosmunder replayed in his head. He decided that it was her voice that had disturbed him. Rather than hearing sorrow for her dead son as he expected, she had sounded frightened.

Dark dreams made his sleep fitful.

He abandoned his bed thirty minutes before his first wake-up call and dressed. The harbor was four blocks away, a straight walk down Posthusstreati—Post Office Street. The sun was long risen. He studied the merchandise in the windows of the tourist shops. Beautiful sweaters and woolens were piled on tables and cascaded off racks. They would make an ideal gift for a woman, he thought, but the only one in his life at the moment was Fay, the wife of FBI director Dick Henna. Mercer and Dick had been friends ever since the Hawaii crisis a few years ago and he decided that he would buy Fay a sweater when the expedition was over.

At the base of the street, across a wide quay, the Geo-Research ship, *Njoerd,* lay low in the water of the protected inner harbor, thick manila ropes securing her to bollards. The wind was a constant force that stung Mercer's cheeks and made his eyes tear. Across the bay, the snowcap atop Mount Esja seemed gilded.

The red-hulled *Njoerd* was a functional vessel about two hundred feet long with a large superstructure mounted well forward. A coil of smoke rose from both her side-by-side funnels. Her aft deck was an open cargo area nearly hidden under the equipment that was going to Greenland with them. Amid the pallets of stores and sections of the base's buildings, Mercer could just see the tops of the Sno-Cats over the gunwale. An overhead crane mounted on rails that ran the length of the ship could shift her cargo as needed, as well as offload her on some hostile coast. Placed transversely behind the funnels but still accessible by the crane was a large oceangoing powerboat that he assumed they used as a fast shuttle. She also had a small helipad.

If not for her oversize superstructure that housed laboratories and accommodations for passengers and crew, Mercer thought she looked a bit like an oil field resupply ship. The Denmark Strait separating Iceland from Greenland had a reputation for being treacherous, but the *Njoerd* seemed more than capable of handling anything the seas threw at her.

He was chilled by the time he returned to the Hotel Borg, and the smell of fresh coffee and the breakfast buffet made his mouth flood in anticipation. The mauve-colored dining room was full of Geo-Research people and members of the other two teams, and the excited conversation made the room buzz. Mercer noted nearly everyone in the room had facial hair of some sort and guessed they cultivated a mountain man look because of what they did. Arctic research attracted a very specific type of person. Igor Bulgarin waved when he saw Mercer enter.

"You are always late, my friend," he greeted.

"I went down to the dock to check out our ship."

"Fine boat," Igor said. "Her bows are hardened to break ice up to a meter thick. I'm afraid this meal is a segregated one. Teams are eating only with each other. That is Marty Bishop at the corner table with the other member of Society team."

"Then I guess I should grab a plate and join them."

"A group are going to Blue Lagoon in a few minutes. Sure you not come?"

"Yeah, I'm sure. Thanks anyway."

"Is okay. See you on *Njoerd* at noon."

Mercer mounded his plate with eggs, smoked salmon, and sweet breakfast rolls before approaching the Society's table. One of the men looked at him suspiciously, then got to his feet. He was short and heavy across the gut, about fifty years old, and he had the pale look of someone who didn't spend much time outside an office. His gray hair was thin at the top and along the front, and it swayed with just a small toss of his head. His neatly trimmed mustache was a few shades darker than his hair and was the only thing that gave his ordinary face any character. Considering his soft appearance, Mercer wondered how much of his being here was his idea and how much was pressure from his father.

"Marty Bishop. Pleasure to meet you." They shook hands. Bishop's palm was as smooth as an accountant's. "Charlie Bryce says you've got one hell of a reputation."

"He exaggerates. It's good to be part of your team," Mercer said, intentionally establishing his subordinate status.

Bishop nodded, obviously pleased that Mercer understood who was in charge. "Glad to have you on board." He pointed to the other man at the table. He was about the same age as Bishop, though had a harder look. "This here's Ira Lasko, U.S. Navy."

"Retired," Lasko added.

Lasko's handshake was like a bear trap and Mercer suspected that he had never been a pencil pusher. Eater maybe, but not a pusher. His hands had deep scars across all the knuckles and white pads of calluses at the base of each finger. They were the hands of a worker. He was about five foot seven and wiry. The sleeves of his flannel shirt were pushed up, and while his arms were thin, ropes of muscle and sinew pushed outward from beneath his skin. He kept his head completely shaved, though there was a fringe of five o'clock shadow circling just above his ears. His eyes were murky brown under dark brows.

"I understand we're missing a team member," Mercer invited as he sat.

"Jim Kneeland," Marty replied, blowing out a long breath. "He was supposed to get time off from the National Guard but was suddenly called back to duty. Kinda throws us off. I asked my dad to consider postponing the search, but he refused." He shrugged. "Considering his health, I can't blame him."

"Charlie said he's in a wheelchair."

"He's now in a hospital bed at home. Cancer. Doctors don't give him more than six months."

"Opening Camp Decade means a lot to him?"

"Actually, he rarely mentioned his time in the Air Force until about a year ago. Suddenly it was all he talked about. When he asked if I was willing to come up here to make a video of the place, I couldn't say no."

"This is a hell of a thing you're doing for him," Ira said somberly. Mercer nodded.

It seemed as if Marty hadn't thought about this situation from another's point of view. He started to smile. "Yeah," he agreed without conceit. "I guess it is. What the hell? It gets me out of the office for a while, and this might actually turn out to be fun."

"I was never told—are you part of the Surveyor's Society?" Mercer asked Lasko.

"No, but I've done some work for Charles Bryce before. He recommended me to Marty."

"What do you do?"

"I used to teach snot-nosed kids how to survive accidents aboard submarines. Now I run the garage at a truck stop. My job here is to make sure all our equipment runs properly. Charlie told us what you do for a living. Why the hell do you live in a cesspool like Washington?"

Mercer laughed. "My first job out of the Colorado School of Mines was for the U.S. Geological Survey. I actually liked living in D.C., so when I went out on my own, I just stayed. All I really need for my work is a computer and easy access to an airport. Have you guys met any of the Geo-Research people coming with us?"

Ira leaned across the table and spoke in a low voice. "They're headed by a real asshole named Werner Koenig. He's got a fistful of degrees and a real superior attitude. Bryce told you how the Danish government forced him to bring us along and move his operation to conform to our mission, so you can believe he ain't too pleased with us."

"His second in charge is Greta Schmidt," Marty Bishop added with a smirk. "A real knockout in a Nordic ice princess sort of way. They're sitting four tables over, next to the bar."

Mercer turned. Greta Schmidt was easy to spot. She was bent over the table passing a folder to someone. Her hair was white-blond and fell past her shoulders. He could see just a portion of her face and got the impression that she was indeed beautiful. Koenig was the man seated next to her. He was speaking to another tablemate, rapping on the table with his hand as he made a point. He had a natural aura of leadership that Mercer recognized even at this distance. Above his dark beard, his face was weathered like old leather, though he couldn't have been much older than forty. His eyes were a cold blue, like polished aquamarine.

"Don't even think about it," Bishop said, incorrectly guessing at Mercer's interest. "I tried to chat her up two days ago. Frigid as an iceberg."

Mercer suppressed a chuckle. He loved how a man like Marty Bishop immediately assumed a woman was frigid when she rebuffed his advances. The skin around the ring finger on Marty's left hand was pinched and slightly discolored where until recently a wedding band had covered it. Opening his father's old military base wasn't the only conquest on Bishop's mind.

They talked all through the long breakfast, forging the rapport that would sustain them for the weeks to come. Although there were forty people total, Mercer's experience was that group dynamics quickly broke down when they were hit by the enormity of their isolation. He wasn't concerned about himself or Ira Lasko—isolation was nothing new to a submariner. He did have some reservations about Marty. While mental character rarely showed on the outside, he felt that Bishop possessed an underlying weakness. He suspected that Marty's father had seen it too and that this trip was more about having his middle-aged son find whatever it was he lacked than taking pictures of a long-abandoned Air Force base.

The meal broke up around nine. Everyone was going back to their rooms to pack up for the ship. Mercer wasn't sure how long he'd be with Elisebet Rosmunder, so he asked Ira Lasko to make sure his bags made it to the *Njoerd*.

He was standing outside the hotel, checking his bearings on a small map, when a female voice called to him from the door.

"You are part of the Surveyor's Society?" The voice was German accented and throaty. Without looking, he knew it had to be Greta Schmidt.

"Yes, I am." Mercer turned and approached her. She was his exact height, and nearly as wide at the shoulders. Her hair was scraped back from her forehead, revealing a widow's peak above her wide-spaced eyes. She wore too much lipstick, he noted, which made her mouth overly full, as though her lips were swollen. She was not as attractive as that first impression. It was the eyes. They lacked focus and depth, as if there was nothing beyond her facade. "I'm Philip Mercer."

"I am Greta Schmidt," she said formally but made no move to shake his hand. "I will not tolerate the way you looked at me at breakfast. You have the same bad manners as your Mr. Bishop."

Mercer took the accusation like an ill-deserved slap. Like most men, he had been caught staring at women many times. However, unlike Marty Bishop, he never crossed the line between admiring and objectifying. And in this case, he had been doing neither.

"You misunderstood my interest, Miss Schmidt. I had just asked Marty Bishop to point out the leaders of the Geo-Research team. I wanted to assure myself that I wasn't trusting my life to a couple of incompetents."

At this, her stare became even harder. Mercer was sure nine times out of ten she was right about what people thought when they saw her and he could understand her anger. What disturbed him was that she enjoyed this anger, seemed to need it. He saw in her expression that she liked that her looks gave her a power to intimidate men.

"And are we," she asked in a brittle voice, "competent?"

"I don't judge people at a glance," Mercer said, throwing her accusation back at her. "But after looking at your ship this morning, I feel safe with Geo-Research."

Greta Schmidt studied him for a long moment, her expression unreadable, and then she reentered the hotel. Mercer went back to his map. Making an enemy this soon wasn't what he had in mind, but he'd done nothing to precipitate the confrontation.

The Tjorn, or Pond, was only a couple of blocks behind the Hotel Borg, screened from Mercer's view by the Town Hall. It was surrounded by buildings on three sides and divided by an automobile bridge about three hundred yards from the cobblestone shore. Ducks and geese filled the air and coated a good portion of the water. They rode the wind-stirred waves like toys. It was obviously a favorite spot for the elderly who fed the birds and for young mothers with their children.

Scanning the crowd, he saw a number of people who could have been Elisebet Rosmunder yet only one paid him any attention. She was a tiny woman, bundled in a long drab coat, a wool hat covering her hair. She sat on a bench near the water's edge, a flock of birds within an easy toss of her position. Like most locals, she looked Scandinavian, with sharp features and clear, though heavily wrinkled skin. Her eyes were as sharp and blue as Harry White's. Mercer guessed they were about the same age too.

"Mrs. Rosmunder?" he asked as he walked nearer. There were a few unclaimed bread crumbs at her feet.

"Yes, I am she," the elderly lady said and indicated that Mercer should sit by her side. "You are the man who phoned me yesterday? Dr. Mercer?"

"Yes, Philip Mercer. Thank you for seeing me."

"Dr. Mercer, it was I who wanted to see you," she reminded him in excellent English.

Mercer didn't recall mentioning his title, but he wasn't certain. "That's right. You said you had something you wanted to tell me."

"That's correct." He didn't get a sense of fear from her like he'd felt during their phone call. Instead, she seemed almost relieved. "I also have something I want to show you as well."

Mercer waited quietly while she threw a handful of bread into the water. A pair of ducks squabbled to get the food, and Mrs. Rosmunder admonished them in Icelandic.

"Do you work for your government, Dr. Mercer?"

"No, ma'am. As I said on the phone, I'm part of a scientific expedition going to Greenland. I was doing research for the trip when I came across the story of a crashed airplane and how your son was part of the search. Because it happened near where we're going, I thought I would speak with him about conditions there."

"Greenland's east coast is a mystery to most people. There are only a few native settlements, and the Danes heavily subsidize them. Where Stefansson went to look for that plane is an area that even the native Inuits don't bother with. You are wise to want to talk with someone who has actually been there."

Mercer said nothing.

"It was the middle of August 1953, I don't remember the exact date, when my husband received a phone call from the American military at Keflavik Air Force Base. They told him about a plane crash and how they needed guides who knew Greenland to help them in their search. Stefan had just returned from another failed attempt to climb Everest and was in no condition to attempt something that strenuous. However, our son, who was twenty at the time and every bit the Arctic expert as his father, agreed to go. Your government was offering unheard-of wages.

"Stefansson was gone for two weeks. As you probably know from the article you read, they never found the plane and they searched by dogsled, on foot, and by airplane."

"Did they happen to go to a place called Camp Decade?"

She looked at him sharply. "You have heard of it?"

"Part of my mission is to reopen the base," Mercer said, somehow knowing this news wouldn't please her.

"You know what the base was supposed to be, yes?"

"It was an experiment to create a town under the ice. To see if such a place could be habitable."

She shook her head as though he'd given her the wrong answer. "Why would your government want to know if such a thing was possible? Have you ever asked yourself that question?"

Mercer hadn't, which was unusual. "Do you know why?"

"No. But I want to show you something." She made no move to show him anything. She sat very still, her mind elsewhere, probably with her dead son. Finally she spoke. "Camp Decade was off-limits to the searchers. They weren't even supposed to know it was there, though they did fly over it once. Stefansson told me he asked about it and was informed by the military pilot that he hadn't seen anything."

"That was the height of the Cold War." Mercer felt a need to explain his nation's paranoia. "My government thought that everything should be classified top secret. To look back now, so much of what they did seems comical."

Mrs. Rosmunder winced. Mercer wasn't sure what he'd said to cause such a reaction. She reached into her handbag and withdrew a leather wallet. From inside, she pulled out two black-and-white photographs. She handed one to him. It showed a handsome young man in a thick roll-necked sweater, his blond hair falling around his head in heavy rings. He was smiling at the camera with the easy confidence of youth.

"That is Stefansson about two months before he left for Greenland," Elisebet Rosmunder informed him, taking back the picture and staring at it before handing over the other.

This shot showed a skeletal figure lying on a bed with sheets drawn up to the neck so all Mercer could see was an enormous head. Bony shoulder blades created sharp ridges in the covers. Whatever was wasting the person rendered its face sexless. Its eyes were sunken, and it had hollowed cheeks and just a few stray hairs covering its skull. Dark splotches marred its skin. Mercer was reminded of pictures of Holocaust victims.

Mrs. Rosmunder held out her hand to take the photo back from Mercer. This time she didn't even glance at it before replacing it in her wallet. Mercer waited quietly for an explanation.

"That was Stefansson six months after returning. He died a couple of days after a nurse took that picture. I never wanted to be reminded what happened to him, but I am grateful that she gave it to me anyway." Her eyes were filled with tears while her voice had tightened. "Doctors told me it was cancer, a very aggressive cancer that he must have had for quite some time but only showed itself in those final months."

"You don't believe what you were told?" Mercer's voice was as gentle as possible.

"It was certainly cancer," she replied. "But I never believed that he'd had it before going to look for that plane."

She spoke with absolute conviction, yet Mercer couldn't help but think she'd fooled herself into believing that something other than cruel fate had stolen her son from her. Newspapers were full of stories about healthy people dying of cancer without having symptoms until the very end. It was the most feared disease for that and many other reasons.

Elisebet Rosmunder turned so she faced him on the bench, taking his hand into her bird-like fingers. "Dr. Mercer, you don't have to believe me. I have long ago given up trying to convince people that there is something on Greenland that killed Stefansson. My government never looked into it, your military never looked into it, and I would never allow my husband to go over there and search for himself. I am certain that my son was exposed to some toxin or some radiation, and that is what gave him accelerated cancer. I also believe it has to do with Camp Decade." She forestalled the question on Mercer's lips by squeezing his hand. "I have no proof. There is no reason for me to think this. And as far as I know, no Americans stationed there suffered the way Stefansson did. I just wanted you to know the suspicions of an old woman who lost her son in the same area you are now going to. In good conscience I could not let you or your team go without warning you."

She turned back and tossed another handful of crumbs to the ducks.

Mercer knew she had nothing more to say. He stood. "Thank you for sharing this with me, Mrs. Rosmunder. You've given me something to think about."

When she looked up at him, her smile was wan. "You are years older than Stefansson when he died, but you remind me a great deal of him. Not your looks. Well, you're as handsome as he was, but I'm talking about your spirit. You both have the same confidence in your abilities." Mercer made a small gesture of denial. "It is true. Yet all the confidence in the world couldn't save my son. But maybe the truth could have. I wanted you to know the truth or as much of it as I know."

Mercer took her hand. "I'm sorry for your loss."

As he turned to go, she stopped him with one more comment. "Dr. Mercer, three months after the plane crash and failed search, Camp Decade was abandoned. Your military didn't dismantle it and cart it away. They deserted it on Greenland for the ice and snow to bury. No reason was ever given. I think it is a mistake for you to reopen it."

Mercer could understand now why he'd detected fear in her voice when they spoke on the phone. More disturbed than he wanted to admit, he left Elisebet Rosmunder with her memories and her ducks. As he walked toward the hotel, he felt a creeping suspicion, a sense of unease that he'd felt all too often. There was something to her story, even if she couldn't provide any proof.

Given the times, Mercer had little doubt the U.S. government might have carried out some sort of experiment at Camp Decade. With its isolation, it would have been the perfect place to test chemical or biological weapons. While the camp was powered by a small reactor, he discounted nuclear testing or an accident because even a small atomic detonation registered on seismographs. He also thought that if something did get away from them, the area around Camp Decade would have been rendered safe by time and the elements; otherwise the Surveyor's Society would not have received permission from the military to reopen it.

Mercer checked his watch. The *Njoerd* was leaving in an hour, which left him just enough time for two stops if he hurried. One stop was a liquor store. Despite Geo-Research's prohibition against alcohol at the Greenland base, he'd bought a bottle of brandy at the airport duty free, and if he was going to spend three weeks with them, he'd need at least one more. The second stop was a matter of suspicion, Mrs. Rosmunder's and his own. Mercer had built his career on risk and didn't mind taking chances as long as he had time to manipulate the odds first. Such was his concern that he headed to the second location before finding booze, a move that would have stunned Harry White or anyone else who knew him.

It was with an unnatural stillness that Klaus Raeder sat in the conference room. His breathing barely made an impression against his suit coat, and his eyes blinked at long, regular intervals. When the phone next to his elbow chimed, his hand made a graceful gesture to pick it up, almost as if he'd paused between rings. In fact, he'd remained motionless for more than an hour.

"Yes, Kara?"

"The board members are here, Herr Raeder. Shall I show them in?"

"Please." Raeder pressed a button on the console built into the blond wood conference table, and the heavy drapes over the large picture windows swept closed, obscuring the view of the Alster River far below.

His secretary opened the door and stood aside for the six members of the board whom Raeder had called in this afternoon. He ignored them as they took their seats. "Kara, has Gunther Rath returned yet?"

"He got back from Paris about an hour ago."

"Tell him I want to see him after we are finished here."

"Yes, sir," the secretary replied.

She closed the door behind her, and Raeder turned his head to regard his guests. At the far end of the table sat Konrad Ebelhardt, the seventy-year-old chairman of the board. Next to him was Anna Kohl, the daughter and only living relative of the company's founder, Volker Kohl, whose portrait stared down from behind Ebelhardt's back. The others were of little consequence to Raeder. Certainly they were wealthy and powerful, but they took all of their cues from Konrad and Anna.

"Good afternoon, gentlemen. Good afternoon, Anna."

"How are you, Klaus?" the elderly Anna Kohl asked. "How are Eva and the children?"

"She's taken them to the lodge in Bavaria for the summer." There was a twinge of loneliness in his voice. "The boys have been looking forward to it."

"Will you be joining them?" she persisted.

"I'm planning on a weekend visit in a week or so." He poured water from a carafe and took a long sip to discourage her from asking any more personal questions.

Raeder folded his hands in front of him, waiting while Anna asked the others about their lives. He wasn't deluded by her interest. Anna Kohl was as tough as any of the men at the table with the possible exception of Raeder himself. She couldn't care less about the board members. The spinster had nothing in the world except the company that bore her name.

"I saw the quarterly projections," Konrad Ebelhardt said to end the idle chatter. He was broadly built with a heavy stomach and a blocky head. He spoke with the deliberation of a Prussian officer. "With our capital reserves as low as they are, I don't like that we are so dependent on getting the Eurofighter's avionics contract. If that deal falls through, we will be in a vulnerable position."

"The announcement for who will be supplying the next-generation computers for the Eurofighter is still a month away, but we have been assured that Kohl's electronics arm will be building them," Raeder stated in such a way that Ebelhardt knew not to ask anything further. The board members wouldn't want to know what their president had done to secure the multibillion-mark contract.

"Does that mean we can forget about the French

attempt to underbid us?" asked Reinhardt Wurmbach, Kohl AG's chief legal counsel.

"Their bid is thirty percent higher than ours," Raeder said. "I'm going to increase our own bid price to cut that gap to ten percent. We'll still get the contract and squeeze another two hundred million marks from NATO."

"Do we have Herr Rath and his trip to Paris to thank for this information?"

Raeder allowed a tight smile, knowing it was expected of him. "My special-projects director was instrumental in learning the amount of the French bid."

"Nothing too illegal, I hope." The lawyer tried to make light of industrial espionage.

The president of Kohl AG said nothing. In his devotion to the company's fiscal strength, very little was beyond his scope, and he would not make jokes about his business practices. An uncomfortable silence stretched for ten seconds. Wurmbach stripped off his glasses to avoid Raeder's stare but he could not hide his bitterness toward the man financial magazines called *Überkind*. Superboy.

When Kohl's previous president announced his retirement eighteen months ago, Reinhardt Wurmbach had worked tirelessly to become his replacement. It was to be his reward for twenty-seven years of loyalty. And yet Anna and Konrad had passed him over in favor of Raeder, an outsider who had amassed a personal fortune buying up marginal companies in the former East Germany and making them profitable in record time. The sting of reporting to this handsome forty-year-old interloper was something Wurmbach had not come to grips with. And yet he couldn't fault the growth Kohl, one of the fifty largest companies in Europe, had enjoyed in Raeder's brief tenure.

"You all know why I wanted to see you today," Raeder said to cut the silence. The six members present represented the core of the board and sixty percent of the company's stock. Collectively, they were Kohl AG. "You are all aware that we are the largest company in Germany yet to cooperate with the reconciliation commission seeking financial compensation for Holocaust survivors and their families. You also know that pressure to turn over documentation for the company's wartime activities is mounting.

"By stalling for as long as we have, public opinion, which had been ambivalent, has shifted away from our company and our products. Our secrecy has had the unintended effect of severely damaging our reputation. Despite a fifty-percent increase in advertising and marketing, sales are down in nearly every division and most strongly in our heavy-construction business. No one is willing to use us until we are out from under the shadow of our legacy."

"Not cooperating with the reconciliation commission was your idea," Wurmbach said and others nodded. "Our losses are your fault."

The outburst had no effect on Raeder. "And it is a decision I stand by. I would not expose Kohl to billions of marks' worth of lawsuits until I was satisfied that I knew everything the company did before and during the war. For that, I needed the time to study the old records."

"It's inevitable we will have to pay something," Wurmbach stated. "Before the war, Kohl was just a small ironworks company with less than a hundred employees. Our expansion was due entirely to military and government contracts from the Nazi regime. We profited from the bloodshed just like Seimens, I.G. Farben, Volkswagen, and all the others."

"And after the war we were a collection of bombed-out factories and ruined equipment," Raeder replied evenly. "What profits we gained during the war were effectively nullified. Despite evidence to the contrary, many believe that we are the same company now as we were before the war and must be held accountable. I needed to know the full amount of our culpability and thus our liability. Putting a few hundred million marks into the collective pot is a lot different than facing an endless number of individual lawsuits worth billions." He looked down the table at Ebelhardt and Anna Kohl. "It is my risk-management skills that attracted you to me in the first place. You knew a day of reckoning was coming and you hired me to protect you."

Anna didn't deny it. "The question is, can you?"

"Yes." Raeder saw Anna slump in relief. "For the past twelve months I've determined our strategy for minimizing the amount of money we will have to pay. I've estimated that a payout of two hundred million marks won't interfere with our long-term growth while satisfying the commission that we are cooperating."

A wave of murmurs and sighs washed across the table.

"I arrived at that number after a lot of exhaustive research," Raeder cut through the dissenting voices. "It's the very minimum we can get away with."

"Have you prepared documents that we can give them that will lead them to this figure?" asked Konrad Ebelhardt.

"Everything's ready now. I've had Gunther Rath and his staff gather one hundred thousand pages of correspondence, shipping orders, and the like. It's all original material, carefully edited so that the commission will determine that we should be responsible for paying roughly a quarter billion marks in reparations."

"You just said two hundred million."

"We'll negotiate down to that number after they have made their findings public. They would be suspicious if we didn't."

"How much of our wartime activity are we keeping from them?" Anna asked.

"Very little, actually. Kohl certainly did profit from the use of slave labor at a few factories, but the practice was not as widespread as in many other companies. If it weren't for one project in particular, I would have felt comfortable disclosing everything to the commission." Raeder noticed the quick glance between Konrad and Anna. He could even read her lips as she mouthed a single word. *Pandora.*

He paused, waiting to see if Konrad would dismiss the rest of the board. He wasn't surprised that the chairman did.

"Gentlemen," Ebelhardt said, looking around the table, "could you please excuse us for a few minutes? Anna and I need to speak with Klaus alone."

Wurmbach shot Raeder a deadly look as he led the three others toward the door. When they were gone, Anna was the first to speak.

"My father intentionally shielded me from the Pandora Project, Klaus, and I ask you to show me the same courtesy. Please don't mention specifics in my presence."

"I can't believe Volker left any records even remotely connected to Pandora." Ebelhardt's face was red with ill-disguised fury. "The damned fool."

"Konrad! He was my father."

"Anna, I only read a bare outline of what was involved," Raeder said, keeping his true sense of horror out of his voice. "Even that little bit was shocking. I have to agree with Konrad. That material should have been destroyed decades ago. God, it shouldn't have been written down in the first place."

"We can't correct past mistakes." Ebelhardt leaned forward, his sharp eyes boring into Raeder.

"We can bury them though." Raeder let his statement hang in the air. "All the paperwork linking Kohl to the Pandora Project has been burned but I don't think that's enough."

"What do you propose?"

"I've made arrangements to have the original site obliterated and any remaining physical evidence destroyed."

"How do you know that by going back to"—Ebelhardt glanced at Anna—"by going back there, we won't give away the secret ourselves? Its location is so remote and has remained undiscovered for more than sixty years."

"Risk management. Just because we burned our evidence doesn't mean there isn't some diary or journal written by somebody involved in Pandora. It could be lying in some musty attic right now, waiting to go off like a time bomb. Our surviving war veterans are all in their seventies and eighties. We can't chance family members discovering such a written record when they go through their fathers' possessions. By hiding Pandora from the reconciliation commission now, we have to make certain that even if a diary is discovered, nothing remains to support the story. By destroying the site, all verifiable links to Kohl are severed."

Konrad looked unconvinced.

"We're about to lie to the reconciliation commission in order to conceal a despicable crime, and we have to make sure that the lie is never revealed. If the world finds out about Pandora and our involvement in it, Kohl's bankruptcy will be the last thing on our minds. They would be fully in their right to seek criminal charges against all of us."

Anna gasped. "Is it that bad? The Pandora Project, I mean."

"It's worse than you can possibly imagine," Konrad answered, placing one of his hands over hers.

"I can make this work," Raeder stated. "I have to. In the current environment, we are liable for billions in reparations, and if people learned what really happened during the war, the company would lose every customer it ever had. The alternative to covering up Pandora and paying the two hundred million is losing everything. Our ten thousand employees would be out of work. Our shareholders would go broke. It's not that inconceivable that the shock waves of Kohl's collapse would severely damage Germany's economy."

"It's not fair," Anna spat. "Why should we be forced to pay for the sins of our fathers? I was a teen when the war ended. I didn't force anyone into slavery. I didn't put anyone into a gas chamber. I've done nothing wrong. There isn't one person left in the company from those days."

"Other than a few old ladies, none of our shareholders were alive then either," Konrad added.

"None of us are responsible," Anna said petulantly.

"It's been determined that all of us are responsible, Anna," Raeder said. "How do you think I feel? I have even less to do with this than either of you. My parents were toddlers in 1945."

When Konrad and Anna hired Raeder, they'd made him aware that Kohl would need to negotiate a settlement with the reconciliation commission, but they had not told him the depths of the company's Nazi involvement. They had specifically withheld Pandora from him, rightly fearing that he wouldn't have joined if he'd known. His reputation for ruthlessness in the business world was richly deserved, but what he'd read about in the old files went far into the realm of the obscene. Now, he knew, he was in too deep to walk away. It was a matter of pride. And ego, he thought. Raeder was equally disturbed by what he'd learned about Kohl and by how easily he'd been manipulated. He'd explore this circumstance once he'd gotten the company out of its present crisis.

"What kinds of steps are you taking to destroy the Pandora site?" Konrad Ebelhardt asked abruptly. "And how sure are you they will work?"

"I don't think you need to know the details, but I assure you that, other than eradicating evidence of Kohl AG's culpability, we will do nothing illegal."

"No one will be harmed?"

"No, nothing like that will happen." Raeder gave a sharp laugh. "My tactics stopped short of physical injury many years ago. Other than a minor setback, my plan is actually nearing the final phase. I bring this up because now is the time we can call the whole thing off and 'come clean,' as the Americans say. Thirty million marks have already been spent getting everything to this stage. A small loss compared to what would happen if we tell the reconciliation commission about Pandora. However, that alternative is still open. I can cancel the destruction of the Pandora site."

He leaned back in his chair, running a hand through his blond hair. By skirting the morality of what they were doing and making this a purely financial decision, Raeder was confident that Anna and Konrad would agree with his plan. Raeder was no more pleased about this situation than either of them and yet he'd cut through the emotions to make the right choice. He had also had a few months to dampen his conscience.

"Do it!" Anna shouted as if she'd been listening to a raging debate in her mind and wanted it to end. She didn't look at Konrad when she continued, confirming Klaus Raeder's instinct that she was the real power behind the company. "Destroy whatever remains to link us to Pandora. I won't allow anything to hurt Kohl."

"Are you sure, Anna?" Ebelhardt asked. "This is a dangerous gamble."

"I'm convinced that Klaus is right. Erasing our ties to Pandora is the only chance we have to save ourselves from financial ruin. You've made it clear that if the commission learns about it, through our own disclosure or from some other source, we are finished. We have to make sure they never do."

"Very well." Raeder nodded. "It will be done."

The wave smashed into the bow of the *Njoerd* like a torpedo strike, blasting up an explosion of white froth that showered the forward windows and fell back to the deck, pooling deep and green before racing for the scuppers. The ship dropped into the following trough, her steep bows cleaving a wedge of seawater at the very bottom before her twin props hauled her to the next crest.

Mercer peered through the shimmering water still sliding from the armored glass in the ship's wardroom. Ira Lasko was at his elbow. As his view cleared, he saw that the sea was calm. The wave had been a rogue. "Where'd that come from?"

"Just Mother Nature reminding us not to get too comfortable," Lasko drawled. "Waves like that are why I went into submarines. Twenty-two years in the Navy and the only times I ever got seasick were on bumboats and sub tenders."

They turned away from the window. Marty Bishop was at one of the Formica tables with Igor Bulgarin and another of his teammates, a German meteorologist named Erwin Puhl. Puhl was in his early forties but looked older because he was so tall and stooped. Little of his hair remained and what fringed his head was gray and poorly washed. He wore thick glasses perched on a large bony nose. His posture and features reminded Mercer of a vulture's, and his gloomy mien did little to dispel the perception.

The Geo-Research people and off-duty crewmen occupied the other tables in the brightly lit wardroom. Greta Schmidt and Werner Koenig held court at a head table. It seemed the segregation that had existed at breakfast would last a while longer. All through dinner and the lecture that Koenig had given afterward, no one other than Igor and his people had approached Marty Bishop's team. In fact, Mercer had noted the *Njoerd*'s crew wasn't overly communicative with them either. Whenever an officer came to tell the expedition something, like their sailing time to Ammassalik, he would go straight to Koenig and have him make the announcement rather than simply telling the whole room. It was strange. Scientific jealousy was nothing new to Mercer, but this continued secretiveness was getting ridiculous.

"When Soviet Union was still a country," Igor said, continuing the story he'd started before the wave had sent a shudder through the *Njoerd* and elicited a collective gasp from its passengers, "I was on research ship much larger than this one. It was cooperative expedition with a dozen French scientists on board. Not only were we not allowed to talk to them unless a KGB watcher was in room, but we had to report everything said if we happened to pass in the halls." He looked to where Schmidt and Koenig were laughing at someone's joke. "I know now how French felt. Is no room in science for egos or secrets. All scientists should be as one."

Mercer nodded. "It's a nice thought, Igor, but you know as well as I do that scientists are some of the most childish and vindictive people in the world."

"*Da.*" The big Russian laughed at a memory. "We discover after expedition that French had stolen much equipment and all of our data."

"What were you doing on a ship?" Ira Lasko asked over the rim of a coffee cup. "I thought you're some kind of astronomer looking for chunks of space rock."

"I was meteorologist, like Erwin," Igor replied. "I give up weather research for planetary geology."

Mercer cocked an eyebrow at him. "Looking for the big one that'll wipe us out like the dinosaurs?"

"If it comes, I want plenty warning. Many women

I need to see before time runs out." He laughed at his own joke.

"Tell me, Mercer," Marty invited, changing the subject. "How do those chemical melters we've got with us work? Charlie said you're the real expert."

"We're going to have to hand dig down to the firn line, that's the demarcation plane between granular snow and solid ice. Then we work with the hotrocks. Once our preliminary shaft is sleeved with plastic to hold back the snow, I mix the chemicals at the bottom. The trick is to layer the stuff so the ice melts evenly. Weights attached to the bottom section of sleeving keep it pressed down to the ice and hold the melt water in the tunnel. Pumps will take care of the water. As the chemicals become diluted and lose their potency, we make sure the shaft's pumped dry and then repeat the process again."

"Why not just use hot water to melt the ice away?"

"Too difficult to control. Without enough pumps, you end up with a big cone-shaped hole that's so wide at the base it'll collapse in on itself. Also, even if you use a hot-water heater suspended on a cable, you need a massive amount of fuel to bore a shaft of any depth. Since Camp Decade is only about thirty feet down, the chemical heat is the most efficient. We need just a single pump, no fuel-hungry boilers, and the chemicals themselves. I counted twenty barrels on the deck when I came aboard, which is more than enough."

"And you think the three of us can handle it?" Ira asked.

"Four would have been better. Since we can borrow someone from Geo-Research, we should be okay," Mercer answered and glanced over Marty's shoulder to see Werner Koenig approaching.

When their eyes met, Koenig smiled broadly and put out his hand. "You have to be Mercer. Willie Haas said to say hello and remind you that, the next time you're in Hamburg, you're buying dinner."

Mercer laughed, totally unprepared for the German's easy use of English and friendly greeting. "You tell Willie that his taking me to McDonald's the last time I saw him doesn't count for a real meal." He shook Koenig's hand. "How do you know him?"

Willie Haas was a staff geologist for a German mining concern that had hired Mercer for a consulting job a few years ago. The two saw each other about once a year, usually at trade conferences.

"We've been friends since our days at university," Werner explained. "He told me you saved his company a fortune when you worked for them. He's convinced you sold your soul to the devil for your geological insights."

"I bartered my soul to escape hangovers," Mercer joked. "The insight comes from a Ouija board."

"Whatever works." Werner smiled. "I'm glad to have you with us. With Greenland's surface covered by a few miles of ice, there won't be much for you to study, but I bet your skills will come in handy anyway. In fact, when we get our ice-coring drill running, I would appreciate if you took a look at the samples we draw up to the surface."

"I'd be delighted," Mercer answered. Koenig was making the first effort to breach the gulf between his team and the others, and for that, Mercer was thankful. That task should have fallen on Marty Bishop since the Surveyor's Society had ruined Geo-Research's plans, but Mercer didn't think Bishop understood how important it was to keep all three teams as cohesive as possible.

Koenig had a cloth bag in one hand, and he reached in to extract a small green bottle of brennivin, the Icelandic version of aquavit commonly known as Black Death. "I've prohibited alcohol at the base camp for safety reasons. However we won't reach Ammassalik until noon tomorrow, so sharing a few bottles tonight won't do any harm."

"Mighty neighborly of you," Bishop said, taking the bottle and twisting off its cap. He poured a measure into his empty coffee cup and passed the bottle to Ira Lasko.

Koenig knelt next to Mercer so only he could hear what he said next. "Greta told me what happened this morning, about your confrontation outside the hotel."

"Ah, I wouldn't call it a confrontation, just a simple misunderstanding."

"Yes, well, she can be . . . difficult. I have not seen her for about a year, and she is very different from the woman I once knew. The woman I almost . . ." He wanted to say "married" but couldn't. "Anyway, she was made number two person on this expedition over my objections, and if she tries to overstep her bounds, please tell me."

"I thought you made all the personnel decisions for Geo-Research," Mercer said to cover his confusion. Koenig's admission wasn't something he had expected.

"Normally, yes. This trip is a little different. You see, I no longer own Geo-Research and my parent company wanted her along. She is dating my new boss. You know how it is." He stood suddenly as if he'd said too much. "Enjoy the brennivin, gentlemen." He moved on to have a few words with those at the next table and give them a bottle of their own.

Igor Bulgarin eyed the caraway-flavored liquor with a glassy look. He stood abruptly. "I must wish you a good night." This startled everyone but Erwin Puhl. "I'm afraid I like alcohol a bit too much. One drink becomes ten and laughter becomes tears. Quickly my hands become fists. Is best I leave now. But watch out for Erwin. Turn your back and bottle gone"—he snapped his fingers—"just like that."

The dour Puhl's face split into an impish smile. "I've never taken that long to finish a bottle of anything." After Igor left the wardroom, Erwin poured himself a dram. "He's been sober for about a year. It's still tough for him to be around alcohol."

"Known him long?"

Before Puhl answered, his eyes swept the room as if he were afraid of being overheard. "Eighteen years or so. I studied at Moscow University when East Germany was still a Soviet satellite, and I worked at the

Soviet Academy of Sciences up until the Wall came down in 1989. We have worked together a few times since then."

"What's the goal of your team?" Mercer asked.

"We are at the end of a particular solar cycle that culminates in an event called the solar max, a time of intense sunspot activity and the ejection of tremendous volumes of charged particles. It'll disrupt communications and power distribution all over the globe. We're going to measure the intensity of the particles as they follow earth's magnetic lines. So far north, the activity should be particularly intense."

"Isn't there some big religious meeting on a cruise ship coming up this way to take advantage of the aurora borealis?" Ira asked.

"The Universal Convocation," Erwin answered at once. "The route's a secret but I heard they're going to circle Iceland from the north. If they want inspiration from above, they're going to get it."

Mercer wasn't really listening to their conversation. He was thinking about what Koenig had told him and decided to do nothing with the information. He had enough to do without worrying about Geo-Research's internal squabbles. Now that he knew what to look for, he could see an undercurrent of tension between Greta and Werner. It was actually more a unidirectional thing. Greta seemed secure in her position. It was Werner who was uncomfortable. Mercer felt bad for him, imagining what it must be like to work with a former lover, especially since it appeared Koenig had yet to get over her.

He finally took a sip of the brennivin and nearly choked. "This stuff's like drinking gravel." As he spoke, he adjusted his Tag Heuer back an hour to put it on Greenland time. "I'm going to call it a night. We should recheck our equipment before we reach Ammassalik."

During a severe winter, pack ice extended all the way from Greenland to Iceland, a distance of about three hundred miles. This ice wasn't the cause of the North Atlantic's famous icebergs. Those calved from glaciers on Greenland's west coast. Rather, the pack ice was a frozen surface accumulation that reached only a few yards in thickness. It melted as it broke up and offered little hazard to navigation during summer. The difficulty reaching Greenland came from the fact that the deepwater fjords that ring the island like a necklace were ice choked until early July and refroze again in late September. The three-month window is the only time that ships can call on the few settlements on the eastern coast.

As the *Njoerd* nosed her way toward the Ammassalik Fjord, thin ice still layered much of the water, which was dotted with huge bergs held immobile like white islands. The ship rammed her way through. None of the expedition members were allowed on the bridge during icebreaking operations, so the best view was from the forward windows in the wardroom.

When Mercer arrived the next morning, he found himself alone except for the cooks preparing breakfast in the galley. He poured a cup of coffee from the continuously refilled urn and took a seat. In moments he realized that the ice was too thin and rotten to make an impression on the *Njoerd*. Even at a slower speed, she knifed through the pack without check. If it weren't for the scrape of ice against her hull plates and the occasional slab that showed above her bows before being thrust aside, he wouldn't have known they had reached the pack.

"Morning," Ira Lasko called as he entered the wardroom. He went to the coffee urn before joining Mercer.

"Looks like you need to shave."

Ira ran a hand around the circle of stubble on his otherwise bald head, and chuckled. "I'm thinking about letting it grow in. How's the show?"

"Icebreaking's more dramatic on television."

"If we'd tried this even a month ago, we wouldn't have made it anywhere near Ammassalik."

"How do people live up here?"

"Most of the fifty thousand people on Greenland are native Inuits. While they've become dependent on Denmark for a lot of their supplies, I think they'd be fine if the Danes left 'em alone too."

"I was reading a guidebook on the flight from the States that said Greenland's Inuits can understand the native languages spoken in Alaska. They're separated by a quarter of the world and fifteen hundred years of isolation and the languages are still recognizable. Remarkable when you consider that we need dictionaries to help us understand the subtleties of Shakespeare and he's only been dead for five hundred years."

"Have you listened to a teenager recently? I can barely understand them, and it's only been a single generation." They laughed and Lasko added, "Speaking of teenagers, I ran into Marty in the hallway next to the bathroom last night and he reeked of perfume. Looks like he's going to have some fun even if he doesn't want to be here."

The dining room filled slowly as others came awake and went in search of coffee and food. Marty was one of the last to come to breakfast, and all through the meal he kept glancing over at a young German girl who was Geo-Research's assistant camp cook. When their eyes met, the brunette would blush and look away demurely.

"Get enough sleep, Marty?" Ira teased.

Bishop looked wolfish. "No, and I don't think I'll get much tonight either."

After breakfast, the Society team went back to their cabins for their parkas and then met on the deck. A steady wind blew across the ship, carrying with it the clean smell of ice and sea. The temperature was thirty-five degrees but the sun was warm. As they checked over their gear, layers of clothes were stripped away. While they were working, Werner Koenig approached to talk about the potential dangers they could face on the ice and warn them about not allowing themselves to sweat.

"If you're away from the camp and your clothes become sweaty, your body heat will leach away so fast you'll be dead before you know it. That goes especially for your boots. We'll be wearing moon boots on the ice, and they heat up fast and take forever to dry out. If your boots get wet from your feet sweating, get out of them immediately or you're going to get frostbite. It takes less time than you think, so just get back to the camp and change." He moved on to give the same advice to Igor Bulgarin's team.

Most of the loose equipment had been stored in the four Sno-Cats or their towed trailers. The machines were big boxy vehicles resembling tracked moving vans, painted red with a decal for Geo-Research affixed to their front doors. Their tracks were heavily notched, like a bulldozer's, and extended beyond the cabins to give them a wide footprint that distributed their weight better over soft snow. Two of the trailers were basically boxes standing ten feet tall and about twenty-five feet long. They were painted a matching shade of red and mounted on spring-cushioned skis. The other two trailers were open and held sections of prefabricated walls for the base-camp buildings. There were also a few preloaded pallets of gear: fuel drums, floors and roofs for the buildings, the Society's chemical heat, and crates of food that would be carried directly to Camp Decade by the rotor-stat.

"Why the hell don't they lug all this stuff right to the site with the blimp?" Ira complained as he rooted through a trailer, looking for lengths of hose for their pump.

"Cost and insurance," Marty said. "The rotor-stat is still experimental and its owners aren't willing to use it to lift equipment from a ship at sea. Liability issues if something goes wrong, I imagine. That means we have to be tied up to a pier. And I guess it's only rated to carry one Sno-Cat and trailer at a time. Fully loaded, these rigs weigh about thirty tons. Geo-

Research wasn't willing to pay for that many trips from Ammassalik to the base camp, so they decided to drive the 'Cats overland and have the rotor-stat make only a couple of runs with the fuel and the other heavy stuff. It's a pain in the ass, but saved about fifty grand.

"And since we're paying for the right to join their expedition," he added, "the burden of driving the 'Cats to Camp Decade falls on us."

"Geo-Research is sending a few of their people with us, aren't they?" Mercer asked.

"Yeah, in case something goes wrong."

"Hey, look at that." Ira had a digital camera to his eye.

"What is it?"

"Land ho!" he shouted, handing the Nikon to Marty.

When it was his turn, Mercer could see a sheer rock peak smeared with snow and ice that rose from above the sea fog like a lonely sentinel. It was one of the thousands of islands that dotted Greenland's jagged, glacier-carved coast. To the others it was an uninspiring sight, but Mercer couldn't help but be intrigued. The rock was certainly granite, some of the toughest stone in the world, and yet it had been ground smooth over hundreds of millions of years. The tremendous pressure of Greenland's ice sheet was a force that even the earth itself could not stop.

"That's Kulusuk Island," a crewman called from the bridge wing high over the deck.

"Kulusuk has an airstrip that was left over from the DEW line station on the north part of the island," Ira Lasko said. "The old Distant Early Warning radar facility was dismantled years ago and the airport was turned over to the locals. It's only about an hour and a half flight from Reykjavik. I think we're pretty close to Ammassalik."

An hour later, the *Njoerd* was surrounded by towering ramparts of stone as she entered Tasiilaq Bay. Here the mountains were as sharp as glass, black silhouettes that cut into the clear sky. She wasn't the first ship of the season into the bay because a wide channel had been carved through the pack ice leading toward the town of Ammassalik. As they threaded their way deeper into the bay, they passed more bergs, twisted sculptures of ice that were as beautiful as fairy castles. The newer bergs were blindingly white, while those that had floated in the bay for a few seasons were shaded the pale blue of a natural gas flame.

The town of Ammassalik appeared off the port side. The first thing they saw was a wall of garbage sloping from the town's dump into the sea. Behind it was a tremendous trash fire.

"Not an encouraging sight," Erwin Puhl said. Most everyone was at the ship's rail watching the approach.

"The natives were used to throwing garbage outside their huts," Igor said. "Mostly bones that dogs ate. After the Danes moved them here and introduce Western packaging, they still do same thing, not knowing metal cans and plastic wrappers don't disappear after one winter. Town used to look like junkyard. Is better this way."

Past a clutch of huge fuel tanks, a small inlet cut into the land, and on the other side lay Ammassalik's concrete pier backed by a large warehouse. The inlet was full of ice chunks and tired fishing boats. At its head, a stream of melt water tumbled under a bridge and poured into the bay. The town itself flanked the inlet, rising above the waters on steep hills that were dappled with snow. The houses were wood framed and colorful, as if to make up for the monochrome blandness of the surroundings. Next to most of the homes stood rickety drying racks covered with fish and chunks of seal. It was a forlorn and isolated place that sixteen hundred Inuit and a handful of Danish administrators called home.

Coming in to the dock, the ship's air horns gave a long, mournful blast that was answered by a chorus of sled dog cries.

"Welcome to Greenland, everyone," Werner Koenig called happily. Greta Schmidt was at his side, her blond hair shimmering like white gold. "First part of our journey is finished. The captain informed me that the rotor-stat should be here in about thirty minutes, so step number two can commence. Is everyone ready?"

"The Surveyor's Society's all set," Marty answered. "Equipment's been checked and resecured."

Werner looked to Igor. "How about it?"

"*Da*. Is all good."

"Excellent. I've been asked to have everyone leave the ship or stay in the wardroom until the Sno-Cats and Land Cruiser have been carried up to the ice sheet. I've posted a manifest in the wardroom so you'll know which 'Cat is yours for the trek to Camp Decade. Since the rotor-stat is still considered experimental, she's not allowed to carry passengers. We'll use helicopters to get us to the ice."

Mercer unzipped the nylon shell he wore and plucked a pair of brand-new polarized sunglasses from an inside pocket. "I can't wait to see this," he said to no one in particular. Both Ira Lasko and Marty Bishop gave him a smile. His excitement about the rotor-stat was infectious.

The airship arrived on schedule, announcing its approach with a deep droning sound that echoed off the bay for ten minutes before it floated into view. There was a defiant serenity to the mammoth dirigible, as if it was immune to the laws of gravity. Unlike the squashed-looking Goodyear blimps, the rotor-stat was torpedo shaped but flattened along her top and bottom. At over four hundred feet long, she was also twice the length of a blimp. Her bow was shaped like a shark's snout, and her tail had a long taper that supported four cruciform fins. Because of her partial internal skeleton, the four streamlined engine pods were mounted along her flank so that noise and vibration wouldn't disturb those in the twenty-passenger gondola slung under her nose. The carbon-fiber skin was white, which made her look like a cloud. She was so new exhaust had yet to darken the sections behind the engines.

It was an unworldly sight and Mercer felt himself grinning as her shadow crept along the bay like an advancing ink stain.

"Jesus!" Ira exclaimed. "That's something you don't see every day."

"More's the shame," Mercer said.

The expedition members joined a growing throng of awestruck locals on the pier when the rotor-stat came to a hover above the *Njoerd,* her engine pods transitioning from forward flight to station's keeping. With the pods tilted skyward, her massive props beat the air like a helicopter's, but until she took on a cargo load her 1.2 million cubic feet of helium kept her aloft.

The rotor-stat maintained enough altitude so the mooring rope dangling from her nose would not interfere with the heavy steel cables that were lowered from the cargo bay amidships. Deckhands on the research ship quickly secured the four cables to the skid placed under the first Sno-Cat and trailer, coordinating their efforts with the airship's pilot via walkie-talkie. When the signal was given, the throb of the rotor-stat's engines deepened as her twenty-five-foot blades took greater bites out of the air. The slack in the lines vanished and the cables vibrated with the strain of the thirty-ton load. As gently as a mother raising a child from a crib, the airship lifted the tracked vehicle from the deck.

A gasp went up from the crowd, and the expedition members cheered. The rotor-stat continued to climb vertically. The Sno-Cat was too big to be drawn fully into her hold, so it continued to hang about twenty feet below the dirigible. She pivoted in place, pointing her nose westward, toward the main bulk of Greenland. In unison, the engine pods tilted forward, giving the great ship some forward momentum while still providing lift. It was then that Mercer realized her hull was shaped like an airfoil that would provide supplemental lift at speed, vastly improving her fuel efficiency.

To the west, a wall of mountains three thousand feet tall separated Ammassalik island from the Greenland massif. The rotor-stat steered for a notch in the mountains, gaining altitude and speed with each passing moment. In ten minutes she was lost from view.

"They'll be back for the second Sno-Cat in less than an hour," Werner told them. "The top of the Hann glacier is our staging area on the mainland. It's only about twenty miles away."

"Provided nothing goes wrong," Marty said, "that puts everything in place at seven tonight. Bit late to start out, don't you think?"

"I've already considered that. We'll sleep on the *Njoerd* tonight and head out tomorrow at dawn. The small advance team leaving from Reykjavik will arrive a day ahead of us, which gives them more than enough time to set up the first building we will use until everything else is constructed."

"Once the base is habitable you'll send for the rest of your scientists?" Mercer asked.

Werner nodded. "It'll take about two days to put together our buildings and stow the provisions. And then your obligation to us is completed and you can begin to unearth Camp Decade and Dr. Bulgarin and his people can begin their own research."

The rotor-stat returned to Ammassalik for the last time at 10:30 P.M., having made its first of two runs to Camp Decade two hundred miles north of the town. The floors and roofs of the base buildings were too bulky for the Sno-Cats and had to be flown up. The last trip was to haul food, the hotrocks, and the fuel. Then the airship would head back to Europe. It would return in September when the entire base was to be dismantled by order of the Danish government.

Mercer was on deck when the airship faded into the twilight. He'd been watching a white smear of light clinging to the distant mountains. He knew instinctively that it was the reflection of the setting sun on the vast ice sheet. He felt a deep pull in his chest and was more relaxed than he'd been in a long time.

When he was prospecting in the field, Mercer was always the expedition leader, and he was forced to deal with the hundreds of details that cropped up on a daily basis. It wasn't an ego issue. He actually preferred to fade into the background. But when a mining company was paying him thousands of dollars a day, sitting back wasn't an option. They expected results. On this trip, it was refreshing not to have that kind of responsibility. Mercer wouldn't have to deal with the burden of command. That fell on Werner Koenig, who seemed more than qualified to handle any emergencies, and Marty Bishop, who was starting to show interest.

Mercer took a deep breath, feeling the burn of icy air in his lungs. It was so clean it left his head spinning for an instant. This was one of those moments of pure happiness, a precious and rare feeling that he savored with each moment it lasted. He laughed aloud as the glow of reflected light faded to blue and then vanished altogether.

Standing atop one of the Sno-Cats so his view wouldn't be interrupted, Mercer swept the vista with a pair of binoculars. Except maybe on the ocean, he couldn't imagine a place with a more distant horizon. The line between ice and sky was as straight as a laser beam. It was only to the east, toward the coast twenty miles away, that the line blurred just slightly as the massive glacier began its three-thousand-foot plummet to the sea. To the west lay 850,000 square miles of frozen nothingness.

Now that the Alpha Air JetRanger had shuttled the last of the team to the glacier and flown back to the heliport at Ammassalik, an eerie silence descended over the clutch of vehicles. The occasional muttered word sounded as out of place and blasphemous as a curse in a cathedral. The wind was a constant whisper not even strong enough to stir snow off the ground, but the temperature was ten degrees below freezing. Mercer kept his hands gloved and the hood of his nylon shell pulled tightly over his head. Beneath it was his leather jacket, a sweatshirt, and two T-shirts. Over his long underwear and jeans, he wore nylon overpants and insulated hiking boots. Since they'd be driving for the next twenty hours or so, he didn't need the heavier Arctic gear packed in his luggage, including the pair of padded moon boots.

Ira Lasko was at the back of the Sno-Cat making sure their ground-penetrating radar sled was secured for the rough overland trek. "What was that line about the moon? 'Magnificent desolation'? Something like that?"

Mercer lowered the binoculars. "I've been on a few glaciers in Alaska, but nothing like this." There was awe in his voice. The variety and beauty of the earth's geography never failed to amaze him.

"They say if the ice covering Greenland were to melt, sea levels around the world would rise about twenty-five feet."

"You're forgetting that the weight of this much ice has actually sunk the interior of Greenland about a thousand feet below sea level. The oceans would rise twenty feet, and this place would become the basin for the largest freshwater lake in the world."

"Last time I trade trivia with a geologist," Ira muttered good-naturedly.

Laughing, Mercer scrambled down the ladder bolted to the back of the Sno-Cat. "Anytime you want, you can stump me about submarines."

Tall marker flags had been attached to the lifting pallets so when the Sno-Cats returned to be retrieved by the rotor-stat, they could be found under the new snowfall certain to bury them. Werner Koenig also got a fix from a handheld GPS and wrote the satellite-derived coordinates into a notebook he carried in his parka. "We're ready to go."

"Let's saddle up," Marty bellowed and gave a cavalryman's closed-fist gesture.

The Toyota Land Cruiser would drive point, since it was the most maneuverable and fuel-efficient vehicle in the convoy. Geo-Research had hired a former European rally racing champion named Dieter to drive it. Werner, Greta, and Igor Bulgarin, who had the most experience on the ice out of anyone on the expedition, would ride with him. Their job was to scout for the easiest routes when the ground became too broken.

The Surveyor's Society team was assigned to the first Sno-Cat and each member would take turns driving it. The vehicle's controls were nearly the same as any truck with the exception of the steering wheel. To change directions, the 'Cats had levers that activated brakes on the tracks.

As team leader, Marty took the first turn in the driver's seat, with Ira next to him. Mercer sat on the large bench seat behind them. The rear portion of the 'Cat was accessible from the cabin but was packed to the roof with personal gear and the radar sled.

"Get the goddamned heater cranked," Ira complained. "I'm freezing already."

The turbo-diesel fired on the first turn of the key, surging for an instant before settling into a powerful growl. A white jet of exhaust burst from the back of the Toyota. Over the sound of their own vehicle they could hear the other three 'Cats come to life. Dieter gave the SUV a burst of gas, and her bulbous, under-inflated tires dug into the snow.

Marty jammed the Sno-Cat into first gear, and they began crawling forward, keeping to the tire tracks left in the Land Cruiser's wake. He worked the levers to test the Sno-Cat's steering response. "It's like driving a tank."

Because of the loads each 'Cat towed, their speed was limited to fifteen miles per hour. The ride in the cabin was smooth if monotonous. After the first hour, everyone but Mercer had lost his sense of wonder. Like a frozen Sahara, ice stretched flat and featureless in every direction, broken only rarely by humps of yet more ice. The sun made the landscape dazzle like a world of diamond chips. Without their dark glasses, the reflection would have blinded them all.

Strung out like elephants in a circus parade, the four Sno-Cats doggedly followed the trail laid down by the Toyota. With the weather clear, it was easy to keep to the track, but as the morning wore on, the wind picked up and a whiteout developed with a suddenness that startled them all. One moment everything was normal, and an instant later the visibility dropped to zero as a swirling maelstrom of ice particles and snow whipped around the cabin. The storm screaming over their heads was strong enough to rock the massive vehicle.

"Jesus, is this normal?" Marty shouted louder than necessary.

Ira chuckled. "According to Igor, this is nothing."

The radio under the dash crackled to life. "How are you doing back there?" Werner was checking on his people. "Igor says this should die out in a minute or two. Or it will go on for a few days."

Ira plucked the microphone from its bracket. "We're hoping for the first option."

A new voice came on the radio. "This is Erwin. I'm in the last Sno-Cat, and the wind's already dying down. We'll be ready to go in just a minute."

The wind dropped just as abruptly as it had risen, but in its wake the men were subdued. This had been just a taste of the Arctic's fury. After a lunch of military MREs, Ira took over the driving. The terrain became more fractured, jarring ridges of ice and snow that the 'Cat hit with kidney-punishing regularity. Their speed dropped to ten miles per hour.

Two hours later, Werner Koenig's voice came over the radio. "This is a call to all Sno-Cats. I just got word from the *Njoerd*. They have reached a position off the coast close enough to Camp Decade for them to launch the helicopter carrying the advance team and the materials to construct our first home on the ice. If we reach the base tonight, we will have a more comfortable place to sleep than these Sno-Cats."

Ira grabbed the radio from Mercer. "Then let's get the lead out. Marty just took his boots off, and I don't think we can stay in the 'Cat tonight without gas masks."

At six, they took a vote to stop for dinner or suffer through tepid MREs again. Werner estimated that they were forty miles from the base, and if they stopped, they'd be forced to spend the night in the vehicles. Grumbling but unanimous, they decided it was Meals Ready to Eat one more time.

Mercer took the Sno-Cat's driver's seat, and Marty

pushed himself into a cramped position between the front seats so he could talk with Ira and him. The sun's fading light caused the ice to glow as twilight crept over the caravan. The sky's soft pastels of purple and rose were mirrored by the landscape, cut only by black shadows cast by frigid hummocks. It was clear enough to see a star's reflection. Like the night before, it remained light long after the sun had vanished. The western horizon was lit as if it hid a vast city below its rim. When the half-moon rose, its ice-born twin doubled its illumination.

Perhaps a half mile away, the beams of the Toyota headlights cast two funnels of light on the ice. It was reassuring yet illustrated their total isolation. The vehicle was the only puddle of light on the ice, a tiny beacon in a land where man was an unwanted interloper. Ira's earlier reference to moonscape was uncannily accurate. The thermometer on the dash showed the outside temperature was –25 degrees Celsius, or about zero degrees Fahrenheit.

"GPS says we're about ten miles from the camp," Werner announced an hour later. "But as you can tell, the ground is pretty broken again."

The range of mountains and hills below the ice sheet had distorted the terrain, so the vehicles were continuously ascending or descending icy upthrusts. The ride was more even than the earlier fractured zone but still their progress was slowed. Dieter needed a few attempts to find the best gaps between the ridges and the Sno-Cats were forced to stop when the Toyota scouted for level passes. Each pause seemed to take longer than the last. With the base so close, everyone's frustration mounted and yet Werner's prompts kept them focused and alert.

Mercer was just reaching for the microphone to suggest that they should stop for the night when Igor's voice filled the Sno-Cat. "On other side of this last ice wall is base camp. We just saw it! We are coming back for you now. Hot meal and warm bed in fifteen minutes."

Like a wraith, the Land Cruiser came out of the swirling snow, ice dust caught in the corona of its lights dancing on the wind. Dieter, who had to be exhausted from nineteen hours of driving, executed a U-turn when Mercer flashed his headlights. The last dash to the camp was surreal. Mercer was tired and should have turned over the driving to Marty. He had to fight to keep himself alert. The falling snow mesmerized him, drawing his attention to individual flakes with alarming frequency. He squeezed his eyes closed, shaking his head to clear it.

"You gonna make it?" Ira asked.

Mercer shot him a crooked grin. "If I don't, you don't."

The first camp building erected by Geo-Research's advance team stood alone. Constructed in sections of insulated plastic, it had been snapped together like a child's toy. Once they all got to work in the morning, this building would be the mess hall/communications shack. For tonight it was their communal bunkhouse. Around the building were pallets for the four ten-person dormitories, two room-temperature laboratories, and two ambient labs used to store and study ice cores. The disassembled ice-coring drill tower was in one of the trailers.

"I just hope Werner's a deep sleeper," Mercer told Ira.

"Why?"

"Because when we get inside I'm having a drink and I don't want to hear him complain."

"We'll join you," Marty said. "I've got bourbon and Ira brought a bottle of scotch."

Dawn broke crisp and clear. After a breakfast of powdered eggs and coffee, Werner Koenig handed out work assignments and the crew set themselves to building their camp. While the Geo-Research team all sported matching black snowsuits with their company's name and their own stitched in gold over their hearts, Igor's people and the Society's group wore a mishmash of Arctic gear, some of it army surplus and some of it store-bought. The only thing they all shared in common was the heavy moon boots. They were cumbersome but with so much fresh snow on the ground they were also necessary.

After running the Sno-Cats over a wide area to compress the snow, the floors of the buildings were laid out in a rough circle with the mess hall at its center. Then the 'Cat hauling the wall sections made a circuit of the camp and the numbered pieces were dropped at each base. It was a matter of standing the walls onto the insulated floor and locking them with a special tool provided by the manufacturer. Roofs were placed with a crane mounted on one of the Sno-Cats. In all, the whole process took three hours per building.

The early energy that sustained the crew waned as the frigid air sapped their strength. And yet they slogged on. By five in the afternoon the last cold lab was finished. They ate in silence that night after loading two of the dormitories with their personal gear.

The following day was spent storing all the provisions and stocking the laboratories. The work was easier than the previous day's and the temperature had risen above freezing. The steadily drifting snow turned into a constant drizzle that soaked anyone outside in a matter of moments. The compacted snow became ice as flat and slick as a hockey rink. Mercer's suggestion to use a Sno-Cat to corrugate the crust with its tracks was met with remarkable success.

At dinner, Werner thanked everyone for their work, praising each one by name for their contribution. He said that Geo-Research would finish the last few chores in the morning, freeing up the others to begin their work. The scientists would arrive by a ski-equipped cargo plane in the afternoon and he asked Igor and Marty for a list of any additional equipment that they felt they needed so it could be put aboard.

"Oh, Igor, I have a communication for you from Dr. Klein." He handed a piece of paper to the Russian.

Igor read it and grunted.

"Looks like bad news," Mercer said, stacking the dishes on the table for Ingrid, the cook's assistant that Marty had bedded aboard the *Njoerd,* to pick up.

"*Da,* she won't make tomorrow's flight here. She must wait two days for the first helicopter resupply."

"What happened to her anyway?"

"I don't know. Some accident is all I was told."

"I don't blame her for wanting to miss the construction party," Marty Bishop said with a tired sigh.

"I do not think she is shy of work," Igor defended. "I have not met her, but her application to join my team was impressive. She has climbed the tallest mountains on four continents, including the Vinson Massif, Antarctica's highest point. And almost made it to the top of Everest. She works as a trauma doctor in Munich's largest hospital and has published several papers on survivor's stress. When I contacted her references, all gave her highest marks."

"Sounds impressive to me," Ira said.

Igor grinned. "She also sent picture with her application. You want impressive? Wait until you see her." He bunched his fingers and kissed them away like an Italian. "Beautiful."

The sled weighed nearly two hundred pounds and had been designed to be towed by a vehicle. When they started their search the third morning, they tried using the Land Cruiser, but the uneven terrain made it too difficult to control. It fell on the men to push the ground-penetrating radar unit, an exhausting task since their search grid was on a long slope. The uphill legs left the men panting and dangerously overheated.

All were thankful that the area wasn't larger than it was.

Because Camp Decade had been secured to an under-ice mountain, it had remained stable as the glacier flowed around it. The Surveyor's Society had requested Geo-Research establish their new base within a quarter mile of where Camp Decade lay hidden. On the fourth pass with the sled they found a corner of the base, a discovery met with cheers but they knew that was only part of the battle. Now they had to map the entire facility and locate the main entrance, where they would sink their shaft.

Camp Decade was laid out like a huge letter H. One long leg contained storage areas and a cavernous garage that once had a ramp to the surface. The other leg was designated for crew accommodations and laboratories, with the bulk of the administration area connecting the two segments. There were countless side chambers attached to the complex as well as a long tunnel running from the garage that led to the small nuclear reactor that had powered the facility. The Air Force had assured the Surveyor's Society that there had never been a single incidence of radiation leakage, and the reactor had been one of the few things removed when the camp was abandoned.

As Mercer watched the monitor attached to the radar set reveal dark shadows thirty-five feet below them, he kept a surreptitious eye on the Geiger counter he had borrowed in Iceland. The unit was an old Victoreen model CDV-700 6A that he had cajoled from Thorsteinn Jonsson, the director of Reykjavik's small geology museum. He hadn't seen Jonsson since the volcanologist had hosted the conference that first brought Mercer to Iceland years earlier, and Jonsson had been reluctant to lend out his only counter until Mercer gave him a hundred-dollar "rental fee."

The photograph of cancer-ravaged Stefansson Rosmunder was too compelling for Mercer to trust the Air Force's assurances. Before first light, he'd gotten up and walked the entire area, sweeping the ice with the Geiger counter. The machine hadn't uttered more than a few clicks, which indicated normal background radiation. There was one spot, presumably over where the reactor had once been buried, that sped up the counter but the levels were far below anything dangerous.

He didn't tell the others what he had done, nor did

he reveal the counter as they worked now. He'd seen people panic at just the presence of one of these little machines. To the uninformed, the slow clicks of ambient radiation sounded as dangerous as the tail shake of a rattlesnake. He kept the counter in a pack hanging from the side of the sled and wore the earphones that Thorsteinn had given him. Since he was the only person who knew how to operate the radar unit, no one questioned the extra equipment. If he'd found something, he would have told them immediately, but after completing half of this slower sweep, he felt that the military had told the truth about the site. There was no hazardous radiation anywhere near Camp Decade.

At noon, Mercer downloaded the raw data they had accumulated onto a laptop computer that would create a digital version of the base. Because of the thick ice, the resolution was poor and the images were grainy and blurred, but there was still enough detail for him to pick out individual features. The radar had penetrated through the roof of Camp Decade, so the pictures resembled an X ray. Inside the facility, he could see wall partitions and even furniture. It was eerie because he was the first person to see inside the camp in fifty years.

He was also very relieved. While the facility was anchored to bedrock and protected from glacial pressure by a peak of rock on its upflow side, he had harbored the fear that the entire place had been ground to debris by the shifting ice. The radar scans showed it had had little problem weathering the past five decades.

"All right, let's wrap this up for now," Mercer said, shutting off the radar and checking the computer and GPS system that was part of the sledge. "We'll compare this data with the original drawings done by the engineers who built this place."

Even without the additional Geo-Research scientists, the mess hall was crowded for lunch, and they had to wait until afterward to clear enough room on one of the tables to spread out their findings. The original drawings had been scanned into the computer, so Mercer brought up the shadowy images recorded this morning and overlaid them with the neat architectural sketches. Instantly, they had the orientation of the base locked down and saw they had only mapped a third of the sprawling complex. Still, it was enough for them to extrapolate the location of the main entrance and determine its GPS coordinates.

Mercer pointed to the spot on the computer screen. "X marks the spot."

"You sure?"

"Do you think I want to dig two holes out there? With your permission, Marty, we can start tunneling through the snow to reach the base."

"That's what we're here for," Bishop replied. "Why don't you go out and mark the area over the entrance? Ira, you go get the Sno-Cat with the crane and plow attachments and haul over the plastic sleeves and hotrocks. I'll tell Werner that we need one of his people for a while."

"That sounds like a plan," Mercer agreed.

"How goes your search?" Igor Bulgarin had appeared with Erwin Puhl at his side. Both men had just entered the mess hall and were covered in snow.

"Oh, God!" Ira made his face into a frightened mask. "It's the Yeti!"

Roaring with laughter, the Russian placed a huge arm on the much shorter Puhl. "And this is my Yetette."

"We've already located the entrance, Igor. We're going to start digging right now."

"So quickly?" Bulgarin sobered. "You Americans, I don't know how you do it."

"I take it you're not having any luck finding meteorites?"

He laughed again. "Is success if I find one or two this trip."

"How's Koenig's group coming?" Mercer asked.

"All morning they work to mount the drill tower on one of the trailers to make it potable."

"Portable," Erwin corrected. "Beverages are potable."

"This coffee isn't."

"*Da,* portable. Is not going well, I think." He frowned. "Germans are supposed to be good engineers. These people, bah! Like children with Legos."

"How about you, Erwin?" Mercer asked. "What's the weather forecast?"

"That I can't tell you." Puhl removed his coat. "But don't expect the satellite phones or radios to have the best range for a while."

"Atmospheric interference?"

The scientist nodded. "And it's just beginning. In another four or five days we can forget about contacting the *Njoerd* except for a few periods of calm when the solar wind dies down."

"Erwin thinks some communications satellites in orbit are going to be kaput because of radiation," Igor added.

Marty stood. "Then let's bust a hump. I want to be able to call my father and tell him we've reached the base before this gets worse."

It took a few minutes to sort out their coats and boots, zip up properly, and secure the Velcro straps around their gloves. It wasn't cold enough to need face guards, but each man leaving or entering the mess hall had all but a bit of his eyes exposed from under hoods and neck gaiters. Mercer put on his glacier glasses and threw open the door, then leaned into the wind that lifted a dense fog of snow.

Waist-high guide ropes had been strung between the buildings, he noted, to help people during whiteouts. It was not unheard of for someone to become lost during a storm and die just a few yards from camp.

After staking where he wanted to drive the shaft, Mercer studied the snowfield while he waited for the others. Judging the angle of the hill and testing snow in his hands, he realized they could use the 'Cat's plow to drag away much of the accumulation.

On the wind, he could hear his long-dead grandfather, a quarry foreman from Barre, Vermont. "Never do work yourself that a machine can do for you." Mercer smiled at the memory. Scraping away much of the surface snow would save them days of backbreaking labor to reach the firn line, where they could employ the hotrocks.

When Ira and Marty arrived with Bernhardt Hoffmann, a young Geo-Research worker, Mercer told them what he wanted to do. By taking thin bites out of the snow, they began digging a trench over the entrance, removing about half a foot of grainy ice with each pass. To keep the slopes gentle, the trench grew to over two hundred yards long. Like a tractor plowing the same part of a field, the 'Cat dug deeper and deeper until the walls of ice flanking the excavation were taller than the vehicle's roof.

Mercer stopped the work and used a shovel to dig into the walls, testing their strength. While he was more familiar with soils and rock, he was confident that the trench was stable enough to continue for another few vertical feet. He would use some of their stiff sheeting to line the trench for added support before boring with the chemicals.

At one point that afternoon an old Douglas DC-3 cargo plane fitted with skis lumbered over the camp low enough to make Mercer duck unconsciously as he stood on the lip of the trench. The aircraft banked away, sunlight sparking off its windows, before returning upwind. It lined up with the makeshift landing strip Werner Koenig's people had packed down with the other Sno-Cats. The plane was at least sixty years old and yet roared flawlessly, flaps down, nose pitched high, and dragon's breaths of snow billowing up in the wake of her radial engines. Her skids hissed against the snow and the pilot had to fight to keep the plane centered as she slowed. It was like a scene in an old movie, Mercer thought, as he watched her pivot for her taxi run back to the camp.

The engines remained at idle as the rear door was thrown open and people began jumping to the ground. They wore the matching Geo-Research snowsuits. They unloaded supplies from the plane with an economy of movement more befitting a well-trained army than a group of scientists. A mound of crates and boxes was stacked on the ice before the door was closed and the plane raced back to the runway. Even as she lifted into the air, two Sno-Cats trundled to the waiting people and the cargo was loaded into the trailers. In all, the plane was on the ground for less than ten minutes.

"They may not be able to fix their drill rig, but they sure can unload an airplane," Ira said, standing at Mercer's shoulder.

"I guess," he replied. "Looks like we get fresh vegetables for dinner and maybe our first mail call."

"Expecting good news from home?"

Mercer didn't answer. Something bothered him about what he had just watched, something he couldn't name. Before he could pull together the thought, another roar shook the site. He caught movement out of the corner of his eye and turned. The mountains that separated the camp from the coast were fifteen or twenty miles away, and yet the air was so clear he could see an avalanche on the flank of one peak begin to build in momentum, a white wave of ice and snow tearing through a narrow valley like a solid wind.

"Look at that!" Marty had a telephoto lens on his video camera.

The avalanche continued to accelerate in undeniable violence as it careened through the valley, its bulk slaloming with each twist in the topography. In seconds, it reached the bottom of the mountain and fanned out onto the snowfield, slowing finally as it expended its gravitational force. A cloud of powder remained suspended above the area.

"Is that normal?" Bishop asked.

"Last night I asked Erwin about avalanches," Ira said. "He said he'd be surprised if we saw any. Global warming has altered the environment up here. He said there's less snowfall than ever and fewer and smaller icebergs. Aerial surveys of the mountains north of us show patches of rock that haven't been exposed for hundreds, even thousands of years."

At six, Marty called a halt for the day. The trench was fifteen feet deep, and the pressure of snow had compacted the material at the bottom enough for Mercer to begin melting operations the next morning.

With the addition of the Geo-Research scientists there wasn't enough room in the mess for everyone, so dinner was served in two shifts. Halfway through the meal, Greta Schmidt approached the table, a bundle of papers in her hand. Mercer had seen very little of her since the *Njoerd,* and when they did bump into each other, he found her demeanor hadn't improved since that first confrontation at the Hotel Borg. He'd also noted that many of the Geo-Research people deferred to her more than Werner. Her relationship with whoever had bought the research company from Koenig had given her a great deal of power.

"The plane carried mail. This is what came for you." She dropped the letters and envelopes on the table, keeping one in her hand. "Also a letter with an American postmark came, but I do not recognize the name on the envelope."

Mercer's guts slid. He knew it was for him and who sent it. "What's the name?"

She checked the address. "Max E. Padd."

Ducking his head as the others laughed, Mercer held up his hand for the thick envelope sent to him by Harry White. Schmidt sensed she had been made fun of and strode away quickly.

"Who's it from?" Ira asked.

"A friend of mine is forwarding my mail." Mercer noted his name was written in tiny script under the boldfaced Max E. Padd. "For years I've tried to convince him he's not funny."

When he tipped the large envelope onto the table, a cascade of junk mail fell like confetti. There were credit card solicitations, sweepstakes entries, catalogs from companies Mercer had never even heard of, and five parking tickets issued since he'd left Washington. In the packet, Harry had also included his own bills, as well as a strongly worded PAST DUE notice for the rent on his apartment a few blocks form Mercer's house. At the bottom of the pile was a handwritten note. Chuckling as he read it, Mercer tried to decide what, if anything, was teasing and hoped to God it was the postscript.

Dear Mercer,

   Sorry, I didn't know what was important so I sent along everything you've gotten so far. I was rushed when I did this so some of my bills might have gotten mixed up with your stuff. If you don't mind, go ahead and pay them and I'll pay you back. Trust me.

   Also, you ran out of Jack Daniel's again, so I forged a check at the liquor store. You do have four hundred dollars in your account, don't you? By the way, I wouldn't have gotten those tickets if you had a handicap sticker for your Jag. Something to consider.

                    Don't let your balls freeze off,
                              Harry

   P.S. Tiny said he'd pay to have the scratch buffed out of your car.

                    *   *   *

It was late the next afternoon when they reached the entrance to Camp Decade. The hotrocks had worked flawlessly, and the single pump they'd brought to the ice was more than capable of drying out the five-foot-diameter shaft as it filled with meltwater. The most time-consuming part of the dig was sleeving the hole with plastic to prevent cave-ins. Mercer and Bern Hoffmann spent most of the time at the bottom of the shaft wearing rubber boots that allowed the cold to leach into their legs, but protected them from the water. Ira and Marty kept up the supply of hotrocks and made sure the pump was fueled.

Mercer had worked it so the shaft dropped about a foot in front of the entrance to Camp Decade. That way the ice wall would act as a barrier to keep melt-water from flooding the facility. Through the distortion of twelve inches of ice, he could see the corrugated metal siding of the entrance and make out that there was a crude sign nailed to the door.

"We're just about set," he shouted up the vertical tube. "I want to lay one more load of hotrocks down her to give us a sump below the level of the base. Our body heat is going to melt some of the ice, and we could have a flooding problem."

"Okay," Marty replied. "I've got another drum in the sling. It's on its way down."

Mercer looked up. Water dripping from above fell like rain. The heavy-gauge plastic that lined the shaft held back the ice, but the joints weren't watertight. Drops pinged methodically off his hard hat, making him feel like he was at the bottom of a wishing well. Above the shaft's lip, the Sno-Cat with the crane was backed right up to the hole, and a forty-four-gallon drum hung from its unspooling cable.

Reaching upward with a gloved hand, he grasped the bottom edge of the drum as it came into range, guiding it down those last few feet. "Okay, Marty. We've got it."

They had done this so many times now their actions were almost habitual. While Bern cracked open the lid, Mercer positioned the pump hose into an intentionally deeper part of the shaft meant to collect the last of the water. The young German was a quick study at spreading the blue granular chemicals. They had to work quickly, for no sooner did the first hand-fuls land on the ice than they began to melt their way into the floor. In moments the entire sump was covered in blue water percolating upward and draining down into the hole. The chemicals smelled like fertilizer as they mixed with water. The pump was at full power and quickly drew the melt to the surface. Mercer expected that the mixture had produced a foul blue stain at the pump's discharge outlet.

Only fifteen minutes passed before the pump began sucking drafts of air. Another six inches of ice had vanished up the hose.

"Well, I guess we're ready." Mercer took a drink of Gatorade from a large thermos. Because there was virtually no humidity on the ice sheet, dehydration was one more constant threat. He cupped his hands to his mouth to shout up at Marty. They'd already decided to have some walkie-talkies brought in on the chopper flight carrying Anika Klein. "Send down the chain saw. We're set to open her up."

"Why don't you come up and let me open the base?" Marty's voice echoed back. "I need Bern to hold my video camera, though, for my father's tape."

"Lower the bucket." Mercer would have loved the honor to be the first one in Camp Decade, but it was right that Marty had the privilege. His father had been stationed here and he was paying the bills.

Snow blew in a constant sheet in the narrow ribbon of sky above the trench, howling just above the Sno-Cat. Yet when Mercer got out of the empty barrel they used as an elevator, the cut protected him from the shrieking fury. Ira handed him a silver flask, still warm from where it had rested against his body. Mercer took a pull of the Scotch, gasping at its smooth burn.

"Good job down there," Ira said.

"Thanks." Mercer took one more snort before returning the liquor to Ira. "Marty should be able to use the chain saw to cut through the ice in ten, fifteen minutes."

The whine of the saw was amplified as it reverberated up the shaft, sending shivers down Mercer's spine as its blade chewed into the ice. It was worse than a dentist's drill. When the chain saw finally cut off, Ira hollered down, "Can you open the door?"

"Yeah, just a second. I'm recording the sign on it."

"What's it say?" Mercer asked.

" 'Camp Decade, United States Air Force.' Below it some joker hand-painted 'Give up hope all ye who enter here.' Once we get the outer door open, you guys can come on down."

"Just say the word."

Mercer could hear Marty talking below him and guessed he was saying something he had prepared for the video, some words for his father. A minute later, he heard a screech of protest, a sound of metal tearing against metal.

"We're in!" Marty whooped. "It's a vestibule of some kind. There's another set of doors about ten feet in front of us. The walls all look good. Just a little buckling."

"How about the floors?"

"They're a little uneven and there's ice in places, but they look good. None of the wood has rotted."

"Can we come down?" Ira demanded.

"Yeah, Bern's on his way back up. Don't forget the flashlights."

Once Bern Hoffmann reached the surface, Mercer used the crane's remote controls to lower himself and Ira back down the pipe. Light spilling down the shaft barely reached the vestibule's far doors, so they each turned on the four-cell Maglites.

Coat pegs lined both walls of the passage and below them grates had been placed to help melted snow drain off boots. This had been a staging area for the crew before venturing onto the glacier. A sign on the wall warned the men to make sure their socks were dry before stepping outside. Beyond the far door would be the camp proper.

"Go ahead, Marty," Ira prompted, his breath clouding in front of his mouth. "Let's do it."

"Just a second." Bishop faced his crew, his Minicam shut off. "You know, it's funny. I didn't want to come here at all. I thought my dad was being a pain in the ass for asking me. But now that we're here, about to enter the base, I'm really glad I did this." His voice was thick with emotion. "I want to thank all of you for doing this with me. Ira, I know you're getting paid for this, but you've already done more than your share. And, Mercer," he said with a smile, "without you we'd still be on the surface trying to dig our way down here with snow shovels."

The second door opened as if it had been oiled just the day before. Their flashlights cut puny slashes through the gloom. Marty had a powerful lamp attached to his camera but there was still more shadow than light. The thin crust of ice on the floor was frozen condensation, the icy legacy of the men who had breathed here all those decades ago. It was so silent, they could hear every footfall they made.

Each of them was subdued by what they were doing, and their chills were not entirely caused by the freezing temperature. It was eerie inside the base. Everything felt muted, as though it was happening at a slower pace than reality. Time had forgotten Camp Decade, and yet they half expected to hear voices or see someone approach from the shadows and demand to know what they were doing here. It was a place for ghosts.

Beyond the entrance lay a short hall that branched at a T-juncture. The camp's entrance had been in the center of the administration area. To the left would be the garage, storage, and reactor room. To the right would be the dorms and laboratories. Without the need to take a vote, the party turned right. The walls were painted plywood backed with a layer of insulation and corrugated metal. In the few places where they had been torn by ice, piles of snow had accumulated on the floor. There were also a few areas where the roof had given way slightly, allowing ice and snow to form solid mounds that nearly blocked the hallway. Many of the blockages were small and could be easily stepped over, but one nearly choked the entire hallway, forcing the men to clamber over on their bellies.

They stopped at each of the doors they came across and flashed their lights around the offices they found. "Time warp," Ira commented once. The Air Force had left a lot of equipment behind like old manual typewriters, a mechanical mimeograph machine, and furniture that dated to World War II.

"My dad told me it was cheaper for them to leave this stuff here than fly it back to the States. All they took was their personal effects, the reactor, and the five Sno-Cats kept in the garage," Marty clarified.

"You're sure about the reactor?" Ira asked, half joking.

"Of course," Mercer said sarcastically. "This is the government we're talking about."

They reached the juncture that bisected one leg of the base. Turning left, Marty led the trio toward the dormitories. There were eight of them on each side of a central hallway; each was an identical room about thirty feet by thirty feet with rows of matching bunk beds. The soldiers who were stationed here had taken their footlockers but there were still a great many personal articles left behind. Near a few of the beds were pinups of women who today would be considered plump and whose bathing suits showed less skin than the average cocktail dress.

The men passed through a mess hall and another space that had been the enlisted men's rec room, which included several pool tables and card tables. Beyond the rec room, the door at the end of the hallway ended in a tiled bathroom large enough to provide for the needs of a few hundred men.

"The officers must have been stationed in another part of the base." Ira stated the obvious.

"That's right," Marty said, chiding himself with a shake of his head. "We passed a door where we turned onto this corridor. That's where they had their quarters. My father lived in room twelve."

Mentally, Mercer adjusted his map of the base.

Where the center of the letter H met the right leg, there would be an additional line extending outward.

Backtracking, Marty rushed to the first juncture. "Check it out." He pointed to the sign on a door they had passed but ignored. "Officers Only." He led them down the corridor, reading numbers off the doors on each side as he went.

Mercer lagged behind. He understood that Marty wanted to see the room his father had occupied, but it went against his instinct to rush headlong. He continuously trained his light on the ceiling and walls to make sure they were solid and took a moment to peer into any of the open rooms they came across. The officers' rooms were luxurious compared to the enlisted men's dorms, but still they were small. Each had a single bed, a desk, and a freestanding closet. As Marty paused in front of room twelve to address the camera for posterity, Mercer craned his head into room ten.

And froze.

"This looks exactly the way my father described," he heard Marty tell Ira Lasko.

Pushing open the door with his shoulder and centering his light on the bed, Mercer turned to the two men. "Does that include this corpse?"

The body of a dark-haired man lay on top of the bed, clothed in a leather jacket. He had been freeze-dried like a mummy.

"My God!"

"Who is it?"

Mercer studied the body for a moment longer, noting the embroidered wings on the fur-trimmed jacket. "Gentlemen, meet Major Jack Delaney, the pilot of a C-97 that crashed three months before Camp Decade was closed."

Sweat pouring down his face, Klaus Raeder leapt back as a callused fist brushed past his jaw, missing him by a fraction of an inch. He pivoted, raised one leg, and fired a counterkick that his opponent swept aside gracefully. Continuing with his spin, Raeder let the first leg drop, cocked the other, and landed a bare foot into the midsection of his adversary.

The man doubled over, his breathing so ragged that for a moment Raeder feared he'd caused injury. He dropped his guard, wiping his hands on the baggy pants of his martial arts *gi*. His opponent saw the momentary lapse and instantly exploded from his position, swinging his arms and feet in a flurry of blows. Raeder was forced to retreat in the face of such an onslaught, blocking shots by pure instinct, for they were coming too fast to actually see. Instinct told him he was nearing the mirrored wall of the *dojo*. When the next punch came at his face, he captured the fist in his crossed wrists, torqued his body so his adversary was pushed off balance, and rammed his knee upward, lifting his sparring partner from his feet. He had been too close to defeat to care about injuries now.

He executed a perfect throw, tossing the other man's two-hundred-pound frame with ease. Rolling with the throw, he came up on his knees, grabbed a handful of the supine opponent's *gi*, and prepared to punch his teeth through the back of his head.

"Give," Gunther Rath croaked.

Raeder's eyes were glazed with bloodlust, his mind empty of everything but absolute victory. He was so close to administering the killer blow that he had to jerk himself away, pounding a palm against the padded carpet to vent a portion of his raw aggression.

Just as quickly as the berserker fury washed over him, it faded. He stood and extended a hand to his special-projects director, a triumphant smile splitting his handsome face. "For a second there, I thought you had me."

"For a second, I did," Rath replied. An injury to his throat during his years as a professional judo instructor had left his voice box severely damaged. Each word rasped as if spoken over sandpaper.

His tortured voice, oft-broken nose, and large build combined to make Rath appear menacing, a man others intentionally avoided. People also thought him slow-witted because of his bulk but he had a street cunning that Klaus Raeder had identified early in their relationship.

He had found Rath in East Germany during a particularly difficult corporate takeover. In 1991, Raeder was trying to buy a factory that made industrial hot-water boilers but a nascent union movement would not agree to terms, putting the deal in jeopardy. The delay caused Raeder's purchase price to spiral to the point where the purchase no longer made economic sense. Yet he would not give up. Never one to let legality interfere with his plans, Raeder went in search of a specific type of problem solver.

A few discreet inquiries led him to Gunther Rath, a former Olympic medal winner in judo working as an enforcer for an underworld leader. When they met the first time, Raeder saw a potential in Rath that went far beyond the petty intimidation he'd been using. The lawless scramble following the demise of communism opened unprecedented opportunities if one had the vision and the will. Raeder had little difficulty imagining the profits to be wrung from East Germany, and he saw that Gunther Rath, with his shadowy contacts, could help provide the means.

Raeder made him an offer. Break the union and he could have a permanent position in Raeder's company. Rath had never considered his particular skills could be used in the legitimate world, so he jumped at the chance to escape his current situation. It was an opportunity for a new beginning and an escape from the mistakes that had tumbled him from the Olympic podium to the streets. The labor problem came to a quick end, following an arson attack against the labor leader's house that nearly wiped out his family.

During his years in the East, Klaus Raeder relied on Rath to be his blunt instrument of corporate coercion. However, by the time Klaus Raeder came to the attention of Kohl AG, the two had tempered their tactics since their reputation alone was enough to intimidate. While Reinhardt Wurmbach, Kohl's legal counsel, questioned Rath's suitability in such a prestigious firm, Raeder would not have accepted the presidency if Rath weren't brought in as his special-projects director.

After a few moments of rest, the two squared off again. Gunther Rath had begun teaching Raeder martial arts early in their partnership. Raeder excelled, very quickly becoming his teacher's equal. In the past few years he'd actually become better than Rath, something he delighted in proving. The two had sparred thousands of times, and yet their workouts had never become stale because each had such drive. It was a contest of ego and desire as much as skill.

Before the first punch was thrown, a buzzing phone interrupted them.

Raeder bowed to Rath and turned away.

The *dojo* was in the basement of Raeder's Blankesene district villa, a hundred-year-old home the size of a castle in Hamburg's best neighborhood. Raeder had purchased the house soon after joining Kohl, renovating the musty wine cellar into a modern gymnasium. The mirrored room was ringed with exercise equipment and benches of free weights.

The phone was on a table near the stairs leading to the ground floor.

"Raeder."

"Herr Raeder, it's Ernst Neuhaus." The head of Geo-Research's support office in Reykjavik sounded agitated.

"Yes, what is it?" Raeder looked at a wall clock, noting it wasn't yet six in the morning. It would be five in Iceland and another hour earlier in Greenland.

"Sir, we've had communications problems from Greenland. Otherwise you would have been informed last night."

"What happened?" Raeder's stomach tightened. Neuhaus was being obsequious, never a good sign.

"The Americans have already opened Camp Decade and they discovered a body that's been frozen there for many years."

"Whose?" he snapped, dreading what he was about to hear. The news, if it was what he feared, would instantly nullify his carefully laid plans.

"It appears to be the body of an American Air Force pilot."

"Thank Christ." Raeder sagged. Had the corpse been of one of the others, Kohl AG would have been destroyed in hours. Gunther Rath approached his superior when he saw the fleeting look of panic on his face. Raeder waved a hand to indicate that everything was all right. "He was a survivor of the cargo plane crash in 1953?"

"That's what they think, yes," Neuhaus answered quickly. "The Americans speculate that he survived out on the ice by living in the plane and eating provisions meant for Thule Air Force Base. Some discussed the possibility that he also ate his crewmates as well."

"Has anyone done a detailed analysis of the body?" Raeder didn't honestly believe that anyone could have survived the accident in the Pandora cavern and ten years of isolation, but he had to make certain.

"Not yet," Neuhaus said. "The corpse is still in Camp Decade. The Americans want to contact their Air Force about how to proceed."

"No!" Raeder shouted. "That can't be allowed to happen. There are already too many people at the site. The U.S. Air Force will want to send in a full forensic team as well as soldiers to escort the body home." He paused, thinking furiously. "The Surveyor's Society group must be prevented from contacting the outside. Use the communications problems as an excuse."

"That won't be much of a stretch," Neuhaus said. "The solar-max phenomenon has made the satellite phones at the base worthless, and the radio works only sporadically."

"Good. Make sure they remain isolated. No one is to use the radio other than our people." That was one problem solved, at least temporarily. "I still want that body examined."

"That may pose a risk. None of our people have a legitimate excuse to inspect it."

"Tell them to do it in secret." Irritation strained Raeder's voice. Neuhaus should have seen such a simple solution. "I don't want an autopsy performed, just a quick examination to confirm that the man is really who the Americans believe." Because of the compartmentalization of this project, men at Neuhaus's level did not know who else could have infiltrated the long-abandoned base. Raeder couldn't afford to say whose body he initially feared had been discovered without compromising security. "Just pass on my orders."

"Yes, sir." Neuhaus paused. "Ah, Herr Raeder, there is one more thing."

"What?"

"We learned the identity of the woman Mercer spoke to here in Reykjavik." Raeder heard his employee snap open a piece of paper. "Elisebet Rosmunder."

"Who is she?"

"Her son was involved with the failed search for the C-97 back in the '50s. Rosmunder herself is more than eighty years old."

"Are you having her watched?"

"Yes, sir. As far as we can tell, her routine hasn't changed since that meeting. She's had no visitors nor has she gone to meet anyone. Do you want us to tap her phone?"

Raeder considered for a moment. He doubted her interest in Greenland went beyond the plane crash. But what of Mercer's interest in her? With no link between the crashed cargo plane and Pandora, the mining engineer was looking up a blind alley. "No, you don't need to tap her phone. Maintain a loose surveillance for a few days, and if she does nothing suspicious let it drop. I believe she's a dead end.

"That reminds me of something, Ernst. The last member of the expedition is due to arrive at the base tonight, right?"

"Anika Klein arrives tomorrow morning," Neuhaus corrected.

"Okay. I'm sending Gunther Rath to Greenland the day after that. I don't know how big our search window will be, so I want to get working as quickly as possible. Thank Werner for me on the excellent job he's done setting up the base. It went better than any of us predicted. Tell him that, as soon as Rath arrives, he will be taking over command of the operation. Once Rath's there, we'll find some pretense to evacuate all non–Geo-Research people from the base."

"Yes, Herr Raeder."

"Neuhaus learned who Mercer met with?" Gunther Rath asked as soon as Raeder hung up the phone.

"A nobody named Elisebet Rosmunder. Her son was part of the search for the missing C-97."

"Considering what's at stake, is it wise to leave her alive?"

Raeder couldn't believe he'd heard correctly. "Jesus, Gunther! Why the hell would you ask that? This whole operation was designed so no one gets hurt, and you casually suggest we kill an innocent woman. What are you thinking?"

Rath gave no physical reaction to the quick rebuke.

"Klaus, this operation goes beyond what we've ever done before. We are more in my old world than your new one. We need to go to extraordinary lengths to protect ourselves. You may have convinced Kohl's board that removing evidence from the Pandora cavern is just a business decision, but we know that's bullshit. Saving the company a ton of money doesn't negate the immorality of your plan."

"Immorality is a far cry from cold-blooded murder," Raeder countered. "No matter how much money we save Kohl, I would never condone such an act."

"She's a loose thread. In this situation she could prove to be dangerous to us."

"Haven't I taught you anything, Gunther? Early on, your tactics were what we required to get what we want. But those days are long past. Despite what you think, our plan to clear out the Pandora cavern is a business decision, pure and simple. We are not going to resort to violence. There's no need for it."

Raeder saw that Rath still looked unconvinced yet said nothing. He had conditioned Rath for unquestioning loyalty and wondered why his orders were now being questioned. His answer came quickly.

"I can't go to Greenland until early next week," Rath said. "The Party's holding an executive committee meeting in Essen Sunday night. I have to attend."

The corners of Raeder's mouth turned downward in annoyance. Gunther Rath had made tremendous progress shedding his criminal image. He favored Savile Row suits, dined at fine restaurants, and had even given up his proclivity for prostitutes to settle down with one woman. Yet all of Raeder's efforts to make him give up his most dangerous trait—interest in the Nazi Party—had failed. For as long as they'd known each other, Rath had been an active member of the fascist organization and worked tirelessly for the cause. Just recently he'd been promoted to an executive committee near the very top of the neo-Nazi movement.

Rath's belief in fascism had its roots in his youth.

His father had been a sergeant in the *Eisatzstab Reich-sleiter Rosenberg,* the professional looter squads charged with plundering Europe's Jews during the war. It was estimated that this little-known organization stole $3.5 billion from Holland alone and their total for all of Europe approached $13 billion in inflation-adjusted dollars. Fully one fifth of the world's recognized Western art had passed through Nazi hands during their systematic pillage.

Unrepentant for what he'd been a part of, Rath's father had raised his son to believe that what the Nazis had done had been fully within their right. Beginning in his teens, Gunther Rath had strived to restore the fascist nightmare that once dominated the Continent.

In a bizarre twist of irony, Klaus Raeder knew from the now-burned corporate records that the gold Kohl AG had used in the Pandora Project had come from a plunder squad similar to the *ERR* that followed behind the advancing German Army in the Soviet Union.

"You were away for a meeting early this week," Raeder admonished. "What could have changed in the past few days to necessitate another gathering?"

"That was an action-council meeting," Rath said stiffly.

Raeder shook his head slowly, his eyes filled with patronizing amusement. "Action council, executive committee—you sound like a bloated group of left-wing rebels. I've never heard of an organization that meets more and does less."

Had this come from any other man, Gunther Rath would have mauled him, but he respected his employer too much. He also had to agree, in part. The neo–Nazi Party spent more time quibbling among themselves than taking their message to the streets. Still, it was difficult to hold his tongue or his fists.

"Harassing Turkish immigrants and salting Green Party rallies with your thugs is good for a few headlines," Raeder continued to mock, "but at this pace it'll take you a thousand years just to build your

Reich. For Christ's sake, Gunther, give it up. Fascism will never come back. People won't give up freedoms like that again. They're too comfortable today to be impressed with fiery oratory and flag-waving spectacles. Besides, Nazism was a personality cult, not a real political movement."

"That was the mistake," Rath challenged. "Hitler made it a personality cult, and when he could no longer sustain the cause, it collapsed."

"The *cause* collapsed because American bombers pounded our cities into rubble, which Allied tanks then overran." Raeder's tone became conciliatory. "I have failed to teach you that capitalism is a preferred method of governing to National Socialism. I suppose I can live with that. But until you obtain your dream, you live in my world and will operate by my rules. Right now I need you in Greenland. If the Pandora cavern is discovered before we empty it, the horror of what your beloved party did sixty years ago will play on every television on the planet. With that many bodies down there, anti-Nazi public opinion is going to soar to an all-time high. You wouldn't be able to rally enough people to hold a game of solitaire."

Raeder climbed the stairs to the master suite on the third floor of his villa. The fury Rath had directed at him was not lost on the industrialist. In the marble shower with its multiple water jets, Raeder wondered if his old friend was the right person for this particular job. Rath's loyalties, divided between Raeder and the Nazi Party, had the same goal in this particular instance, but Rath was acting as though his interest and thus his tactics lay with the Party—proof being his suggestion to kill Elisebet Rosmunder. The corporate Rath never would have made such a proposal.

Stepping from the shower, Raeder realized that Gunther had never questioned one of his orders. He was thinking like a Nazi thug and Raeder worried that, once his special-projects director reached Greenland, he would become even more defiant. When this operation was over, he hoped Rath would again return to normal. But for as long as it took to erase part of Kohl's Nazi past, Raeder would have to keep a tight rein if he wanted to avoid bloodshed.

Mercer was sitting on his bed, going over the computer maps from their survey, when the dormitory's main door crashed open. Though his room was at the far end of the structure, he felt a noticeable temperature drop.

"Mercer! Mercer!" Marty Bishop shouted. "Are you in here?"

"Back here," Mercer called.

"Thank God. Igor's dead."

Stunned by those words, Mercer's guts gave a hollow slide. Igor dead? Injury or even death wasn't unheard of in the dangerous world of polar exploration, but Igor Bulgarin? He was the most experienced person in the camp. Somehow, Mercer was not surprised it was the big Russian. Coming on the heels of their discovery of Major Delaney yesterday and Mercer's findings this morning, he knew something was very wrong with this entire expedition. It being Igor who died seemed like the appropriate third link in a chain of bizarre events.

Quickly, before his thoughts became clouded, Mercer set aside his personal feelings of loss and suspicion. There would be time for that later. His relaxing, don't-need-to-be-in-charge vacation was over. Marty's coming to him in such an obvious panic meant that the leadership of the Surveyor's Society team was about to shift to him. Mercer didn't hesitate. He owed it to Igor and he owed it to the Surveyor's Society. He was on his feet and zipping up his coat by the time Bishop appeared at his bedroom door.

"What happened?" His voice crackled with the authority he'd intentionally hidden from the others.

Marty paused, looking Mercer in the eye. For an instant he resisted answering, knowing that he was supposed to be in charge and should be demanding explanations. Yet he had rushed here, pushed by instinct, to report their discovery to the man who was the natural leader of the group. He could not sustain Mercer's steady gaze, and rather than resentment, his voice was filled with gratitude.

"When we went into Camp Decade this morning, Bern Hoffmann and I found there had been a cave-in overnight. Part of the roof collapsed in the main corridor, right beyond the area that was already partially blocked by snow. Remember where we had to crawl to get to the barracks and officers' quarters?" Mercer nodded. "Just past there, about ten feet of the hallway was filled floor to ceiling with ice and snow. We were using shovels to clear away the mess when we found Igor at the bottom of the pile. He must have been right under the avalanche when the ceiling let go. He was frozen solid."

"Show me."

Outside, the sun was hidden by clouds so thick there were no shadows. The wind was a raw force that knifed its way through the few gaps in Mercer's Arctic clothing. He drew his hood tighter and refastened the Velcro at his sleeves to prevent the icy air from reaching inside his gloves. He snapped a lead from the safety line to his coat and began trudging across the snow toward Camp Decade's entrance. It was impossible to hold a conversation in these conditions, so Marty walked silently in his footprints.

Mercer's mind raced with speculation. Because Igor had the room next to his, Mercer had heard him leaving the dormitory in the middle of the night. Assuming he was headed for a late-night snack or possibly a romantic encounter, Mercer had quickly fallen back asleep. When he awoke, Igor wasn't in his room and Mercer guessed he'd already gone to the mess for breakfast. He put the incident out of his mind, working instead on a problem he'd discovered with their subsurface radar survey.

Now the Russian meteorite hunter was dead, killed by an avalanche that shouldn't have happened in a section of the camp he had no right to be in. Mercer couldn't shake the feeling that, had he questioned Igor last night, Bulgarin wouldn't be dead this morning. There were a great many deaths on Mercer's conscience, mostly trapped miners he'd been unable to rescue, but there were others too. Soldiers. Refugees. Friends. And even without knowing the full truth yet, he added Igor Bulgarin to the list.

Behind him, Marty shouted for him to slow down but Mercer ignored him, lengthening his stride in a futile race to reach the Sno-Cat poised above the tunnel. A race Igor had already lost.

Mercer didn't pause before climbing into the waiting bucket and lowering himself into the ice. Marty would have to recall the makeshift elevator when he reached the 'Cat. He leapt from the bucket as soon as it touched bottom, his boots splashing through accumulated meltwater.

"Hold on," Marty called down from the rim of the shaft.

"Start the topside pump," Mercer shouted savagely. "There's too much water down here. You should have done it first thing this morning."

When he reached the second set of doors, he heard the low thrum of a portable generator running somewhere in the maze of the complex. Mercer cursed under his breath, fury sparking behind his slate eyes. He checked his watch and calculated that Marty and Bern had been working down here for a few hours.

At the first intersection he turned right and saw the glow from several portable spotlights rigged to the ceiling farther down the corridor. The sound of a small generator grew with each step toward the light. So did the reek of exhaust.

The young German didn't hear Mercer approach.

He was at the far side of the generator shoveling chunks of ice and compacted snow into an empty office. Mercer grabbed up a flashlight left on the floor next to the portable generator and flicked off the gasoline-powered engine. The floodlights dimmed to orange before failing completely. The beam from Mercer's flashlight was nearly swallowed by the darkness.

"Who's there? Who shut off the generator?" Hoffmann peered into the flashlight.

Mercer fought to keep his anger in check. "Get the hell out of here right now. This drive is fouled with carbon monoxide." Unconsciously Mercer switched to the vernacular of hard-rock mining, where a tunnel was called a drive.

"Didn't Mr. Bishop tell you? Igor's dead."

"And you will be too if you don't get out of here." Mercer grabbed Bern by his collar, heaving him to his feet, where he swayed for a moment, pressing his gloved hand against a wall to hold himself steady.

"Whoa." He slammed his eyes as a blinding headache raged inside his skull.

"Your lungs are full of gas. Didn't you smell it?"

"*Ja,* but I thought we'd be okay."

Bern could barely stand, so Mercer continued to drag him by his jacket, maneuvering him toward the exit. In the spill of light coming from the surface, his face was gray and his eyes weeped. The fresh cold air made him cough in fits so powerful that he vomited.

"Marty," Mercer yelled up the shaft. "Where's Ira?"

"During breakfast Greta asked him to help fix the engine on one of the Sno-Cats."

That explained why these two had been so stupid. Ira Lasko would have known not to run a generator inside the base. Because carbon monoxide was heavier than air, the gas had pooled where the men were working and had been slowly suffocating them. In a sense, Mercer saw that Igor Bulgarin had saved their lives. Had Marty not gone to get him, he and Hoffmann would have been asphyxiated as they attacked the blockage, and their corpses would have been found next to the Russian's.

"Go get him and tell him we need to rig wiring into the base for lights. Then come down here and give me a hand wrestling the generator back topside."

Marty didn't argue. Bringing the Honda generator into the tunnel had been his idea. Listening to the Geo-Researcher's racking coughs, he knew what a deadly mistake that had been.

Mercer turned to reenter the facility, clamping a hand on Bern's shoulder. "Just stay here and keep taking deep breaths to clear your lungs. In a few minutes Marty'll give you a hand getting back to your dormitory."

The floor of the hallway was covered in water melted from the snow that had broken into the base. He didn't know how many BTUs the little generator pumped out, but it was more than enough to cause a pretty good flood. Once they had the sump in the main shaft drained he wanted a hose snaked in here to get rid of this water too. It would refreeze soon and make working conditions dangerous.

He moved slowly as he neared the cave-in, stepping over the silenced generator and the shovels and other tools brought down to clear the passage. In the sharp beam from the light, he could see the gaps in the roof, where the relentless pressure of snow had broken through the structure. It was logical that this would be the area that let go—part of the ceiling had already collapsed in the years since the camp had been abandoned. And yet he couldn't think why it had failed at the very instant Igor Bulgarin walked underneath it. The odds were too long. He studied the twisted metal and jagged teeth of torn plywood, wondering if Igor had done something to the roof to precipitate the failure.

That made no sense either. And what was Bulgarin doing down here in the first place?

He trained the flashlight on the body. Igor lay facedown on the floor, wearing his blue parka with the hood pulled down. The lower half of his body was still buried under the ceiling-high snow. Although Marty and Bern had removed much of the snow around him, Mercer could see where blood had stained the ice near the back of his head. He knelt to examine the spot. It looked like a large slab of ice had hit him at the base of his skull. He could see a thin but deep depression in the bone under his matted hair. Depending on the force, it could have easily been a killing stroke.

Mercer had seen enough head wounds to know how much they bled, and there wasn't enough blood to make him believe that Igor had survived the blow. The first impact had most likely killed him instantly. He hadn't suffered. For that Mercer was thankful. He could easily imagine Igor's agony if he'd slowly frozen to death in the dark.

"Hey, are you all right?" Ira Lasko had approached silently, only announcing his presence after Mercer stood and brushed off his gloves.

"Yeah," he answered. "How are Marty and Bern?"

"Marty's lungs cleared when he went to get you, but Bern's back in his room, sicker than a dog. He'll be fine in a few hours." Ira's expression soured. "It's my fault. I never should have let them come down here alone. Marty doesn't have the common sense of a Boy Scout."

"He said you were fixing one of the Sno-Cats."

"Greta grabbed me at breakfast. Said they needed help with a clogged fuel injector. Dieter and a guy named Fritz are still working on it. What happened here?"

"Hanging wall let go." Mercer used a mining term for the roof. Then he swept the flashlight to show where the ceiling had collapsed. "Igor was right underneath it. When the snow came pouring in, it looks like a chunk of ice caught him in the head. He didn't have a chance."

"This place has been pretty secure for fifty years. What could have caused it?"

"We did," Mercer answered.

"Come again?"

"We caused it. The climate down here had been stable until we entered the base. By us moving around and the heat we gave off by working and breathing yesterday, it's likely that the ice above this area shifted just enough to rip through the roof."

"So Igor was in the wrong place at the wrong time?"

"Yes."

"What was he doing down here in the middle of the night?"

"I heard him leave his room, and I think it was more like early morning than late night," Mercer corrected. "But I didn't know he was coming down here, nor do I know why."

"He could have come down anytime he wanted with one of us," Ira remarked. Like Mercer, he'd seen too much death to be rattled.

"Doesn't make sense," Mercer agreed absently, noticing that Igor Bulgarin's arms were stretched out in front of him as though he'd been walking with his hands touching the ceiling. He wondered if that was an important detail and decided it probably wasn't.

"The body?"

Mercer looked at Ira, understanding what he was asking. "It's possible he wanted to check it out, but why would Igor be interested in a dead pilot? And why come down here secretly?"

"Booze?"

"That was my first thought," Mercer said sadly. He didn't like to think the worst of Bulgarin. "Maybe he didn't want anyone to know he'd fallen off the wagon, so he came here to get drunk." He bent to pat down the body, but couldn't feel the distinctive shape of a bottle. "Could be he stashed it someplace when he decided to leave."

"Lot of ground to cover to prove it."

Mercer flashed the light down the tunnel to make certain Marty hadn't returned yet. He felt that Ira, with his experience on submarines, could handle what he was about to say, but he wasn't sure about Marty. He spoke in a low voice. "We've got another problem too. It's not important why, but I brought a Geiger counter with me from Iceland." He paused, waiting for a reaction.

Ira made a gesture with his hand for Mercer to continue. Mercer was correct about the former Navy man. Nothing got to him. "When we were using the radar sled, I also made a radioactivity map of the facility. None of the radiation I detected was dangerous. It was mostly ambient background noise, but there was an area that spiked a bit. I assumed it was where the old reactor had sat. On another hunch, this morning I compared the radar sled readings to those from the Geiger counter and found that the spike occurred over the room with the pilot's body, nowhere near the old reactor site."

That got a reaction. "The body's hot?"

"Call it warm, yeah." Mercer nodded. "Just enough to tickle the counter now, but back when he died he would have been glowing like a neon sign."

Ira knew that radioactive contamination didn't cause a person to physically glow but he understood what he was saying. He looked at Mercer skeptically. "You've got some pretty accurate hunches."

Mercer shrugged and told him about Elisebet Rosmunder and her son's search for the downed C-97 and his subsequent death from cancer. "I guess you could call it more of a warning than a hunch," he concluded.

"If there was something that radioactive on the plane, the government wouldn't have stopped until it was found," Ira said after giving the problem a moment of thought. "There was quite a flap when the Air Force lost a couple of nukes from a bomber off the coast of Spain in 1966 and again when an armed B-52 crashed over in Thule in 1968. I remember for that one they hauled off nearly a million cubic feet of ice, snow, and debris. No, the Air Force would have moved heaven and earth to locate that plane and clean up any spill."

Mercer regarded Lasko for a minute. "You could be right. I don't know. But the evidence suggests that the C-97 was carrying radioactive material that leaked when the plane crashed, poisoning Jack Delaney and later killing Stefansson Rosmunder."

"So what do we do?" Ira asked.

"Finish unburying Igor and bring his body to one of the cold laboratories and then try to contact the Air Force again. Maybe the communications are back up."

"What about Delaney?" Ira turned, hearing someone approaching down the corridor. It was Marty.

"We'll keep that to ourselves," Mercer said quickly. "The body's not hazardous to handle, but until we hear from the military, he should be off limits."

"Agreed," Ira said out the corner of his mouth before addressing Bishop. "Bern okay?"

"He took some aspirin and is asleep right now." Marty Bishop looked ravaged by guilt. His eyes were dull and he spoke as if each word caused him pain. "Mercer, ah, listen, I, ah . . . It was my idea to bring the generator down here. This whole thing wouldn't have happened if I had talked to you or Ira first. I nearly got us killed."

"You're right," Mercer said mildly, not letting Marty flinch from his responsibility. "It was a stupid thing to do and you two were lucky. This hallway is probably still full of fumes, so for the next twenty-four hours I want the entire facility off-limits."

Mercer caught Ira's eye, making sure he would agree with the lie. The base would be safe in just a few hours.

"That's a good idea," Lasko agreed. "That should give us the time we need to notify the Air Force too."

"Okay," Marty said. "I think I'm going to lie down for a while myself. I feel like shit."

"Go on ahead. We'll take care of Igor."

Two hours later, Igor Bulgarin's body had been placed in one of the cold laboratories. Mercer and Ira had also wandered through Camp Decade, looking for evidence that the Russian had gone there for a drinking binge. Other than some old bottles hidden fifty years ago in the enormous garage, they found nothing. Neither man was surprised. There were tens of thousands of square feet of rooms and passages and closets where Igor could have hidden an empty liquor bottle. Giving up, they used a length of chain and a padlock from the Sno-Cat to secure the base's main doors. No one would be able to enter Camp Decade without them knowing it.

Mercer and Ira met up with Erwin Puhl in the mess hall. The German scientist was still in shock over Igor's death. He sat in an almost catatonic state, his eyes unfocused and unblinking. He hadn't even bothered removing his parka or gloves. A cup of coffee in front of him had gone cold. The only words he'd spoken were, "My brother." It was obvious that he and Igor were a lot closer than anyone thought. He seemed inconsolable.

Greta Schmidt was at the back of the hall, speaking with some of her people. After an appropriate amount of time had passed, she approached the table.

"Dr. Puhl?" Erwin looked up into her blue eyes. The juxtaposition of her vibrant beauty and his desolation was unsettling. "I just learned how long you and Dr. Bulgarin have known each other. It is a terrible thing to lose a friend. I am very sorry for you."

Erwin said nothing but continued to stare at her. His lower lip quivered. She placed a hand on his shoulder. "As soon as we reestablish communications with the *Njoerd,* I'll have a helicopter sent to remove his body and make arrangements to have him flown back to Moscow."

"St. Petersburg," Erwin said softly. "He was from St. Petersburg."

"Yes, of course. How could I have forgotten?" She glanced at Ira and then her gaze settled on Mercer. "Is it safe for your people to be working in Camp Decade?"

"It will be," Mercer replied. This was the first sign of any tenderness he'd seen from her, and it was surprising. "I've closed it for twenty-four hours to let the gas fumes dissipate and to let the avalanche that struck Igor settle. Tomorrow we'll go back in and shore up the ceiling where glacier movement has weakened it."

"Werner and I have already discussed calling the Surveyor's Society and asking them to cancel your expedition. In light of Dr. Bulgarin's death, we feel the base may be too dangerous."

The gentleness she'd just shown Erwin had vanished. There was a challenge in her voice. Mercer responded in kind. "That will be up to Marty Bishop's father and Charles Bryce. You can't order us to leave."

"I can, Dr. Mercer. And if it becomes necessary, I will." She executed a military-style snap turn and stormed away.

"Talk about Beauty and the Bitch," Ira mumbled.

"It might be best if we did leave," Erwin said. "Igor's death . . ." His voice trailed off.

"Not even when Brunhild there tells me to," Ira snarled, nodding as Greta retook her seat at the other end of the mess hall. "I don't like to leave a job unfinished."

"Neither do I," Mercer agreed. "But I'm beginning to wonder what our mission really is."

He spent the remainder of the day with his Geiger counter, traversing the snow piled on top of Camp Decade to get a more accurate fix of any radiation readings. Mercer didn't expect to find anything new, but he needed the hours of solitude. He tried to put what had happened in some sort of perspective and found there wasn't any. Igor was dead and no amount of thought would change that fact. He could only hope that, when he discovered why the Russian had gone to Camp Decade, he would be able to dispel his misguided feelings of responsibility.

Every few hours Mercer returned to the mess hall to inquire about the communications problems. Each time he was told that they had only received broken transmissions from the *Njoerd* and absolutely nothing from the office in Iceland. The technicians doubted that their own signals were getting out and all agreed that the problem would persist for a few days at least.

It was at dinner that the first clear call came through. Mercer and the rest of his team were trying to keep Erwin's mind occupied by playing lazy games of poker over stale coffee when the short-wave transceiver in the corner of the room burst to life. Even through the squawking distortion of static, everyone could hear the hysteria in the voice.

". . . ayday! Mayday! Geo-Research base camp! . . . eo-Re . . . rch . . . camp! . . . is inbound helo from *Njoerd*. I am . . . ixty kilometers east. Turbine is . . . ailing. We are . . . oing down!"

The comm officer scrambled to get his headphones on. Around him a dozen people clustered shoulder to shoulder. "Inbound helo, this is base camp. We understand you are sixty kilometers east of our location and are declaring an emergency."

". . . ank God!" the pilot of the helicopter screamed through the ether. "Storm approaching. Tried to beat it. Engine o . . . heat. I can't keep us in the . . ."

Mercer pulled Werner Koenig away from the group of anxious listeners so his voice wouldn't disturb the radio operator. The Geo-Research supervisor was shaken by what he was hearing. Not wanting to add to Werner's distress, Mercer spoke calmly, reassuringly. "You still have Sno-Cats out there, right?"

"Yeah." Koenig couldn't tear his eyes away from the radio, his concentration on the drama that was unfolding too quickly for him to comprehend. "There are two teams on the ice."

"Where?" When Werner didn't answer immediately, Mercer grabbed his arm, allowing his voice to rise slightly. "Where?"

"Ah, team one is coming in from the south." He looked at his watch. "They should be here in another twenty minutes."

"And the other team?"

Werner suddenly understood why Mercer was asking about the 'Cats. He sounded miserable because the answer was one he did not want to give. "They're due west of us, maybe fifty kilometers away."

"Damn it." Any chance of a successful rescue depended on each second Mercer could gain. "Where's your rally driver, Dieter?"

"He's with team two. What are you going to do?"

Thinking furiously, Mercer's brain shifted back to the pilot's strident call. ". . . titude down to one thousand feet. Dr. Klein says . . . smoke . . . air vents."

That did it. His moment of hesitancy evaporated. There was a passenger on board. The pilot had made the choice to fly through a storm, but Anika Klein was different. She was simply along for the ride. Deep down he knew he would have gone even if the pilot had been alone. "Ira, get on the other radio and keep me updated. I'll be in the Land Cruiser."

Mercer was at the door before anyone realized he'd moved. He didn't bother with the moon boots. His sneakers would have to do. He thrust his arms into a lightweight outer jacket that was the topmost coat on the rack near the exit.

"Dr. Mercer!" Greta Schmidt shouted, running toward him. "I forbid you to go. We will organize a proper search."

"And when you're done you can follow me," he snapped, jerking the zipper to his throat. "Ira, you with me?"

The wiry mechanic had already muscled his way to the short-range set they used to coordinate communications with the Sno-Cats. "Move your ass."

"No! You will wait." Greta grabbed Mercer's sleeve in a fierce grip that felt like it went all the way to the bone. "This is a wasted gesture. Wait until we know where they land. Going alone is suicide."

Mercer had just a second before two more Geo-Research workers joined her. Though he had never struck a woman, he was sorely tempted to break that rule. Why couldn't she see that the only chance the pilot and Anika Klein had was if someone left now?

He yanked free and reached the door. The pressure of wind slammed it open when he turned the handle. The wind was a solid force that made him stagger back until he got better traction, hunched his shoulders and bulled his way forward. The blowing snow and gathering dusk swallowed him.

Despite her fury, Greta made no move to follow. She slammed the door closed again, her body shivering with just that brief contact with the frigid gusts. She stepped over to Ira, her expression one of ill-disguised contempt. "That was the most stupid thing I have ever seen."

"No need to tell me," Ira said with a smirk. "But at least he's doing something. Get your damned search party ready and follow him."

A few minutes later, Mercer came over the radio. "Ira, you there?"

"Nice and snug," he drawled. "How about you?"

"I'm going to need the Jaws of Life just to get my testicles to drop. According to the thermometer in the cab it's fifteen degrees below zero out here. Any word from the chopper?"

"They're still in the air and still heading this way. Pilot said the GPS puts him twenty-one miles due east. How's your speed?"

"I'm pushing it now. Doing twenty."

"Take it easy out there. I don't think Greta's gonna stop for you if you get stuck."

"She'll never see me," Mercer replied with a graveyard chuckle. "Visibility's pure shit. I can't see more than fifty feet in front of me."

"How do you expect to find a crashed helicopter?" Ira asked, alarmed.

"Tell the pilot to have Dr. Klein fire a flare just before they crash." He didn't need to add that neither would likely be in any condition to do it afterward.

"Roger, good idea," Ira was shouting into the microphone because Mercer's transmission kept fading.

His radio had much less power than the chopper's. "I'm telling the comm officer to relay your message now."

It took two minutes for the pilot to acknowledge the request. But even if they were able to do it, Ira had doubts that Mercer would see the flare. The helicopter was down to three hundred feet and Mercer was still between five and ten miles away.

Ira kept his misgivings to himself. "Mercer, the pilot will comply. He estimates he can hold her aloft for another five minutes." He heard nothing but static. "Mercer, do you copy? Over."

There was a small window above the radio sets. It was dark, but with the floodlights on, he could see how the wind raced first in one direction and then another. The captured snow and ice looked like it was caught in a tornado. Ira estimated the gusts at forty miles per hour. He prayed Mercer brought back the pilot so he could kill the stupid son of a bitch for daring to fly in this kind of weather. No resupply mission was worth it.

"Mercer, do you copy? Over."

The comm officer was listening hard to his own earphones, talking with the pilot in easy tones despite the fear they all heard from the speaker.

". . . ifty feet . . . iring flare now." It was a cruel twist of atmospherics that the last seconds of broadcast from the helicopter came in so crisply that it sounded like the pilot was in the room with them. His scream was piercing enough to shatter crystal.

"Mercer, chopper's down! Chopper's down! They fired the flare. Did you see it?" Ira mashed the earphones to his head. "Mercer, are you receiving? Over."

Nothing.

He tried again every thirty seconds for the next half hour. And the results were always the same. Mercer was gone.

Amid the rusting tankers, bulk carriers, and container ships, the *Sea Empress* gleamed like a new Rolls Royce parked in a junkyard. Her upperworks were snowy white, trimmed with black and gold, with twin raked funnels topped by aerodynamic wings not much smaller than those on a private jet. She was longer than most of the ships around her, and her eight-story superstructure towered above every vessel in the busy port. Designed as a catamaran, her two hulls were nearly a thousand feet in length and each had a ninety-foot beam. The cavernous gap between them was used to lower any number of watercraft, from two-hundred-passenger lighters to glass-bottomed excursion boats to Jet Skis.

She could comfortably accommodate four thousand passengers as well as her full-time staff of three thousand. Her list of world records for a cruise liner included everything from number of restaurants—thirty-nine—to casino square footage to having a four-hole pitch-and-putt golf course. Her cost too was a world record likely to hold for years—$1.7 billion.

Despite the ascetic beliefs of many of those who would be sailing on her, few could help but be awed by the sight of her snugged against a concrete pier. The *Sea Empress* was a high expression of the beauty mankind was capable of creating.

Because of the tight security surrounding the Universal Convocation, the quay was quiet except for the guards posted all along the length of the ship. Harbor patrol boats buzzed along her starboard side, and overhead military helicopters kept the roving media

choppers at a safe distance. So far there hadn't been
a single credible threat against the ship or her passengers, but with so much world attention focused on the
greatest religious meeting in history, the authorities
were taking no chances. After lengthy interrogations,
her crew had been sequestered aboard for the past
week, and she was searched daily with bomb-sniffing
dogs.

Getting the ship ready and secure had been a massive operation, and now that the passengers were embarking, those in charge of security had redoubled
their vigilance. Each passenger, from the pope down
to the lowliest secretary, was escorted through unob-
trusive metal detectors calibrated to allow nothing
bulkier than religious medals to pass through. The latest generation of chemical-sniffing devices was also
used to detect the most minute amount of gunpowder.
Even if someone sneaked a ceramic pistol past the
metal detectors, traces of gunpowder from the bullets
would be picked up on these machines.

It had been agreed earlier that only the pope's Swiss
Guard would be allowed to carry weapons on the *Sea
Empress*. There had been some difficulty with the
thirty Sikhs attending the convocation since their tradition demanded each carry a small knife at all times.
The pope had gladly given them permission to maintain the practice.

Neils Vanderhoff was a guard at a manifest check-
point assigned to verify each of the lesser-known passengers against a master list, authenticating their
identity with a computer database of photographs
compiled from six different sources. The pictures
dated back at least a year before the Convocation's
announcement to prevent terrorists from using carefully built false legends to slip aboard.

In front of him now was a tall, middle-aged man wearing a shiny suit that cost more money than Vanderhoff
made in three months. His face was deeply tanned
and smooth, and he had the whitest teeth the
Dutchman had ever seen. He sported a diamond-en-

crusted Rolex and an elaborate ruby pinky ring. While his hair was thinning and silver at the sides, on top it was as dense and jet black as a sable's pelt. Neils wondered why the man spent so much on his wardrobe, teeth bleaching, and jewelry yet wore such an obvious toupee.

Clutching his elbow was a sight Vanderhoff would never forget. The man's wife might have been pretty once, but her fight against time had been a long, bloody campaign that had left the battlefield in ruins. She wasn't that much younger than her husband but her face had been so frequently lifted that it was as tight as the head on a snare drum. She looked like a poorly cast wax model of herself. Behind black false lashes, her eyes bulged from one too many tucks. Her makeup was as overvibrant as that applied to a corpse by a color-blind mortician. Above her eyes were thick slashes of blue and yellow, her cheeks were so rouged they looked sunburned, and her collagen-puffed lips had been troweled over with layers of frost white. Her big hair was brass blond and piled six inches high. She had maintained her figure, or possibly had it maintained for her, but still her hips and backside strained against a skirt sized for a woman fifteen pounds lighter. Her breasts were silicone fantasies that threatened to spill over the top of her lamé blouse.

In her arms was a nervous Pekingese that yapped continuously. The woman made no move to quiet her rodent-size dog.

She popped a piece of chewing gum as her husband passed over their passports. Tommy Joe and Lorna Farquar from Nashville, Tennessee, USA. As if Neils couldn't tell they were Americans. He stared at the caricatures slack-jawed.

"I know what you're thinking, son." Tommy Joe's enormous teeth flashed like a mirror pointed at the sun, and he spoke as if addressing a crowd of ten thousand. "You've seen my ministry on television, and you can't believe you've gotten a chance to meet me."

"Honey, they don't carry our show in Europe, 'cause

they don't talk American here." Lorna Farquar had a little-girl voice with an adult's ignorance. "Do they, Pookie? They haven't been saved yet. No, they haven't." The Pekingese's whine was deeper than its mistress's.

"Sure they do, Lorna. It's on satellite feed, don't you remember?"

"I'm sure I don't," she simpered, her eyelashes tangling like fighting spiders when she blinked up at him.

Neils Vanderhoff shook off his amused incredulity and typed their names into his workstation. Instantly a series of pictures appeared on the screen, mostly publicity shots of the couple at a blue satin altar adorned with the words MIRACLES OF JESUS CHRISTIAN MINISTRIES. He noted wryly that Mrs. Farquar's bosom had been noticeably smaller last year.

Craning her head to see what the customs man had chuckled at, Lorna wailed, "Oh, sweet Jesus! Those pictures are from before I had my titties done."

"There, there, dear." Tommy Joe patted her hand.

Vanderhoff checked to see the most recent entry stamps on their passports as per his orders. He was on the lookout for any suspicious travel since the Convocation had been announced. The Farquars' passports had numerous stamps to Caribbean islands but nothing in the past six months. He handed them back without a word, praying they would move on without braying at him again.

The next person in line was a large man traveling alone, and by the dark robes he wore, heavy silver cross hanging from a chain around his neck, and his full beard, Neils recognized him as a member of the Eastern Orthodox Church. The priest must have heard the exchange, so Vanderhoff gave him a conspiratorial smile. The black-robed figure didn't change his stony expression. He handed over a Russian passport.

Feeling rebuffed, the customs agent noted that Father Anatoly Vatutin had been in Germany before coming to Holland for the Convocation. He punched up the name, comparing the fierce-eyed cleric in front of him to photographs taken a few years earlier at an Eastern Rites meeting in Istanbul. Vatutin had more gray in his beard and hair now but time had not softened his hawkish features. Giving back the passport, Vanderhoff felt a chill when the intense priest nodded in acknowledgment.

Anatoly Vatutin slid his passport back into his battered shoulder bag and hurried along the corridor. Before reaching the exit, he passed the obnoxious television minister, who had stopped so his trashy wife could let her dog lift its leg against a wall. A dark puddle formed on the carpet, and the woman scooped up the Pekingese before its feet became soiled. The thought that these people worshipped the same god he did made Vatutin wince.

Unlike many who had preceded him, Father Vatutin did not pause when he got his first look at the luxury liner. He paid scant attention to the guards either. Head down and cheap shoes clomping, he moved across the pier toward one of four embarkation points, his expression one of anxious determination. The sun soaking into his black clothes was only partially responsible for the sweat that caught in his beard and trickled down his flanks.

He presented his ticket to a uniformed woman at the top of the gangway, not returning the cheery greeting. "You are in cabin E429, Father Vatutin," the assistant cruise director said in passable Russian. "That's on the starboard hull. Go straight into the ship, and when you reach the first atrium, you'll see a broad hallway to your right. That's the Champs Élysées, one of four main throughways connecting the two hulls. When you reach the atrium on the other hull, another attendant will direct you to the elevator bank closest to your cabin."

"*Spesiva,*" Vatutin grunted, clutching at his shoulder bag as if afraid the bubbly attendant would take it.

He moved quickly through the ship, pausing for a flicker of a second to gaze upward when he reached the lofty, glass-crowned atrium that was the center-

piece of each side of the vessel. The balconies ringing
the upper floors dripped with flowering plants, reminding Vatutin of an artist's rendition of the Hanging
Gardens of Babylon. He found the long corridor
called Champs Élysées, then threaded through clusters
of people conversing in excited bursts. He noted that
the men outnumbered the women by a factor of fifty.

At the next atrium, he again presented his ticket
and was directed to an elevator bank near the stern
of the vessel, where he took one of the cars downward
to the lowest of passenger decks. While his Spartan
cabin had a small porthole, it presented a shadowy
view of the channel between the hulls. The cabin
pulsed with the vibration of the *Sea Empress*'s engines.
He paid no attention to the view or the vibration. His
heavy antique wooden chest had already been deliv-
ered and sat in the middle of the tiny room, taking
up so much space that Vatutin had to tuck his legs
under the bed to face it. He checked the lock carefully, relieved to see that it hadn't been tampered
with. He had no idea what kind of scrutiny the luggage
was given, and he had been concerned that if the contents had been examined, he wouldn't have a ready
explanation for what lay within.

He used a brass key on the lock and lifted the lid.
The case was a clever disguise, meant to look solid
and heavy when in fact it was made of wood veneer
over an aluminum shell that weighed just ten pounds.
It was what was at the bottom of the trunk that gave
it such weight.

Below the few items of clothing and toiletries that
Vatutin needed for the two-week cruise were a pair
of gloves, a hood, a type of smock, and a specially
designed metal flask. The gloves almost looked like
medieval chain mail except they were crafted of tightly
woven gold thread and weren't yet a hundred years
old. Each one weighed three pounds. He knew from
experience that they were clumsy and awkward to
wear and even harder to work with.

Next to them was a long hood similarly fashioned

of gold thread. Two eyeholes were woven into the mesh, and over them, a special flap could be drawn down to completely cover the eyes if necessary. Fortunately for Vatutin, the cowl's original owner had had a larger than normal head, so he could slip on the hood without difficulty. He set the glittering gloves and hood aside and strained to withdraw the last item of clothing. This was a recent addition to Vatutin's collection because the original smock had long since disappeared.

This one weighed almost ninety pounds. It was composed of lead-impregnated cloth with hundreds of small lead plates sewn in place to form a solid shield extending from the waist to the throat. The sleeves were banded with lead rings of various sizes that allowed limited movement at the shoulder and elbow.

Anatoly Vatutin wished that the Brotherhood could have afforded to assemble the garment out of gold, like the original, but they no longer had anywhere near that kind of money. As it was, if they failed in the next two weeks, the Brotherhood would not have the funds to continue their work.

A high-strength stainless-steel flask was left at the bottom of the trunk. Though it was the same size as the trunk and about a foot tall, only half its volume was filled. Its liquid contents had been smuggled at tremendous cost from the Chernobyl nuclear plant before its closure. He looked at it with dread before lowering the smock back into the chest and replacing the gloves and hood. He had just started a prayer of thanks that his secret was still safe when there was a knock on his cabin door.

His heart slammed against his ribs. *Oh, God, no!* It had to be the Swiss Guards coming to question him. Either he had been betrayed or they had X-rayed the trunk. *Not now that I am so close,* he cried silently to God. *Please, this is your work I am doing.*

Frantic, he threw his other clothes into the trunk, slammed the lid, and turned the lock again. "Moment, please," he croaked in English.

"Father Vatutin?" a man called from the other side of the door. "I am from the purser's office. Please open the door."

"I am on the toilet," Vatutin improvised, eyeing the porthole as a possible escape route. It was much too small, of course. Trapped, he resigned himself to trust in God to see him through. "I am coming."

On the way to the door, he had the presence of mind to reach into the closet-size bathroom to flush the toilet, maintaining his thin veil of deception. If there was only one of them outside the door, Vatutin wondered if he could kill him. For what he needed to do on this trip, taking the life of a purser was a small price. He had the element of surprise, and even without a weapon, he was formidable at six foot three inches tall and two hundred thirty pounds. He composed himself, wiping sweat from his face. The door swung smoothly and standing in the corridor was an innocent-looking young man wearing a white uniform and holding a bunch of flowers.

"Father Vatutin, these are compliments of the cruise line." He smiled and offered the flowers to a befuddled Vatutin. "When the sailing arrangements were made, your bishop, Bishop Olkranszy, assured us that you wouldn't mind being on the lowest deck. However we felt brightening your cabin with flowers was the least we could do."

"The cabin is fine," Vatutin stammered, his relief immeasurable. They knew nothing! "Perhaps you can give the flowers to the person in the next cabin."

"We have them for all guests staying on the inside of E deck, Father," the young man said and smiled again.

"Ah, thank you, then." Vatutin closed the door, leaning his back against it as he tried to slow his breathing. He wished he had brought along something to settle his stomach. He wanted to vomit.

Get hold of yourself, Anatoly, he thought. He felt like he was having a heart attack. *No one knows why you are really here.*

He knew he would not relax until he took possession of the icon being presented to Bishop Olkranszy by the Vatican and confirmed what lay hidden behind its golden cover. Anatoly gave little thought to his own death if he mishandled the relic just as long as he accomplished his mission. It was little wonder that knowing the secret of Satan's Fist had driven the Brotherhood's founder insane. Grigori Efymovich had handled dozens of such icons while Vatutin was responsible for only one. It would be days before he received the icon, and the tension was already tearing him apart.

Over the anemic throb of the helicopter's faltering engine Anika Klein could hear her grandfather's voice in her head. "Go to Greenland, *liebchen*. There you will be safe."

She could never remember a time when *Opa* Jacob had been more wrong.

The chopper lurched again, a sickening plunge that made her restraining harnesses dig into her shoulders. The pilot, a young Dane contracted by Geo-Research, fought to keep the dying craft in the air. The grim set to his jaw and the undisguised fear in his eyes told Anika that he wasn't likely to win the fight. Around them, the storm that the *Njoerd*'s meteorologist promised wouldn't hit for another six hours raged with banshee fury. Anika had been on enough helicopters to know that, even if the engine wasn't about to let go, they had little chance of reaching the research camp. The snowstorm was too intense. For the hundredth time she cursed herself for flying, cursed the daredevil pilot for thinking he could beat the storm, and cursed *Opa* Jacob for convincing her she'd be safer in Greenland than at home pursuing Otto Schroeder's killers.

While she had lost all details of the drive from Schroeder's house to Ismaning, where her friend had picked her up to bring her home, Anika vividly recalled everything that had come before that. The gunfire. The blood. The pain. And most of all the anger that had grown to a fever pitch.

As a doctor, she had dedicated herself to the preservation of life, and witnessing the torture Schroeder had endured sickened her to the very core. She vowed to see that the man responsible, the man Anika admitted she hadn't really gotten a good look at, was convicted for his unspeakable crime.

When she had phoned *Opa* Jacob after a full day of recovery, she had related everything, including the presence of the unknown snipers and the fact that Schroeder died believing he possessed a secret more valuable than gold. She also asked if the name Philip Mercer meant anything to him.

"I've never heard of him," Jacob Eisenstadt had said. "This is someone Schroeder mentioned?"

"Yes. He said a mysterious caller a few weeks ago told him that this American could be of help. Does he do what you do, *Opa*?"

"Not that I'm aware of but he could be new to the field or work for someone else, like Wiesel's Peace and Justice Center."

"Well, Schroeder was convinced he could help. And what about the Pandora Project he mentioned? Does that sound familiar?"

"I've not heard of that either," Eisenstadt confessed. "But I bet it's the code name for a specific Nazi looting program. Remember that Schroeder was an engineer, not a soldier so it could even be the name given to an attempt to build a secure stash for art and precious metals like they did at the salt mines in Austria."

The idea was an alluring one. "So what do we do now?" Anika had asked, the scent of treasure added to her desire for justice.

"We," Jacob thundered, "do nothing. I will continue working and you get out of Germany. You aren't safe there. You said yourself that the men who killed Schroeder have seen your face and could at this very moment be learning who you are. You should go on your trip to Greenland. You will be safe there, and by the time you get back in a few weeks, I will know enough to go to the police and get you proper protection."

The following argument lasted nearly an hour with

Opa's partner, Theodor Weitzmann, and Frau Goetz, the housekeeper, joining in on the other phones at the Institute. They were unified in their appeal, which was a first as far as Anika knew. That day Anika had called Geo-Research's main office and told them that she would not be able to make the rendezvous in Reykjavik due to an accident. She didn't add that she would spend the days letting the bullet graze in her thigh heal.

After the plane ride to Kulusuk and a chopper to the *Njoerd*, here she was on another helicopter that was minutes away from crashing. Yet her thoughts weren't on her situation. She thought only of the guilt *Opa* Jacob would feel when he learned she died following his recommendation. It very well might kill him.

"There's a rescue effort under way right now," the pilot shouted into the headphones. "They want you to fire a flare when we get close to the ground. They're in an emergency pack under your seat."

Anika was in the copilot's seat and had to loosen her shoulder restraints to reach under her chair. She waited until the gyrating craft stabilized for a moment before attempting the maneuver. As her fingers brushed against a plastic case, the chopper bucked suddenly, dropping farther into the raging clouds of snow blowing by them like random tracer fire. Her head hit the control stick, deepening their dive, which forced the pilot to jerk back hard, hitting her once again.

"Schiesse!" she cried, rubbing the knot already forming under her hair. She checked her glove to make sure she wasn't bleeding.

On her second attempt she brought out the orange box and retightened the straps before she could be thrown bodily out of the seat. The flares were in individual firing tubes that could be activated by pulling a short lanyard at their base. She gripped one firmly, getting ready to open the small window next to her. "Tell me when."

"No. Not up here. You have to go in the back," the pilot told her, jerking a thumb over his shoulder at the cargo compartment. "The flare will destroy my night vision."

From her vantage she could see there was an operable window in the hold's side door.

"Okay." She pulled off the headphones since the cord wouldn't reach; then she unbuckled all her safety belts.

There was no pattern to the helicopter's erratic flight, so there was nothing she could do as gravity either tossed her toward the roof or crushed her to her seat. As if she was mountain climbing, Anika maintained three contact points at all times, only moving a limb when she was certain the other three had a secure purchase. In this fashion, she crawled over her chair and slid into the only open space in the chopper's hold, bracing herself by pressing her back to the floor and jamming her feet against a built-in shelf on the forward bulkhead.

"Can you hear me?" Anika screamed, testing whether she would be able to hear the pilot when he gave his order to fire the flare.

"Yes!" His reply sounded as if it came from outside the aircraft. "About five more minutes, tops."

Okay, AK, this is it.

As long as the engine held together, they had a chance to find a break in the storm and land safely. She kept that hope alive by praying to God, Who had kept her safe in situations like this. She thought of the time when a climbing rope had parted two-thirds up Eiger. She recalled when a white-water raft she'd been paddling had been split open in the middle of Class-4 rapids, dumping her and three companions into a liquid maelstrom. Then there was the case of food poisoning that had forced an end to a hiking expedition in Peru. Anika had eaten the same native stew as the four others with her, and while they had to be choppered back to Iquitos for medical treatment, she hadn't felt the slightest ill effect.

She liked to brag about her outdoor skills, but she knew so much of what she had survived was due to luck, an ally she sometimes disdained. Not now. She was terrified and would need whatever last shreds of good fortune she'd managed to preserve.

Reaching up, she slid open the small Plexiglas window. She gasped at the raw blast of air that sucked her breath away as if the chopper had just gone through explosive decompression. Intellectually, she knew if they survived the crash, they wouldn't last more than a few hours on the ice, but that didn't impair her desire to see the chopper down safely. She would worry about rescue afterward.

The wind rattled the tub of mail left near the door. In the worst bit of irony about this whole ill-fated trip, she'd noted when the crate was put aboard that the topmost envelope was from New York City and had been posted to none other than Philip Mercer. The odds that the man mentioned by Otto Schroeder was on the same trip as her were too long to be coincidental. The anger that had begun at the isolated farmhouse nearly exploded. Though she immediately knew she'd been set up, she didn't know if it was by Schroeder, his killers, or the snipers. Or maybe even by Philip Mercer himself.

Until the storm struck the helicopter, she had been quietly brooding about this development, determined to find the truth.

"Get ready!" the pilot yelled from the cockpit.

Anika stuck the end of the flare out the window, stripping off one glove so she could get a better grip on the lanyard. From her position she couldn't see outside and this was better. Let the crash come as a surprise, she thought. If she didn't know it was coming, her body wouldn't tense involuntarily.

"Now!"

She jerked the string and the glowing ball of fire arced into space, its red corona flying away like the spectral trail of a meteor. Ten seconds later the chopper's skids slammed into the ground. The collision was

like a full swing of a sledgehammer against Anika's
spine. Momentum made the craft's nose pitch forward.
Its blades sliced through the granular snow until they
hit solid ice and came apart. The engine's torque continued to spin the unbalanced rotor head with enough
power to slam the helicopter over on its side. Anika
was thrown into the door, her body pinned by boxes
forced loose by the first impact.

The ragged bits of blade left on the main shaft
chewed into the ground. Teflon-coated shrapnel exploded off with each contact with the ice. The smaller
tail rotor hit the snow, digging in before it too disintegrated in a deadly swarm of fragments. Most flew
away harmlessly, but several cut through the chopper's
thin skin, one slicing by close enough for Anika to
feel its passage. She screamed.

The engine finally died when it became starved for
fuel. The sound of the chopper's frenzied destruction
was replaced by the noise of the storm's full force. It
assaulted Anika's ears like a hurricane, with hail-size
chunks of ice rattling against the fuselage. Battered
but unhurt, she began to shift bundles of clothes and
boxes of food off of her. It seemed that the more she
moved, the more the gear shifted and wedged around
her. It was like trying to dig in quicksand. The agony
radiating from her back wasn't helping. Then she remembered she hadn't heard anything from the pilot.

"Hello!" she called. "Are you okay?"

She got no response and called again and again,
raising her voice until she was shrieking and tears
were spilling down her cheeks.

"Get a grip on yourself, AK," she said aloud, wiping her eyes. "He's gone."

This time she attacked the pile of equipment with
deliberation, thinking through each move before exe-
cuting it. There was a small amount of light spilling
from the cockpit, and she balanced her need for cau-
tion with the urgency to get to the radios. When the
batteries died, so would her chance of contacting the
base camp.

Twenty minutes later, with cargo balanced precariously around her, Anika was almost free when the cockpit lights faded to nothing. Darkness enveloped her. She had to fight to keep panic at bay and was succeeding when a gust of wind slammed into the chopper, upsetting its center of gravity enough to topple the cargo back on top of her.

This time she could not stop the tears. They came in salty waves even as she again began to work, her jaw clamped tight to prevent her teeth from chattering. Without power, the radios were worthless. There was no need to move from where she sat, since there was little chance of a rescue. The moment of pessimism passed and left her infuriated with herself. She would not give up. Life was too precious to squander because of personal weakness.

It took another hour to extricate herself from the helicopter. Anika confirmed that the pilot was indeed dead—killed by the piece of rotor blade that had narrowly missed her—and fired the last flare into the darkness. On her walk around the chopper, she didn't smell any fuel and assumed the self-sealing fuel bladders had not ruptured. She knew her luck was still holding when she found cans of jellied cooking fuel to keep herself warm.

Propped up in the hold, Anika Klein tucked her head into her arms and prepared to wait out the storm. She had to remain awake so she could light new cans of fuel when they went out, but the struggle became too much after only half an hour. Even as the first can guttered to a weak blue flame, her eyes closed. She jerked herself upright, cursing her weakness, and lit another one.

Her exhaustion was deeper than simple fatigue. She fingered the knot on her head again and decided that she had a mild concussion. Hope of rescue was the only thing keeping her going. It would be so easy to just lie back and let the inevitable overcome her.

"To sleep is to die," she said aloud, mesmerized by the little tin of fire next to her. "To sleep is to die."

She kept repeating the mantra, unaware that each utterance was a bit quieter, her voice more slurred and the pauses longer. She fell asleep with only ten minutes of heat remaining. When that second can burned out, the temperature in the chopper crashed to the ambient temperature of the Greenland ice sheet: minus fifteen degrees Fahrenheit—nearly fifty degrees below freezing.

Something woke her an hour later. She found frost coating the front of her parka, and her body had stiffened. She didn't dare open her eyes to look at her hands. She could feel they were frostbitten, as were her ears, the tip of her nose, and her cheeks. She felt more tired than she could possibly imagine and knew that she was dying. She'd survived the crash and the first few critical hours only to succumb to exposure.

She sniffled once and winced. Her nasal membranes were frozen. Still, she could detect a faint odor, a musky fragrance that was completely out of place with her predicament. It smelled like a man's aftershave, something subtly masculine and diluted with the scent of the wearer himself. Anika smiled at the smell. It was like a last treat before she died.

"If you don't mind me saying, Dr. Klein, your smile makes you look like a pixie."

The voice galvanized her. She opened her eyes and saw a grinning man next to her. He had entered through the shattered cockpit. The noise she had heard must have been him crawling into the hold. She was too emotionally wasted to react to his presence. She merely looked at him in the glow from his flashlight, studying the planes of his face and how his gray eyes were shielded by dark brows. Ice glittered in his hair like gems. He was handsome in every sense of the word.

"Looks like you've built quite a nest for yourself in here," the man said, noting the blankets piled on top of her and the cans of Sterno she'd neglected to keep lit. "If you want to stay, I'll understand, but I think you'd be more comfortable in the Land Cruiser. The heater's cranked and the base camp is only about an hour away."

"Who are you?" Anika managed to ask.

"Philip Mercer at your service. Other than that touch of frostbite on your face, are you all right?"

Anika was thankful that her face was frozen so she could not show her shock. This was the very man she was looking for! Yet she was in no condition to question him. She had no idea who he was or whose side he was on. But if he wanted her dead, he wouldn't have driven through the storm to rescue her. Meekly she held out a hand. When she tried to say thanks, her lips couldn't form the word.

A minute later, Mercer had lifted her from the chopper and led her to where the Toyota was idling nearby. He got her buckled into the passenger seat before swinging around to the driver's side. By the time he stepped into the rugged, cross-country vehicle, Anika was sound asleep, her head cocooned in the hood of her parka.

Without the need to replace a tire that had shredded about two miles from where he'd seen Anika fire the second flare, and with the storm all but over, Mercer made it back to the camp much quicker than the drive out. The whole time he was behind the wheel, he couldn't get the gratified smile off his face. Anika Klein would not join the list of people he felt he had failed.

The following morning, Mercer roused Ira Lasko at sunup, and the two of them commandeered one of the Sno-Cats to return to the site of the crash. The couple hours of sleep had done nothing to alleviate his exhaustion, so he let the former submariner drive while he dozed in the passenger seat. Ira navigated by driving in Mercer's tire prints from the night before, which were already being obscured by the constant wind. Because the tracked vehicle was much slower than the Land Cruiser, it took them two hours to reach the downed helicopter.

"We there yet?" Mercer asked, blinking sleep from his eyes when Ira tapped him on the shoulder.

"I told you to pee before we left, young man," Ira quipped.

"I didn't have to then."

The humor vanished from Ira's voice when they saw the helicopter sitting forlornly on the ice like an over-turned insect. "Hard to believe anyone survived that."

Mercer just grunted and opened the 'Cat's door. Other than a few bits of debris, the snow around the crash site was a clean white blanket that hid the violence of what had happened. But when he looked closer, Mercer saw footprints that circled the downed helo and then vanished off to the north. For a split second he thought that the pilot hadn't been killed in the crash and he had abandoned him out here last night.

He knew that couldn't be true. He had seen the chunk of rotor blade sticking through the man's neck and the frozen blood that coated his flight suit. The pilot had been dead long before he'd found the chopper. Because the footprints were nearly buried by snow he couldn't tell where they originated or what size feet had made them. It was possible Anika Klein had made them, but that made as much sense as the dead pilot pulling a Lazarus act. She had been near death herself.

"You thinking what I'm thinking?" Ira asked when he saw what Mercer was studying.

"I don't know what I'm thinking," Mercer admitted. "Did someone beat us out here this morning to check out the crash?"

"I didn't see any tracks besides yours, but it's possible. Maybe they left right after you got back."

"But why?" The pilot's body was still strapped in his seat, his recovery being the principal reason Mercer and Ira had come out.

"Something on the chopper they didn't want discovered?" Ira offered.

Lifting his feet to clear the powdery snow accumulated on the ground, Mercer started following the trail
of prints. He was back at the crash site in just a few
minutes. "They disappear about fifty yards away,
blown clean by the wind."

"What about a stowaway?"

"I was thinking that myself."

The helo had a rear door that opened at the back of
the cargo hold. It was sealed now, but it was possible
someone had exited through it following the crash and
closed it afterward to hide their presence.

"Given her injuries and the noise generated by the
storm, Anika might not have heard anything," Ira said
after examining the door. "But we don't need to worry
about it."

"Why's that?"

"You think someone could still be alive out here
after twelve hours?"

Mercer considered the question. "Given the right
gear, yeah, they could, but they'd be in for one hell
of a long walk."

"You want to go look for him?"

"Not in the slightest," Mercer growled. "He wanted
to get away so badly he'd abandon an injured woman.
I say let the son of a bitch keep going. Let's load up
the pilot's body and anything else we can stuff in the
Sno-Cat and get back to the base."

They were ready forty-five minutes later. The pilot
had been wrapped in a plastic tarpaulin, and every
square inch of the Sno-Cat's cargo area was filled with
boxes of perishable food, Anika's luggage, and anything else they felt was needed back at the camp. Despite his earlier vehemence, Mercer steered a zigzag
search pattern for the first hour of the drive while Ira
scanned the monotonous surroundings through a pair
of binoculars. They saw no footprints or track marks
left by another Sno-Cat. If it had indeed been a stowaway who had walked from the helicopter, he wasn't
headed toward the research station.

Ira put away the binoculars and reached for the mail

bucket, shuffling through the parcels and envelopes looking for anything addressed to him. He sniffed appreciatively at a letter from his wife that still carried traces of perfume she must have sprayed on the paper. "Sorry, nothing for you. Doesn't appear that anyone loves you."

"Did you check for names that didn't sound quite right?" Mercer asked. "Remember my last letter was sent to Max E. Padd."

"Ah, here we go." Ira held up a large envelope. "It's from Arlington, Virginia."

"That's me." Mercer winced when he asked Ira to tell him the name.

"Juan Tzeks Withasheep."

It took Mercer a second to decipher Harry's lame joke. Want sex with a sheep.

"You've got one warped friend there, Mercer."

"Tell me about it. Open it up and let's see what he sent."

"A confirmation for your new *Playgirl* magazine subscription, a couple receipts from a strip joint in Washington, another envelope forwarded from Munich, and a police citation for a noise-ordinance violation."

Mercer wondered what was in the envelope from Germany and was about to ask Ira to open the envelope when he remembered the mysterious e-mail he received before leaving for Iceland. This must be the material the lawyer said he was sending for his unnamed client. He thought it was best if he opened that in private. "When our communications are back up, I think I'll call the Arlington police to report a squatter has taken over my house. That'll show the old bastard."

"Oh, that's mean."

"If you knew some of the crap he's pulled over the years, you'd know he's getting off light," Mercer replied.

There was a crowd waiting for them when they got back to base and halted the Sno-Cat near the mess hall. Not everyone was happy to see them. Werner Koenig and Greta Schmidt stood apart from the others, scowling. Leading the group who cheered them on was Marty Bishop and a much recovered Anika Klein.

"Let's keep those footprints to ourselves," Mercer said when he killed the engine.

"People find out all the secrets we're sharing, they're going to get jealous," Ira said in a singsong voice.

Mercer threw open his door. "Mail call."

Greta Schmidt pushed through the crowd to confront Mercer. "That is the second time you have taken a vehicle without authorization," she snapped.

"Which makes it two times I've done your job," he replied with a mocking smile. He noted that again it was Schmidt, not Koenig, who was the most upset by his foray, and he wondered exactly which one was running the expedition.

"Relax, for Christ's sake," Marty boomed. "He saved Dr. Klein's life last night."

"I am aware of that, but there are procedures. Discipline must be maintained. I am going to report you all to the Surveyor's Society with the recommendation that you be airlifted back to Iceland immediately. This is no place for cowboy heroics." She stormed off.

"Your rescue was ill-advised, but appreciated." Werner shook Mercer's hand when Greta was out of sight. "I don't think I will be able to stop her from ordering your evacuation. I'm sorry." He followed in her wake.

Marty turned to Mercer. "Don't sweat it. When we have the radios up again, I'll square it with my old man."

"Thanks, Marty," Mercer said. "But I doubt it'll make much difference. With the chopper crash coming so close to Igor's death, I won't be surprised if Geo-Research has their entire operation shut down by the Danish government."

Neither man had noticed Anika Klein had moved

close to them and overheard what Mercer had just said. "Igor Bulgarin is dead?" she cried.

Mercer turned, stunned that no one had told her and guilty that he'd mentioned it so casually. Even though she was in moon boots, the top of her head was below the level of his chin. Her eyes were wide with shock and he was struck again by how much she looked like a mythical imp. A tough, resilient imp, to be sure.

"I'm sorry, Dr. Klein. I didn't know you were there," he stammered. "Yes, Igor died in an accident yesterday morning."

She just stared at him for a moment, her gaze wary. "I didn't know."

"It came as a shock to us all," Marty said, extending his hand. "I'm Martin Bishop. I head up the Surveyor's Society contingent here."

"Anika Klein," she replied absently, her mind far away from social niceties.

Mercer took her hand when she offered it. "I doubt you remember much from last night. I'm Philip Mercer."

"I remember," she answered cautiously. "You came out to get me. Thank you for what you did. That was brave."

"It was foolish, but you're welcome." He studied her for a second. "Looks like it wasn't frostbite after all."

Anika touched her cheeks and nose where the color had returned to near normal. "If you'd been any later, it would have been."

"I'm glad you're okay." She didn't seem like someone meeting her rescuer, Mercer thought. She seemed almost afraid of him.

"What's that?" Anika pointed to the manila envelope in Mercer's hand.

"Huh?" The odd question threw him. "Oh, it's just some junk mail from a friend."

Unlike the night before, this time Anika couldn't hide her surprise. She eyed the package for a long moment before dragging her focus back to Mercer's face. "You probably want to go read it. I'm sorry for delaying you."

"No, actually I'd like to talk with you. Are you sure you're all right?"

Anika stiffened. "Yes, I'm fine." Then her shoulders sagged just a fraction. "That's not true. I have a vicious headache, and I keep thinking about the pilot. Tell me more about Igor's death. How did it happen?"

"There was a cave-in inside Camp Decade," Mercer said. "He was struck by falling ice. We don't think he suffered."

Anika immediately grasped the part of the story that had bothered Mercer since the accident. "What was he doing there? He was a meteorite hunter."

Mercer was right about her resilience. A helicopter crash last night, a delayed rescue that left her half dead, and now the shock of her team leader's death and still her mind cut incisively. "We don't know," he admitted.

Ira Lasko had been helping others unload the Sno-Cat during the conversation. They were done except for one item, and he approached the trio. "Begging your pardon, ma'am. Mercer, do you want me to put the pilot's body in the cold storage lab with Igor's?"

"Yeah, that'll be fine."

"I just spoke with Erwin," Ira continued. "The radios are still out, so there's no word yet from the Air Force about the body you found in Camp Decade."

"Another body?" Anika's eyes bored into Mercer.

"An Air Force pilot lost in the 1950s. He's still down in the camp where we found him."

"I'd like to examine him." Her voice had firmed as she came to grips with the past few minutes, regaining the professional edge she used in the emergency room.

"Camp Decade is sealed until we shore up some of the roof," Marty said. "We feel it's too dangerous to go down there."

In an effort to impress her, Marty was trying to reclaim his control over the group by answering her request. Anika wasn't fooled. She'd already realized that Philip Mercer was in charge of these men. She addressed him directly. "I would consider it a favor if you would let me examine him as well as the body of Igor Bulgarin."

"I can let you see Igor, but the base is off-limits for a while." He doubted her examination would detect that Jack Delaney's corpse was radioactive, but until he had some answers, no one was getting near him.

When she was disappointed, Anika had the habit of sucking on her lower lip. While not a calculating gesture, it had a certain effect on men.

"Before the Air Force comes," Mercer relented, "I promise you a chance to check him out."

"Thank you. May I examine Dr. Bulgarin in a couple of hours? I'd like to get something to eat and then sleep for a while longer."

Mercer rolled back his glove to look at the Tag Heuer slung around his wrist. "I'll meet you right here at 2:30."

Marty Bishop followed after Anika when she started off for the mess hall, leaving Mercer alone with Ira Lasko.

"What do you think, Ira?"

"I think that's one tough little lady," he said thoughtfully. "And I also think she's one scared lady too."

"I noticed that as well. Any guess why?"

"No idea."

"This whole thing has been screwy since the word go. I shouldn't be surprised that our latest addition is a mystery too."

"Why does she want to examine Igor?" Ira asked. Mercer had no immediate answer. "I wonder if maybe she knows something about his death. Like why he was in Camp Decade when he shouldn't have been."

"How would she know that when we don't?"

This time it was Ira's turn to remain silent.

Yesterday, this trip had seemed like a great vacation for Mercer and he'd been enjoying himself. But since

Igor's death, that had all vanished and his frustration had mounted. He'd paid little attention to the small inconsistencies since his arrival here, and now they plagued him. He doubted that Anika Klein would shed any light on what was happening. In fact, her demeanor and requests added to his concern. "This trip is one snafu after another," he muttered.

"Amen. You think the Danes are going to pull us?"

"I hope to God they do."

At the appointed time, Mercer saw Anika approaching the mess hall from the direction of the dormitories. She was bundled in a red one-piece Gore-Tex snowsuit with a hood pulled tight around her face. With her back to the wind, snow dusted the knapsack over her shoulder. For the past hour he had been sitting with the radio operator trying vainly to get a message out to Reykjavik. Other than static and a burst of conversation that sounded like it came from the *Njoerd,* they had received nothing. The electronic interference from the sun's massive coronal ejections ensured the base was completely isolated. When he saw Anika through the steam-clouded window, Mercer thanked the radioman, pulled on his parka, and stepped out into the gale.

"How are you feeling?" he shouted over the wind.

"Fine. Let's go."

Mercer led her to the cold-temperature lab at the far end of the camp, first making sure she was clipped to the guide rope. The blowing snow swallowed their feet with each step, so they appeared like legless torsos gliding through the swirling ice. Once Geo-Research got geared up, the cold lab would house ice cores and snow samples. For now it held just the two bodies.

The building was made of plastic, with a couple of windows on each side. Drifts had grown on the windward flank, piling almost to the eaves, but the structure had been placed in such a way that the entrance was mostly clear of snow. Like all the buildings, there was a wide-bladed shovel clipped near the door, and after a few minutes of digging their path was cleared. Mercer didn't need to worry about warmth escaping the lab, so he held the door for Anika to enter first.

He snapped on the overhead lights, long banks of fluorescents that provided plenty of light but generated little heat that could damage frozen samples. Under tarps at the far end of the room, two recognizable shapes were laid out on adjacent worktables.

Out of the wind, Mercer and Anika pulled back their hoods and shook snow off themselves. She ignored his gesture to sweep snow off her back in a rush to reach the bodies. The first tarp she drew back covered the pilot's corpse, and after just a second she replaced the shroud. She already knew what had killed him.

She said nothing as she uncovered Igor, looking first at his ghastly white face before beginning to examine him with single-minded intensity. It was as if Mercer wasn't there. Starting with his booted feet and moving upward across his still-clothed body, she ran her hands over every part of him. Mercer had no idea what she hoped to accomplish since the body was as stiff as the table beneath it. Because Igor's mouth was open, she pulled a penlight from her knapsack and explored his teeth and gums, grunting when she saw something of interest.

"What is it?" Mercer asked.

"Russian dentists. These are the worst fillings I've ever seen. Igor had to have been in constant pain."

She removed her thick outer mittens and replaced them with a pair of surgical gloves, probing his mouth with her finger. From deep in his throat she withdrew out a bit of frozen saliva mixed with snow. She studied it for a second before dropping it on the table. Without a proper lab to examine the material, it did her little good to keep it. Next she bent close to look at the deep scrapes on his nose and forehead, grunting again, but this time Mercer kept his silence.

He was fascinated by her. With her eyes narrowed and her brows pulled down in concentration, she looked like a child worrying at a particularly tough school problem. But she was an adult, examining a corpse, and he was captivated by the dichotomy of her appearance and profession. He imagined that she'd been underestimated many times in her life and pitied the people who did it.

Finished with Igor's face, she ran her hands over his skull, pressing various points with her fingertips. "Can you give me a hand?" she asked without looking up.

"What do you need?" Mercer moved to her side.

"I want to roll him over."

They did, and because Igor Bulgarin was so heavy and broad, it was like flipping a king-size mattress.

When Mercer retreated again, she combed aside the frozen knots of blood and hair at the base of his skull, tracing the wound with a finger. She scowled and reached into her bag for a magnifying glass. There was a palpable tension in her as she scrutinized the wound under the glass, her face so close to Igor's head that her breath snaked through his hair like steam. After two minutes, Anika straightened and looked around the room intently.

"What did you find?" Mercer closed the gap between them, infected by whatever had so unsettled her.

She said nothing, moving by him to grab a crowbar left on another of the worktables. She looked at the piece of steel for a moment, feeling its weight, not caring that the metal was freezing her hand. Unsatisfied, she dropped it unceremoniously, and rummaged under the table, where more tools had been left in plastic crates. She came up with a twenty-inch-long handle from a portable screw jack. It was only then she remembered Mercer was in the room with her. She looked at him clinically, as if weighing a decision, and nodded when he passed some sort of unspoken test. She couldn't hide the fear lingering in her eyes, but she spoke in a calm tone.

"Igor was murdered," she stated. "He was then

dragged from where it happened and left in a place where someone could stage an avalanche to cover the killing."

On some intuitive level Mercer wasn't surprised. Somehow it made sense to him. Though he'd not voiced them, not even to himself, he'd had misgivings about the entertaining Russian. But his professional skepticism wouldn't allow him to accept her statement without proof. "How do you know?"

She hefted the jack handle, carrying it to the body. "This is a little thinner than the murder weapon— shorter and lighter too, I would guess—but it'll give you an idea what happened." She placed the handle into the long wound at the base of Igor's skull. "As you can see it fits almost perfectly in the gash, a straight impact line that runs from side to side beneath the occipital bulge. This wound wasn't the result of ice hitting him. It's too symmetrical. He was killed by a very strong person swinging such a tool like a base-ball bat. The blow would have crushed a portion of the cerebellum and the medulla spinalis, killing him instantly."

Mercer peered at the injury. Quelling his uneasiness, he lifted the handle, and then placed it back in the wound as Anika had done. He had to admit that it was indeed a pretty damn good match.

"If you notice, the scrapes on his face all go in the same direction. Add the fact that he rigored with his hands over his head, and it's logical to conclude that someone dragged him by his hands, facedown, over a rough surface like a wooden floor. The snow I found jammed down his throat is consistent with this hypothesis."

Mercer remembered thinking how strange it was that Igor's arms had been over his head when they found the body. At the time he'd assumed the cuts on Igor's face had been from falling ice hitting him. But now? She presented a plausible scenario. As he looked at Anika, his eyes asked his next questions.

"I don't know why he was killed, Mr. Mercer. Or who did it."

"It's Dr. Mercer, actually, but everyone just calls me Mercer," he said automatically.

Who would have done this? A strong person, she had said. That description fit nearly everyone at the camp. If the timing had been different, he would have considered the stowaway who'd left the tracks around the helicopter, but the crash occurred well after Igor's death. He was left with the unpleasant option that apart from everything else going wrong, there was a killer in their midst. Now he knew where Anika's fear had come from. He shared it.

"You're getting your wish," he said after a moment.

"Wish?"

"You wanted to examine the corpse we found in Camp Decade. That's the only thing of even remote interest in the facility. If Igor was killed for a reason, I bet that body's it."

"You said the base wasn't safe."

"You just told me that someone caused the avalanche to cover Igor's murder. If you're right, the ceiling in Camp Decade's still structurally sound."

"What if I am wrong?" Suddenly it seemed the thought of going into the underground base wasn't quite as appealing to her.

"You should trust your instincts," Mercer said. "Considering what you've just discovered, I'd say they're right on."

Leading Anika once again, he made his way across the base, this time walking into the wind. The flying ice felt like glass shards when it hit his face below his tinted goggles, and no amount of tugging could tighten the hood enough to eliminate all the gaps. It was like being attacked by a swarm of wasps. They reached the long trench carved over the entrance of Camp Decade, and once they were below ground level, the punishing wind would release its hold. They could walk upright again and hold a conversation.

"Before you left the *Njoerd,* did you learn how long

this wind's supposed to last?" Mercer climbed into the Sno-Cat to fire the engine and power the winch.

"All day today and they think there's only a couple-hour gap tomorrow before an even stronger storm front hits."

"Erik the Red was one hell of a salesman," Mercer joked. Anika looked at him quizzically. "When the old Viking was banished from Iceland in 982 A.D., he sailed west and landed here. He wintered someplace on the east coast. When he returned home, he told people about the beautiful island he had discovered, calling it Greenland to describe its lushness. That probably wasn't the first marketing lie ever told, but it certainly was one of the most effective. He convinced twenty-five ships' worth of settlers to follow him back."

He jumped down from the 'Cat and reached across the twenty-foot void to grab the dangling bucket they used to get to the bottom of the shaft. Anika stepped in without a moment's consideration with Mercer right behind her.

"Not afraid of heights?" he asked as the bucket started its slow descent.

"I climb mountains for relaxation. I could probably climb down this tube faster than this contraption of yours."

Mercer didn't doubt her. At the bottom, he checked the chains he and Ira had used to secure the doors after removing Igor's body. It didn't appear they had been tampered with, so he jammed home the lock's key and twisted. Once inside, he handed one of the flashlights left there to Anika and kept another for himself. Cutting through the darkness, their powerful beams were like lances.

The feeling that ghosts were watching him was stronger this time. Memories of Igor Bulgarin flooded Mercer's mind. He led her toward the officers' quarters, where Jack Delaney's body had lain undisturbed for five decades. When they had pulled Igor out, Mercer and Ira had cleared a lot of the snow that had once clogged the passage, but still they had to clamber over heaps of ice. Even in her snowsuit, Anika moved with fluid efficiency, not slipping or misplacing a hand or foot as she climbed. Mercer was having a harder time. He was used to tight spaces like this, made his living in them, but he wasn't as deft at judging the slick surfaces.

Once they cleared the final obstacle, they trained their lights at the floor. Anika got on her knees for a better look and spotted what she'd expected. The claret streaks on the floor were blood. Igor Bulgarin's blood. The faint marks continued down the dark passage.

"You were right," Mercer said, not knowing how he felt about that.

"So were you. Igor was checking the body."

They reached the officers' annex in a moment and passed down the hallway until they came to room number ten. Jack Delaney looked as he had when Mercer first found him. His face was gaunt to the point of starvation, drained of all color except around his mouth, which was a lighter shade, almost gray. His hands were clutched at his chest, skeletal fingers interlaced as if he'd been praying at the final moment of his death. It took no imagination to think of the bitterness he must have felt after surviving for so long only to discover Camp Decade had already been abandoned. The loneliness of his death was in the vacant stare of his long-dead eyes.

"Does he look like he's been disturbed?" Anika's question snapped Mercer from his grim reflections.

"No." He checked the floor and found more blood, a few drops scattered near one wall. He could tell by the pattern and their tearlike appearance that they had sprayed from the wound. "Igor died in this room. Either attacked by someone preventing him from examining the body or murdered to cover up someone else's investigation."

"But before he could do anything to the body?" Anika persisted.

"Yes, neither person appears to have touched the corpse. Thinking about the timing, Igor would have gotten down here at about 4:30 in the morning. His killer could have been a few minutes behind, seen him in here, bludgeoned him, and immediately started hiding the evidence. Since people get up about six, that only gave the murderer an hour and a half, barely enough time to stage the avalanche and get back to his dorm before anyone noticed."

"We're lucky." Anika set her knapsack on the desk next to the bed. As with Igor Bulgarin, she began her examination at Delaney's feet and slowly worked her way up. Mercer stood at her shoulder, following her hands with his flashlight so she could see what she was doing. When she reached his mouth and studied his teeth, she called him closer. "Look at this."

Delaney had only a few teeth remaining in his mouth, black stumps so cracked it was doubtful the airman could have used them to chew. His gums looked like raw meat. For a few seconds Anika tried to find traces of dentistry, but there was nothing left. "He's very thin."

"Considering what he'd been through, I'm not surprised."

Anika said nothing and took a tape measure from her bag. Delaney was just five feet six inches tall in his boots. Awfully short, Mercer thought, but since he didn't know what kind of height restrictions the military maintained for its pilots, he didn't say anything. Next, Anika pulled up Delaney's sleeves.

"You shouldn't move him until the Air Force arrives," Mercer admonished but not very sternly. He was just as curious as she was.

He checked his watch. They'd been here for ten minutes. He would give her five more before leaving. He was conscious of the body's mild radioactivity. He realized that could have explained the tooth loss and the fact that under his woolen hat, Delaney was completely bald—another symptom of acute radiation poisoning.

"What do you think?" Anika pointed to a rectangular scar on his left forearm.

"Looks like a burn."

"More like a brand mark," she countered. "But there's nothing to it except scar tissue, no symbols or words."

When she tugged his sleeves down again, a piece of paper that had been clutched in Delaney's hands came loose, a small corner showing from under one long finger.

"What's that?" Mercer asked.

"Good eyes. I would have missed it." She used a pair of surgical forceps to slide out the folded piece of paper, careful not to dislodge the original position of Delaney's hands.

The smoke hit them as she handed it to Mercer. It came in a solid black wave sweeping through the underground base, dense and impenetrable. In moments the beams from their Maglites were nothing more than feeble spots of light unable to cut more than a foot into the roiling haze.

"What the . . . ?" Anika started coughing before she could finish the question.

Mercer pushed her to the floor, where the air was marginally cleaner. Anika's eyes were red rimmed and weeping. Her lungs convulsed for a few more seconds until she could purge the worst of the smoke.

"What happened?" she gasped, fighting not to throw up.

"Fire. I don't know. We've got to get out of here."

"How?"

Mercer crawled to the door. Even through the pall of smoke he could see the dancing glow of a fire at the exit of the officers' quarters. The fire appeared to grow in ferocity in the few seconds he stared transfixed. On the other side of the advancing wall of flames was the only way out of Camp Decade.

Anika joined him at the door. "We're trapped!"

Mercer didn't need to voice his agreement.

Everything was happening too fast for panic to be

a problem. His mind was sharp and ready to figure a way out, but as he watched the growing flames, inspiration remained beyond his grasp.

You're trapped underground by fire. There's one way out and it's blocked. The flames have plenty of fuel considering this whole place is made of wood and it won't starve for oxygen before you're cooked. Like a natural chimney, smoke would be billowing up the access shaft at the same time the fire sucked down more air to keep itself going.

"Mercer!"

You've been here before, he reminded himself. *At different times and at different places. How did you get out?*

He knew the answer to that was an unlikely solution. The underground fires he'd faced before had been in coal mines where teams of trained experts battled the inferno to save him.

You know how to get out of this. You've done it before. How?

It came to him. "Air shaft," he shouted over the noise of Camp Decade being consumed from within.

"It's in the middle of the fire." Anika choked. "We won't make it."

"Not the main shaft we came down. With this much smoke, we'll never find it. We have to go all the way through the fire to reach the garage on the other side."

"How?"

"Run like hell."

"Why not try to find the exit doors?"

"Anika, there's nothing down here that could have started this fire. It was intentionally set by whoever killed Igor to stop us from proving his murder." A paroxysm of coughing racked her when she gasped. "We can't risk stopping in the middle of the blaze to search for the doors because they are most likely blocked. We have to reach the far side. There will be air shafts in the garage used to vent engine exhaust when the military stored Sno-Cats there. It's our only chance."

Mercer shuffled to the bed holding Delaney's body and unceremoniously shoved the corpse aside to strip away the blankets he'd been lying on. The encroaching fire had melted a tremendous amount of ice and snow, so water rippled down the hallway and past the bedroom door. Mercer dumped the blankets in the stream, soaking them through. The water was near freezing and burned his exposed hands like acid. "Take off your snowsuit," he ordered.

"Are you nuts?"

He turned to face her. "Yes. Take off your snowsuit."

As she did what he asked, Mercer took off his own parka, sloshing it in the torrent of meltwater. Before he put it back on, he dropped onto his back, gasping when he came in contact with the icy river. Even as he splashed more water on his legs, he could feel crusts of ice forming and breaking with each movement.

"We'll freeze to death."

He splashed handfuls of water on his face and hair. "I'd rather freeze than burn." He took Anika's red suit and soaked it, motioning her to douse herself in the water as he worked.

Her lips were blue by the time she was done, her jaws chattering uncontrollably. Mercer imagined he looked as bad. If they made it through the fire, they would have only a few minutes before hypothermia overcame them. He handed her the one-piece and worked his arms back into his dripping parka. The garment weighed at least ten pounds more than it had. He could only hope it retained enough water to insulate him.

The fire roared only fifteen yards away by the time they were dressed again, their delay caused by numb fingers that refused to work properly. Assuming that it spread evenly, they would need to run through a sixty-yard gauntlet before reaching open air again.

He pulled his hood around his face, covering his eyes with his goggles and making sure that Anika was similarly protected. "Be careful when we reach the middle of the fire. I don't know if all that snow has melted completely, so there could still be piles of it."

"What happens if the fire's bigger than you think?"

Mercer's gallows humor didn't fail him. "Then all those people who've told me to go to hell will get their wish. Are you ready?"

"No."

Mercer gave her a reassuring smile and draped a few wet blankets over her. "We'll make it."

"Okay, AK, let's do it," Anika said softly and watched Mercer launch himself down the hallway like a javelin. She waited for a heartbeat and went after him.

Mercer kept his eyes open for as long as he dared. When the heat hit him full blast, he pulled his own blanket over his head, hunched his shoulders, and ran as fast as he'd ever run in his life. Behind his closed lids and through the now-steaming blankets, light still danced against his vision, ragged swirls of flame that licked upward from the floor. Over the raging inferno, he could hear the blankets sizzling as the water boiled away. Ten yards into the blaze the heat intensified. He hadn't considered that parts of the roof would be collapsing at any moment, creating obstacles that could trap them in the middle of the fire.

Twenty yards and he knew he was approaching the avalanche that had buried Igor Bulgarin. His boots sloshed through a thick slurry of snow and water that pulled at each step. It was like wading through liquid mud. Yet he started to drag his feet, pushing aside the slush to clear a path for Anika. Somewhere behind him he heard a rumbling crash. A portion of ceiling had succumbed to the flames and given way. If Anika was on the other side of the blockage, he would never be able to reach her. He continued to run. The blanket felt like it was starting to smolder.

Mercer's foot hit a snow pile at full stride, pitching him forward. Had he not been prepared for it, he would have sprawled headlong. As his center of balance shifted, he tucked his shoulder, still clutching the blanket around him. He hit hard, shoulder rolled, and heaved himself back to his feet. His momentum was too much, and he was about to go down again when a steadying hand grabbed his arm.

Miraculously, Anika had been running even faster than he had. She saw what happened and was ready to keep him on his feet. Mercer chanced opening his eyes. It was like standing at the very bottom of hell. Flames encircled them, racing up the paneled walls to meet at the roof in shimmering sheets. The heat seared his breath. He managed to regain his orientation before a veil of smoke closed off his vision, saving him from seeing that they had covered barely a third of the distance.

Side by side, they ran onward, spurred by the primal fear of fire. The water saturating Mercer's clothes began steaming. He could sense Anika Klein at his shoulder, running hard.

In the few seconds they'd been in the conflagration, Mercer had become accustomed to its consuming roar, so when the sound receded behind him he knew they had cleared the fire. He didn't dare stop, but he let the blanket fall from his shoulders and opened his eyes. He saw nothing but blackness. Smoke.

"Anika, get down," he shouted, diving like an All Star for home plate.

She followed his slide and at the floor they found fresher air. Although her blanket was smoldering, her snowsuit seemed untouched. Together they crawled onward, finally reaching a set of heavy doors at the end of the corridor. Once through, they slammed them closed.

Even without light they could tell by the way their coughs echoed that the garage they stumbled into was huge. The air, mercifully, hadn't yet been fouled by smoke.

"Are you all right?" Anika wheezed when she regained her breath. She snapped on her light.

Mercer nodded, his head down, tarry smoke coming from his mouth with each cough. "I have a friend," he panted. "He smokes two packs a day. I bet he would have gone through that and had a nicotine craving afterward."

Getting to his feet, Mercer began to undress, retrieving his flashlight before discarding the parka. Next went his sweaters and shirts. "You know we have to," he said when Anika hadn't started doing the same. "It can't be below freezing in here because the snow covering the base acts like insulation. We can stand that for a while as long as we minimize heat loss. Wet clothes will draw heat away from us many times faster than the air."

"I know." Anika started to strip. "I was just wondering about the bullet scar on your shoulder."

"Oh, that. Ancient history." The furrow cut into the top of Mercer's shoulder was from an assassin's bullet years earlier. "Thanks for what you did back there. If I had gone down, I wouldn't have gotten back up."

"We're even." A trace of a smile lifted the corners of her mouth. "Do you think we'll be okay until they get the fire out?"

"Not unless we let them know we're here. Remember, we didn't tell anyone we were headed for Camp Decade."

Wearing nothing but boxer shorts, with his breath condensing around his head, Mercer tried to organize his thoughts, fighting not to let the cold sap his energy. He couldn't help but feel vulnerable and he imagined Anika felt even more so in her cotton panties and sports bra. She didn't appear to be self-conscious about her lack of attire.

"First things first." Mercer hadn't spent much time in this section of the base, but he recalled that there were a few lockers located next to a small washroom.

Snapping open the doors, he found what he wanted. Because so much equipment had been left behind in the 1950s there were still some mechanics' overalls in a couple of the lockers. He grabbed four of them and tossed two to Anika.

"You knew about this?" she asked, gratefully pulling on the stained garments.

"Other than the reactor that powered the facility, the Sno-Cats, and the men's personal gear, everything was abandoned here. I wasn't sure we'd find these but I knew there'd be something we could use."

A minute later he found some boots. He started to feel like they had a chance. He handed Anika a cigarette lighter.

"Don't tell me you smoke." She scowled with disgust.

"Never, but I carry a few when I'm on an expedition like this. Boy Scout training. Can you make us a fire?"

While she got to work, he wandered around the garage. He noted that in one corner of the room sat a large fuel cylinder for the military's Sno-Cats. He rapped it with a hammer left on a workbench. The dull thud indicated it was at least half full. A long coil of rubber hose with a standard nozzle hung from a bracket welded to the tank's support cradle. At the far end of the workshop was a series of wide doors that had once led to snow ramps to the surface. Next he played his light on the trussed ceiling fifteen feet over his head, discovering several large air vents. They were more than big enough for what he had in mind. All he needed now was a ladder and a long pole, like the center post for an army tent. He found both items in a utility closet.

The smell of burning wood was becoming distracting. It would take a while to reach a dangerous level but it was a constant reminder that on the other side of the fireproof doors was an out-of-control blaze.

Anika huddled next to the fire she'd built from packing crates, cupping her hands as if receiving a gift from the flames. "Strange to think this would feel good after the run through the hallway," she joked.

"We're not done yet. It's time to put an old adage to work." She shot him a questioning glance. "Fight fire with fire."

After he explained what he had in mind, she had

only one question. "How do you know the diesel will still burn?"

"Fuels don't lose their combustibility over time, just their efficiency. Once we drain the sediment and water from the bottom of the tank, we'd be able to fill our own vehicles with it and suffer just bad mileage and burned piston rings." That was an exaggeration, he knew, but it was close enough.

"Let's do it." Anika got to her feet, convinced because Mercer seemed so certain. He'd said earlier that he trusted her. For now, she had no choice but to reciprocate.

Mercer set his ladder near the largest of the air shafts, climbing up to remove the circular grate protecting it. The vertical tube was more than large enough to accommodate him and Anika. Flashing his light upward, he could see the vent had been battered and dented by glacial movement, but it was still clear for a good fifteen feet before becoming clogged with ice. He estimated that there would be ten additional feet of snow above it before he could see daylight.

Anika spent her time unfurling the fuel hose, using some rope she'd found to secure the end of the flexible pipe to the tip of the ten-foot tent pole. Her knots were tight and professional. While Mercer checked the spigot attached to the tank, she used his pocketknife to cut the gas nozzle from the hose. The rubber was brittle but remarkably resilient, demanding all her strength.

With the tank resting four feet above the polished concrete floor, Mercer knew it was gravity driven rather than relying on a mechanical pump to fill the vehicles that were once stored here. Without the restricting nozzle, an arcing jet of diesel would spew from the hose once he opened the tap.

"Are you ready for a test?" Mercer asked Anika, who was fifteen yards away, silhouetted by her flashlight.

"Okay." She pointed the open end of the tube away

from her, not knowing how powerful the stream would be.

"Here we go." Mercer needed both hands and the considerable power of his shoulders to crack the initial seal on the spigot. Once the wheel began to turn, it spun freely.

"Jesus!" Anika screamed in surprise, prompting Mercer to close the tap quickly.

He raced to her side. "Well?"

She raised the focus of her flashlight, following the shimmering wet streak staining the floor. The trail led for fifty feet before it vanished beyond the light's range. "Powerful enough for what you had in mind?"

"Overkill." Mercer laughed, delighted that his idea might just work.

He sobered quickly when a thick wave of smoke reached them. The temperature in the garage was starting to climb. The doors segregating the garage from the rest of the base weren't nearly as fireproof as Mercer had hoped.

"Get on the ladder," Anika said, already in motion. "I'll operate the valve."

Mercer moved the ladder away so he could hold the hose under the air vent while staying away from the fuel that would be pouring back down. High above the floor, the air was fouled with smoke. He pulled the collar of his coveralls over his mouth, but the musty cloth was ranker than the air.

"Just give me the word and I'll start the fuel flowing," Anika yelled, her voice echoing.

Mercer heaved the pole into position, resting the tip into the vent shaft to balance it, the hose tied to it dangling to the floor and away toward the storage tank. Bracing himself against the sturdy ladder, he could maintain a firm grip without the pole's weight becoming too much to hold steady. By pressing the end of the pole into his stomach, he managed to free one hand. Once Anika turned the tap, he would need that hand for only a moment.

"Open her up."

Through the pole he could feel the attached hose pulsate as diesel fuel surged toward the outlet, forced across the garage and upward into the vent shaft by the tremendous impetus of its own weight. His make-shift flamethrower shuddered, nearly dislodging him from his perch before he got a better grip. In a rush, diesel climbed the hose and exploded up the shaft, splattering the underside of the ice plug like it had exploded from a fire hydrant. As soon as the fuel started falling back to the floor, Mercer snicked open the Zippo lighter and tossed it into the incendiary liquid raining from the roof.

The fuel ignited in a concussive whoosh, an explosion of orange and red and black that blinded him before he could turn away. It looked like the exhaust from a rocket motor. Even from ten feet away the heat was intense, and Mercer felt sweat begin to pour into his eyes. Beneath him, the widening lake of fire found the gutters cut into the concrete and began to run in rivers to underground waste tanks.

Amid the flaming fuel draining from the vent, water too began to flow, ice that had melted under the brutal thermal onslaught. Mercer had no way to judge how quickly the ice plug was being dissolved, but each second brought an acceleration to the amount of water diluting the fiery pool.

"It's working," he heard Anika shout over the noise of the fire.

"Did you have any doubts?" Mercer grinned down at her. He looked like a demon backlit against the pillar of flames.

Swept up in the euphoria of the moment, Anika returned his cocky smile. "Not for a second."

With the burning fuel ducted into the drainage hollows under the floor, Mercer's fear of starting a fire worse than the one they had just escaped were unfounded. He let the flaming jet of diesel bore into the ice for five minutes before shouting to Anika to kill the flow. They didn't need to wait for him to move the ladder under the vent to see they had been successful.

Shining into the puddle of flames on the floor was a perfect circle of daylight.

They were through!

It took a few minutes for the fire on the floor to extinguish itself completely, and as it died they could see smoke being drawn up the vent from deeper into the base.

"It's just a matter of time before someone fighting the fire at the main entrance sees smoke billowing out of this vent and comes to investigate," Mercer said, looking up at the sky.

He turned to Anika. She had an enigmatic smile on her face, a mixture of astonishment and respect.

She placed her arms on his shoulders and drew him down, planting a feather-soft kiss on his cheek. "That's twice you saved me. Now I owe you."

Mercer's heart tripped. He believed she was going to kiss him on the mouth. He thought he had recognized that look and for a selfish moment he wished she had. But he was glad she hadn't. Shared danger did strange things to people, created instant bonds, and he'd learned that such passions weren't real. The emotions were usually nothing more than the after-effects of adrenaline and relief.

He recalled some of her accomplishments that Igor had mentioned, realizing that she probably handled this kind of stress much better than he did. It was his own relief he'd seen reflected in Anika's expression, not hers.

"We're even." His gruff tone covered his embarrassment.

From above, a voice called, "Hello." It was Erwin Puhl.

Startled that their signal had been seen so quickly, Mercer checked his watch. Thirty minutes had passed since the fire had started, more than enough time for the expedition members to begin combating the subterranean blaze at the facility's entrance.

"Erwin, it's Mercer."

"When you weren't leading the firefighting efforts,

we feared you were trapped down there. Is Dr. Klein
with you? No one has seen her in a while."

"Yeah, she's with me. Can you lower a rope? The
smoke is getting pretty thick, and the heat's rising."

"Back in a minute."

"Hurry. Once the flames break through the fire
doors protecting the garage, there's going to be one
hell of an explosion." Mercer eyed the diesel tank
hulking behind the wavering glow of Anika's campfire.
"Also warn the others who are working at the main
entrance to clear the area."

Ten minutes later, they were pulled up the air vent
by the winch mounted on the front of a Sno-Cat Ira
had driven out to rescue them. "Everyone's back at
the base camp," Ira said as they jumped into the
boxy vehicle.

"Let's go. We've only got a few more minutes. The
fire doors can't hold much longer, and it must be over
a hundred degrees in the garage already." The drop in
temperature from inside to out had left Mercer light-
headed and trembling.

Ira didn't need to hear anything further. He put the
Sno-Cat in gear, twisted it around on its axis and tore
off across the ice, feathers of churned snow blooming
from under its treads. He circled around the long access trench near Camp Decade's entrance. Smoke
streamed from deep underground and a huge swath
of snow was stained with soot.

He braked once they reached the mess hall a quarter mile away. Mercer was just stepping down when
out across the frozen plain, the fuel tank erupted like
a volcano, vaporizing a ragged eighty-foot circle of
glacier. Chunks of ice the size of automobiles blasted
into the sky, propelled by a towering column of flame.
The concussion hit a second later, rocking the Sno-
Cat on its suspension and tossing Mercer onto his
backside.

Powdered ice drifted for many minutes before falling back to earth. When the last of the snow finally

settled, smudge continued to billow from the hole, smearing the pristine horizon.

"What the hell were you two doing down there?" Ira asked sharply after hauling Mercer back to his feet.

Mercer fingered the scrap of paper they'd retrieved from Jack Delaney's dead fingers. "I'm not sure yet."

As if enraged that its power could not rock the great cruise liner, the North Sea surged ferociously, generating huge waves that would have swamped a commercial fishing boat or pitched the largest freighter. Because of her wide-spaced twin hulls and tremendous length, the *Sea Empress* had several distinct wave patterns under her at any moment and their opposing crests and troughs canceled each other out. This phenomenon allowed her to sail serenely under the pewter skies as if the swells were nothing more than ripples.

Father Anatoly Vatutin had spent the first days of his journey safely in his cabin, having an occasional light meal sent to him rather than venturing to one of the many restaurants or eating in the vessel's four enormous dining rooms. He'd left word with Bishop Olkranszy, his superior, that he hadn't felt well since the ship had gotten under way. That wasn't far from the truth.

Vatutin had come from peasant stock, with farmer's hands and shoulders like a plow ox. Yet his imposing size, fierce countenance, and unwavering strength masked the fact that he possessed a delicate stomach. Even the ship's gentle motion made him ill. Such was his dedication to his mission that he rode waves of nausea stoically, spending hours either in his bunk or hunched over the toilet bowl.

He skipped the Universal Convocation's elaborate opening ceremonies and what some said had been the most beautiful papal blessing ever given. His rare forays to the deck to get fresh air were all under the cover of darkness, and he intentionally avoided any of the attendees he saw. Vatutin had become a nonentity at the most famous meeting in history and he was glad for it.

He had only one thing in mind. The icon.

Other than the waiters who brought him broths and bread and calls from Bishop Olkranszy inquiring about his condition, the only person Vatutin had spoken with was a cardinal named Peretti who was the pope's secretary of state, the Vatican's number two man. Peretti had been charged by the pontiff with returning thousands of religious artifacts belonging to other faiths that the Catholic Church had in its possession. He was the only person at the Convocation that Vatutin cared about.

Because of the sheer volume of items being returned, only a portion of the hoard was actually on the ship. These were the most precious relics—ancient texts, rare books, the most valuable statues and icons. Peretti's shipboard office had been deluged with requests from various people to obtain an item early in the voyage rather than at its end, which had been the plan. In the name of cooperation and fellowship, Peretti had granted all such requests, detailing a dozen *floreria,* members of the Vatican's technical services department, to search through the shipping containers stored in the vessel's holds.

Peretti's office had finally gotten to Father Vatutin's request, and now he found himself following the broad back of a *floreria.* The workman wore crisp coveralls and had a pair of white gloves tucked into his belt for handling the more fragile objects. While the worker strode with arm-swinging ease, Vatutin shambled down a carpeted hallway with one hand brushing the wall for balance, although the ship was rock steady. His mouth brimmed with saliva.

They descended into the working section of the liner, where the hallways were sterile and narrow and the lighting came from institutional fluorescent fixtures affixed to the ceiling. The air had a humid chill that told Vatutin they had moved below the water line.

At a set of large watertight doors the *floreria* exchanged a few words with the Swiss Guards stationed there and produced a ring of keys from his pocket. A sign on the door proclaimed this to be Cargo Hold 3. As the workman unlocked and then opened the door, one guard made a joke that Vatutin believed was at his expense and the others laughed. He didn't care. His chest felt hollow, and as he stepped into the vast hold, his pace involuntarily slowed. He couldn't believe he had come this far. In a few moments he was about to end his lifetime quest.

Vatutin couldn't possibly put into words what he was feeling. Everything he saw took on an added dimension of holiness. It didn't matter that the dimly lit hold was like an industrial warehouse that managed to smell musty despite its newness. He felt he was walking into the greatest cathedral in the world, a sacred place because of what lay within. The *floreria* spat on the floor, and Vatutin almost struck him before realizing that this man had no idea what he was about to give back to its rightful owner.

No, Anatoly thought, *there is no rightful owner except Satan himself. I am nothing more than a temporary trustee.*

Checking a large manifest, the worker guided the priest through the rows of containers and boxes. Peretti's organization had been impeccable. The manifest detailed everything from the largest painting to the smallest set of prayer beads. After a moment they were in front of a steel shipping container. The *floreria* produced his keys again and unlocked the mammoth crate. He waited while Vatutin unfolded the seventy-year-old photograph of the icon he was here to recover. The picture was stained in one corner with brown spots that even the priest didn't know was blood.

Taking the photo and motioning Vatutin not to enter the container, the workman ducked inside, snapping on a small flashlight he'd carried in his other pocket. He returned in just a few minutes.

The icon was only about two feet long and one foot wide, yet the *floreria* staggered under its weight. It was nearly six inches thick. Vatutin knew immediately that this was the relic he sought. The workman laid it on a nearby table. Although Vatutin took back the photograph he didn't need it to verify the piece's authenticity. He knew the icon better than any man alive. He could reproduce it in his mind any time he chose. From where it had been created near the city of Vanavara, Anatoly Vatutin had traced the artifact's century-long journey to St. Petersburg to Stalingrad to Berlin and finally to Rome. It had entered a thousand dreams and kept him awake on a thousand nights. He knew it better than his own face.

Unlike most icons, this was no wooden painting covered by a gold veneer. The relic was almost solid gold. He traced his finger over the bas-relief of the Virgin Mary holding her crucified son, noting the distinctive drape of her robe and the vividness of Christ's wounds, especially the blood that leaked from his side. He bent close to study the mark over Mary's shoulder, verifying that it was indeed a faint comet's tail.

Anatoly Vatutin fell to his knees, his seasickness and every other hardship he'd endured for the past forty years forgotten. He prayed harder than at any time in his life, giving thanks to God, Christ, Mary, and Brother Grigori. His decades of exacting research had been correct. The icon had ended up in the Vatican following the Second World War, given to them by a mistaken American soldier working for a repatriation commission. It had been one of thousands of items looted by the German Army and returned to the wrong owners after the war.

He was physically exhausted by the time he got back to his cabin, his muscles aching from the effort of carrying the icon from the hold. His spirit, however, had never felt more invigorated. He laid the icon on his bed, the mattress springs protesting at such a dense object. Tossing aside the clothes at the top of his trunk, he removed the chain-mail garments fashioned for Brother Grigori.

First he opened the special flask at the bottom of the chest. The liquid inside was as clear as water. It was actually "heavy water," or deuterium, a substance used for handling the most dangerous elements on earth. He could only hope it would add protection for him from an element that was not of this world. Lying in the deuterium bath was a hammer and a six-inch molybdenum awl. He went to the bathroom and retrieved an item from his toilet case. The fact that a man who hadn't shaved since his teens owned an electric razor was one more inconsistency he was thankful had not been noticed. Of course, it wasn't a razor at all.

He needed to strip to his undershirt to put on the lead-armored mantle. He used a liberal amount of petroleum jelly to work his hands into the golden gloves. Before donning the priceless gold hood, he tested his grip on the hammer and awl and made sure that the golden plug that he'd had in his pocket matched the diameter of the spike. He was ready.

He pulled the icon off the bed and groaned as he lowered it into the pan at the bottom of the trunk, ensuring that the artifact was fully awash with deuterium. He brought the cordless razor close to it and turned it on, satisfied when nothing happened. He'd know in a moment if his crusade was successful. Again he prayed.

Placing the metal spike over Christ's heart at the center of the icon, Anatoly Vatutin lowered the hood's visor over his eyes, took a deep breath, and brought down the hammer with all his strength. Quickly he checked the razor again, dismayed that it hadn't reacted. Hands trembling, he replaced the tip of the spike in the dimple his first blow had created and hammered it again.

This time the razor emitted a steady series of clicks coming so close together they sounded like a continuous tone. The instrument was a disguised Geiger counter, and it had just encountered a radiation source unlike any on the planet. Considering the origin of the radiation, Anatoly hadn't been sure if the device would work. Balanced between elation and fear, he fumbled for the small plug and set it in the scar, bringing down the hammer to seat it properly. The Geiger counter fell silent once again.

Father Vatutin chanced rolling up his visor so he could accurately tap the plug more firmly in place. Only then did he look at the counter. Through three inches of gold, the second densest natural element in the universe, and several more inches of a fluid meant to absorb radiation, the device had registered a dose that equaled a lifetime worth of X rays. He swept the Geiger counter over the trunk and the cabin's walls. As predicted by Grigori, and later proved by another, Brother Leonid, the radiation had not been absorbed by inorganic material. It was only when he pointed the counter at his own hand that it began to click again. The exposure had been less than five seconds yet would likely rob Vatutin of a few years of life.

Enshrined within the icon, and protected by an abnormal reaction it had with gold, was a fragment of what the Brotherhood called Satan's Fist. Anatoly knew that hundreds, maybe thousands of people had been victims of this piece or the others like it. The realization that he now possessed the power to kill everyone on the *Sea Empress* made him shudder. From Brotherhood records, Anatoly knew that before Brother Grigori was murdered, he had amassed fifty such icons in Vanavara and all but one had been destroyed later by Brother Leonid. This was the last one.

He tidied the cabin, hiding his protective clothing in the trunk once again. He was too emotionally wasted to finish his mission. In fact, he was ravenously hungry and checked his watch, thinking that maybe he would finally venture out for dinner.

Before he took care of his body's needs, he had to pray. Thankful for his success, Anatoly Vatutin knew that his mission would be a wasted gesture if another endeavor far from the exclusive confines of the cruise ship failed.

The Brotherhood didn't yet have all elements of Satan's Fist. There was still one other source.

"This is not a point of debate," Greta Schmidt snapped. "If you had been here when the communication window opened, you would have heard that the Danish government is calling for your evacuation. It is not a Geo-Research decision."

Marty Bishop's face reddened another shade. "And I'm sure you did everything in your power to argue our case," he said sarcastically.

"What case?" she scoffed. While her arms were crossed in a defensive posture, her attitude and tone were belligerent. Werner Koenig was at her side as they stood over the dining table. He said nothing. "Two people were almost killed this morning, and Camp Decade—your whole reason for being here—is a smoldering hole in the ice."

"We can still go down there once it cools," Marty sputtered.

"Mr. Bishop, there is nothing left." She seemed to be enjoying herself. As she showed more and more control over the expedition in the past days, her once attractive features had turned as hard as the ice outside. In contrast, Koenig seemed to have physically shrunk since establishing the base. "The fire Dr. Mercer accidentally started destroyed it."

Mercer had told that lie shortly after their rescue as a delaying tactic. Anika had agreed to go along with the deception because she was equally determined to discover the real arsonist and murderer. Had they told Werner and Greta that it had been intentionally set, they were certain that Geo-Research would have ordered them from the ice as a safety precaution.

Which, as it turned out, was happening anyway.

Mercer's expression remained unchanged when she looked at him, her face made ugly by a superior smirk. "Then why," he asked deliberately, "are you also sending away Erwin Puhl, Dr. Klein, and the other members of their team? The loss of Camp Decade doesn't affect their research."

"Without Igor Bulgarin to lead them, Dr. Puhl has done nothing but sit in his room. The other two meteorologists haven't accomplished much of anything either. And Dr. Klein has no function here, no real job except for some foolish interest in stress research. With you and Puhl's team gone, she has nothing to study. Besides, she is only here because of Bulgarin's insistence."

Mercer opened his mouth to reply but stopped himself. That last fact was something new. Igor had made it sound like Anika had been the one to petition him to join their expedition. Schmidt's statement meant it was the other way around. While he hadn't gotten the impression that she knew more than she'd admitted, he wondered again if she did. When he thought about it, she hadn't told him much of anything about herself or her interest in coming to Greenland.

Werner spoke for the first time. "There is no reason to continue this conversation. Tomorrow morning the weather is going to clear for a few hours and the DC-3 that came out a couple days ago will return to take you back to Reykjavik. I am sorry."

"This according to the same weatherman who sent a chopper into a hurricane?" Ira asked sardonically.

Greta glared.

Mercer wondered what Werner Koenig had ever seen in her. He was easygoing and caring and seemed like a dedicated scientist. She strode around the camp like a dictator. He suspected that dating the new owner of Geo-Research had somehow changed her because he couldn't imagine a guy like Werner ever loving the woman she was now.

He cleared his mind of unnecessary speculation and

concentrated on the problem at hand. He cocked a questioning eye at Marty. "This is your show. What do you think?"

"My father shelled out a ton of money for this expedition. He won't be happy, but since Camp Decade's gone there's no real reason to hang out here."

"Ira?" Because Ira knew more about what was going on, Mercer was confident how the ex-Navy man would vote.

Lasko cracked his knuckles before answering. "I say we get back to Reykjavik, have ourselves a decent night's sleep, and call Mr. Bryce in New York. I think he'll have us back here in a matter of hours. There's still a lot we can do. Not all the base was burned."

Greta watched the vote but didn't wait for Mercer to voice his opinion. "This isn't a democracy. You are being ordered back to Iceland. The plane will be here in the morning. You will be on it when it leaves."

She turned to go. Werner paused for a second, looking apologetic. He was about to speak when he closed his mouth and followed her out of the mess hall. The Society's team was left to themselves at their table. There were a few others scattered around the mess, mostly scientists who'd shown no interest in the argument.

Mercer went to get a cup of coffee. Ingrid, the cook's assistant who was sleeping with Marty, motioned him into the kitchen when no one appeared to be looking. Standing with her was Hilda Brandt, the other assistant chef. A heavy woman, she'd learned her craft in the German Army but her skills had improved since then. Both looked anxious. "I heard what just happened," Ingrid said in her delightful lisping accent. "That witch is also sending away the contract employees: me and Hilda."

"You don't work for Geo-Research?"

"No, only the head chef is their employee. We work for a commercial catering company."

The implication was clear. "After tomorrow the only people left here are actual Geo-Research staff?"

"*Ja.*"

Just what the Danish government wanted to avoid, Mercer thought. "Thanks for the info."

He returned to the table, accepting a shot from Ira's flask to fortify his coffee. He was quiet for a moment, his gaze lost in the black pool swirling in his ceramic cup.

"You with us, Mercer?" Ira asked.

"For what it's worth, I think Ira's idea has the most merit." They looked at him, waiting for him to continue. "The fire that leveled Camp Decade and nearly killed Anika and me wasn't an accident."

"You started it on purpose?" Marty cried, nearly coming out of his chair.

"Quiet down!" Mercer said. "I didn't start it."

"Anika?" Ira asked.

"She was with me the whole time." Mercer shook his head. "It was started deliberately by the same person who murdered Igor Bulgarin."

Jaws dropped around the table. "Igor was murdered?" Marty finally gasped.

Mercer explained Anika's findings, concluding that the fire was most likely set by the murderer to cover his trail. He had probably seen Mercer and Anika headed toward the underground facility, realized that they might be trying to prove the murder, and started a fire that would trap them. "Ira, did you get a chance to check the doors leading into the camp when you were fighting the blaze? I suspect they were chained shut to prevent us from escaping if we somehow managed to reach them."

"There was too much smoke coming up the access shaft. We never got down that far before you were found by Erwin."

"Damn. That would have been the proof I needed."

"Sorry, none of us were looking for evidence."

"It was my fault." Mercer's voice was thick with self-recrimination. "I forgot to go back after the diesel tank blew up. If they'd been locked, the killer's had plenty of time to remove the chain."

"Why'd you say my idea has the most merit?"

"Because Ingrid just told me that she and Hilda are being evacuated with us. Geo-Research is going to have this whole place to themselves, a situation they've wanted all along. When we land in Iceland, I'm calling Charlie Bryce. He's got the leverage to get us back out here."

"Why bother?" Marty said. "None of this has anything to do with us."

"I don't like leaving unsolved mysteries," Mercer replied. "And I especially don't let people trying to kill me get away with it. Because of the solar-max effect we can't communicate with anyone, which means until I'm in Reykjavik I can't get the answers I want. Geo-Research isn't what it's pretending to be, and Charlie's the only person I know who can find out who they really are. And just because Igor was a virtual stranger doesn't mean I won't find the son of a bitch who murdered him."

Mercer decided he would also contact Dick Henna. He hated using his friendship with the director of the FBI but since he was looking into a murder this was more than a personal request. If Bryce couldn't find out what Geo-Research was up to, Henna certainly could.

"What are you now, a cop or something?"

"No. I just don't hide behind my father while people are dying around me." The fury in Mercer's eyes made Marty look away guiltily. It wasn't Bishop he was particularly angry with. In other circumstances he would agree with him. But this situation had Mercer on edge and anxious. Marty was just a convenient target to vent some of his bottled emotions. "You don't want to come back, that's fine. I am."

"I'm with you," Ira said, directing a long look at Marty.

He was silent for just a few seconds, but the change in him was profound. Mercer had hit his most vulnerable spot—his fear that he couldn't live up to his father. The accusation stung. For his entire life, Marty Bishop had argued that he didn't mind being under his father's shadow, and he would have shrugged off Mercer's comment. But for the first time he was prepared to face it and himself. Here was a chance to go beyond what was expected of him, and he wanted to take it. Shoulders squared, he met Mercer's gaze and nodded.

"Looks like we're both with you," Ira remarked. Having shepherded many young recruits onto the path of responsibility, he poured a congratulatory dram from his flask into Marty's coffee. That Bishop was learning this lesson at fifty and not twenty was fine— many people never learned it at all.

"Thanks." Before they returned from Iceland, Mercer would tell Marty about everything—Elisebet Rosmunder's warning, the radioactivity in Jack Delaney's body, the stowaway on the chopper, and his own misgivings concerning Igor Bulgarin. He wouldn't blame Marty if he recanted his decision to return to the base.

The front door blew open, and a bundled shape was propelled into the mess hall. It was Anika Klein. She shook snow off her parka and danced from foot to foot to remove her moon boots. After slipping on a pair of sneakers and filling a coffee cup at the urn, she came over to the table. "Looks like I came at a bad time."

"We're being kicked out of here," Marty said.

She glanced at Mercer. "Because of the fire?"

He nodded. "You're leaving too, along with Erwin and the others with him."

"What? Why?" Her dark eyes went from sympathy to anger in an instant. "The fire has nothing to do with my work. They can't make me leave. I paid Geo-Research nearly ten thousand dollars for my part of the expedition. I'm not going anywhere. Whose idea is this?"

"Greta claims it's by order of the Danish government."

"Is the radio working again?" she asked quickly.

"Not anymore."

The communication gear in the corner of the mess

had been abandoned. Geo-Research hadn't posted an operator to listen if the constant static that had assailed them for days would lift. They had even locked the cabinet to prevent unauthorized use of the equipment. As Mercer studied the stack of electronics in the Plexiglas case, it occurred to him that only Geo-Research personnel had been around when any messages had come through. His jaw hardened.

"Ira, where's the closest Sno-Cat?"

"The one I used to save you is parked between here and the main lab. All the others are out on overnight survey for Werner's people."

"Be right back." Mercer stood and left the mess, donning his parka but not bothering with the cumbersome moon boots. His work boots would do for the thirty-yard walk.

He returned in a few minutes, carrying a pair of heavy bolt cutters from the Sno-Cat, strode right to the radio cabinet, and snipped the lock as though it were tissue paper.

"What the hell are you doing?"

"It just occurred to me that the radio only works when none of us are here. Could be a coincidence or maybe not." He sat at the operator's station and flicked on the main power switch. The set was state-of-the-art and came to life instantly.

One of the technicians who'd been on the DC-3 flight came over and grabbed Mercer's shoulder. "You cannot do this."

Mercer smiled disarmingly. "Won't be a minute, I promise."

"*Nein.* It is not permitted."

The radio returned nothing but white noise. Anika came over and said something in German to the irate lab worker. A shouting match quickly developed. Mercer used her distraction to begin scanning frequencies. He had a minute at most, and every time the SCAN function paused at a frequency, static burst from the speakers. The Geo-Research technician saw and heard what Mercer was attempting and reached over to kill the power. He called to one of his own people. Mercer heard his name and that of Greta Schmidt. The other worker threw on his coat and raced for the door.

"I was done," Mercer said, pushing back from the radio. "You didn't need to send for your den mother."

Something about this crop of Germans had bothered him from the time they stepped off the plane, and now he saw what it was. As scientists went, the man standing over him had to be the toughest he'd ever seen. Polar research was a hard field, but this guy looked more like a soldier than a lab rat. He was beardless, and his brown hair wasn't much longer than a military buzz cut. He had wide shoulders, a deep chest, and a rather dim expression. He scowled down at Mercer as if inviting a physical confrontation. After a moment, the German spat a curse and walked away.

Mercer turned to Anika. "I assume he just insulted my manliness."

"Yours and a few past generations' also."

"In case her walk back here hasn't cooled her off, I'm going to my room before the Abominable Greta comes storming in."

"I think we should all call it a night," Ira agreed.

Their dormitory was on the opposite side of the mess hall from the one the senior Geo-Research people used, so they didn't run into her. Mercer asked Ira to tell Erwin Puhl about the evacuation and walked down the building's central hallway to his room. Once he'd decided he needed sleep, his exhaustion nearly overwhelmed him. His stamina had held him together through Anika's autopsies, the fire, and the escape but he was at his limit.

For whatever reason, Geo-Research didn't want anyone at their base and they were playing their final hand by forcing the two teams thrust on them to leave Greenland. Mercer was determined to learn why. He harbored the suspicion that this evacuation had nothing to do with the Danes. He wasn't convinced that his failure to pick up any broadcasts meant the radio was being blocked by atmospherics. It could have been altered somehow to stop others from reaching the outside world. He was impotent until they reached Reykjavik.

There were no locks on the dorm room doors, so he pushed against his and crossed the threshold. He stopped dead. While not exactly torn apart, his quarters had been thoroughly searched. His bed had been stripped and the mattress pushed off its frame. The contents of his luggage lay strewn around the space. The Geiger counter was left on the single plastic chair as if the searcher had studied it before leaving.

Stunned, Mercer knew there was no way this was random. The vandals had been looking for something specific and he was sure they hadn't found it. From a compartment in his wallet he removed the folded piece of paper he'd recovered from Jack Delaney. It was a map of sorts with accurate lines of longitude and latitude. In the center was a pencil drawing of the crashed C-97 and off to the left was another drawing of what appeared to be Camp Decade as it had been fifty years ago with a number of chimneys and air vents poking from the snow.

On the right side of the map was an X with a drawing of a man's hook-nosed profile above it. The distance from the mysterious mark to the plane was given as twenty-eight kilometers in a direct magnetic heading of 187 degrees. If the map was done to any sort of scale, Delaney had walked nearly three hundred kilometers from the plane to Camp Decade on the same azimuth, an amazing feat of endurance. The only other item Mercer had that could interest anyone was the bundle of papers forwarded to him by Harry White, which he also carried in the inside cargo pocket of his parka. Because they were written in German, the only thing Mercer had managed to decipher from the pages was their authorship by a man named Otto Schroeder.

His first thought—that someone from Geo-Research had rifled his room—dissolved as soon as it came to

him. The undeniable fact was that Anika Klein was
the only person who'd shown any interest in the bundle of papers. She was also the only one, other than
him, to know about the scrap of paper, even if she
hadn't yet learned it was a map.

"Ira?" Mercer shouted down the hall.

"Yeah."

"Can you come over here?"

"What's up? Did the vodka fairy visit and leave you
a present?"

"Just pop over and bring Erwin."

"Coming, dear." Ira appeared at Mercer's side and
peered into the ruin that was his room. "I like what
you've done with the place."

"Wish I could say I did it myself, but this was someone else's decorating job." Mercer turned to Puhl.
"How are you doing, Erwin?"

"Oh, ah, fine," Puhl mumbled. He looked terrible.
What little hair he had was awry, and his glasses
hadn't been cleaned in a while. His breath reeked of
stale alcohol. "What happened here?"

"I was hoping you could tell me," Mercer said gently, recognizing how fragile the meteorologist appeared. His grief over Igor Bulgarin's death had
deepened. "You've been here for most the night. Did
you hear or see anyone enter my room?"

Looking like he was about to lie, Puhl thought better of it. "I've been in the bathroom for a while," he
admitted. "I got drunk a while ago and wanted to
sober up. I think I used everyone's hot-water ration."

"That's fine," Mercer soothed. "You didn't hear
anyone over the sound of the shower?"

"I don't think so. I don't remember. I fell asleep
for a while." Erwin looked down miserably, ashamed.
"Actually, I passed out."

"Don't worry about it." Mercer smiled, touching the
scientist on the arm. "Why don't you go pack for tomorrow? I'll give you a hand in a minute."

"Poor guy is reeling," Ira said after Erwin returned
to his room. "When I went in to tell him we're being

booted he just sat there staring at his Bible. I never saw him and Igor as being that close."

"There's no proper way to mourn," Mercer stated.

"I get the impression you've been there a few times yourself."

"Yeah."

A silence hung for a second.

"Since it wasn't the vodka fairy making a delivery, any other suspects?"

Mercer gave a quick laugh, thankful that Ira had broken the black mood coming over him. "My list includes our arsonist/murderer but I'm betting on the lovely, though enigmatic, Dr. Klein."

"What about the stowaway from her chopper?"

"I don't believe there was a stowaway after all."

"So who left those footprints at the crash site?"

"I think Anika did when she went to bury something out there. I'm guessing some mail that was actually addressed to me." Mercer held up the envelope that Harry had sent with the joke name on it. "She missed this one because I've got a friend who fancies himself a comedian."

Ira was quiet as he absorbed this. "If you're right, what does that mean about the rest of her actions here? I mean, if she steals your mail and ransacks your room, lying about Igor being murdered would be a much gentler crime."

Mercer looked down the hall to make sure Erwin was still out of earshot. The last thing he needed in his brittle state was to learn the truth about Bulgarin. "I don't know. Should be an interesting conversation on the plane back to Iceland though."

Ira chuckled. "If you think you can talk on a DC-3 it's obvious you've never been on one. Those things are louder than hell, and that's before you get airborne."

Mercer turned serious. "I want to thank you for backing me in the mess hall and for everything else you've done so far. You've had no reason to trust me and yet you have."

Lasko looked abashed. "Don't sweat it. Twenty years in the Navy trained me to follow an officer's orders."

"But I've never been an officer," Mercer pointed out.

"Which means," Ira said, "you actually know what you're talking about."

"Thanks." Mercer guessed that receiving a compliment from Ira Lasko had the same odds as winning a lottery. "What about you? What was your rank when you got out?"

"Nothing but a lowly chief," the submariner dismissed. "Clean up your room. I'll give Erwin a hand pulling himself back together and find the two other guys from his team who're getting the heave-ho." Ira turned to go, then paused at the door. "Mercer?"

"Yeah?"

"You have any idea what's going on here? Honestly?"

Mercer didn't need to think about his answer. "No clue."

Roaring in from the east, the antique DC-3 Dakota shattered the peace of the morning. The weather had cleared for the first time in days. The sky was nearly cloudless and the wind was a negligible caress. According to the experts, the calm wouldn't last for more than an hour or so.

It was barely eight, which meant the pilot must have left Iceland before dawn to reach the base so early. Those leaving for Reykjavik were assembled in the mess hall and had a view of the makeshift landing strip. Werner had had a crew out at first light to plow aside the drifts of snow that had accumulated overnight. No one from Geo-Research was waiting with the evacuees. It was as if they had already left.

"Our chariot awaits," Ira said, trying to make light of the situation, but the attempt fell flat.

"I hate leaving so much gear behind," Marty complained for the tenth time.

Werner had spoken with him that morning about the need to load the plane quickly and assured him that once they had a proper weather window the plane would return all Surveyor's Society equipment to Iceland. Koenig had said the delay wouldn't be more than a day or two and Geo-Research would pay any additional fees incurred by the arrangement.

"We'll be back by noon tomorrow," Mercer said.

"If we're not," Anika Klein chimed in, "I'm suing Geo-Research for my money."

"We all are," Marty agreed. His father's investment was twenty times hers.

Ingrid approached the crowded table, not sure how to greet Marty outside her bedroom. *"Guten Morgen."*

"Morning," Marty boomed, adding a significant look. "You all packed up and ready to go?"

"Ja. Hilda *und* I are ready but neither is happy."

"Welcome to the club. We were just deciding the lawsuits."

"But it is Danes who said we have to leave, not Geo-Research. Hilda heard radio earlier this morning when Greta Schmidt spoke with office in Reykjavik."

"You heard them?" Mercer asked, leaning forward intently. He directed his gaze at Hilda Brandt, whom he saw standing a little behind the younger, slimmer cook. She blushed.

"Ja." Ingrid answered for her friend. "She heard her speaking to a Danish official from their embassy in Iceland. It sounded like Danes want entire facility shut down for good."

Mercer's immediate reaction was to think the conversation had been faked. Greta could have easily been speaking to one of her own people pretending to be a Danish diplomat, staging the conversation so Hilda would overhear. It would help convince the Society's team that she was innocent of ordering their removal from Greenland. And then he thought he was being paranoid.

"Even if the evac order is legit," he said at last, "I'm still going to fight it when we get to Iceland."

Anika was at the window for a better look at the landing. "The plane's down and I can see Werner motioning to us."

"Then I guess this is it." Mercer got to his feet and everyone followed.

Their luggage had already been ferried to the landing strip, so they trooped out like a defeated army, trudging through newly fallen snow in the worn paths. Even at low idle, the sound from the plane's engines was deafening. A blizzard of ice particles blew around the spinning props. Both pilots were on the far side of the aircraft, relieving themselves in the snow.

Once they reboarded the aircraft, Mercer saw Bernhardt Hoffmann, the young worker nearly asphyxiated in Camp Decade, and a passenger he didn't recognize jump from the rear door. Even with his feet encumbered by tall boots the stranger moved through the snow as if born to it, like a wolf. Greta Schmidt cried out when she saw him and ran into his embrace. This had to be the sometime-boyfriend Werner had mentioned. Greta, who was nearly as tall as Mercer, vanished in his arms. The man was huge. He had the hood of his black snowsuit down around his wide shoulders, so Mercer could see that his nose had a misshapen look that only came from being broken.

They stayed away from the evacuees as they waited for their turn to climb the ladder into the plane. Werner Koenig did come over to Mercer to relay the message Greta had gotten that morning from the office in Reykjavik about the Danish attaché. If he was lying about the conversation, his performance was Oscar quality.

"The Danes are adamant about nonessential people leaving until they can send someone to determine if our facility is safe," he shouted over the growl of the old Dakota's radial engines.

"What about your team?" Mercer held his mouth close to Koenig's ear.

"Most of them are out with the core drill taking samples. I'm hoping a safety inspector will be sent soon, so I don't have to recall them and lose a few days of work."

"So we're your sacrificial goats to Denmark's bureaucracy?"

Werner shrugged. "I'm sorry. My hands are tied."

If he was telling the truth, Mercer could understand Koenig's position. "All right," he said. "No sense blaming the messenger."

Anika was right in front of him at the boarding ladder when Mercer turned to take perhaps his last look at the camp. If not for traces of cooking smoke rising from the back of the mess hall and the generator enveloped in its own exhaust, the base would have looked completely deserted. The only motion came from the breeze lofting wisps of snow like dust in an old Western movie. Mercer felt like whistling the theme from *High Plains Drifter*.

Greta Schmidt caught his eye. She must have said something to her companion because he strode over to the plane, cutting the distance in a few strides. In a burst of vindictiveness, Mercer went up the ladder so the German would have to stand in the buffeting prop wash if he wanted to speak with him. He tapped Anika on the shoulder before the Geo-Research official reached the hatch.

"Would you save me a seat? I'd like to talk to you."

Anika stared at him for a second, a shadow of apprehension behind her fixed smile. "Okay."

"You are Philip Mercer?" The German's accent wasn't bad, but he spoke in a low, rasping snarl as if afflicted by a terminal case of laryngitis.

"I'm Mercer." Neither man made a move to shake hands. There was an instant antagonism between them. It was instinctive, the coming together of two rival animals.

"I'm Gunther Rath. I recently had a nice talk with Elisebet Rosmunder. She gave me something to give to you. It's taped to the bulkhead behind the cockpit." Before slamming the door closed, the man gave Mercer an ugly smile and said, "Have a good flight."

What the hell was that all about? Mercer turned to find a seat and slammed into Anika, who hadn't yet moved from the entrance. She looked terrified.

"I'm sorry." He tried to help her to her feet at the same moment the pilot gave the engines a burst of power to begin taxiing. They both fell back into the slush left melting on the cabin floor.

The pilot's voice came over the tinny speaker mounted in the ceiling, his Icelandic accent made more unintelligible by the motors' thunderous bellow. "Sorry about that. With another weather system moving in, I want to get back in the air as quickly as possible. There isn't even time to unload the supplies we brought."

As the DC-3 bounced over the uneven glacier, Mercer fought to get Anika and himself into a seat and belted in. He thought he'd hurt her when they bumped because her normally pale face was as white as the snow outside and her eyes refused to focus. He took her hand and found it quivering.

"Anika?"

"I know that man," she said as if in a trance. "I recognized his voice. I don't think he realized who I am." Then she broke out of it. The wellspring of determination he'd seen during the fire in Camp Decade rushed back. Her grip tightened. "Did you get the package from Otto Schroeder?"

Mercer blinked, stunned that she all but admitted her guilt. "So it *was* you who searched my room."

"Yes," Anika replied defiantly. "Did you get it?"

"As a matter of fact I did." It suddenly occurred to him that she couldn't know who had sent the package because it hadn't left his sight since Harry had forwarded it. "How do you know Otto Schroeder?"

Anika paused as the plane's skis came unstuck from the ice and the DC-3 strained into the air. "I watched that man back there order his death."

As soon as the hatch closed and the DC-3 began lumbering across the ice, Greta took Gunther Rath by the hand and led him toward her quarters at an urgent pace. He knew by the predatory gleam in her eye what she wanted, and his need surpassed hers. However, now was not the time. He snatched his arm away after a few steps.

"Later, Greta." His voice was made harsher by the suppression of his own desires. "We don't have time."

"Yes, we do," she breathed, her hand reaching for his groin, not caring if others saw. "It has been far too long."

"Not for me," he snapped with intentional cruelty, which only seemed to inflame her more.

"I've had to deal with Werner's sulking for a week. We're going to my room right now and you are going to screw me until I can't walk."

"Keep this up and I'm taking you back to your room to slap you unconscious."

"You can do that too," she simpered demurely, reveling in the presence of his overwhelming strength. It was the old game they were playing and invariably she would win. She knew his needs far outstripped hers. And the longer he held out the more violent, and satisfying, was their eventual sex. The heat between her legs grew with anticipation. Touching his groin again, she could feel him swelling.

This time Rath couldn't stop himself. He grabbed her by the arm. "Which is your dorm building?"

Greta knew not to gloat. She lowered her eyes and pointed.

She wondered who had seduced whom last year when the company Gunther represented negotiated to buy Geo-Research. At the time she had been with Werner for nearly two years, happy, and yet couldn't explain why she was putting off his marriage proposals. They lived a vagabond existence aboard the *Njoerd*, working wherever his contracts took them. In all it had been satisfying, but somehow she felt she was being rushed to normalcy. Werner wanted children and a home to come back to from his voyages. Greta had mouthed she wanted those things too and knew she was lying. She didn't know what she wanted. And then Gunther Rath had come into their lives with a blank check and the promise of noninterference in the company. He'd said purchasing Geo-Research was merely an investment for Kohl AG, a way for them to defer taxes.

She'd known from the first that the expensive suits he wore hid something far different from his corporate image. He retained the unstudied social disdain of the wanna-be rebels who had thrilled her and her girl-friends as teenagers, but grown-up and with a lot more to offer than exciting rides on shoddy motorcycles and small bags of low-grade marijuana. At that first meeting, when Werner stared wide-eyed at the figures Rath was willing to pay for Geo-Research, Greta found herself showing off. Nothing obvious, nothing that Werner would even detect, but Gunther had known it the way a lion can sense a female in estrus.

Whenever the three would meet in the weeks it took to sign over the company, Greta had thought she was just playing a game to see how far she could push the flirtation. But like any game without rules, she had to act more brazen to elicit the same animal reaction she'd felt the first day. She believed she was controlling him with her ploys, not once realizing she was manipulating herself into what he wanted. In the end, when she was nearly throwing herself at him, he had finally sought her out, allowing her to think that she had done the seducing. But now, a year later, knowing what their relationship had become, she realized he had gone to her only to prove his dominion. The relationship was almost that of master and slave, and she found herself greedy for any degradation he heaped on her.

At the dorm, she first made sure the building was empty. A minute later they were naked in her room, with no others around to hear the slaps or the cries of pain and climax. Rath's practiced hands did not leave marks where they were visible, but it would be a while before Greta could sit comfortably.

While she cleaned up in satisfied euphoria, Gunther Rath searched for Werner Koenig and found him in the mess hall with Dieter, the rally driver. "What's the status of the search?"

Werner looked up, feeling the old pang of jealousy. He could tell by Rath's expression that he'd just taken Greta. Since the day she'd left him, Werner had held out hope that some vestiges of his former lover remained. He knew now that wasn't the case. Rath had reduced her to nothing more than a vessel for his warped dysfunctions. The once-sweet Greta had become a whore, yet he continued to mourn the loss of the woman who might have been his wife. Making it worse, Rath had insisted she come along on this expedition to be his eyes and ears. Werner suspected that Rath enjoyed this humiliation more than anything else—it was the kind of primitive behavior that would appeal to his Neanderthal mentality.

"Three teams have been out for a few days now, but as you suspected we are too far south to find anything."

"With the others gone," Gunther said, "we can end this charade and move a portion of the base northward. I passed on the fake weather report to the pilot of the DC-3 so they'll swing far to the north before turning to Iceland. They'll never see the rotor-stat flying in to ferry us."

"How is that possible? The airship is under tight flight guidelines until it receives its certification."

"Because it's owned by one of Kohl's subsidiaries. We can do anything with it we want. It should be here in another couple of hours. There actually is a fog prediction for this area that'll last for at least a day, so moving a building and the 'Cats is going to be tricky. It should be a good demonstration of the airship's capabilities. With the Surveyor's Society out of the way, we have two and a half weeks until their replacements arrive and we have to return everything back here."

"Damn Danish government," Dieter said. He was actually a longtime Kohl employee. "If they hadn't amended our permit, none of this would be necessary. We should have fought them harder when they told us to move our operation to Camp Decade to accommodate the Americans."

"If we'd argued they might have barred us from Greenland completely." By his tone it was clear Rath didn't want to debate the point again. "Pressure against Kohl in Europe is mounting. We have to find the cavern."

Werner didn't want to hear how the recent buyers of Geo-Research had perverted his company for their own ends. He had agreed to sell at the overvalued price because Rath and a battery of Kohl lawyers had assured him that Geo-Research would continue to operate as it had in the past. He was told they would do nothing to damage the hard-won reputation he'd built for clear scientific research.

That promise had lasted until this mission, just one year later. Trapped now by a moment of greed, he and Geo-Research were being corrupted by Gunther Rath and his boss, Klaus Raeder, for a mission Werner didn't fully understand. He had no idea why they were searching for a cavern or what was inside. Nor did he care. He just wanted the operation to be over so they would give him his company back and leave him alone.

"Werner, you don't look well," Rath mocked.

"I was just thinking how glad I'll be when you are gone."

"It won't take us long. Once we finish clearing out the cave, our interest in Geo-Research is over. Your company will continue under the Kohl umbrella but in a much less hands-on role."

"What happens if you don't find the cavern before the next team of researchers arrives from Japan?"

"For their sake, let's pray we do." Rath looked out the window in the direction the DC-3 had vanished. "Go make preparations to move a dorm building and Sno-Cats."

Bern Hoffmann was stationed in the communications alcove, a pair of sleek headphones covering his ears. He'd just finished rewiring a couple circuit boards and was replacing an access panel at the back of the set. Rath walked over and touched his shoulder to draw his attention. "Have you fixed our solar-max problem?"

"Just about, Gunther." While he used Rath's Christian name, there was subordination in Hoffmann's voice. Like most of the people at the base, he was actually part of Rath's security force. "There are legitimate atmospheric problems, but nothing like what we led the Surveyor's Society to believe. We can communicate with the *Njoerd* just fine."

"And you're sure the plane's radios are dead?" While the pilots were outside the aircraft, Rath had watched as the young technician sabotaged the radios.

"I doubt the pilots will realize they've been wrecked until they're halfway to Iceland."

"Which is as far as they'll get."

Anika's statement extinguished any anger Mercer had been harboring. Even when they were facing the fire in Camp Decade, he hadn't seen such naked fear. She was like a raw nerve, exposed and pained. By admitting that she had searched his room, he no longer had a reason to doubt her. She hadn't gotten the name Otto Schroeder from him, which meant she had additional information from another source, information that he needed. He said nothing, studying her with his depthless gray eyes, a patient, nonjudgmental scrutiny that invited her to continue. Emotion continued to play across her face as she struggled to regain her composure. He knew she was deciding how to overcome her natural suspicion and take him in her confidence.

Only the forward half of the DC-3's open cabin had seats. The rear portion was given over to cargo, which lay under mesh netting secured to eyebolts in the floor. Mercer and Anika were in the rearmost seats. Forward sat Marty and Ingrid, who were talking with their heads almost touching. Ira was a couple rows behind them, looking around nostalgically, obviously transported to another time and place by the utilitarian aircraft. The remainder of the passengers either stared out the square windows or had already settled in to a book.

"Anika, please," Mercer said as gently as the rattling aircraft would allow. "I think between the two of us we know what's going on, but alone we know nothing. We have to share if we're going to figure out who killed Igor and why." He had already assumed a connection between Bulgarin's murder and Otto Schroeder's.

Anika looked into his face, searching for the strength she hoped he possessed because hers was gone. Everything had come full circle too quickly. Hearing Schroeder's killer outside just now had abolished any desire she had for justice. She wanted to run from all of this, to go to Vienna to be with her *Opa*. He would know what to do.

"I hadn't heard of Otto Schroeder until I opened the package from Germany," Mercer continued, his gaze never leaving Anika's eyes although the plane pitched and vibrated. "I was warned by an e-mail before I left the States that something was being sent. I had no idea what it was. I still don't. This journal Schroeder sent me is written in German."

"You haven't read it?" Anika asked. It was a neutral question, one that gave nothing away.

"I can barely read English," Mercer joked, but Anika didn't respond. "All the German words I know are either food related or naughty."

"What did that man say when you got on the plane?" There was a sudden urgency in her voice. She had a premonition that this wasn't the time to compare notes. Not yet anyway. There was a more pressing issue. There were now two murderers at the base camp, and she was beginning to see conspiracies behind everything.

"He told me his name is Gunther Rath and wished us a good flight."

"We don't have time to go into the whys, wheres, and hows but that man put a bullet in my leg last week and presided over the torture of Otto Schroeder, an old soldier I was interviewing for my grandfather. Just before Schroeder died, he mentioned your name and said you were someone who could help. It can't be a coincidence that you, me, and Rath are in the same place at the same time. We've all been manipulated."

"Does Rath know Schroeder was going to send me something?"

"No, he'd been driven away by snipers."

Mercer's eyes widened. "Remind me to ask you the whole story sometime. Rath probably didn't recognize you because everyone looks the same under ten layers of clothes. Yet you still think he's a threat."

"Don't you?"

Mercer did, but he didn't know how immediate a threat. It wasn't a great leap of deductive reasoning to guess that Rath was working with Igor Bulgarin's killer. Greta Schmidt? Possibly, but unimportant right now. He put himself in their position and knew the murderers' first priority would be to eliminate all traces of the crime. The physical evidence, Igor's body, lay unguarded at the base. And the only two people who had firsthand knowledge of the killing were on the same antique plane. With another convenient fire in the cold laboratory and a plane crash, the killers would be in the clear.

Mercer didn't forget that Gunther Rath had been on the DC-3 while the pilots were peeing in the snow. And then he remembered Rath mentioning Elisebet Rosmunder. He unstrapped his seat belt and ran for the cockpit. If his sudden hunch was wrong, no harm done, but if he was right . . .

Taped to the bulkhead was a manila envelope. He tore it away from the wall. Unsealing it with trembling fingers, he tipped out the contents. Photographs. The first was the shot of Mrs. Rosmunder's son, Stefansson, before his ill-fated trip to Greenland. The second was the one a nurse took shortly before his death. And the third picture, Mercer balled in his fist after just a glance. The bullet hole in the old woman's forehead was like an obscene third eye.

The rage began someplace deep inside, and he let it come, let it grow until it filled every fiber and nerve. He vibrated with it. For long seconds he allowed it to consume him like an internal fire, waiting for that moment of transmutation when rage became hate. And it came too, sharper than any he'd felt before. Unfocused anger was corrosive, worthless, but the hate was a weapon he could control. The ability to harness it was the gift that had allowed him to face so much ugliness in the past without destroying his soul.

He looked down the length of the cabin, knowing that his responsibility lay here. His revenge for Mrs. Rosmunder's murder would come once he was sure these people were safe.

The door separating the cockpit from the rest of the plane was open. Out the windscreen, Mercer could see that the black ocean far below them was dotted with icebergs, as murderous a sea as he'd ever seen. The pilots were both young Icelanders dressed in vintage-looking bomber jackets.

"Have you been in touch with anyone on the radio?" Mercer asked, his voice calmer than it had any right to be. If communications had been intentionally blacked out at the camp, he was sure Rath would have interfered with them here too.

"Sir, you should be in your seat," the copilot said automatically. "This crate wasn't designed for stability."

"Just tell me if your radios work."

Mercer's urgency prompted the pilot to dial Reykjavik tower. "Papa Sierra 11 to Reykjavik, come in please." The headphones he wore prevented Mercer from hearing the reply but when the pilot repeated his call he knew there hadn't been one. The pilot tried a third time before dialing another station and then another and another. His glance at his copilot told Mercer everything he needed to know.

"The radios are dead, aren't they?"

"Could be the solar-max effect. We've been having problems for a while." The attempted reassurance sounded flat.

"Don't bet on it," Mercer replied grimly. "How far are we from Iceland?"

"About two hours with this head wind."

Mercer doubted they had that much time. "Not an option. What's the closest airport?"

"Kulusuk is a bit closer, but we're flying northeast to avoid a storm front we were told about at your research base. In a few minutes Iceland will be closer."

The trap had been set and they'd flown right into it. There was no storm. It was another fabrication, like the Danish evacuation order. *Okay, Mercer, think. They didn't have time to damage the engines or contaminate the fuel supply, so how would you crash a cargo plane with perhaps the greatest safety record in history?*

The answer was as obvious as it was chilling.

A bomb.

"There's no storm front," he said, forcing the terror out of his voice. "Keep on course for Iceland, but be prepared to turn back because we may not have the time."

Mercer returned to the cabin and prodded Ira, who had slumped against a skeletal frame member as if it were a pillow. "Wake up. We could have a problem."

"Stewardess forget your drink?"

"I think there's a bomb on the plane." Mercer didn't care that the others heard him. They would know soon enough.

Their search was systematic and quick. After checking under all the seats and behind any removable panels in the cockpit and cabin, they began shifting the stacks of cargo in the rear of the plane. Marty and Anika were helping by this point while everyone else had been ordered to their seats, their frightened stares never leaving the searchers.

Mercer unhooked the netting over the last cargo pallet, a neatly stacked pile of boxes at the very rear of the hold. The cabin's heaters couldn't overcome the chilling drafts, and yet he was covered with sweat. It felt like a lead weight had settled in his stomach. He checked each box thoroughly before lifting it from the stack to hand to Ira. Had the bomb been motion activated, the plane would have exploded as soon as it began moving across the ice, so his biggest concern was a booby trap around the device.

Ira and Anika were carefully examining the tape seals on the boxes to see if any had been opened but they hadn't found anything. Mercer reached the last carton. He nearly missed the filament of wire running from a tiny hole in the cardboard to a bulkhead, where it had been glued to the steel. It was an anti-tampering wire designed to detonate the bomb if the box was moved.

"Got it!" he called, both relieved and sickened.

The tape on the box's lid had been slit open. Ira held the box steady while Mercer lowered himself until the top of the carton was at eye level. Gingerly he opened one flap, mindful that there could be another trip wire attached to its underside. It appeared clear, so he opened the other side. Anika gave a startled gasp, and he nearly jostled the box.

Rath had made a hollow in one corner of the container by removing a bundle of paper towels. In their place was the bomb. It consisted of six dynamite sticks bundled with tape and a high-tech detonator held in place by wires and more tape. The trip wire attached to the plane disappeared into the side of the activator, so Mercer couldn't tell how it was pretensioned. Cutting the wire or moving the bomb could conceivably obliterate the plane.

The LED numbers spinning backward in a window at the top of the device read sixty-eight minutes, twelve seconds. Eleven seconds. Ten seconds.

"You can deactivate it, right?" Anika asked hopefully. "You're a mining engineer. You know all about explosives."

"Ah, no." Mercer's voice caught in his throat, and he had to swallow heavily to clear it. "I don't know the first thing about bombs. Ira, any suggestions?"

"Land."

"Marty, go tell the pilot we have a bomb on board and we'll never make it to Reykjavik. Have him turn back to Greenland."

"What happens when we return to the Geo-Research camp?" Anika asked. "Rath's trying to kill us now. What's to stop him from just doing it later?"

Mercer made sure that Ira had a firm grip on the box before he stood, bracing himself as the DC-3 went through a steep banking turn. "Because we're not going back to the base. Give Ira a hand packing stuff around the bomb so it doesn't shift and pull the trip wire. We're not out of this fight yet."

The plan was a desperate one, but as Mercer reached his seat he felt there was a slim chance of hope. Because the DC-3 was equipped with skis, he wasn't worried about landing. What concerned him was the amount of time they might be stranded on the ice. Once the bomb went off, he doubted there would be enough of the plane to protect eleven people from the elements. He had to find them shelter. Mercer had a location in mind, but finding it depended on a man who'd been dead for fifty years.

He unfolded the map he'd recovered from Major Delaney and studied the figures the airman had penciled in. Mercer's immediate urge was to tell the pilots the heading Delaney had used to reach Camp Decade from the crash site. Finding the wreck would have been a simple geometry equation.

And it would have been wrong.

A fact largely ignored by modern navigators because of global positioning satellites and other artificial aids is that the magnetic North Pole is not a stationary point. It can migrate up to fifty miles in a single day and averages a northwestern drift of approximately nine miles every year. Earth's iron core, which generates the magnetic field, is slightly out of phase with the rotation of the crust, creating this observable movement. To find the plane, Mercer had to factor fifty years' worth of drift to Delaney's heading, a difference of about four hundred and fifty miles.

With a calculator and a pen, he did the math as quickly as he could, aware of the bomb's remorseless countdown. He could do nothing about Delaney's estimate that he'd walked three hundred kilometers to reach the abandoned Air Force facility. Once they established themselves above his route and began backtracking, Mercer could only hope they would spot his plane. Erwin had said a few days ago that the region around where Mercer believed the C-97 had crashed had less snow cover now than at any time in decades. That was just one of the many lucky breaks they would need.

He felt a hand on his shoulder and looked up. It was Erwin Puhl. "Anything I can do?"

"Get Marty's sat-phone."

Erwin shook his head. "Marty already tried it. He can't get a lock on any satellites. It's the solar max."

"In that case, are you a praying man?"

"I am now."

"Me too."

The pilots didn't question Mercer's orders when he told them the new course to fly because he was the only person who had an idea how to save them. He returned to the rear of the plane, where Ira, Marty, and Anika had buried the bomb under as much cargo as they could pack around it. It was a makeshift redoubt, but any bit would help. "How much time?"

Ira checked the timer on his digital watch. "Forty-five and a half minutes."

"We'll be feet dry over Greenland again in fifteen and over our target area a couple minutes after that."

"Doesn't give us much time," Marty pointed out.

"If we don't find Delaney's plane, we'll still be able to put down and hope there's enough of this one left to sustain us."

"We pulled some of the better food stores, camping supplies, and cooking fuel away from the bomb," Ira explained. "We can each grab an armload when we make a run for it."

"Good idea. I hadn't thought about that."

"Don't thank me. It was Dr. Klein's idea."

Mercer smiled at Anika. "Intelligent, brave, and quick thinking. Do you have *any* faults?"

"I get drunk on a single glass of wine."

"You call that a fault?" Mercer chuckled, trying to reduce the gloom that had permeated the cabin. "I call that a reason for a weekend together in the Napa Valley."

Anika made a face of mock horror. "Ugh. You Americans sicken me. The Loire Valley or nothing."

The banter didn't last. The enormity of their situation overshadowed everything. Once they cleared the ramparts of the Greenland coast, Mercer had everyone at a window watching the snow and ice and rock below. Even though they had a few more minutes before reaching Delaney's reported path, he wanted them accustomed to the rough topography so they were better prepared to spot anything anomalous.

To intercept Delaney's route, they had to fly thirty miles into the hinterland before swinging north-northeast, back toward the coast at a shallow angle, their altitude reduced to a thousand feet above the ground. Hunched between the pilots' seats with the Geiger counter in his hands, Mercer estimated they were about forty miles south of where the plane went down.

Watching the terrain scroll under the DC-3, everyone kept a lookout for a flash of sunlight striking a metallic surface or any unnatural straight edges, like a wing. As Erwin had predicted, there wasn't anywhere near the amount of new snow here as had been around the Geo-Research camp. Large patches of bare rock appeared at irregular intervals, jagged peaks that showed above the ice. There were still enough snow-covered sections to land the plane, which also meant there was an increased possibility that the C-97 had been buried as deeply as Camp Decade. They'd know soon.

Far ahead he could see a fjord carved deep into the ice sheet, protected on all sides by sheer mountains. A quick guess put the plane wreck just south of where the narrow bay terminated. Mercer checked his watch. They had ten minutes before he would call off the search and order the pilots to land. He'd cut the margin as close as he could, balancing the need to locate the wreck with the time it took to find a safe landing site.

"Mercer!" It was one of Erwin's teammates, Wilhelm Treitschke, seated immediately behind the lavatory. "Ahead about four kilometers, just before that rock that looks like a shark fin."

Looking out the windshield, Mercer spotted the feature Will described and concentrated on the shadow staining the clear ice in front of it. For an instant he thought they'd found it. The size was right and it had an airplane's cruciform shape, but as he looked closer, he could tell it was just a rocky projection that hadn't quite broken through the surface. His mouth turned bitter.

"Good eyes, but that's not it. Keep looking."

A minute later, the copilot hit Mercer on the shoulder with the back of his hand and pointed. "There!"

Near where a wall of mountains rose before falling off into the fjord was a piece of debris sticking up from the ice like a tombstone. Battered and bent by decades of glacial movement, it was still recognizable as a section of an aircraft's wing. There was another piece of wreckage sitting on top of a low ridge of stone maybe a hundred yards from it.

The shape of the mountain looming over the wreck indicated that the plane had had the added misfortune of coming down in an avalanche channel. He imagined that when the C-97 crashed in the 1950s, its impact must have triggered an avalanche that buried it, hiding the wreckage from both air and ground searches. But now, with temperatures on the rise and record low snowfall, the aircraft had melted out of its frozen tomb. Since this part of Greenland went largely unexplored, it was possible the plane had lain exposed for years.

The dial on the radiation monitor hadn't twitched since he'd turned it on but Mercer was still concerned that the old plane was contaminated. He'd earlier instructed the pilot that if they did find the aircraft to land no closer than three miles from it. He looked at his watch again. Two minutes remained on his search timetable, which gave them only twelve minutes to land and get clear of the DC-3.

He tapped the pilot, pointed to the ground, and went to the rear to strap in. "We found it," he announced as he reached his seat. "We're landing now. Everyone, tighten your seat belts."

He sat next to Anika in the last row of seats, accepting a bundle of clothes to use as a cushion when they assumed the head-down crash position. "I'm scared," she said as the pitch of the engines changed.

"You shouldn't be. What are the chances that you survive a helicopter crash only to die in a plane crash?"

"How can you be so calm?"

"I'm faking it. Don't forget, this plane is designed to land on ice and snow, and the pilots know what they're doing. We'll be fine."

A moment before the landing, the copilot ordered the passengers to brace themselves. Mercer tucked his head into his lap, grabbing the back of his thighs as tightly as he could. He knew the landing would be rough and he thought he was prepared.

He wasn't. None of them were.

Flared nose up, the DC-3 skimmed the ground for a moment, its skis hissing and banging across the uneven surface. Then one of them hooked into a hardened piece of ice. The plane slammed hard, a jarring impact that nearly tore the fuselage apart. No longer moving in a straight line, the aircraft skipped and skidded, scrubbing off airspeed in a rapid deceleration that pitched the tail high. Amid the screams of the passengers was the explosive sound of the windscreens imploding. A solid wall of snow filled the cockpit and erupted through the connecting door. The two seats behind the bathroom tore free from the floor and launched themselves into a bulkhead. Wilhelm Treitschke and his companion, Gert Kreigsburg, were crushed against the metal wall, their necks snapping in identical pops.

As its momentum expended, the tail of the DC-3 dropped to the ground in a wrenching crash that bent the airframe and blew open the rear hatchway. The plane finally came to an uneven stop. The lash of cold air whipping into the cabin revived Mercer. He looked behind him. Ira had done a remarkable job securing the cargo. Despite the violence of the crash, the stack of crates hadn't shifted under the netting and pulled the trip wire.

Mercer unbuckled his lap belt and stood, swaying against a wave of nausea. The sounds assaulting his ears were pitiable. Several people were still screaming in pain and fear while others sobbed uncontrollably. Worse was the silence from the front of the plane.

The wall of snow filled the door leading to the cockpit. Buried somewhere inside were the pilots.

"We've got two minutes," Mercer bellowed, hoping to galvanize the survivors with his voice. Each word felt like a hammer pounding against his temples. He ached everywhere. "Anyone who can move grab a bundle of supplies and get the hell away."

Ira Lasko was the first to find his feet. He had to lift Erwin Puhl from his seat and hold him steady for a moment before they each took handfuls of gear and disappeared outside.

"Come on, Anika. You're next." Mercer tugged at her seat belt, freeing her.

"I'm okay," she said groggily, a trickle of blood escaping from her hairline, where she'd hit her head against the seat back in front of her.

"We've got to add 'lucky' to your list of attributes. We made it," Mercer said before turning serious. "Can you get out on your own?"

"I think so."

It was clear that she couldn't. "Ira," Mercer yelled out, "I need a hand in here."

Ira dashed back to the plane to help Anika and unload more gear while Mercer went forward to check on Marty, Ingrid, and Hilda. He didn't need to check the two meteorologists or pilots. Their fate was all too apparent.

"Let's go, Marty," Mercer shouted when he reached his seat and then fell silent. Marty had pushed Ingrid back in her seat and was trying to get her head to remain erect. He couldn't. The delicate bones in her neck were as pliable as rubber. She was dead. He looked up at Mercer blankly.

Mercer's voice dropped. "We can't help her, Marty. I'm sorry."

"I think she looked up just as the plane hit." He spoke with an unsettling monotone. "I even think I heard her neck break."

The clock was ticking. "Can you get out by yourself?"

"Yes, I, ah, yes." He stood and walked toward the rear exit as calmly as a seasoned passenger coming off a regular flight. He was in shock.

The heavyset Hilda, who Mercer recalled could move fifty-pound bags of potatoes with one beefy arm, was still folded over in the crash position, her arms dangling to the floor. He suspected she was dead until he saw that her shoulders were shaking. There were only a few seconds left.

He roughly pushed her back in her seat and unhooked her belt. The woman neither helped nor hindered his efforts. She was unconscious. And she weighed about two hundred pounds. Bending so he could dig a shoulder into her ample belly, Mercer heaved her limp body into a modified fireman's carry and strained to straighten again. His body had been pummeled by the accident and it protested every inch he rose but he managed to stand, staggering to find his balance.

"Oh Jesus," he groaned, moving down the aisle in a faltering lurch. "Did you have to sample every dish you prepared?"

On the way out the door he grabbed his leather sample bag by its strap. Ira had returned to the plane once again and helped Mercer jump to the snow. Together they hefted the inert chef away. They made it fifteen yards before the beeper on Ira's watch went off.

"Down!" he shouted and fell flat, collapsing the woman and Mercer.

The explosion was muffled by the cargo stacked around it, and its detonative energy was concentrated on the far side of the aircraft. Still the concussion hit with enough force to suck the air out of Mercer's lungs. Bits of debris and a hail of snow pelted him as he lay over Hilda to protect her from the worst of the blast. The bomb was far enough from the fuel tanks that there were no secondary detonations, which had been Mercer's biggest fear. He looked over his shoulder as the rumble died away.

The entire tail assembly was twisted away from the remainder of the fuselage and the roof above the bomb had vanished. Such a blast during the flight would have dropped the DC-3 out of the sky like a brick. Thankfully, the explosion wasn't powerful enough to completely destroy the aircraft. Enough remained to provide shelter until they were rescued. If they were rescued.

Mercer felt something warm and wet on his cheek, and he turned his head quickly. The chef lying beneath him was awake and her mouth was pressed to him in a grateful kiss. Her voice was muffled but he could hear her muttering, *"Danke, danke."*

The harder Mercer tried to lift himself from her, the tighter she held him in an embrace. She had a pleasant face, he noticed, and tears made her soft eyes look liquid, but her mustache was thicker than his if he skipped a day of shaving. She planted a long kiss on his mouth, easily smothering his struggles to free himself.

"Taking advantage of a woman in such a vulnerable state," Ira teased when Mercer finally regained his feet. "I expected more from you."

Mercer smiled, relieved at being alive despite the awful deaths of the pilots and the three others. He would not give in to survivor's guilt. "You okay?"

Lasko stood and brushed snow off his spare body. "I will be as long as she doesn't realize I helped save her."

"We lost five, Ira, including Ingrid."

"And we saved six," the ex-submariner replied sagely. "Don't think of the names. Just consider the numbers. It's the only way."

Anika Klein approached, limping slightly. She'd smeared some of the blood on her head trying to stanch the flow. She studied the wreckage before turning to Mercer. "I've got a feeling that one of us is jinxed, and I think it's me."

"If you knew what I've been through in the past couple of years, you'd know I'm the one with the bad juju." Mercer was only half joking. "Hey, Ira, can you check over the plane and make sure nothing's on fire? Erwin, how about an inventory of everything we've got that'll help us?"

"You got it."

"What about me?" Anika asked.

"As the only doctor in our ranks who can actually doctor people, you're in charge of our medical needs. Which begins with yourself. Your head's still bleeding. Then check on Marty. Ingrid died in the crash and he's . . . I don't know. Just check on him."

Mercer's next words were cut off by a shout from Ira Lasko. He was kneeling on the half-buried nose of the plane, scooping away snow as fast as he could. "One of the pilots is still alive!"

Marty Bishop reacted quicker than any of the others, racing to the entombed cockpit. He pushed aside Ira and attacked the snow clogging the windscreen as if frenzy alone could somehow expunge whatever he felt about Ingrid's death. In moments he was able to thrust his upper body through the shattered glass and touch the leather-clad arm thrusting out of the snow and ice. From the position of the arm, it was the co-pilot who grabbed on to Marty's offered hand and refused to let go.

Mercer and Ira swung around the plane and approached the cockpit from the cabin. Using pieces of torn fuselage as shovels, they began the laborious digging. Whenever they paused, they could hear Marty reassuring the stricken aviator through the snow. It took twenty minutes to clear away enough of the frozen debris for Anika Klein to worm her way into the cockpit to administer whatever aid the copilot needed.

"Mercer," she called from the hollow they had dug, "I need two lengths of metal or wood for a splint. His arm is broken. Also, get my bag. I've got medical supplies in there I'll need."

Hilda had already retrieved the kit and passed it forward. The next ten minutes passed in anxious silence punctuated once by a single shrill scream when

Anika reset the arm. It seemed the despair over the deaths of the others had been suspended while she worked.

Slowly, Anika's backside emerged from the cockpit as she half led, half dragged the wounded man from where he'd been trapped. His arm was bandaged and strapped to his chest, and the countless lacerations on his face had been cleaned. She'd already stitched closed the worst. His skin was stained with antiseptic. "He's going to be fine. I've got him pretty doped up," she said. "He's got to be kept warm to minimize shock." She turned to Marty, who had just entered the cabin from his vigil outside. "I need someone to stay with him. Are you up to it?"

Marty looked from the prone figure on the floor to where Ingrid still sat under a blanket Erwin had draped over her. His voice was iron. "I'll take care of him."

"Nice job," Mercer told Anika when they were outside. "With the copilot, and with Marty."

"He's stronger than you give him credit for. Only he doesn't know it, so neither does anyone else." She used snow to clean her hands.

Ira came up to them. Whatever mental trick he had used to get over the horrors of the past hour had worked. He seemed as unruffled and composed as always. "What's our next move?"

"I need to check on the crashed C-97. I want you to get this wreck site into shape. It's going to be our home for a while. Make sure Marty's sat-phone is okay so that when the solar max lets up we can get ourselves rescued."

Once everyone was organized and working, Mercer decided it was time to go. He made sure he had his Geiger counter and a few protein bars stuffed in his sample bag before beginning his walk to the other plane crash. He also took an ice ax, a silver "space blanket," and a small can of Sterno in case he couldn't get back before nightfall.

The trek was brutal. Each step broke through the

crust of snow, sinking him to his knees. It was an exhausting process to lift his foot clear to take another pace, and quickly his motion more resembled wading than walking. The wind scouring the flank of the mountain range hit him full in the face as he walked, oftentimes powerful enough to arrest his forward progress. He began sweating, and his breaks became more frequent. At each rest stop he would check the Geiger counter, mystified that it had yet to show any radiation. He began to wonder if Delaney's contamination had come from another source.

Although the wreckage of the C-97 Stratofreighter was only three miles away it took him two hours to reach it. From the air, they had seen only part of one wing and a scrap of fuselage, but as he approached he could see other pieces of debris—a landing gear assembly, a section of the retractable flaps, and a blade from one of her four props. Fifty years of ice movement had obliterated any semblance of order to the debris field, and Mercer was surprised to find as much as he had.

Two hundred yards beyond the wing fragment, the Geiger counter began to click. Mercer clamped his hand to the earphones, checking the display on the handheld unit. The amount of radiation was barely detectable, and his heart slowed again.

Using the counter as a guide, he searched for the area that showed the highest readings. In this fashion he found the bulk of the plane. It lay in a saddle of rock, wedged in place and nearly covered by ice. Only the stump of its vertical stabilizer sticking from the ice was exposed. He swept the Geiger counter along the length of the plane, noting the readings were strongest where he estimated the cockpit would be.

"Why there?" he wondered aloud. If there was a radiation leak on the plane, surely it would come from the cargo section at the rear.

Under the mantle of ice, he could see places were the fuselage had been ripped open by either the crash or avalanche that once covered the plane. He selected one of these darker shadows close to the cockpit and began working with the ice ax. Soon he had settled in to an easy rhythm. He rested every hour, aware that the sun could go down before he got back to the others, but he had to make certain he didn't get overheated, an ironic condition considering the temperature had dropped below freezing.

By three in the afternoon, he'd chopped his way to the aircraft's metal skin. The rip in the aluminum wasn't large enough for him to crawl through, forcing him to hack at it with the ax. Strips of metal tore away each time he heaved back on the handle. It took a further half hour to open a large-enough hole. The slightly elevated radiation reading when he'd penetrated into the plane was still well below a dangerous level.

All the time he'd been working, he'd mentally prepared himself to enter the plane. Yet now that he was ready, apprehension struck. He didn't know what he would find inside or what it would mean to the survivors relying on him. Resigned to the task, Mercer lowered himself into the aircraft's belly.

The interior was dim and he flicked on a small penlight. It revealed a ruby-crusted corpse staring at him sightlessly. Mercer scrabbled backward, tripping over his feet and falling heavily. He remained on the floor, ignoring the pain of freezing air in his lungs as he hyperventilated. He'd known there were bodies on the plane, but he hadn't been ready.

When he was calm again, he levered himself upright and flashed the light at the body that he assumed had been the radioman/navigator. The ruby effect that had so startled him was the result of frozen blood around the man's mouth and splashed over his flight jacket. It looked like he'd also bled from the nose and . . . Mercer leaned closer. *Jesus, his eyes. He had bled from his eyes.*

There was more blood in the snow on the cabin floor, pools and strings of it like some obscene abstract painting. He flicked the beam toward the cockpit.

Nearly all the windscreens had been smashed in by the crash fifty years ago. The snow forced into the cockpit had solidified into a misshapen block of ice. The copilot was strapped in his seat, his head turned away as if the light could still bother him. The snow piled up to his chest was stained crimson. He too had mysteriously bled out.

Mercer had been right. With the navigator in his seat and the copilot focused in the beam of light, the body he'd found in Camp Decade was the pilot, Jack Delaney. He flicked the light to the pilot's seat to make sure. What he saw made him stumble back again.

Major Delaney sat there as if still flying the plane, his cap still in place although he no longer wore his leather coat. Much of his face had turned gray and shriveled over the years, so his dazzling teeth looked particularly gruesome. A death's head smile with aviator glasses.

A nika didn't know how many times she had checked her watch or cleared the condensed breath from the window. The routine had become automatic, although with the setting of the sun her pace had increased. Her lower lip felt raw from constant chewing.

Mercer hadn't said anything about staying at the other wreck until the next morning, nor had he taken enough supplies to sustain him. The thick ground fog that had settled in the past hour only served to increase her anxiety. Since they could be stranded for weeks, they couldn't waste anything for a signal fire, and if Mercer lost sight of his footprints coming back, he'd never find the DC-3.

Initially, she'd told herself her concern had come solely from the fact that Philip Mercer was the undisputed leader of the group. His actions had saved them all, and his absence, even for a few hours, had left the others sullen and pessimistic. Their dinner had been eaten with a minimum of conversation, and everyone had retreated to separate areas of the fuselage to sleep. Anika had stayed awake to check on Magnus, the thirty-five-year-old Icelandic copilot. Marty had been by her side until he too had succumbed to exhaustion. Ira Lasko had remained awake the longest, falling asleep only an hour ago and telling her she should do the same. He'd also assured her that Mercer knew what he was doing.

She wasn't so sure. While she'd never been to Greenland, she'd spent more time in harsh conditions than any of the other survivors. She knew the dangers of hypothermia, had seen the effects of deep frostbite, and knew how fragile a lone man was outside with the temperature down well below freezing.

Now that she was in the second hour of her lonely vigil, Anika allowed her mind to wander to the other reason for her concern, a more personal reason. She didn't know Mercer well enough to think beyond the physical, but on that level she was attracted to him. His was a natural masculinity that other men strove to attain through bravado and swagger. Yet there was a self-deprecation in him, as if he tried to hide his talents. He was a year or two older than her but he was like a buoyant teen who hadn't yet gotten used to becoming an adult. It was charming.

Anika remembered the look he'd given her after they had run the gauntlet of fire. It had been a reflection of her own desire. Experience told her to temper her feelings because of the drama surrounding their first meeting and everything since. She'd taken lovers whom she'd shared dangers with, mostly fellow rock climbers, and every relationship had crumbled under the weight of the subsequent normalcy. While it was unfair to compare Mercer to these other men, she suspected the results would be the same.

Still, it was fun to think otherwise.

She didn't know she'd fallen asleep until a noise startled her awake. The survivors had built a snow wall to screen the gaping hole at the rear of the aircraft, fashioning a crude door at the bottom with a section of bent metal. They used tarps found in the remaining cargo to cover the other holes in the fuselage. As a result the plane, though chilly, was warm enough to keep them alive. It was the door being pushed aside that woke her.

The apparition who entered in the faint glow emitted by their single gas lantern looked like some mythical creature. It was covered from head to foot in snow, with icicles dangling from the scarf covering its mouth. The fur trim around its head was a solid halo of ice.

As it moved, knots of snow fell away like it was shedding its skin. It was Mercer.

Without a word, he lumbered down the aisle and doused the lantern, plunging the cabin into total darkness.

"Mercer, what is it?" Anika asked, confused and still half asleep.

"Quiet!" His labored breath sounded as though he'd run a marathon.

Then she heard it—a steady and deep thumping that seemed to come from every direction at once. She didn't recognize the strange sound, but the others who'd been roused by Mercer's entrance did.

"It's the rotor-stat," Ira said at last.

"I heard it about half an hour ago." Mercer unwound his scarf and pulled down his hood. "I was afraid you might have a signal fire going, so I ran back as fast as I could. Even with the fog, I could see the lantern through the window a good way off."

"What is it doing here?" Erwin could be heard fumbling for his glasses. "Looking for us?"

"They don't know we're here." Mercer's parka was so ice crusted it remained erect when he dropped it on the floor. "And I think the airship is miles away. We're just hearing its echo ricocheting off the mountains."

"Then why is it in the area?" Marty asked.

Chills racked Mercer before he could answer, his body quaking so strongly that he had to clamp his jaw. "I assume it's moving Geo-Research's base northward like they wanted all along."

"Are they looking for Delaney's downed Strato-freighter?" Ira had a towel to hand to Mercer, whose hair was a mass of frozen sweat.

"I think they're searching for something else, considering Jack Delaney and the rest of his crew are still sitting in the plane."

Mercer's bombshell was met with a collective gasp. In the following silence, the sound of the dirigible began to fade. It was Ira who finally asked the question on all their minds. "If Delaney's in his plane, whose body did we find at Camp Decade?"

He let the question hang for a moment before turning to Anika. "You want to answer that one?"

Anika's stomach gave a sickening slide, and she had to grab on to a seat to steady herself. Earlier, she'd thought that hearing Gunther Rath at the base camp had brought everything full circle. That hadn't been quite true then, but it was now. This had started with her grandfather's search for hidden Nazi treasure and an interview with a man who had been an engineer. The two together meant a secret cache someplace, obviously in Greenland since Rath, Mercer, and she were here. Until this instant she'd never considered whom the Nazis had forced to dig their repository and never imagined that any of them could have survived on this bleak wasteland long enough to reach Camp Decade. Ten years had passed from the end of the war until the base was abandoned and yet there was no other explanation.

Her voice was barely above a whisper. "He was the last victim of the Holocaust."

Mercer relit the lantern, setting it to a weak flicker, and crawled into his sleeping bag. "Tell us what you know."

"My grandfather has spent his life trying to recover property looted from the Jews during the Nazi occupation of Europe. Recently he received some information from an unknown source in Russia about a shipment of gold taken from Stalingrad and sent to Hamburg. The documents also revealed that an engineer named Otto Schroeder had played a role in this transfer, an operation I learned was called the Pandora Project." As she got further into the story, Anika's voice firmed and her outrage returned stronger than ever.

"Up until ten days ago, Schroeder was living outside of Munich. I went to interview him about the gold. When I arrived at his house, he was being tortured by a group of men led by Gunther Rath, the man who planted the bomb on this plane. With his dying breath, Schroeder said that the gold—and I'm talking about tons of it—was only part of the operation and that Philip Mercer was someone who could help me." She looked to him, searching for an answer in his eyes as to why.

"Around this time," Mercer said, "I received an e-mail from a lawyer in Munich telling me that an unnamed client was sending me a package of documents." He dug them out of his sample bag and held them close to the lamp for the others to see. "Until this journal arrived, I'd never heard of Otto Schroeder. Nor do I know why he would send it to me. And since it's written in German, I have no idea what's in it."

Anika picked up the tale again. "Just before I left the *Njoerd*, I learned that Mercer was at the Geo-Research base. I knew that somehow we had been set up. Right after the helicopter crash, I went through the mailbag and buried anything addressed to him. I couldn't take the chance that Schroeder's information might be passed to someone I didn't know or trust. I had planned to go back later to retrieve the letter I'd hidden a hundred meters from the chopper."

Ira looked at Mercer. "Our stowaway wasn't a stowaway after all."

"She told me just before we discovered the bomb." Mercer shifted in his sleeping bag. "Because of a practical joke played on me by my friend Harry, she never got the letter she was looking for. I suspect the envelope Anika took was from Charlie Bryce." He indicated that she should continue.

"Because Schroeder was an engineer, my grandfather and I believe that he was involved with creating a secret storehouse for Nazi plunder far from where the Allies would find it. An enormous hoard of treasure was recovered in old salt mines at the close of the war, but there are still billions of dollars' worth of art, antiques, jewelry, and gold bullion that was never found. Schroeder's statement that the gold we sought was only part of the project made us think we had stumbled onto another of their hidden depositories."

"Here on Greenland?" Marty Bishop asked. "Seems a bit excessive even for the Nazis."

"I would agree if Mercer and I weren't here with Rath."

"How did Schroeder know the two of you were coming here?"

"I don't know," Anika admitted.

"It was part of the setup." Mercer took a sip from his brandy bottle, which had survived the crash. "The Russians who sent the information leading Anika's grandfather to Otto Schroeder chose him rather than better-known Nazi hunters because they already knew the gold is on Greenland and that Anika was coming here. I'm willing to bet that they were the ones who told Schroeder that Anika could trust me."

"You're right," she cried. "He said that he received a mysterious call about you a few weeks before his murder."

"That doesn't explain how they knew Mercer would be here," Ira pointed out.

"Either they got that information from the Surveyor's Society Web site and just chose to include me," Mercer said. A dark implication came clear and he hesitated. "Or because Charlie Bryce engineered it so that I was here at the same time as Anika."

"That would mean Charlie's part of this too," Marty said doubtfully. "I've known him for years. He's not a Nazi hunter or anything like that."

"I've known him a long time too," Mercer agreed. "As unlikely as it sounds, that's the only explanation that works."

"So what did you mean that the body at Camp Decade was the last victim of the Holocaust?" Hilda asked. Because she didn't speak English, Erwin Puhl had been translating the conversation for her.

"I think he was a Jewish slave laborer used to excavate some sort of cave for the Germans to hide their plunder." Tears welled in Anika's eyes. "Somehow he was left behind and managed to survive for ten years until he discovered Camp Decade. I can't imagine the horror and isolation he endured only to find his one chance at rescue had already been abandoned."

The bitter irony left a long vacuum in their discussion, each thinking about the terror of such a death.

"He could have been a German soldier," Ira offered after several long minutes.

"No," Mercer replied. "The evidence was on his arm."

Anika sniffled and wiped her cheeks. "You noticed?"

"I didn't think anything of it at the time, but now its significance is apparent." Everyone hung on his words. "The body we found had a scar on the inside of his arm as if he'd been burned. I think it was self-inflicted to erase the identification number the Nazis tattooed on his skin when he became a victim of their Final Solution."

"Is there any proof to this?" Marty asked.

"If there is, it'll be in here." Mercer handed Schroeder's journal to Anika. "Figure out what you can. We've got other problems to discuss."

Moving close to the lamp, Anika took the leather-bound manuscript and began thumbing through to the relevant sections.

"So what about—"

Mercer cut Ira off. "We'll get to the other questions later. With Geo-Research moving their operation up this way, we can't risk staying with the plane. They're going to spot it once the fog lifts."

"The number one rule of survival is staying with your vehicle," Marty reminded.

"We don't have a choice," Mercer countered him. "If Rath finds us, we're dead. Our only option is to keep moving."

"How long do you think we'll last without shelter?" Marty snapped. He'd been prepared to fight Geo-

Research to return to Greenland, but Ingrid's death had once again sapped him of his drive. He didn't care about Nazis and looted treasure and Holocaust survivors. He wanted this nightmare to end.

"Longer than we'd survive if Rath finds us," Mercer flared before checking his irritation. He had to remind himself how far the survivors were out of their league. He studied the others and saw fear reflected in their eyes. "Sorry. None of us deserve what's happened, but that doesn't change the fact that we're in this together. We've managed to hold on this long, and I think I know a way to keep us safe."

"How?"

"It all depends on what Anika finds in that journal," Mercer answered. "It's pretty clear that Geo-Research's scientific cover story is just that—a story. They, or whoever's behind them, are on Greenland to find the treasure. Now, in order to save themselves thousands of man-hours, I suspect that the Nazis expanded an existing cavern for their warehouse rather than mine a whole new chamber. It's my experience that if there's one cave in an area, there are bound to be more. We can hide out in one far from the one the Nazis used until Rath and his merry band leave or we get the sat-phone working again."

"Sounds reasonable to me." Ira looked around the dim cabin for agreement.

"How far do you estimate we are from the cave?" Erwin asked anxiously.

"About thirty kilometers," Mercer said and just then realized something he'd overlooked earlier. The distances on the map he'd discovered in Camp Decade were written in the metric system. An American pilot would have used standard or nautical miles. He shook his head in self-reproach. He should have noticed such a discrepancy immediately. He'd already calculated the deflection in compass headings, so the navigation had been done. His earlier foray told him that they were in for a grueling march.

"Can you lead us there?" Hilda asked through Puhl.

"No." Mercer wasn't going to risk their lives by pretending he had all the answers. "But Anika has experience in these conditions. I trust her to get us to safety."

"We've got a problem." Anika looked up from Otto Schroeder's journal, her eyes pinched from the strain of reading in such low light. "I haven't finished the whole thing yet but I have something that makes your plan unfeasible."

"What's the problem?"

"Otto Schroeder was a combat engineer in the German Army. Before that he had trained as a mining engineer. He was sent to Greenland in 1943 as part of the Pandora Project to help expand a network of caverns discovered under a glacier. The orders had been cut by Hitler himself. He never knew what became of his work, because two months into the project he was caught in a rockslide and had to be evacuated. He says in his journal that a thousand Jewish and Gypsy slaves were being used in the excavation and that the scope of the mining was increasing. He also said that they were dying off at an average of ten a day."

The figure was sobering. With his intimate knowledge of mining practices, Mercer had a better grasp at the unspeakably brutal conditions those poor souls had faced.

Anika continued. "Schroeder's principal task before tunneling commenced was to mine an air shaft to the surface through an estimated thousand feet of ice."

"Hold on." Her statement didn't make sense. Mercer thought she'd read it wrong. "Are you sure he had to mine an air shaft first? That would mean they started underground and worked their way up."

"That's the problem." Anika paused. "The cavern is buried under a mountain at the end of a fjord and was accessible only by submarine. After completing the air shaft, Schroeder was to create a dock for the supply submarines and hack out more space in the cave for dormitories and other work spaces."

Mercer cursed. "The air shaft is what Rath is looking for."

Anika nodded. "Which means there aren't any other caves for us to hide in."

"And we haven't addressed one issue that we need to." Ira shot Mercer a significant look. Mercer knew what he was about to say and nodded. "We didn't tell you that the body we found in Camp Decade is radioactive. He may have picked up the contamination from the C-97 when he took Delaney's flight jacket but Mercer and I already discounted the idea that the U.S. military would leave atomic materials lying around."

"I checked the plane," Mercer interrupted. "Readings were the same there as in Camp Decade. It's not the source."

"That means the radiation came from the cavern we're going to be humping our way toward," Ira concluded. "Since he still gave a reading on the Geiger counter after fifty years, whatever's down there has gotta be hotter than hell."

Mercer looked to where Erwin Puhl huddled silently in his sleeping bag, the lantern glow reflecting off his glasses like tiny sunbursts. "How about it, Erwin? Are you ready to drop your cover story and tell us what you know?"

It was such an unexpected question that they all turned to the German meteorologist. For his part, Erwin tried to look shocked, but he'd experienced too much trauma in the past few days to sustain the facade. "How did you know?" he asked simply.

"Your friendship with Igor Bulgarin," Mercer said. Erwin knew what he meant but the rest waited for an explanation. "When Igor and I first met, he told me he was coming to Greenland to search for meteor fragments. The only problem with his story is that finding meteorites on Greenland is next to impossible. They do it in Antarctica all the time because there's so little precipitation that much of it is considered a desert. Chunks of space rock can lie around for years waiting to be picked up. Here, they're usually buried in minutes."

He looked around the cabin. "I read about an expedition in 1998 that spent six weeks on Greenland's west coast looking for microscopic bits of the Kangilia meteor. That one weighed an estimated one hundred tons and there was a video and satellite information telling them where to look. They didn't find a trace. There's no way that one man walking around the ice could ever hope to find extraterrestrial debris." Mercer returned his gaze to Erwin. "I figured that, since you were friends for years, you already knew that Igor's cover was bullshit and knew what he was really doing here."

Puhl didn't deny the accusation.

Mercer took his deductions to their obvious conclusion. "He must have known about the Nazi cache and gone into Camp Decade because he suspected the body might have come from the cavern. Someone in Geo-Research knew what he was doing and murdered him to keep it a secret."

Erwin's lack of reaction told Mercer that the meteorologist had already figured out Igor's "accident" was premeditated murder. His near-catatonia in the past few days was likely due to the fear that his friendship with Bulgarin meant he was next.

"Do you know who killed him?" Ira asked Mercer.

"Since Igor was struck on the back of the head, the murderer had to be someone he didn't suspect and would turn his back to. The killer also had to be strong enough to bludgeon a man who was the largest in the camp. And finally the killer dragged the corpse out of officers' area and abandoned it when he reached the first major obstacle. This means he wasn't strong enough to actually carry the body."

"Makes sense. So who was it?"

"The only person who fits all three criteria is Greta Schmidt," Mercer answered and received a number of dubious looks.

"I think he's right," Erwin said after a moment.

"Although Igor and I didn't think Geo-Research knew who we really were and why we were on Greenland, we did discuss people we should be careful about. Neither of us considered that Greta could be part of this."

"Erwin, do you know if Geo-Research is affiliated with a company called Kohl?" Anika asked. "Schroeder mentioned the name in his journal as the company given the actual contract to dig the cavern. He was among a handful of military experts sent to help."

"Kohl bought Geo-Research last year so they could hide behind their scientific credentials and execute their true aim."

"Which is the recovery of the gold?" Marty asked.

Erwin echoed Schroeder's words. "The gold is only a small part of what's going on."

"What were the Germans hiding?"

"They weren't hiding anything. They were trying to recover something, something that was never meant to be on this planet."

Mercer put it together quicker than the others. "A radioactive meteorite that landed here in 1943?"

"Not quite," Erwin said. "Most of it slammed into Russia in 1908."

The sudden insight came to Mercer in a rush, and despite the horror surrounding this search and the loss they had already felt, he couldn't help but be excited. They were talking about one of the greatest scientific mysteries of the twentieth century. There was a hushed awe in his voice. "Tunguska."

"Yes, Dr. Mercer. The Nazis were looking for a piece of the Tunguska meteor that exploded over Siberia on June 30, 1908."

"How? Why?"

Puhl looked at the blank faces of the others. "For those of you who aren't familiar with it, the Tunguska explosion has remained an enigma since it occurred. Some theorized it was an asteroid, others a comet or black hole. Some even believe it was the detonation of a UFO's nuclear power plant. What everyone does agree on is that it leveled a thousand square miles of forest, although trees at the very epicenter were left standing like certain buildings in Hiroshima after the atom bomb. Seismographs as distant as Washington, D.C., registered the shock wave, and an unearthly glow was seen as far away as Copenhagen. Furthermore, eyewitness accounts say that a portion of the object was observed continuing in a northwesterly direction and was actually gaining altitude *after* the explosion.

"To answer Mercer's questions as to how and why the Germans were searching for the wayward fragment those witnesses saw, I have to give a bit more history." Erwin accepted the brandy bottle when Ira passed it to him. "The first scientific expedition to search for the site wasn't conducted until 1927 by a man named Leonid Kulik. He is important to remember because he was captured by the Germans and died at a prison camp in 1942. During weeks of brutal interrogation he revealed everything he knew about the mysterious impact.

"After they learned the truth about the blast, the Germans spared nothing to secure his research notes. In fact they sacrificed thousands of troops in what became one of the most desperate battles of the entire war just to find a couple of notebooks." He paused again, more contemplative than dramatic. "When the war broke out, Kulik had sent his more secret findings to an associate in Stalingrad."

"Are you saying the Battle of Stalingrad was all about a couple of notebooks?" Marty scoffed. "Give me a break."

"No, but hundreds of commando teams were sent behind Russian lines during the fighting to find them. Thousands of men died in the search. When it came to Hitler's obsessions, fact is a lot stranger than fiction. Let me tell you another story to illustrate this." Erwin lectured as if to a child. "In April of 1942, he sent a team of scientists equipped with state-of-the-art radar gear to Rugen Island in the Baltic Sea to test a new theory that he had. Hitler had become convinced that while the Earth was indeed round, we didn't live on its outer surface but on the inner curve of a hollow sphere, like insects in a salad bowl. The scientists spent weeks beaming radar waves into the sky hoping for a rebounded signal from the British naval base at Scapa Flow.

"You must realize at the time Germany lagged far behind the Allies when it came to radar equipment and yet *Der Führer*," Puhl mocked the title, "wasted valuable resources on a quest doomed to fail."

"What's this have to do with Tunguska?"

"Not all of the ludicrous scientific avenues the Nazis pursued during the war were such dismal mistakes. The Pandora Project was much more successful. As I said, the first official investigation into the Tunguska blast didn't occur until 1927. However, there had been a great deal of local interest. The first unofficial search was sent out a year after the celestial impact, although they were turned back because of weather and the site's inaccessibility. It wasn't until two years after that, in 1911, that anyone saw the devastation first hand.

"While Tunguska is one of the most remote tracts in the Siberian taiga, news of this success reached the Imperial capital of St. Petersburg in 1912 because so many of the explorers died in the forest or shortly after their return from the site. Their deaths were horrifying, a mysterious disease that dissolved the flesh from their bodies. They ended up as nothing more than skeletal figures."

Mercer's mind flashed to the photograph of Stefansson Rosmunder lying in a hospital bed in Reykjavik, knowing now what had killed him.

"The peasants believed," Puhl continued, "that the devil had punched the forest, leveling the trees, and it was his residual evil that killed their men. Some returned from the impact zone with pieces of a strange rock that was warm to the touch, claiming it was pieces of Satan's skin. Entire settlements where this unknown rock was stored died of the same wasting disease, usually just days after the explorers' homecoming. Priests called in said they knew what dark forces were at work and had all the samples encased in golden icons, confident that they would contain the evil that had killed an estimated one thousand people. Their idea worked."

His statement was met with skepticism until Mercer spoke. "That was a hell of an idea even if they didn't understand why. If the rocks they collected were radioactive fragments from the meteor, gold would act as an effective shield because of its density. Not as good as lead, but efficient nonetheless."

Erwin nodded his head. "Kulik's research later proved that gold dampened the radiation much more effectively than lead. He was never able to explain why this radioactivity behaved so differently, and in his defense, little was known about radiation at this time. It was a mysterious force only a few were even aware of."

Mercer's scientific background allowed him to see the hole in Puhl's story. "How is it such a potent radiation source didn't kill *all* the men who went to the impact site?"

"Kulik knew that all radioactive material decayed in what is termed 'half-lives.' His theory was that the meteor pieces decayed unevenly, from the outside in, and as the surface becomes inert in a few months, it shields itself from more decay. He believed this phenomenon was caused by a reaction with our atmosphere or perhaps an effect of solar radiation breaking down something within the fragments. Neither he nor anyone else is really certain. He guessed that only those chunks the peasants handled roughly and broke away the nonreactive coating were the ones that caused the deaths."

Noting a number of flaws with this theory, Mercer held his tongue. He wasn't a planetary geologist. They were talking about an element that had never been seen on earth before and had never been examined by modern science. He didn't know what fantastic substances could be swirling around the universe on the backs of interstellar comets. Every few years, scientists working with particle accelerators added new elements to the end of the periodic table. It was possible that the meteor was composed of some stable element we hadn't yet discovered.

"Okay, back to my story," Erwin said, and the group became attentive again. Few of them understood or cared about the physics. They just wanted to hear the rest of his enthralling tale. "In 1912, Czarina Alexandra sent her most trusted emissary to Vana-vara, the city closest to the blast, to discover what was killing her people. The man had a religious background and quickly adopted the idea of sealing the fragments in golden icons. He had teams sent into the forest to scour for more bits of 'Satan's Fist,' as he called it."

"I'll be damned," Mercer exclaimed. "That explains why nothing of the original meteorite has ever been found at Tunguska. Someone cleaned the site before Kulik or any subsequent expedition ever reached it."

"Precisely," Erwin agreed. "Even with protective boxes to seal the meteorites as soon as they were discovered, hundreds more perished in the task. This priest had a golden suit made for himself so he could work with the samples, making sure that they would never again harm another soul."

"Who was the priest?" Ira asked.

"His given name was Grigori Efymovich Novykh."

Anika Klein was so wrapped in the story it took her a second to realize she knew that name. Or at least the more famous one the man was known by. "Rasputin!"

"Yes, Rasputin was the Czarina's emissary and he spent two years at Tunguska recovering the meteorites. Upon his return to St. Petersburg, he refused to tell anyone about what he had found. World War One had just begun and he feared that his discovery would be used as a weapon. Even when the Germans first used poison gas at Bolimov in January 1915, he would not divulge the presence of this extraordinary killer. As the war dragged on, rumors surrounding what he'd found grew and he knew it was only a matter of time before he was tortured to reveal what had killed the villagers in Tunguska. With pressure against him mounting, Rasputin formed the Brotherhood of Satan's Fist, enlisting a few trusted priests so they would continue to protect the secret after he was gone. Rasputin was murdered in December of 1916, not because of his influence over the royal family as the history books record, but because he wouldn't tell certain military men what he knew."

"So he wasn't the psychotic demon people think he was?"

Erwin chuckled with dark humor. "Oh, he was that too. Tales of his debauchery are, if anything, milder than the truth. But those in the Brotherhood saw him as a man who might have saved humanity from its own destructive impulses."

"So how does this involve the Nazis?"

"The first Russian revolution swept through St. Petersburg a few weeks after Rasputin's murder, and those who knew the rumors about Satan's Fist were exiled or executed. Interest in the Tunguska blast waned. The Brotherhood hid the fifty icons containing the meteorite fragments in various churches and monasteries around the country, moving them often as communist forces either confiscated or razed the buildings. And as members grew older, new people were brought in. Leonid Kulik was one of them, the first who wasn't a priest. He was asked to join so he would not reveal some of the anomalous findings he had made at the impact site, like the fact that he knew others had been there before him."

"How many members were there at any given time?" Mercer asked. Like the others, he'd already deduced that Erwin Puhl and Igor Bulgarin were part of the Brotherhood.

"Usually never more than six or eight. Our small

size helped ensure our anonymity. It was Kulik who determined the true nature of what the Brotherhood safeguarded, and it was his recommendation shortly before Germany invaded the Soviet Union that the icons be destroyed. He would not allow this horror to be unleashed on the world. Much more was known about radiation by then and he feared that physicists could build an atomic bomb from the fragments.

"All but one icon were encased in cement and transported far out to sea, where they were dumped. Because gold won't corrode in seawater, they will remain dormant forever. At the same time this was going on, Kulik calculated the trajectory of the piece of meteor that eyewitnesses said skimmed off the atmosphere and vanished. His next goal was to track down this other piece to ensure it didn't get discovered by anyone else. That is when the Nazis launched their lightning strike into the Soviet Union. Kulik was captured before the last icon could be shipped from the isolated abbey where it had been hidden and before he could organize an expedition to find the other fragments."

"Which landed here?"

"Yes." Erwin soothed his throat with another sip of brandy. "The Nazis eventually learned of the missing icon from Kulik, sent a commando team deep into Russia to steal it, and secured his notebooks from Stalingrad, which gave the coordinates to where the last piece of Satan's Fist had landed."

Anika's dark eyes shimmered with the same passion that so infected her grandfather. "Then they launched the Pandora Project using looted gold to build their own storage boxes for any radioactive material they discovered. Once they found the meteorites, they sent Otto Schroeder to dig them out of the ice."

Nodding, Erwin polished his glasses. "By this time the allies were regularly flying over Greenland in aerial convoys ferrying aircraft to England."

"The 'Lost Squadron' we were talking about earlier was just such a flight," Mercer added.

"Yes. The radioactive heat generated within the stones had melted the fragments down to bedrock. Because of these flights, the Germans couldn't risk tunneling to them from the surface, so they approached from the sea in submarines, eventually finding a cavern under a glacier that was within five miles of where the meteor landed. They planned to use the cave as a staging area before driving a long tunnel through ice and rock to reach the fragments." Erwin looked over to Anika, who still had the journal open on her lap. "You don't need to finish Schroeder's journal. I've already read it. They had completed the air shaft and pier for the sub and had just commenced the tunnel to the cache when Schroeder was injured. He didn't know what happened here after he was injured."

"Do you?" Marty asked.

"No one knows except the poor slave Mercer found in Camp Decade."

Something Puhl had said struck Anika. Her brow furled and her thin eyebrows arched. Her tone was accusatory. "When did you read Schroeder's journal?"

Erwin looked away, pained. "Shortly after you went to interview him," he said evasively.

"How shortly?" Her anger rose because she was pretty sure of the answer.

"We found it in his house after driving off Rath and his neo-Nazi thugs."

Anika exploded. "Those snipers were your people? You son of a bitch! You were there the whole time and you let Schroeder die. You let me get shot." And then everything else came clear. "It was you who set this whole thing up—my *opa*, me. You fucking bastard!"

She lunged from her seat and would have reached Puhl had she not gotten tangled in her sleeping bag and fallen. Mercer dove to pin her to the deck, holding her arms over her head so she couldn't squirm free. She was a foot shorter than he, eighty pounds lighter, but for a few desperate seconds he was afraid she'd beat him. Fury augmented her strength, so she was like an enraged animal.

"Anika, stop it," Mercer pleaded, his teeth gritting against the pain as she bit his shoulder.

She got a hand free and went for his eyes, her fingers cocked like talons. Mercer ducked his head and felt her try to tear a piece of skin from his cheek. And then it was over. Anika went completely limp. Mercer opened his eyes, confused, wondering what had calmed her. Chef Hilda stood over them massaging one fist. She said something over her shoulder for Erwin to translate.

"She knew you would never strike a woman, so she did it for you."

Hilda gave Mercer a proud smile and a wink.

"Danke," he replied, checking on Anika. She had a growing bruise under her left eye, but otherwise she'd be fine. He moved her back to her seat, secured her seat belt to stop her from charging the instant she woke and leveled a gaze at Erwin. "She's right, you know. You are a son of a bitch. What gives you the right to drag innocent people into your fight?"

"In this fight, no one is innocent. The Brotherhood of Satan's Fist has spent nearly a century protecting the world from what we know. I think for that kind of dedication we should be allowed to involve others if we need them."

"But why involve Anika and her grandfather? Or me?"

"I will answer your second question first," Erwin said calmly. "We did not get you involved. You were already scheduled to come to Greenland with Geo-Research. It was just luck on our part. We mentioned your name to Schroeder as a possible ally in case something went wrong with our plans. You have a reputation for being a very capable man."

Mercer remained unconvinced, but if Erwin was revealing the truth about the cavern and Anika's grandfather, why would he lie about him?

"I don't know this Charles Bryce you mentioned

earlier," Puhl continued, "so I think his invitation for you to join the expedition to Camp Decade was legitimate."

"And Anika?"

"We sent information to her grandfather that would lead him to Schroeder in the hopes that he would be able to expose the Kohl Company and the Pandora Project. It wasn't until we followed Anika to Schroeder's house that we realized our security had been compromised. Gunther Rath, who is the special-projects director for Kohl, somehow learned about Schroeder and had beaten us there. We suspect that Anika's grandfather's office in Vienna was bugged.

"Igor and I chased off Rath and his group. Well, Igor and another Brother chased them off. I don't know the first thing about guns. We broke into Schroeder's house and found the diary he kept hidden. We gave it to a lawyer in Munich to forward to you. The operation was falling apart and once we reached Greenland we feared we would need your help, considering Rath's brutality. By this time Anika had vanished, so we couldn't warn her off. I didn't know her whereabouts until we heard the SOS from that helicopter. We never intended for anyone to get hurt. None of us were supposed to be here. Geo-Research's expedition would have been canceled had Anika been able to reveal what we intended her to learn." His voice trailed off.

Mercer sat back in his seat, trying to absorb everything. It would take a while, he knew, maybe forever. It was an amazing story. Meteors, radiation, secret brotherhoods, Rasputin, Nazis, neo-Nazis, Nazi hunters, and a planeload of innocent people trapped on a glacier between a Gunther Rath and his goal. "What do you think, Ira?"

"Since we kicked ass in W.W. Two, we can assume that the Germans never got the meteorites. Which means they've been down there for the sixty years since the start of the Pandora Project."

"Go on."

"Makes me wonder why this Rath character is so hot to find them now. This thing's been in the works for a while, considering Kohl bought Geo-Research to spearhead their hunt a year ago. What I want to know is what happened last year to make this such a priority. Any ideas, Erwin?"

"We don't know," he admitted.

"Ah, guys," Marty called. "This has been very interesting but it doesn't help us. We've survived one murder attempt but I doubt we'll survive the next if we stick around."

"We should try for the air shaft," Mercer said, looking at Puhl. "Rath knows that Igor Bulgarin was part of the Brotherhood because of his interest in the body. Do you think he's aware you're part of it too?"

"Since they didn't kill me at the base, I doubt it. There have been only a few Brothers who weren't Russian and Rath knows I'm German. When Igor set up our being here, he falsified some of my records so it didn't show I had studied in Moscow when East Germany was their vassal state. Rath has nothing to connect me to the Brotherhood."

Mercer remembered Erwin making certain that none of the Geo-Research people were in earshot when he explained how he knew about Igor's alcoholism aboard the *Njoerd*. In retrospect, his secrecy seemed well warranted.

"Better and better. Rath doesn't know we're aware of the cave. When he finds this plane abandoned, he'll assume we made a run for the coast, our only logical choice. If we can reach the air shaft before him, we can seal ourselves inside and wait until he gives up looking for it. He can't search forever because Geo-Research has obligations to other scientific teams coming to their camp in a few weeks. We can make it until then."

"How?" Marty asked. "That cave is full of deadly radiation, for Christ's sake."

"No, it isn't. And the survivor we found at Camp Decade proves it. He lived down there for ten years, eating supplies left by the Nazis, no doubt, until loneliness or madness forced him to leave."

"And how do you know a sudden radiation leak didn't force him out?"

"Erwin said that Russian villagers exposed to the radiation died within days. If he'd been dosed, he never would have made it to Decade."

"Okay, but why do you think we can beat Rath? His company dug the damned air shaft. The rotor-stat is probably moving them there as we speak."

"I doubt it. Remember, they brought four Sno-Cats here as well as the Land Cruiser. There's no need for that many vehicles if they know the vent's exact location. They need to search for it, and thanks to the map I found at Camp Decade, we know right where to look."

"You'd make a good detective." It was Anika. She'd been awake, listening, but hadn't stirred.

"Are you okay?" Concern lowered Mercer's voice to a whisper.

"Yes. I'm sorry about that." She included Mercer and Erwin in her apology. "I just . . . I don't know. It was all too much for a second."

"You had every right," Erwin said. "I am more sorry than I can ever tell you."

Ira scraped some snow off the wall and bundled it in a handkerchief for Anika. She gratefully pressed it to her swollen eye. "Who hit me?"

"Hilda, Germany's finest combat chef. If her Wiener schnitzel doesn't get you, her right cross will."

Switching to German, Anika addressed the stout woman with a smile. "Remind me never to insult your cooking and get you really angry."

"It's nearly midnight," Mercer announced. "If we leave at first light we'll only need to spend one night on the ice to reach the cave. I for one am exhausted. I'm usually in bed by ten on days I'm in a plane crash."

When Mercer had been returning from the C-97 crash scene, the survivors had slept far from one another. With him back now, they huddled close, drawn into a cohesive group by his strength. This didn't go unnoticed by him. And he was glad for it, because as much as they looked to him for leadership, he needed them for the encouragement to keep going. They had been through a lot together and he knew the worse was yet to come. He also noticed, as he settled into his sleeping bag, that Anika was at his side, her delicate face turned to him.

"Anika," he whispered and her eyes fluttered open. "Can you do me a favor? I'm pretty sure Hilda has a crush on me. Do you think you could be my bodyguard?"

She suppressed a laugh. "My hero." Then her expression turned serious, a worried frown pulling at her mouth. "I'm thankful for what you said earlier about me being able to lead us to the cave, but I don't think I can do it."

Mercer could see how much this admission cost her. It was in her eyes. The defiance she normally showed the world had evaporated. "Why?"

She was wrenched by such doubt that she questioned the very thing she had always believed defined her. "When I go mountain climbing or hiking in some rain forest, I think I'm being daring," she said, "but I'm really just pretending. None of it's real. It's make-believe. With a rescue chopper only a radio call away, I'm never in any actual danger unless I do something stupid. This is different. Lives depend on us reaching the cavern. I can't take that kind of responsibility. I've been kidding myself to think I'm brave, Mercer. I'm a fake, a fraud."

He snaked a hand out of his bag to stroke her short hair. "Anika, we've barely met and yet I can tell you that you're one of the bravest people I've ever known. You've already proven that you are cool under fire. Literally. You can think on your feet and"—he touched the red mark on his cheek where she'd raked him—"you have unbelievable determination. To me, that's the definition of courage. Only a fool goes in search of danger. A brave person avoids it when he can but faces it when he has to. Your hobby is dangerous to be certain, but that's not what makes you brave. You're brave because you know the difference between fantasy and reality. And when reality hits you, you strike back.

"I won't patronize you by tossing around platitudes like 'I'm sure you'll do fine' because I don't know. However, I *believe* you can do it. For me that's enough."

She simply said, "Thank you," because there was no phrase that fully expressed her gratitude.

"You're welcome," Mercer said because any other reply would have betrayed how much he wanted to kiss her. Anika fell asleep with a trace of a smile on her lips and he wondered if she already knew.

The following morning, Mercer found Marty Bishop standing over the graves the team had dug while he was investigating the Air Force Stratofreighter. The others were preparing for the trek, packing everything from sleeping bags and extra Arctic clothes to a cooking stove, propane cylinders, and as much food as they could carry. There had been a few arguments over items individuals felt they had to bring—Marty's videotapes for his father, Erwin Puhl's thick journal, even Hilda's personal recipe book. Mercer won them all. They stripped themselves to the absolute essentials, and even then they were dangerously overloaded. Only Magnus, the Icelandic pilot with the broken arm, would walk unencumbered. Mercer made up for him by carrying the heaviest pack at sixty pounds.

"I didn't really know her," Marty said when he felt Mercer's presence. Ingrid's tombstone was a piece of metal with her name scratched on one side.

"Doesn't matter. For a few days she was part of your life. That's more than enough time to feel grief."

"We were just having some fun, you know. It would have ended as soon as we got to Iceland." He wiped his cheeks with a glove. "I would have walked away. Now I can't."

"No, you can't," Mercer agreed. "She's going to be with you for a long time. Nothing is as casual as we'd like to think. Especially people."

"I've never spent much time thinking about consequences."

"I have a feeling you'll be thinking of nothing else

for a while." Mercer put a hand on his shoulder. "I'll give you a couple more minutes. Then we have to go."

"Thanks."

While the fog had lifted, the tracks Mercer had left on his trip to the C-97 had been nearly obliterated by Greenland's constant wind. For this, he was grateful. It meant that by tomorrow there'd be no trace of their trek, no trail Rath could follow. They reached the Stratofreighter before noon and spent a couple of hours burying what pieces of wreckage were exposed. No one wanted Rath to make the same discovery Mercer had about Major Jack Delaney.

Because he knew the route to the plane, Mercer led, but when they started the long march to the air shaft, each member of the team took a turn at point. Trailblazing in the deep snow was exhausting work that only he and Ira could maintain for more than an hour at a time. Anika spent the day behind the leader, keeping track of their course with a handheld compass taken from the DC-3's emergency kit. When not at the head of the column, Mercer walked with Marty as he helped Magnus. Anika had found a balance of painkillers to keep the aviator alert yet comfortable for the march. He was young and strong and could maintain their pace despite being unbalanced by his slinged arm.

Protected in the latest foul-weather gear, they had no problem handling the cold. It was exhaustion that slowly ground them down. Because of her size, he'd expected Hilda to have the greatest difficulty, but it was Erwin who needed the most encouragement. By five, the group had covered only a third of the distance, and their pace was a quarter of what it had been when they'd commenced. Mercer's plan to spend only one night in the open wasn't going to happen.

Rather than push them beyond their level of endurance, he decided to find cover for the night. Mercer was at point when he made the decision and he veered toward the jagged mountains on their right, hoping to find protection from the strengthening wind. It would have been too much to hope for a cave, but a natural windbreak would have been sorely welcome.

It took another hour of marching to stumble across a V-shaped outcropping of rock that would shield them from the gusts. Gathering storm clouds created a false twilight. Taking a lesson from sled dogs, they began to burrow individual holes in the snow on the rock's leeward side.

"Not like that," Anika cautioned when the work began. "We need to double up to share body heat. We won't survive the night if we don't."

She had removed her tinted goggles and her eyes met Mercer's as the group began to pair off. The invitation was there but she had a duty to her patient. "Magnus, you're with me."

The pilot was ashen from the ordeal but managed a cocky grin. "I knew breaking my arm would have a benefit."

Anika spoke to Hilda, and the chef began expanding her burrow so it would have room for the three of them together. She then whispered to Mercer, "I'll make sure she doesn't sneak over to you while you're asleep."

Even with the added snow insulation, the night was miserably cold. If not for their deep exhaustion, none of them would have slept. Sometime after midnight, the wind reversed directions and quickly stripped the snow cover from their dens. They scrambled to dig new ones on the other side of the low ridge. This time they hollowed out one large chamber and slept in a tight, uncomfortable ball.

At daybreak, it took several minutes to tunnel back to the surface through the two additional feet of snow that had accumulated above them. They continued onward after a meager breakfast of protein bars and snow melted on their single stove. The wind was driving at their backs. Behind them, their footprints vanished like a jetliner's dissipating contrail, scoured away by the relentless gusts. Hour after hour they marched north, mindlessly following the person in front of them. It was a demonstration of faith in Anika as their navigator and in Mercer as their leader.

That was why he pushed himself the hardest, taking point when the snow became deeper or the trail more difficult. The responsibility was a weight the others didn't carry, and for him it was far heavier than the overloaded pack on his shoulders.

At eleven they came across the first really tough terrain. The ice was broken with pressure ridges that had to be climbed and long crevasses measuring at least fifteen feet deep. While some could be jumped, others had to be crossed by descending into the glacier and climbing up the other side, with ropes slung to assist Magnus. Most polar expeditions carried light-weight ladders to cross such formations but Mercer and the others didn't have the luxury. Their pace was cut in half.

Yet no one complained openly. Their frustration and pain were evident in every movement, but no one said they'd had enough. These five men and two women, strangers until a few days ago, were willing to suffer indescribable agony and deprivation for one another because the others were willing to do it for them.

Surrounded by ice and bitter cold, few of them expected the raging thirst they felt. Not only were they sweating from the exertion, dangerous in itself, but every breath expended precious fluids because the air was desert dry, devoid of all but a trace of humidity. They kept canteens close to their bodies to prevent them from freezing, and still they had to stop every couple of hours to boil snow to replenish them. When they found shelter that evening, an hour later than the first night on the ice, Mercer estimated they hadn't yet covered the second third of their trip.

Erwin Puhl seemed to be suffering the most from the exposure. The wind had found a chink in his face mask so the tops of his cheeks were showing frostbite.

When Anika had him remove his boots, several toes were an unnatural pale white.

"Don't play hero," she said angrily as she began to work on him. "If your feet freeze, call a halt to warm them again. If you get severely frostbitten, we won't be able to carry you."

"But our pace is too slow as it is," Erwin countered through gritted teeth as pain splintered his warming toes. "I won't be the one to let the others down."

"You will if we have to leave you," Anika snapped as she rubbed the blood into his feet.

High above, the clouds that had hidden the sky for two days finally cleared. The night exploded in a dazzling display of northern lights, dancing curtains in an otherworldly light show. On the scientific level, Mercer knew the ribbons of color were a result of the solar wind striking certain molecules in the atmosphere—red for nitrogen, violet for ionized nitrogen, and green for oxygen—but it was the aesthetics of the borealis that made him gape with the others. The aurora was visceral, pulsing and seemingly alive.

They watched the show for five minutes before Mercer realized the wind had died.

The pitaraq *is a gravity-driven wind. It starts from south and then there is calm. You have about ten minutes to find shelter.* It was Igor Bulgarin's voice Mercer heard in his head.

"Everybody, find cover! Now!" Mercer was in motion even as he spoke.

Like the previous night when the wind had shifted, their hideouts would be on the wrong side of a ridge when the *pitaraq* struck. Mercer dumped the food he was cooking, cinched his pack, and lunged over the rocky crest. He tumbled down the other side until he landed in deep snow. Quickly he began to dig, scooping out armfuls of snow in a frantic race. A few seconds later, the others joined him. Mercer didn't bother to explain his actions. His frenzied digging was enough to galvanize them. They tunneled into the snow, burrowing toward the protection of the rocks. Mercer had no way to judge how deep they needed to be. Even when he heard a gentle whisper of wind whistling across the entrance to his tunnel he continued mining snow, trying to pack it behind him as he dug downward.

He flipped on a flashlight, and glittering snow crystals reflected the light like jewels. For an illusionary moment he felt safely cocooned in the snow's embrace. His breathing was ragged and his hands felt stiff and frozen. He'd dug his tunnel without his gloves. He donned them, massaging his fingers to get the blood flowing again.

"Can anyone hear me?" His voice was deadened by the weight of snow.

"Yes," Anika replied. She sounded like she was many yards away but was doubtlessly much closer.

"Can you reach me?"

"Yes, I see your light through the snow."

That was the last voice Mercer heard for the rest of the night, even when Anika bored her way to him and Ira and Erwin found them a short time later. A few feet over their heads, the millions of tons of air that had been blowing northward to form a massive high-pressure area came back in a screaming fury. The transition from a dead calm to a hurricane-force gale was measured in seconds. Snow and ice that had accumulated for years was whipped away, exposing rock that hadn't seen the surface in decades, if ever.

The noise was a banshee cry that scraped along nerves like an electric current. Even though they were screened by layers of snow, it was still impossible to speak into the shrieking onslaught. Anika burrowed into Mercer's arms, her body pressed to him as if he could somehow protect her if the wind found them. Ira was mashed to Mercer's other side and by the other man's movements Mercer could tell he was clutching one of the others. Marty was on the far side of Anika, lost in Hilda's panicked embrace.

No power on earth could sustain the amount of energy the wind carried for very long, and after five minutes Mercer was certain the storm had expended itself. The sound seemed to be fading.

He could just barely hear Anika crying.

Then the true wind hit them. The first gust had merely been the prelude to the actual *pitaraq*. Driven by its own weight, the collapsing high-pressure front acted like water, pouring across the ice, ripping away everything in its path at a speed approaching a hundred and fifty miles per hour. Torn and tortured, the glacier's surface came alive with raking barrages of snow and ice and rock. They could feel the ground shudder as large chunks of ice slammed into the wall of rock protecting them. Ice cracked like exploding artillery shells. Mercer pressed his gloves to his head, trying to save his hearing from the sound of ten thousand steam whistles erupting at once.

It went on without letup for an hour. Then two. Then three. Screaming just above them with a rapacious hunger unlike anything they had ever heard. Nestled below the surface, Mercer knew that if the wind found them he'd never know it. They'd be pulled from their burrow and tossed miles before the act could register. It would be a quick way to die, and by the fifth hour he was wondering if death would have been preferable to the relentless fear of surviving the storm.

Slowly, slowly it began to register that he could hear Anika again. She was mumbling, a prayer perhaps, but what mattered was that her voice could be heard above the storm's screech. Mercer sagged in relief. He pulled her face from where it was buried under his arm. Her eyes were enormous, and yet he could see determination in them.

"The wind's dying."

She nodded in understanding, barely able to hear his voice. Her grip relaxed to a hug that in any other circumstance Mercer would have enjoyed. He reached across her and felt for Marty's hand, giving him a reassuring squeeze before turning so he could speak to Ira.

"Think we can chance digging ourselves out?" the submariner asked before Mercer could pose the same question. "Erwin's on the other side of me, and it turns out he's claustrophobic. I don't want to be here when he regains consciousness."

"What happened to him?"

"He held on until about an hour ago and then he freaked out. I had to put a choke hold on him."

Mercer was impressed by the unorthodox cure. "You learn that trick in the Navy?"

In the glare of the flashlight, Ira flashed a wry smile. "Actually I did. The current captain of the attack sub *Tallahassee* owes his career to me for getting him over his fear of cramped spaces."

As the *pitaraq* subsided, Mercer and Ira began to claw at the surface of their den, compressing the fallen snow to the side or beneath themselves as they expanded the burrow. In ten minutes they could kneel upright, and in twenty they could stand, using the hollows where they'd waited out the storm for the waste snow.

"I feel like a goddamn mole," Ira said.

"You go a few more days without a shower, you'll smell like one too." Mercer felt they were almost to the surface. "Any idea about Magnus?"

"I lost track shortly after the storm hit."

"While I'm digging, see if you can find him."

"You got it."

By Mercer's watch, it was a quarter of three in the morning when the tunnel face collapsed on him. He thrashed against the snow and suddenly found himself free. He stood, quickly shaking snow off himself like a dog after a water retrieve, not realizing how warm the tunnel had become until he tasted the crisp Arctic air once again. In the dim light of a hidden moon he looked around. It appeared as if nothing had changed but the drift that had entombed them was substantially deeper and longer than it had been. Other than that, the snow ripped from the ice had been replaced by identical snow from farther up the coast. Even in the face of such an awesome force as the *pitaraq*, Greenland remained virtually unchanged.

Erwin was the next to emerge, clawing his way out like a monster in a 1950s B movie, and then came the others. Marty was the last to crawl out of the hole. While Mercer dug, they had spent the past hour in a vain search for Magnus. Mercer feared the worst.

A hundred yards south was another outcropping of rock similar to the one that had protected them. Its windward side was cleaned of all traces of snow. Mercer fished a pair of binoculars from his pack, but there wasn't enough light to discern details on the ridge's shadowed face. He told Ira to reorganize the remaining gear and started out, swimming through the snow as much as walking. Twenty yards from the crest he saw what remained of the pilot.

The *pitaraq* had plucked Magnus from his tunnel like a raptor snatched its prey and slammed him into the rock. The wind had acted like a sandblaster, stripping him nearly naked and ripping away much of his skin so that frozen blood pooled around the crumpled body. From a distance, Mercer could see that the pilot's skull had been flattened by the collision.

Returning to the tunnel entrance, where the others had gathered, Mercer told them that the pilot had been killed by the storm. They slept for the remainder of the night in the tunnel, and this time Mercer didn't make any excuses for Anika not to rest in his arms. It felt too right not to let it happen. He drifted off with the memory of her lips on his cheek and her whispered "You saved six of us. Don't think about the one you didn't." She knew he would take Magnus's death personally.

They emerged from their underground shelter when the sky was still a shimmering canopy of stars. By the looks on their faces, many of them had already come to grips with Magnus's loss. Rather than dwell on their failure, they took strength from knowing the icy island had thrown the worst it had at them and they had survived. They had another twelve miles to cover.

Just before they started out again, Marty took Mercer aside, his face a mask of shame. "I lost the satellite phone," he mumbled. "I was testing to see if I could get a signal when the wind hit us. I managed to keep my backpack, but the phone . . . I'm sorry."

Mercer remained silent. There was nothing he could do or say to change what had happened. They had just lost their only means of communication, and the odyssey facing them had become doubly difficult. It was no longer enough to evade Rath until he abandoned his search for the Pandora cavern. Now they would have to trek back to civilization again.

Once Anika had navigated them back to their original course, the pain-racked journey continued. Without cloud cover, the temperature dropped dramatically, and every breath was like inhaling acid. It froze tender lung tissue and caused nosebleeds if air was drawn through unprotected nostrils. Mercer had to continuously rotate his scarf when the fleece became clogged with frozen mucus and condensation.

"Where's that global warming we were promised?" Ira grumbled at lunch.

The terrain eased some, quickening their pace, but it took its toll. Legs that seemed fresh following a break began aching after only a few steps and they constantly had to adjust their clothing as frigid air found tiny entrances, piercing right to the flesh before they could recover themselves. Urinating was done only when absolutely necessary. The women suffered the most during the act but the men made a bigger deal out of it. Ira had the best line when he described the process as making a "dickcicle."

His humor and positive outlook helped keep the exhaustion at bay.

At four that afternoon, Mercer's estimate put the air shaft a half mile ahead. He could see that their

march had led them to the mountains thrusting
through the glacier at the head of the fjord he'd seen
from the cockpit of the DC-3. The mountains—bald
round hills really—were a thousand feet high and had
been so ravaged by glacial movement that their domed
sides were riven with scars. He was looking to the west,
toward the interior of Greenland, to survey the surroundings, when he suddenly dropped flat to the snow,
screaming at the others to do the same.

If the sky hadn't been free of clouds, he never
would have seen the distant speck. It was the rotor-
stat plying its way serenely northward. Knowing the
clarity of polar optics, he guessed the dirigible was five
miles away.

"Bury yourselves!" Like a beached seal, Mercer
paddled snow onto his back, struggling to camouflage
his red parka and green pack. His heart pounded painfully, and he took a bite of snow to moisten his dry
mouth. *Jesus, that was close.*

He peered over his shoulder and saw the team had
followed him without question. In seconds they were
nothing more than six innocuous-looking lumps in the
snow. He couldn't chance reaching for his binoculars
because the sun's reflection off the lens would flash
like a beacon. Since the airship was continuing past
his estimated position for the air shaft, Mercer's earlier opinion that Rath didn't have its exact location
was true. They were moving their secondary base too
far north. This would buy Mercer the time they desperately needed.

"Be thankful the weather has been so rotten," he
said when the airship vanished around a promontory.
"It's delayed them as much as it has us."

"How much time do you think we have?" Anika
asked, brushing snow off his back.

"I don't know," Mercer replied absently, watching
the spot where the rotor-stat had disappeared. "Not
as much as I'd like."

"Figure they'll bring three Sno-Cats up here and at
least one building," Ira said. "Four round-trips, six

hours flight time, an hour loading. That's a little over twenty-four hours if they fly around the clock."

"Or half that if they'd already moved stuff before the *pitaraq*," Mercer added.

With a renewed urgency, they continued walking. Mercer had the point and pushed at a brutal pace. His legs burned from the strain of clearing a path for his people, and yet he maintained a gait not much slower than a trot. He kept watch for the rotor-stat and studied the rock formations as he moved. The mountains were like a string of beads impeding the glacier from reaching the sea, and as they rounded one more in the long line, a wicked smile split Mercer's chapped lips.

"Anika, you still have that map?"

"Yes."

"Take a look at it and tell me what you see above the X."

"Looks like the profile of a face. A face with a big nose."

"Kind of like the one on the side of that mountain up there?" Mercer pointed at a natural design cut into the stone by aeons of erosion. It looked remarkably like a human face in profile. The lips were out of proportion, but the nose was unmistakable, as were the deep-set eyes. The formation loomed like a sentinel high above the ice.

"My God," she breathed.

"The last piece of the puzzle." Mercer grinned. "I wondered about that drawing when I first saw it. Now I get it. It was the laborer's way of telling us exactly where to look."

"With a little imagination you can even think the face up there is Jewish."

"If you're referring to the nose, that's an ugly stereotype."

"I'm Jewish. It's okay. You ought to see the beak on my grandfather." She smiled up at him. "You think the air shaft is beneath the face?"

"We'll know soon enough." Before Mercer let them proceed, he spent a few minutes with the Geiger counter checking for radiation. As they followed far behind him, he kept his eyes on the monitor, fearful that the counter would peg over at any second. So far it was giving just faint chirps of background radiation.

A hundred yards from the near-vertical mountain, the Geiger began to tick a little more rapidly. Mercer held up his hand to halt the others and paused to see how far the readings would go. The level was slightly higher than he'd encountered in the C-97 but a few weeks' worth of exposure would be below the danger level provided no one got X-rayed for a while.

There were certain fears Mercer couldn't purge from his brain, and radiation was one of them. He hated it. It reminded him of firedamp gas in coal mines, invisible in its touch and insidious in its death. There was no defense except avoidance.

He walked slowly. The snow near the base of the mountain had become ankle-deep slush. He wondered how close Stefansson Rosmunder had been to this very spot fifty years ago during his search for the C-97. Close, he estimated, considering the dose needed to kill him so swiftly. Not knowing the half-life or dissipation rate of an extraterrestrial element, Mercer proceeded with deliberation, like he was walking through a minefield.

Tick. Tick. Tick, tick, tick. Tickticktick.

Mercer's eyes dropped to the Geiger counter. Twenty-five RADs, about a quarter of the dose needed to cause radiation sickness or about eight times the average yearly exposure people received from background radiation. They would be safe for a while, but each moment brought an increased possibility of cancer later in life.

Nothing around him looked like a likely radiation source. There was no meteor impact evidence on the side of the mountain nor were there signs of Otto Schroeder's air shaft, no tailings of waste rock from their mining. He looked up and saw he was still ten yards to the left of the face. Moving laterally and trying to ignore the clicking counter, Mercer knew he was close. The ice had become even more watery, as if heated from below. Erwin had told them that pieces of the meteor kept in the Russian villages melted snow even in winter.

Without warning, the ground opened up and swallowed Mercer in a wet rush. He fell about ten feet and landed heavily on his backside in a small ice cave. It was an antechamber at the head of the Nazi air shaft. Ahead of him was the long tube descending into the glacier. A wall of icy slurry surged down the eight-foot-diameter tunnel. Had this cave not had a level floor, it would have carried him headlong into the earth as though he'd been flushed down an enormous drain. The moment of terror that had tripped his heart gave way to awe as he surveyed his surroundings. He wasn't even aware of the pain from the fall.

Then he saw the body.

It was badly decomposed, merely a skeleton dressed in gray rags adorned with brass buttons and piping and medals. He recognized the rotted insignia on the corpse's uniform. He had been a sailor in the German Kreigsmarine, specifically the U-boat service. If Mercer needed any more proof that Erwin Puhl's story was true, here it was. But that wasn't what filled him with wonder. It was what lay next to the seated body: the two-foot-square box of pure gold stamped with the swastika-clutching eagle of the Third Reich.

"I'll be a son of a bitch," he breathed, superstitious ripples charging his skin like static. The Nazis had called their operation the Pandora Project, meaning he was looking at a true Pandora's box, its contents as deadly as the evils the mythological one once contained.

"Mercer? Are you all right?" Anika yelled from above, her voice strained by concern.

"Yes," he replied. "Stay back."

The Geiger counter had been turned off by the fall and he flipped it back on. The meter thankfully registered the same dosage as he'd found before his sudden plunge. He held the probe first to the box and then the corpse, finding that it was the sailor's body emitting radiation and not the container of Satan's Fist. The reading was significantly higher than from the survivor he'd found at Camp Decade, meaning this man had received a much more powerful dose, fatal in minutes rather than weeks.

But what about Stefansson Rosmunder and the crew of the C-97? Mercer wondered. How strongly had they been hit? Was it exposure to the corpse or the meteor itself that killed them? Rosmunder had lasted six months after returning from this area, so Mercer guessed it was an acute dose of residual radiation from the body. Considering how they had all bled out, he presumed the airmen were killed by a radioactive blast from the fragment sealed in the box. The sailor must have opened it, killing the flight crew and himself.

Why, after surviving for ten years, did he commit suicide and murder? Madness? Desperation?

Mercer put his hand on the gilded crate, noting that its surface was warm to the touch. Then he realized why the shaft hadn't been buried any deeper. The environment and the box had come to a kind of balance, melting away much of the snow that fell here but leaving enough to cover the tunnel's entrance. That was why there weren't hundreds of feet of ice blocking the shaft. It wasn't until he came along that his added weight overcame the equilibrium between Arctic cold and radioactive warmth and exposed the air vent. Eventually, as the meteor fragments decayed, the heat would diminish and the glacier would forever seal the tunnel.

He gave the box a shove and realized that, while it was heavy, it wasn't solid. Straining to gain traction on the slick floor, he pushed it against the corpse, pressing the disintegrated pile of bones into the wall of the excavation, partially shielding the space from its deadly rays. The Geiger counter dropped noticeably. Next he unfolded the thermal blanket from his pack and draped it over the box to reduce the amount of heat it radiated. He would use the other blankets each person carried to further dampen the warmth, so when they blocked the entrance, the container wouldn't melt away their effort.

"Hey down there, what'd you find?" It was Ira.

"What's left of a German sailor and part of his set of golden luggage. Mind tossing me a rope?"

"Have you out in a second."

Back on the surface, Mercer changed his wet parka and snow pants for the spare ones they'd brought for an emergency, and he told the others what he'd found. The idea of walking past the radioactive body had a chilling effect on them even after he explained that their exposure wouldn't be too dangerous. Like him, they were all terrified by radiation.

It took a half hour to pile enough snow near the opening to seal the hole and erase their presence. With the Pandora box, as Mercer already thought of it, covered by the "space blankets," the slush would freeze to concrete hardness in a few hours. Rath would need weeks and a lucky break to find them. Both of which, Mercer mused grimly, he would no doubt have.

They lowered each other one by one into the antechamber until only Mercer remained on the surface. He mounded snow around the hole, shrinking the aperture until it was barely large enough to admit him. He took one last look at the setting sun and allowed himself to fall into the ice, his landing cushioned by waiting arms below. Flashlights had already been snapped on, their beams vanishing into the bowels of the glacier.

"We ready?" he asked brightly, hoping to dispel their apprehension.

"I've got a bad feeling about this," Marty said as he looked down the stygian air shaft.

"It drives me nuts when they use that line in the movies." Mercer stopped and turned, his eyebrows raised in a mocking expression. "Marty, do you think any of us have a *good* feeling about walking through an oversize Nazi sewer pipe that leads to a radioactive chamber filled with God knows what?"

Together, they started the long descent into the unknown.

Klaus Raeder waited a moment before answering Reinhardt Wurmbach's question. He carefully unlaced his fingers and placed his hands palms down on the tabletop, fixing his stare as if pondering his response. "No," he said at last.

"No, you won't agree to pay the reconciliation commission two hundred and twenty-five-million-mark settlement, or no, you won't counter with two hundred million like you promised before?"

"No to both," Raeder replied, delighting in the veins that bulged like tumors on Wurmbach's forehead. "Tell the lawyers that we'll consider one hundred and seventy-five million."

"Damn it, Raeder, what are you doing?" The lawyer did nothing to hide his anger. "We agreed at the last board meeting that we would pay out the two hundred and consider ourselves lucky. Why make this more difficult by prolonging the negotiations with the Jewish groups?"

"Because we have a fiduciary responsibility to pay as little as absolutely necessary,"

"What about our moral responsibility?" asked Reinhardt's deputy counsel, Katrine Groener.

"Our shareholders don't pay us for that," Raeder answered, annoyed that the woman would ask such a ridiculous question. "Too bad if we offend some delicate sensibilities. This is a business decision."

"Which is costing the company money," Katrine persisted. "Our increased expenditures to marketing and advertisement have yet to stem the loss of customers. And in the past week we've seen NATO cast doubts over Kohl receiving the contract to build the computers for the Eurofighter unless we come to a quick resolution with the reconciliation commission."

Raeder remained impassive, refusing to betray his anger over the possibility of losing the Eurofighter contract. That had come as a complete shock a week ago when a friend at NATO headquarters in Brussels had telephoned with the confidential decision. Now the deal was being openly discussed in capitals all over the Continent. The French especially were putting pressure on NATO to pull the contract from Kohl, a company they screamed had yet to make amends for its Nazi past. The irony was that the electronics firm in Toulouse that would fill the order if Kohl lost out had made a fortune selling radio gear to the wehrmacht right up until D day.

Katrine Groener waited for Raeder to respond, and when he didn't, she continued. "Our warehouses are filling with products we have no buyers for as our market share diminishes. Kohl Heavy Construction has no new work lined up for the remainder of the year. And"—she sifted through some pages in front of her—"ah, here it is. While the corporation is hemorrhaging money, I've found we've spent roughly twenty million marks on a project with an accounting number I can't find in any of our books: 1198-0."

Wurmbach did a poor job hiding his astonishment that she knew about 1198-0. He wasn't even sure what the code signified, only that it was being handled by Raeder's pet fascist, Gunther Rath. "Katrine, that's a special project still deemed too secret to put through normal channels. It, ah, has to do with, ah, a new steel-milling process," he improvised lamely. "Forget you know about it."

"Fine, whatever," she said, looking from the sputtering Reinhardt to the glacially cool Raeder.

"Just to satisfy your curiosity," Raeder said when he saw that the young attorney wasn't impressed with Reinhardt's pathetic explanation, "there will be no further expenditures on 1198-0. As to the Eurofighter contract, we're not out of the running yet. Once we come to terms with the reconciliation commission, we'll get that deal. If they won't go for the one seventy-five, Reinhardt will give them two hundred million and they'll leave us alone. It's my decision to wait them out a little longer and save ourselves money we sorely need."

"And in the meantime?"

"In the meantime we'll be denounced by fringe groups and lambasted in the media for harboring Nazi secrets, but in a few weeks no one will remember any of this." Raeder's confidence wasn't forced. He was as certain of his plan now as he was when it had been conceived. His intercom buzzed. "Yes, Kara?"

"Herr Raeder, I know you asked not to be disturbed, but Herr Rath is finally on the line from Greenland."

"Thank you. Put him through." He clamped his hand over the mouthpiece to address Wurmbach and Groener. "Excuse me please." He didn't speak again until the two lawyers had left his office. "Gunther, what the hell is going on out there? I've been getting panicked calls from Ernst Neuhaus at the Geo-Research office in Reykjavik. The plane with the Surveyor's Society people and the other team is two days overdue. What happened to the evacuation?"

"The evac went as planned." Rath's voice was faint as the solar max stripped power from the radio he used to patch through to the *Njoerd* and then on to Hamburg. Raeder couldn't be sure of the emotion in his special-projects director but it sounded like defiance. "They left right on time."

"Where are they?" Raeder feared what he was about to hear.

"There was an accident on the flight back to Iceland. The plane was lost with all hands."

The full horror telescoped in on Raeder so quickly he felt like he was going to be ill. He knew there had been no accident. Gunther Rath had killed those people, murdered them in cold blood. *Oh, God, it isn't supposed to be like this.* Raeder and Rath had done many illegal things in their career together but nothing approaching murder. Yes, there had been that arson early on, but that was the only time. And since then their tactics had lost any trace of brutality. Industrial espionage and veiled threats were one thing, but this?

What have I done? Raeder finally saw that he didn't control Gunther Rath, never had. Thinking he was using Rath's special propensities in the business world, Raeder had allowed the neo-Nazi into corridors of power he'd never known existed, showing him the real meaning of strength. Now Rath was turning the tables, unveiling to Raeder what depravity actually lurked in his heart. And Raeder had handed Rath the tools he needed to execute the plans of his fascist masters.

"We are proceeding with the rest of the operation," Rath continued, misunderstanding Raeder's silence as tacit approval for his actions. "From corporate records we have the general area of the air vent, but a weather front has delayed our establishment of the northern base. Using the rotor-stat and Sno-Cats we'll find the tunnel in a day or two."

What is the man talking about? He's killed a dozen people and thought that everything was going according to plan. How could I have possibly thought that I could civilize a man like Rath? He's an animal who worships a cult of evil and death. Raeder knew he had to put a stop to this. He couldn't let Rath continue. Not like this. He made his decision quickly. It was an effort to keep revulsion from his voice when he spoke. "I'm leaving for Greenland immediately, Gunther."

"Why? We haven't found the cavern yet."

"Watch what you say! This is an open channel." Like facing a rabid dog, Raeder had only one choice: put the animal down. He would send Rath back to Germany and take over the recovery of the Pandora boxes. Once that was done, he would decide what to do with his special-projects director.

"I will be there sometime tomorrow," Raeder

snapped. "I don't want you to take any more actions until I arrive. Is that clear?"

"Klaus, I'm close. You don't need to be here."

He had another agenda, Raeder realized. The only thing that made sense was that Rath wanted the boxes for his Nazi bosses. He'd told them what was in that cavern and was under orders to recover them so they could either be used or sold. Either option was too horrifying to consider

Raeder softened his voice. He had no idea what the neo-Nazi hierarchy had in store for him if he interfered. "I know I don't need to be there, my friend. It's just that I want to be. I'll see you tomorrow."

He killed the connection before losing control of his emotions. He raced for the private bathroom next to his office because he thought he was going to vomit. He heaved and heaved but nothing came out. Responsibility and remorse couldn't be so easily purged. He studied himself in the mirror above the gold-and-marble vanity. He looked the same. His hair was in place, his complexion smooth, his teeth brilliantly white. It was in his eyes that he saw the corruption.

"Get through this and you'll be fine," he told himself. He liked how that sounded so he repeated it, adding, "I didn't kill those people. He did. It was his choice, not my order. No matter what, I am not a murderer. We'll pay the commission, destroy all the Pandora boxes, and I'll fire Rath. He'll remain silent because to reveal what he knows would be an admission of guilt. He's trapped himself."

He drank a palmful of water and went back to his desk, hitting the intercom. "Kara, is Reinhardt still out there?"

"Yes, Herr Raeder. Would you like me to send him back in?"

"No. Tell him to pay whatever the commission is currently asking for. I think it's two hundred and twenty-five million marks. Then page our pilots and have the company jet ready for an immediate flight to

Iceland. Have my car brought around to the front of the building."

"Yes, sir."

Raeder dialed his summer house in Bavaria, hoping to reach his wife. His eleven-year-old son, Jaegar, answered the phone. "Papa!" the boy cried before restraining his emotions as his father had taught him. "How are you, sir?"

Squeezing his eyes at hearing how he'd turned his son into an automaton, Raeder needed a moment to answer. When this was over, a lot of things in his life were going to change. *Oh, God, please let me see them one more time.* "I miss you. I miss all of you. Is your mama home?"

"No. She went shopping with Frau Kreiger from next door. Fatima is watching Willi and me." Willi was Jaegar's six-year-old brother; Fatima, their Turkish housekeeper.

"I need you to take a message for me. Tell Mama that I had to go away this weekend on a trip."

"You aren't coming to Bavaria?" The boy's engrained reserve could not contain his fierce disappointment.

"I'm sorry, son. I just can't."

"When will you be coming?"

Reader considered his reply, knowing a lie would only add to his family's disillusion. "Not for a long time, I'm afraid. I love you, Jaegar. I'm sorry. Tell your brother that I love him too. And your mother"— *God, this hurt*—"give her a big hug for me."

Raeder knew his uncommon burst of concern would confuse the boy. But if things didn't go as planned in Greenland, he'd be glad he'd made the call. It could be the last his family heard from him. On his way out of the office, he opened his safe to retrieve his licensed pistol, a holdover from the kidnapping threats he'd received before coming to Kohl.

THE PANDORA CAVERN

The flashlight beam pushed back the gloom for only a few dozen yards before being swallowed by impenetrable darkness. With Mercer in the lead, the group chased the retreating ring of light, marching downward at a steady pace, protected by a thin bubble of illumination in an otherwise cold black realm. Otto Schroeder had engineered the sloping tunnel so those walking through it would never lose traction on the icy floor, and every hundred feet the entire shaft leveled out for a yard or two in case someone did fall.

Without the wind, the air was a constant thirty-two degrees, and after so long in below-freezing conditions, many of them had unzipped their parkas. None of them were yet comfortable enough to speak. The walk through the passage was punctuated only by the rustle of equipment and the slap of their boots. Even the Geiger counter in Mercer's free hand had remained silent since they'd slipped past the corpse at the tunnel's entrance. They continued ever downward, wending through living rock and glacial ice.

After thirty minutes, Mercer estimated they had walked nearly two miles into the mountain and had descended a thousand feet. He knew they had to be approaching sea level. Suddenly the light that had cocooned them no longer brushed the walls. It had vanished into an enormous gallery. Mercer stopped, checking the floor to see that it had leveled out. The ground was bare rock, mined smooth during World War Two.

"I think we've reached the bottom."

Training the light upward, he could just barely see

the underside of the cavern, an ugly mixture of ice and rock hanging fifty feet above them. Others snapped on their own lights and more details emerged. The cavern was roughly circular, at least five hundred feet in diameter, and domed. All around them, huge tongues of glacial ice were being forced into the cave through fissures in the stone. In a few centuries, the ice would eventually reclaim the space that the Nazis had carved for themselves. Ahead, the floor dropped off to still black water. Mercer imagined that somewhere across the water was another entrance to the cavern, a submerged grotto accessible only by submarine. He strode across the cavern to the water's edge. By the high-tide lines staining the edge of the quay he knew that the path to the open ocean had remained clear after all this time.

"Must be the tides that keep it open," Ira said as he approached. "If you look closely you can see currents in the water."

Mercer dropped to his belly so he could reach over the side of the pier that Otto Schroeder had built and dipped his hand in the frigid water. He tasted it and spat back into the pool. "Typical salinity. It hasn't been diluted by ice melt."

"I bet if we had a submarine we could get out of here without Rath ever knowing it."

Mercer's attention was fixed on a large gray shape in the water at the far side of the pier. "I'll be goddamned. Wishing it makes it true."

Ira Lasko had to jog to catch up. Mercer called to the others with lights and they converged at the water's edge, close to one side of the chamber. "I can't believe it."

Low in the water sat a German U-boat that looked like she'd just slipped down the ways. The paint on her upper works seemed freshly applied and there were only a few streaks of surface rust along the side of her outer hull. Her conning tower stood about twelve feet above her flat deck, ringed halfway up by a tubular steel railing. Her designation, U-1062, was stenciled on her tower, and she looked as sleek and deadly now as she had generations ago.

"No deck gun," Ira said after a moment's examination.

"What?"

"This is a type VII, the most widely constructed version. Over seven hundred, if I remember correctly. She should have an 88mm cannon just forward of the conning tower." He rubbed the sprouting beard on his chin. "I think this is one of the special torpedo resupply subs the Germans built. She wouldn't need armament if they were using her to transport cargo in and out of this cave. Notice the rubber membrane on the conning tower. That's Tarnmatte, an antiradar coating. She was built for stealth."

"I'm glad I never took up your trivia challenge about submarines," Mercer said, impressed by the breadth of Lasko's knowledge.

"When you spend your life in one of these monsters, it's good to know their history." The gangway spanning the narrow gulf between sub and shore was a short distance away. Ira shot Mercer a look.

"Let's explore the rest of this place before we board her."

"You have a plan?"

Mercer grinned. "Always."

"A good one?"

"Rarely."

For the next hour, they split into teams and scoured the chamber. There were four separate caverns carved off the main cave as well as a long tunnel bored parallel to the air vent. This shaft did not rise up into the glacier but ran level for eighty yards until ending abruptly in a pile of loose boulders and chunks of ice, obviously the result of a cave-in. One of the side chambers had been a machine shop for repairing mining equipment, such as generators, pneumatic drills, lights, and small utility loaders. Ira Lasko remained in the workshop while the others continued their exploration.

Another cavern, about half the size of the central one, had been a dormitory and was filled with rows of bunk beds stacked four high. Mercer confirmed the slave laborers had used it when he found a Star of David painstakingly carved into the underside of one of the beds. There were enough bunks for five hundred people, double or even triple that if the workers were forced to sleep in shifts. Most were neatly made, the single blanket stretched taut. A few were rumpled and he could see the outline of the last person to sleep there. That was all that remained of the man or woman. An impression.

It was all that remained of any of them.

Fists clenched, he backed out of the dormitory, refusing to turn away until he returned to the main cavern.

Buildings for administration, planning, and housing of the Nazi overseers had been erected in the central chamber. Walking through them was like stepping into a museum. Uniforms hung neatly in closets, dishes were stacked in cupboards, and a deck of cards had been left on a table as if the players had just stepped away for a moment.

"Where are the bodies?" Marty Bishop asked when they left the Germans' dorm.

"I'm not sure." Mercer had been scanning everything with the Geiger counter and had yet to find any trace of the Pandora radiation.

"Hey, Mercer." Erwin Puhl was at the water's edge, standing between a storage dump of forty-four-gallon fuel drums and crates of other cargo.

As he approached, Mercer could see that Erwin had stripped a tarpaulin from a pile of boxes. When his light fell on the topmost, a golden reflection flashed back at him. Pandora boxes. He estimated there were at least thirty of them, and all were larger than the one they had found at the surface. These measured about five feet square and were three feet tall. He waved the counter over the neat stack, detecting nothing. The Germans had obviously learned how to properly seal the meteorite fragments.

There was a palpable amount of heat washing off the gilded crates. Meltwater dripped from the ceiling high above them, running off the pier and into the sea.

"Look at this." Erwin indicated the top box, and Mercer climbed the pile.

This one did not have a lid and he could see that the interior was baffled with diminishing sized boxes like a Russian nesting doll, though all were made of sheets of pure gold.

"Any idea why they made them like this?" Erwin asked.

"Heat dissipation," Mercer replied, jumping back to the ground. He felt along the edge of another box, where its internal structure would be attached to the outer shell, and found it was warmer there than on the flat sides. "They couldn't make the boxes solid for cost and weight reasons, so they used as little gold as possible, designing them this way so the whole thing didn't become too hot to handle."

"Clever bastards," Marty remarked sardonically.

A shrill scream pierced the air. Mercer led the two men as they raced across the chamber to where Hilda stood with Anika Klein. The chef's face was pale and tears were running down her rounded cheeks. Anika stroked Hilda's hair, trying to calm her.

"What happened?"

"In there." Anika gestured to a small aperture in the towering rock wall that Mercer hadn't noticed before.

Tensed as he ducked into the hole, Mercer held the Geiger counter at the ready. He moved through the cramped space, twisting his body as he scraped along the rough stone, the beam of his light showing nothing. The passage ended at a ledge overlooking another cave, the bottom of which was littered with tens of thousands of cans and a heavy scattering of bleached white bones.

Closing his eyes and taking a deep, calming breath,

Mercer braced himself for a more careful examination. He studied the bones for a moment and fell back against the wall, a wave of relief momentarily robbing him of energy. He backed out of the passage to rejoin the others.

"It's a garbage dump. Hilda saw bones in there and thought they were human. They're not. They're seal bones."

"Seal?"

"To supplement the food the Germans brought here, the two survivors hunted seals that ventured into the cavern through the submarine tunnel."

"That's how they survived for ten years down here," Ira said, wiping grease from his hands. "The provisions couldn't have lasted from the war until 1953."

"I bet they could," Mercer countered. "With a thousand people working in here, they needed tons of stores. If the accident that killed everyone occurred right after a supply run there would have been more than enough canned goods to support two men for ten years. Especially if they killed an occasional seal."

"That explains why the man at Camp Decade had such rotten teeth," Anika said as Hilda composed herself once again. "Even with fresh meat, ten years without fruits and vegetables would cause scurvy."

"But where is everybody?" Marty asked for the second time.

"Since I haven't found any radiation," Mercer answered, "I think the corpses have been moved to another chamber and sealed inside to protect the two men who survived the accident."

"You think it was a radiation leak that killed them?"

"What else could it have been?" Mercer said. "They all died at the same time. Otherwise, they would have escaped on the sub. The man we found at Camp Decade and the one at the entrance must have been on the surface when the cave was dosed with radiation. They could have waited up there for the radiation to dissipate to a safe level before returning underground.

Then they could have moved the bodies to a side chamber and buried them."

"How is it they didn't get killed by the residual radioactivity still in the bodies?" Anika asked. "The ones we found are still radioactive after sixty years."

"I don't know."

"The Germans must have had protective clothing for themselves," Erwin offered.

"Why didn't the Navy officer use it when he opened the box when the C-97 flew over?"

No one had an answer to Ira's question.

"Let's get closer to the Pandora boxes, where it's warmer, and discuss our options," Mercer suggested. "I have a surprise and an idea."

"I'll meet you there in a second," Ira said and went back to the repair shop.

Once they were settled, Mercer pulled a nearly full brandy bottle from his pack. "Surprise."

"I couldn't take my father's videotapes and you brought booze?" Marty said angrily. "That's not very fair."

"I said essentials only." Mercer took a pull. "I consider alcohol an essential. If you don't want any, feel free to give up your share."

"I didn't say that," Marty backpedaled. "So what's your idea?"

A low rumbling sound prevented Mercer from replying, and from the side of the chamber, a bright glow appeared in the machine shop before being suddenly doused. "Damn!" Ira cursed. A moment later the light returned and stayed on.

"What did you do?" Mercer shouted as Ira appeared from the shop. Lasko's grin went from ear to ear.

"Played a hunch," Ira said. "I noticed the uniform shoulder tabs on the body up the tunnel were the brass cog wheels of the Kreigsmarine engineer corps. The guy had been the sub's chief engineer. As a mechanic myself, I guessed that he spent the last ten years of his life making sure everything in this place was in perfect running condition. It's what I would have done."

"But in the fifty years since he died, wouldn't everything rust? And wouldn't the fuel go bad?" Erwin asked.

"In normal conditions this place would resemble a scrap heap but the low temperature means there's virtually no humidity. Nothing rusts. Hell, the brass buttons on the uniforms are barely tarnished. As to the fuel, the Germans used diesel with a low cloud point for Arctic conditions. All I had to do was drain the water at the bottom of a can as a result of phase separation, strain out the sediment, and preheat it over a can of Sterno to put the paraffin back in the solution. I had to crank the generator like a bastard to flush the kerosene our German friend used as a rust inhibitor, but it should smooth out in a minute or two as it lubricates itself."

"I just can't believe it," Erwin persisted. "My car won't start after just one cold night."

"You're hearing and seeing the proof. The generator works like a charm. With proper care, you can leave an engine for decades and all you need to start it is a good battery. That's what prevents your car from turning over. Cold temperature saps their power. Since the portable generator starts off a flywheel, all it required was about fifty pulls on the cord. It's the lightbulbs that have lost their seals over time. The first one blew as soon as the electrical current hit it."

"Well this changes a few things," Mercer said as his original idea evolved. "I had a feeling we'd find a sub down here when Erwin first mentioned that's how this base was supplied. The Germans would have kept one here at all times so they could transport the fragments as soon as they were ready, which means its crew would have died with everyone else. I'd thought that we could hide from Rath in it by submerging in the lagoon."

"Without power how would we have surfaced again?"

"By opening a hatch and swimming out," Mercer answered. "Can't be that deep in here. Now I wonder if we need to hang around at all."

Ira guessed at Mercer's intention. "Just because I got a one-cylinder generator running doesn't mean the sub'll still work."

"If the engineer took that much time on the generator, it stands to reason his U-boat is in excellent condition too."

Ira weighed Mercer's logic for a second and nodded. "Possibly."

"You're proposing we sail it out of here?"

"Without Ira I never would have considered it, but he used to teach submarine operations at the Navy's sub school in Groton, Connecticut. If he can train teenagers to run a nuclear vessel, he can teach the six of us how to maneuver this antique. Correct me if I'm wrong, Ira, but the principles haven't changed much in fifty years."

"Haven't changed much in a hundred years really," Lasko agreed. "Nuke boats have a lot more automated controls. That fish over there is bare bones, uses muscles to open and close valves."

"If nothing more, we can use the U-boat to hide ourselves. But if we can get her running, I think our best bet is to get the hell out of here." Mercer looked each of them in the eye as he spoke. "Without Marty's satellite phone we're still stranded when Rath and his goons leave here. It'll take weeks to walk the six hundred miles to Ammassalik. Considering we barely survived the past couple of days, I doubt we'd make it a quarter of that distance."

"Why the hell did you bring us up here instead of having the pilot land us closer to Ammassalik?" Marty asked angrily. "None of this needed to happen. Radioactive bodies. Golden boxes filled with Christ knows what. Maybe Ingrid would have—"

"Marty, calm down!" Ira shouted right back. "Mercer had a good goddamned reason. The plane would have crashed a hundred miles from the town. We'd have died closer to it—that's all. Ingrid would have been just as dead. I'm sorry. At least now we have a chance."

"But my sat-phone?"

"Probably wouldn't have gotten a signal until long after we froze," Ira stated. "Mercer's been buying us time every step of the way, so cut him some slack. All right?"

Marty fell silent.

Capping the brandy bottle, Mercer looked around the circle of expectant faces, proud of them all for handling the past days so well. "Here's my plan. I would like Anika and Erwin, since you read German, to search the administrative offices thoroughly for evidence. I've noticed Kohl's name is stenciled on a lot of the equipment lying around, and now I'm pretty sure Rath's job is to destroy it and erase any link his company has to this place. We need paperwork and documents that implicate Kohl for when this nightmare is over. Just make sure you don't leave any indications that we were here. Marty and Hilda can give Ira a hand with anything he needs."

"What about you?"

"I'm going to work with Ira." He looked at Anika. "As soon as your search is done, join us. We don't have much time."

"Okay, boys and girl, let's get busy," Ira said with the mock cheer of a drill instructor.

"What's first?"

"I'm going into the boat to check it out. I want you three to start on the fuel. You need to drain the bottom few inches of water from each drum without stirring up the sediment. There's a chain fall in the machine shop you can bring out to lift the barrels. Later, we'll devise a filtering system. I should be able to jury-rig a preheater aboard the boat so we don't need to cook each drum when we're ready to load."

"How much fuel do you think we need?" Marty asked, eyeing the hundred or more barrels stacked next to the U-boat. It would be an exhausting job.

"Let's see. The typical type VII has two six-cylinder supercharged G.W. diesels that could push them along at about sixteen knots on the surface and double-commutator electric motors that produce about five hundred horsepower for a top submerged speed of approximately seven knots." Ira looked upward as if doing mental arithmetic and then grinned sadistically. "That means we need all the fuel we can get into her."

"I was afraid of that."

By the light from the portable lamps wired to the generator, Mercer and the others got to work while Ira disappeared into the U-boat. After establishing a system and a rhythm, they had managed to prepare fifty of the drums when the slender submariner re-emerged from the vessel. His parka and snow pants were streaked with grime, and his face was tiger-striped by smudge marks.

"How's she look?" Mercer called to Ira, who stood atop the conning tower surveying their progress.

"That engineer knew what the hell he was doing." He laughed. "I've seen new cars fresh off the assembly line in worse condition than this old girl."

"You think this is going to work?"

"I honestly think it will. I was worried about the rubber gaskets and hoses, but they've been treated with something. While they're stiff as hell, they should hold okay once they warm up. Just in case, I'm only going to run one engine and have the hoses from the other ready as spares."

"What about the batteries? We'll need to charge them if we're going to get out of here."

"He drained the hydrochloric acid from them and stored it in big glass bottles, so none of the batteries have been eaten away. I've just started refilling the sixty-three cells in the aft battery room. That should be enough juice to clear the tunnel and reach the surface."

"Our priority is to make sure we can submerge her once Rath shows up. We'll worry about getting out of here later."

"In that case, we'll start loading the diesel into her main tanks as soon as I check them for water seepage. This way we can use her Junkers compressor to fill the air tanks for when we want to surface again."

Mercer checked his watch. He was stunned to see it was past midnight. Without the sun to guide his circadian cycle, he hadn't realized that they'd been on the move for twenty straight hours. "We'll start that after we grab a few hours' sleep."

Hilda sagged when she recognized the English word sleep. *"Danke."*

"Where the hell are Anika and Erwin?" Marty asked, dropping to the stone floor and propping his back against a barrel.

"Obviously they found something of interest." Ira climbed down the conning tower and crossed the gangway to the dock.

Hilda took over cooking duties from Mercer when he started gathering provisions from the packs, freeing him to find Anika. He found her slumped over the desk in the administration building's largest office. Erwin Puhl was asleep on a threadbare couch. Mercer touched Anika's shoulder and she came awake with a guilty start.

"Oh, God. I am so sorry." She saw that Erwin had also succumbed to exhaustion. "We were reading and took a quick break"—she looked at her watch— "three hours ago."

"That's okay." Mercer smiled. "We've just knocked off outside. Have you found anything?"

"Everything," Anika replied, fire replacing the sleep in her eyes. "Names, dates, orders, procedures, the works. If we get out of here, Kohl AG is finished."

"What about the two men who survived the accident that killed everyone else. Did they leave any kind of a journal?"

"That's what Erwin was reading."

The scientist came awake when he heard his name. He slipped on his glasses. "You were right about a great many of your conjectures, Mercer. One of them was a Jewish slave laborer named Isidore Schild. The other was the submarine's chief engineer, Wolfgang Rossler. They were on the glacier when one of the Pandora boxes dropped from a crane and spilled its contents. The radiation blast killed everyone in the chamber an hour after they got the fragments safely into another box. Schild and Rossler remained outside for two weeks, freezing and starving until they felt it was safe to enter again. The protective suits the Germans brought couldn't take a direct blast of radiation, but it did shield them when they moved the contaminated bodies into the excavation and backfilled it by blowing up what they called the hanging wall."

"That's a mining term for the ceiling of a tunnel," Mercer explained. "They must be talking about the shaft leading to where the meteorite fragments came to a rest after melting down to bedrock."

"Yes, that's right. They couldn't operate the submarine with only the two of them, so they were marooned. Necessity ended any animosity between the two men. They lived off the food supplies and killed the few seals that came into the cavern. For the first few years they tried to signal Allied aircraft that ventured nearby on their flights to and from England, but it was rare any planes came this far north. They assumed after several years that when no more planes approached the war had ended."

"Jesus." Mercer shuddered at the idea of being isolated for so long.

"Schild's journal is filled with anecdotes about their time here. He was a remarkably generous man toward Rossler, considering the circumstances. I'll tell you the details later if you'd like. They decided that the only way to attract attention was if they could shoot down one of the passing planes. Since they had only small arms from the submarine, the only weapon capable of crashing an aircraft was the radiation from one of the boxes. They dragged the smallest one to the surface and took turns every day waiting for a plane to fly low enough and close enough for a direct dose of Pandora

radiation to kill its crew. For eight long years they
waited until the C-97 flew over. Rossler was at the
entrance, so Schild doesn't know the exact details. He
guessed that maybe the plane had engine trouble.
Anyway, Rossler opened the box, sacrificing his own
life for Schild's, and downed the plane.

"As soon as the radiation dissipated enough for his
suit to protect him, Schild went in search of the plane
but couldn't find it. After two weeks he returned to
the cavern. Despondent, he finally gave up a short
while later and left, packing up enough provisions to
sustain him for a week. The seals had long stopped
coming, so he was dying of scurvy anyway. He wrote
a beautiful suicide note at the end of his journal,
which leads me to believe he knew nothing of Camp
Decade."

"Want to know the sickest part of this?" Mercer
said when Erwin fell silent. "Had he stayed in the
vicinity of the cave entrance after the plane crash, he
probably would have seen Stefansson Rosmunder as
he searched for the wrecked Stratofreighter. He
passed near enough to this place to give himself a fatal
dose of radiation from Rossler's body."

The tales of Japanese soldiers surviving on remote
islands long after the war were tame compared to the
hardships Rossler and Schild endured only to die so
close to rescue.

"There are other parts of Schild's journal," Anika
said, "that are much, much worse." She held out her
hand to Erwin for the journal. She thumbed through
to the passage she wanted, pausing to build the
strength to reread it. "This takes place at the height
of the mining operation." Her translation came fluidly,
as though she'd already memorized the passage.

August 11, 1944
*Can the Nazis leave any beauty uncorrupted? We
learned again today that they cannot. We fooled ourselves
into thinking the guards didn't know about Sara's preg-
nancy. Yes, her belly was hidden under loose clothing, but*

*there were more obvious signs of the life within her. She
was happy. An unknown aberration from this living hell.
That she'd been raped by guards who planted this seed no
longer vexed her as her time approached. She'd been beautiful and the guards' favorite. We didn't understand why
they had left her alone these past months. Now we realize
they were under orders not to touch her. She gave birth
this morning, straining as much to free the child as to
maintain her silence. Many of the older women who knew
midwifery helped her. And as if they knew the due date,
Herman Kohl, nephew of the industrialist Volker Kohl
and here on an inspection tour, appeared moments later
with Sturmbannführer Kress. They took the child to the
dock. The wailing infant was forever silenced by the still
waters. I write now to the sounds of the old women crying
and the snuffling of the guards once again raping Sara. I
pray for the strength to hide from the suicidal thoughts
plaguing me since my first day here so that mother and
child will never be forgotten.*

The heavy silence in the room served to amplify
Anika's sobs. Mercer too felt the salty sting of tears
in his eyes. A handful of the abstract six million had
names and faces for him now. He made a silent vow
to stop at nothing until Kohl paid for what they had
done. For him there was no ambiguity about responsibility. "Kohl AG is going down." He was unaware he
spoke aloud.

Anika looked at him and was a bit frightened by what
she saw. His rage was unlike anything she'd ever experienced. It shimmered off him like heat waves. For the
first time she realized Mercer's capacity for revenge.

Since they didn't know how long they would remain
isolated, their meal was a light one. Their rations
would be proportioned to sustain them for a week to
ten days. Too exhausted to let rumbling bellies distract
them, they slept like the dead until Ira Lasko's watch
alarm roused them six hours later.

Because of the physical strength needed to move
the three-hundred-fifty-pound fuel drums, Erwin and

Anika were given the job of degreasing the machinery in the U-boat with rags under Ira's guidance. He spent the morning cleaning the sub's port diesel engine and checking that her electric motor would operate by jumping it with the portable generator. Ira had to scavenge wiring from the starboard power plant to get it running smoothly but was satisfied with his efforts. Mercer spent part of the morning rigging a trip wire device near the surface entrance. He formed a sheet of lead into a tight ball that would roll down the tunnel once a lanyard was brushed by passing feet. He placed a metal plate at the bottom of the tunnel that would reverberate like a bell when the ball struck it. Even if Rath's men sprinted down to the cavern, the ball would beat them by ten minutes, giving Mercer and his group enough time to submerge the boat. The whole setup looked innocuous enough to evade suspicion once Rath found it.

They put in eighteen hours of work that day and slept, if possible, harder that night. Before Mercer would let them into their sleeping bags, he made certain that all evidence of their presence had been erased and that everything was packed for the dash to the U-boat if necessary. They'd considered sleeping on the boat but didn't have enough people to move one of the heavy Pandora boxes into it to provide heat.

The following morning, the exertion and cold made them lethargic and ill-tempered. They loaded fuel all morning, a filthy job that left them reeling from the fumes. By lunch, Ira had tested all the sub's valves and he was confident that, when the time came, she would dive. With her air tanks charged off her compressor, she would resurface too. He'd also managed to coax a few minutes of running time off the port engine and knew what needed to be done to get it running at full power. He announced that they were ready with the exception of her batteries.

He'd filled a few with acid so they would hold a charge for lighting the boat but the rest remained empty. That job would have to wait until they were ready to leave. Most of the batteries had cracked in the past decades and were unusable. Those that Ira salvaged still tended to seep acid. Because it was impossible to completely dry the bilge spaces, the leaking hydrochloric acid would mix with the seawater contamination. The resulting clouds of poisonous chlorine gas would quickly fill the U-boat's pressure hull. To limit their exposure, Mercer decided they would fill the batteries just before leaving the cavern.

After his meager meal, Mercer gave his team a few hours' rest before tackling the batteries. As they gratefully fell into their sleeping bags he made the long trek up the tunnel to check his warning device. He'd thought of a better system to release it and wanted to make the modification. Climbing a thousand feet in a two-mile-long shaft wouldn't normally bother him, but he was more tired than he could remember. The lack of food and cold so sapped his energy that two-thirds the way to the surface he decided to turn back. He couldn't afford to waste his dwindling reserves on building what amounted to a better mouse trap.

With a fraction of a second's warning, a bounding shadow flitted through the beam of his flashlight. Mercer tried to dodge out of the way as his ten-pound lead ball came bouncing out of the darkness toward him. It smashed his thigh like a baseball bat at full swing, crumpling him to the ground like he'd been shot. The ball continued its plunge to the cavern a mile and a half away.

He bit his lip to keep from crying out and tasted blood. Lying on the floor of the tunnel, he strained to see anything farther up the pipe, cursing his stupidity for coming up here. Even if he couldn't see Rath's men, he knew they were coming. As he lurched to his feet, his right leg would barely take his weight. It was dead all the way to his toes.

"Son of a bitch," he grunted and began loping down the tunnel, a shuffling gait that hammered pain to the top of his skull with every step.

Mercer knew the leg wasn't broken and tried to convince himself that he could run through the agony. With a half-mile advantage he could only hope that Rath would need time to assemble his men at the entrance before descending into the earth. At his pace, Mercer's lead would vanish fast. There were no tricks he could think of to lessen the pain, nothing he could do to increase his speed except push himself harder.

Ira and the others must have heard the ball slamming into the metal plate at the bottom of the tunnel. He wondered if they would wait for him and prayed they wouldn't. To be captured now because of his mistake was something he couldn't take. He knew, though, that they would wait right up until it was too late.

The thought that their lives hung in the balance carried him the next half mile. He was two-thirds home, but knew he was tapped out. His breathing raged painfully. His thigh throbbed even stronger, an agony that made him cry with each footfall.

He reached the cavern floor before he knew it, his determination able to push him far beyond what he knew where his limits. The cave was completely dark, and he could hear nothing over his own pained gasps. Up the shaft he could just discern a faint ghost's glow of light, a distant flicker that warned him he had only a few minutes. He left his own light off, relying on years of subterranean experience to guide him across the cavern to where the sub should be. When he thought he was close, he splayed his fingers across the Maglite to diffuse its beam and flicked it on.

His sense of direction was perfect. He stood a couple yards from the gangway. He looked up to see Anika Klein standing atop the conning tower. She saw him and her face lit up with undisguised relief. "Come on."

Beyond the sub, the lagoon was littered with a hundred empty fuel drums that would disguise the one Ira had bolted to the top of the U-boat's snorkel and the gas can he'd mounted to hide the attack periscope.

"Tell Ira to dive," Mercer wheezed.

"We heard the ball fifteen minutes ago. We're ready."

He swept his light across the dock. Nothing remained of their equipment. Rath would never know they were here. Using his arms and one leg, he climbed the ladder welded to the conning tower, grateful that Anika was there to drag him up the last few rungs.

Mercer didn't waste seconds he didn't have by climbing into the sub. He launched himself through the open hatch and fell to the floor of the fire-control space located above the main control room. Anika followed him through, stopping to dog the hatch above them. The sub was watertight.

"Ira, now!" she shouted down to the control room.

A steady hiss echoed throughout the U-boat as Ira opened valves to the sea, flooding them with enough water to put the sub on the bottom of the lagoon, sixty feet below the keel. He knew to trim the flooding to compensate for the sub's tendency to sink stern first because of her engines. She went under with barely a ripple.

Mercer gingerly lowered himself into the control room. As cramped as the room was, it was the largest space on the U-boat, but the low ceiling, clutter of pipes, wires, and conduits as well as the myriad duty stations made it claustrophobic. Around the large tube for the boat's second periscope, Ira stood in front of the dive controls, adjusting the dizzying array of flow valves and knobs. Marty was seated at the planesmen's station, his hands kept well away from the twin wheels. The others were in the forward torpedo room to distribute weight.

Gently, the sub settled on the bottom. Ira forced a little air into the saddle tanks to prevent suction forming against the silty seabed. For fifteen minutes he continued to trim the U-boat, set the depths for the snorkel and periscope, and generally made certain they were secure. He scampered around with the agility of a man half his age. It was clear that retirement hadn't deadened his training. Because no one had his specialized knowledge, the others wisely stayed out of his way.

"By the end of the week," he said at one point, "all of you are going to know how to run this tin can in your sleep."

"If sleep is a prerequisite, after I do a little spying through the periscope, I'm heading for a bunk to get a jump on everyone else," Mercer joked but pain clipped each word.

"No, you're not," Anika snapped with clinical professionalism. "You're getting to bed right now. You can barely stand."

Mercer made to argue and thought better of it. Anika had to support his shoulder as she led him to the captain's cabin, the only private spot on the two-hundred-fifty-foot relic.

"You or Hilda should have this cabin," Mercer said when Anika stripped off his parka.

"Sweet gesture." She smiled. "But we took a vote yesterday. By unanimous decision, this one's yours."

She gave him several painkillers, which he washed down with a mouthful of brandy. "No operating heavy machinery for twelve hours," she admonished.

"I promise I won't even lift my eyelids."

Her more-than-concerned kiss lingered on his lips long after she'd closed the curtain on the wood-paneled cabin.

"Say again?" Gunther Rath snarled into the static-filled radio. "Your last transmission not understood."

"We have located the cavern," came the response from Dieter, the driver of one of the Sno-Cats. "Advance team has penetrated the access tunnel and verified contents."

Rath looked up from the radio and caught a smile on Greta's lips. Klaus Raeder stood behind her, but his expression did not change. He had just arrived at the base after a series of weather problems delayed his flights. "Excellent, Dieter. We have your location from the tracking device on the 'Cat. I will recall all vehicles and converge on your location."

The solar max swallowed Dieter's reply. The tenuous link was gone.

Rath got to his feet. "Klaus, I told you I could handle this."

"I didn't doubt it," Raeder replied sarcastically. Face-to-face with Rath, his confidence and certainty had returned. "It's your tactics I question, not your abilities. Greta, would you excuse us?"

The northern camp was composed of only one of the dormitory buildings flown up from the main base by the rotor-stat. By removing a few partitions, they had converted four of the bedrooms to an operations center and makeshift galley. Greta Schmidt didn't like being ordered to leave but knew Gunther would tell her later what Raeder had to say. She went to her room without a word.

Raeder's voice was tight. "You will now explain

why you felt it necessary to murder a planeload of
people."

"Maybe I should start by explaining why I murdered a man named Otto Schroeder outside of Munich
first. And why Greta had to kill the Russian scientist,
Igor Bulgarin, here in Greenland." Rath smirked at
Raeder's stunned expression. "You don't know how
close this expedition was to being compromised from
the very beginning."

"Obviously not," Raeder said when he found his
voice.

"In the Kohl archives we burned, do you remember
transcripts of Leonid Kulik's interrogation by the Ge-
stapo where he said he belonged to a group called the
Brotherhood of Satan's Fist? Far from dying out during the war, the Brotherhood exists to this day. I
learned through contacts I maintain in Russia that this
group has been feeding information to a Nazi hunter
in Austria in an attempt to stop us from securing the
Pandora boxes. We weren't able to stem the flow of
documents, so I had a team eavesdrop on the Jew
and learned that Otto Schroeder had been a mining
engineer who worked on the cavern, apparently the
only living person with firsthand knowledge of what
happened here.

"During our"—Rath paused to find the right
word—"discussion, not only did a group of snipers
open fire on us, but Anika Klein, who I have since
learned is the Austrian Jew's granddaughter, showed
up. Schroeder was silenced, but Klein escaped and
frustrated our attempts to locate her before she arrived in Greenland. Somehow she discovered the connection between Geo-Research and us after she
arrived here and obtained the support of Philip Mercer. I had no choice but to silence them all."

"And what about the Russian you mentioned? The
one Greta killed?"

"On your orders to check the body in Camp Decade, she discovered him already checking the corpse

for clues about his true identity. Realizing that Igor Bulgarin could be a member of the Brotherhood, Greta beat him to death with a tire iron.

"Dr. Klein didn't believe the false clues Greta left to make the murder look like an accident, and she tried to return to the scene of the crime with Mercer the day after she arrived here. Greta almost succeeded in stopping them by burning Camp Decade with them inside. However, luck was with Dr. Klein again and they survived."

"Why didn't you tell me any of this?" Raeder demanded.

"These were details you pay me to handle," Rath said smoothly, knowing that his superior's anger was evaporating. "The evacuation plan we'd put together earlier was no longer viable since at least two people knew the truth about Bulgarin. I had to kill them before they reached Iceland. The only way to do that without causing even more suspicion was destroying the transport plane en route."

"There had to be another way," Raeder said, though he had already seen that there wasn't anything else Rath could have done.

Rath put as much sincerity in his voice as he could muster. "I thought long and hard about what I did, believe me. It wasn't an easy decision. I admit I was a little rough with Otto Schroeder, but his death was the result of the sniper attack. Bulgarin died because Greta panicked. I've been reacting to a situation out of my control. We both know my past, so I won't pretend that violence isn't an option, but I drew the line at murder long ago. I took no pleasure from what I did."

Raeder searched Rath's eyes, hoping to see truth in them. He decided to believe Gunther. It was easier than the alternative. Since he was here, he could better control his special-projects director. While he would allow Rath to coordinate the destruction of the evidence in the cavern, Raeder was still wary about the fate of the Pandora boxes. When it came time to dispose of them, he would make sure Rath couldn't implement any hijacking scheme he might have planned. "Okay. What happens now?" he said at last.

"My men will empty the cave of everything we can move and burn what we can't. Explosive charges will seal the place forever, so even if there is another survivor like Otto Schroeder, there will be no way to find the base. Then we'll haul the Pandora boxes out to sea with the rotor-stat and dump them in the deepest water we can find."

"How long do you think it will take?"

"Just a few days. We'll have this building and the Sno-Cats back to the main base near Camp Decade in plenty of time if the Danish government decides to revoke our permit. And if they don't, we'll turn everything over to the Japanese team as scheduled. Don't worry, Klaus." Rath smiled. "No one will ever know what we've done. Kohl can pay the Jews a pittance compared to what we really owe."

When Raeder went to the bathroom, Greta Schmidt returned to the op-center. "Well?"

"He bought the whole thing." Gunther struggled not to laugh.

"We knew he would," she purred, massaging his shoulders. "I was thinking. Werner Koenig is the only person here not under our direct control. He knows that we aren't in Greenland for any scientific research."

"Dr. Koenig's 'accident' is already planned."

"I want to do it," Greta said quickly, her face flushed.

Laughing, Rath pulled her down to his lap and bit her ear. "You liked killing Bulgarin, didn't you?" There was no need for her to reply. "I bet you got off when he died."

"Not then," she said hoarsely. "But later, in the shower."

"You are a sick bitch."

"That's why you love me."

"I don't love you."

Her breath was coming faster now, her eyes glassy. She was near orgasm just thinking about murdering her former lover. "All right. That's why you fuck me then."

THE PANDORA CAVERN

Torn between his fear of cramped spaces and being choked again by Ira Lasko, Erwin Puhl chose to crush his claustrophobia by acting as the crew's lookout on the periscope. By watching the activities of the black-clad Geo-Research men working in the cavern, he could pretend that he wasn't trapped in an elongated coffin sixty feet under water. The powerful floodlights the Germans had installed gave him a small measure of security. It was only when he returned to the main part of the U-boat to sleep that the terror threatened to engulf him once again. Lasko made sure that Erwin's bunk was above his own in the amidships officers' quarters, just in case.

He had his face pressed against the eyepiece when Mercer came up the ladder from the control room.

"How's the view?" Mercer asked and handed him a cup of water.

"Same as it was yesterday and the day before." Erwin stood. "Take a look."

Mercer replaced him on the steel seat and studied the cavern through the lines of the scope's crosshair reticle. All the Pandora boxes had been moved to the air shaft entrance on dollies Rath's men had brought, and several had already been dragged to the surface by winches anchored at regular intervals along the tunnel's length. The three wooden buildings had been dismantled and burned, and Rath had had teams of men remove Kohl's name from each piece of equipment with torches before dumping it into the water. A few pieces of gear had hit the submerged U-boat, producing a hollow echo that startled everyone inside the first time it happened.

From the wavering glow radiating from the slave annex, Mercer could tell that the five hundred bunk beds were also being reduced to ash. He carefully turned the scope so the fuel drum bolted to it didn't act too unnaturally as it pivoted through the water. He was searching for Gunther Rath and spotted him near the remains of the administration building, talking with Greta Schmidt and a fortyish man with brushed-back bronze hair whom Mercer didn't recognize. He flicked a lever on the scope to double its magnification. The stranger had the sleek look of someone with power and he guessed that this was Rath's boss, the head of Kohl AG.

Mercer committed his face to memory.

Although the interior of the sub was thirty-one degrees and their breath was like clouds around their mouths and noses, Erwin Puhl was sweating when Mercer looked up from the periscope. "Thanks, Erwin. Take back your window on the world." The German jumped back to his normal position.

The stiffness had gone out of his leg, but Mercer still didn't put his full weight on it when he descended back to the control room.

"What's happening topside?" Ira asked. He was training Marty and Hilda how to operate the planesmen's stations. Anika Klein was at the small chart table rereading the captain's logbook. She had already translated the sections pertaining to how they would negotiate the twists and turns necessary to escape the cavern through the submarine channel. It promised to be an interesting trip.

"Rath has already dragged a few boxes to the surface, and everything else is about destroyed. I bet they'll clear out within twenty-four hours."

"How is Erwin doing?" Anika asked.

"Fine as long as he has his periscope."

"Mercer!" Erwin called from above them. "They're about to shoot at the barrels."

"What?"

"There are three men with assault rifles at the edge of the dock. Rath's talking with them. I think they're going to sink the fuel drums in the lagoon."

"Shit. Rath's a thorough son of a bitch, isn't he?" Mercer recognized the implication immediately. "Stand by to lower the scope."

"Why?" Puhl's voice cracked.

"Because of the barrel covering it. They'll know something's up if it doesn't sink when they shoot it." Ira had already moved to the snorkel controls

"I . . . I can't." He was terrified. "They're shooting now. Barrels are sinking."

"He has to tell me when," Ira said. "You go up there."

"No. Erwin needs to do this or he won't last five minutes once we're cut off."

"Oh, God, they're aiming right at me," Puhl screamed.

"Lower your goddamned voice," Mercer hissed. They all heard a fusillade of rounds pound the barrel above them. *"Now!"*

"I can't."

"Now!" Mercer snapped. "Or so help me Christ, claustrophobia's going to be the least of your problems."

"They hit the snorkel."

Mercer nodded at Ira to retract their only access to fresh air. "Lower the scope, Erwin."

The terrified meteorologist didn't reply but the hydraulics activated and the attack periscope sank into its well. Erwin came down a moment later and ran forward, staggering at the circular hatch leading out of the control room. He almost made it to the tiny lavatory before he threw up.

"I should check on him." Anika got up from her seat.

"Leave him," Ira said. "Mercer's right. He needs to get through this on his own."

Blind, cut off from oxygen, and stuck in what

amounted to a narrow tube, even Mercer felt the walls start to close in. Filling the batteries with acid would do them no good now because they couldn't run the charging generator without fresh air and a way to vent the exhaust. They were trapped on the bottom until Geo-Research left the cavern.

"Never thought I'd say this, but I hope Rath hurries the hell up."

"Amen."

There was no reason for the crew to sleep on a regular schedule except habit, but at midnight the U-boat was lit by a single red bulb in the control room. The only sound came from the patter of condensation dripping from nearly every surface. They had spent the day under Ira's gifted tutelage learning everything they would need to guide the sub out of the cavern when the time came.

Anika lay awake in her bunk above Hilda Brandt's. The tension of the past days, the horror of it all, was finally cracking her resolve. Erwin had his burning drive to prevent the meteorite fragments from falling into Kohl's hands to give him strength. Marty sustained himself by knowing he'd become more of a man in the past week than he'd ever been. As a trained sailor, Ira Lasko seemed immune to the stress. She didn't know how Hilda held herself together, her time in the Bundeswehr, Germany's army, perhaps.

And Mercer? He accepted every situation so calmly that Anika couldn't envision a crisis that would faze him. She was sure he was as scared as the rest of them but his impassive demeanor allowed him to work through it effortlessly. Anika recalled her first shifts on ER duty and the near-paralyzing fear she'd felt. It took months of experience to build the confidence necessary to overcome her anxiety. She wondered at Mercer's experience—what he'd done in the past to let him handle bomb threats, plane crashes, infernos, and everything else thrown at them.

It was in the solitude of the nights that Anika realized she needed some of his strength. She paused to listen to the boat and heard nothing but drips and an occasional snore from Ira farther forward. She tossed aside the World War Two–era blankets and unzipped her sleeping bag. She slept clothed in everything but her boots, and she gave a little gasp when the cold of the deck plating leached through her socks. In the ruddy light from the control room she could see the curtain covering the entrance to Mercer's cabin. She took a tentative step, wondering how far she would take this.

"Where are you going?" Hilda Brandt whispered.

Anika swallowed an unexpected jolt of guilt. "I have to pee."

"The toilet is behind you past the wardroom," Hilda reminded with a trace of humor in her voice. The chef knew where she was going.

Thankful for the dark because her face was flushed with embarrassment, Anika turned and padded to the bathroom.

"Better?" Hilda teased knowingly when Anika returned to her bunk.

"No."

The first explosion came a little past seven the next morning. Mercer was alone at the chart table, cleaning Cosmoline from the pair of MP-40 *Schmeisser* machine pistols he'd found in his cabin along with a broom-handled Mauser—a pistol that had been an antique even when the sub was built. He'd already checked and matched the ammo. He looked upward as if he could see through the hull and the water. Not that he needed to see to know what was happening. "Garbage dump," he said. At the second rumble he added, "Slave area." The third would be the excavation that was already partially blocked, and then came the longest detonation, a rolling thunder that went on for five minutes, amplified by the acoustics of the cavern, the lagoon, and the U-boat. The main access tunnel had just come down, blasted into an impenetrable wall of rubble by explosive charges. Working around the clock the Germans had completed their task and sealed the cavern forever.

"What the hell was that?" Ira charged into the control room from the radio shack, where he'd been attempting to fix the wireless or the sonar gear. He'd had no luck with either.

"Gunther Rath burning his bridges, Chief," Mercer replied passively. He'd started teasing Ira by using his former rank during their days of training. "We'll give it an hour or two to let the dust settle and then surface the boat."

"They're gone?"

Mercer nodded. "Unless a few had a death wish."

In a swirling vortex of air bubbles, the U-boat rose from the bottom two hours later, black water streaming off her outer hull. Erwin Puhl was in the conning tower and he threw open the hatch, not caring about the torrent of water that doused him. Although the cavern was pitch-black, he took the first deep breaths he'd enjoyed since losing the use of the periscope.

"How's that?" Mercer asked from below.

"Heaven," he sighed, fingering water from his glasses.

Within a few minutes, Ira fired the port diesel. The engine ran rough from fuel contamination and tar-thick oil, but he felt he could keep it running long enough to reach Iceland. Mercer went ashore to check the cavern, finding it much as he'd predicted. There was no evidence that anything man-made had ever been in the chamber, and all the alcoves were blocked with debris. Boulders and loose rock from the entrance tunnel spilled far onto the main floor, indicating a great deal of its length had been dynamited. He was confident that Rath and his men had collapsed a similar amount of the tunnel near the surface.

If they couldn't negotiate the sub through the zig-zagging underwater channel, they would die here in the darkness. He returned to the U-boat to help Ira

fill the battery cells with acid. Once they recharged—
if they recharged—they would be ready to leave.

After an hour of noxious work in the cramped aft
battery room below the galley, Ira announced that
they were in trouble.

"Considering our circumstances, you're not telling
me anything new." Mercer's eyes streamed tears from
the caustic fumes.

Lasko's normal humor had abandoned him. "I mean
real trouble. Most of these batteries are worse off than
I thought. The ones taking a charge leak like sieves.
Once we close the hatches, the sub's going to fill with
chlorine gas a lot faster than I anticipated."

Mercer tensed. "How long do you think we can
stand it?"

"Depends on the individual. But after an hour or
so the boat's gonna be a coffin ship."

"Can you rig some breathers for us?"

"I can, but that's not the problem. With acid eating
into the functioning batteries, the boat's electric motor
will lose power long before the first of us checks out.
Have you figured out how long it takes to get through
the tunnel and out to open sea?"

Mercer's expression darkened. "According to the
captain's log, about an hour and a half."

"Figures," Ira said sourly.

"All's not lost. All we have to do is push our speed
over what he wrote to shave off some time. It won't
take me long to make corrections in the timing of our
turns to compensate."

"You're forgetting that his figures are based on
traveling a certain amount of time at certain RPMs
before making a turn. Back then his boat was loaded
with stores and a crew of fifty. We're at least a hundred tons lighter, which will make us faster. I can double the RPMs but that won't necessarily mean that
you can halve the time."

"I hadn't thought of that," Mercer admitted.
"Any suggestions?"

"Factor in a speed difference of about half a knot

faster than the captain used and hope to Christ you're right."

"What do you mean 'hope *I'm* right'? It's your idea."

Ira smirked. "I don't want the others blaming me when we plow into a tunnel wall because we missed a turn."

It took a further two hours to get ready. Once the batteries were charged and any electrical faults repaired, Ira made certain that the air tanks were topped to their maximum pressure tolerance. Using the diesel, they swung the antique away from the pier and lined up with the entrance to the submerged channel out of the cavern. Hilda and Anika would operate the planes while Marty was at the helm to control the rudder. Ira had stationed himself at the ballast control. Mercer stood at the plotting table, where he could watch the gyrocompass. On the table were a pair of dividers and the captain's log, which lay open to the chart of the submerged passage. The rough sketch of the tunnel showed a twisting tube filled with numerous obstacles the sub would have to avoid as it wormed its way to the outlet in the fjord.

"We're in position," Erwin called from the conning tower. He had noted their distance off the dock using the attack scope's range finder.

"You know what you have to do," Mercer shouted back up to him.

The scope sank back into its mount and a second later Erwin sealed them in. This time he actually walked calmly to the bathroom and had time to close the door before he began retching.

Without the pounding throb of the diesel, the boat was remarkably quiet.

"Chlorine gas is already starting to build up," Ira said, though it would be a while before they would smell it.

Mercer consulted his chart, noting how sharply the cavern floor had dropped off from the pier. "Ira, make your depth sixty meters. Helm steady. Planes at neutral." Mercer thought he sounded like an actor in an old war movie, but his crew responded to his orders without question.

"Hold there, Ira," Anika called, her eyes riveted to the fathometer at her station.

"Gotta tell me earlier or else we'll sink past our target depths," Ira said, compensating for the mistake.

"Aye, aye. Okay, depth sixty meters."

"Here we go, boys and girls." Consulting his revised propulsion figures, Mercer spoke crisply. "Give me ninety RPMs for ten minutes starting"—he checked the ratcheting second hand on his TAG Heuer—"now!"

Silently the U-boat began to creep across the lagoon, a washing hiss sounding through her hull as she cut the water. "I'll need two degrees up on the planes when I give the command in about five minutes."

"We're ready," Anika said.

"I'll be damned, Chief." Mercer grinned, momentarily overcoming his uneasiness. "You actually did it. You got this thing going."

"Don't thank me. Wolfgang Rossler's the man we owe our lives to. If the Nazis had had a few more like him, they could have won the war on maintenance alone."

When it was time, Mercer gave the order to raise the bow planes to reduce their depth. Ira asked if he should vent water from the tanks, but the log indicated that this maneuver was done only with the planes. After another five minutes the tunnel took its first turn to the right.

"Marty, steer right ten degrees. I'll tell you when to ease off." This was a shallow turn in what the chart said was the widest part of the passage. Mercer wasn't concerned about hitting anything yet. That fear would come later. He watched the compass next to him. "Okay, ease her back. A little more. That's it." He let out a breath. "Increase to one hundred and thirty revs and prepare for a hard turn to port in two minutes."

They were well inside the sunken conduit, surrounded on all sides by rock and ice. A miscalculation in any direction would kill them all. No one knew if the tunnel was still wide enough to allow the sub passage, so they were forced to crawl along blindly, unable to reduce their speed because of the chlorine gas filling the bilge.

"Marty, coming up is a ninety-degree corner, so bring us to port as fast as you can spin the wheel. Now! Anika, ten degrees down on the planes. Make your depth eighty meters."

"That's two hundred and fifty feet," she said. "Can this old hull take it?"

"We'll know in a minute."

Creaking like a sailing ship caught in a typhoon, the U-boat spiraled deeper into the abyss. Her moans reminded Mercer of whale song. "All right, straighten her back out. Reduce RPMs to one hundred. We've got a long stretch at this depth. Make sure she doesn't drift."

Like steel nails drawn across a chalkboard, the U-boat scraped against the side of the tunnel. The impact made them clutch their seats. The sub veered away from the wall and then drifted back again, harder, the hull plates screaming. Dislodged rocks hit the hull like cannon fire.

"Shit! Marty, bring us to starboard two points." The unholy screeching died as soon as Bishop spun the wheel.

"What happened?" Erwin cried. He'd run into the control room at the first impact, too scared to remain in his bunk despite his claustrophobia

"We needed to scrape some barnacles off the side of the boat," Mercer replied. "We should be back in our lane again. Marty, bring her back to eight degrees magnetic."

"You did take the North Pole's drift into account, didn't you?" Bishop asked.

"And the fact we're moving with the current, which according to the chart runs at two knots."

They continued on this course for twenty minutes when Erwin, who was at the back of the control room, began to cough. Mercer looked over his shoulder and saw a sickly green mist rising from the engine room behind him. Chlorine gas. The first tendrils seemed to wrap around Erwin's stooped form like tentacles of some wrathful creature.

"Hold out for as long as you can before using the air tanks I rigged," Ira reminded.

Mercer got his first stinging taste of the chlorine. His eyes burned. They had another fifty minutes before they reached the open. It was going to be close. In order to protect their vision, everyone donned the protective goggles they'd used to combat the arctic weather.

"The tunnel floor's about to rise," Mercer said. "Prepare to blow tanks to bring us to fifty-five meters, ten degrees up on the plane. Marty, we've got a quick series of turns coming up, port, starboard, port. You just turn the wheel when I tell you. Increase to one hundred and thirty RPMs again when we level out."

They went into the turns at the increased speed, the old sub tilting first one way and then the other on Mercer's commands. He didn't tell them that the channel through the S-turn was just wide enough to allow the maneuver.

The tail slammed into a rocky pinnacle coming out of the first curve, slewing the boat like it had been torpedoed. Mercer's call for a quick correction wasn't fast enough. They went into the second turn and the bows veered into the rock face, reverberations booming like the inside of a church bell. Erwin shrieked and Anika's knuckles whitened on the plane control wheel.

"We're doing fine," Mercer said, choking when he took a lungful of gas. "Marty, bring us to port, bearing ninety degrees."

Marty nodded, unable to speak around the accordion tube from his air cylinder. The hull creaked.

Mercer didn't understand what had happened. The

chart said that they shouldn't have hit anything that second time. The pipe was supposed to have widened. The next turn was in five minutes, and he wasn't sure if they were traveling in the middle of the passage or along one side. They didn't have the luck to consider they were in the middle, so Mercer had two choices. Were they far left or far right?

The control room was filled up to their knees in heavy chlorine gas, wisps rising up like fog from a haunted moor.

"Marty, are you right- or left-handed?" Mercer asked and finally started drawing breath from his own cylinder. Marty held up his left hand. "Bring us two points to starboard for a minute and on my command crank us to port."

If Mercer's guess was wrong, they would plow straight into the far side of the turn at roughly six knots. That kind of blow would crumple the bow like aluminum foil. "Helm, steer us to one hundred and thirty degrees." Everyone felt the tension in his voice.

Angled over so they had to brace themselves, the sub went through the turn, gas pooling against the bulkheads like a liquid. Mercer held his breath. They all did. The beat of the propellers through the water sounded like a distant drumroll. By Mercer's watch they were halfway through the turn. He checked the chart and lurched. The bottom of the tunnel had dropped away and the ceiling had lowered. They were supposed to be at seventy meters!

"Dive!"

Ira twisted open valves to flood the bow ballast tanks at the same time Anika and Hilda cranked the dive planes as far as they could go. The sub seemed to stand on its nose, loose articles crashing to the deck all along the length of the vessel. Mercer's feet came out from under him and he swung free, dangling from a steel pipe.

They didn't quite make it. The top of the conning tower crashed into the underside of the subterranean channel, ripping away both periscopes in a wrenching squeal of torn metal. Water flooded the attack center located in the sail and would have filled the ship if it weren't for one more watertight hatch. A wall of chlorine gas as dense as smoke raced down the boat, cutting visibility to almost zero until Anika brought the bow back up, leveling her out at eighty meters just as her keel began to scrape the bottom. The noxious cloud settled again, reaching up to Mercer's waist.

"Bring us to seventy meters. Ira, neutral buoyancy again." Mercer checked the compass and saw that Marty had them perfectly on course. "Good job. That was my fault. Sorry."

Mercer paid for complimenting them. Seared by gas, his lungs went into convulsions and vomit shot from his mouth. He sucked great drafts from his air bottle, cleansing the tortured tissue. They had only one more change of depth to clear a peak in the channel and fifteen more minutes to go.

He knew they wouldn't last that long. Marty had been on his bottle much longer than he had, and Mercer could imagine poor Erwin had been hyperventilating since they'd left the cavern. He changed the figures on the chart, making a quick guess rather than an accurate calculation. "Maximum revolutions!"

The tachometer peaked at two hundred twenty RPMs. "Bring us to thirty meters on my mark." Mercer could feel the sub racing along the bottom of the tunnel, careening toward a bump on the seafloor that rose nearly a hundred feet. Come up too soon and they slammed into the ceiling of the passage. Too late and they would barrel into the mount. "Ten degrees up on the planes. Mark!"

Mercer made up for his earlier mistake. His timing was perfect. Like a crop duster swooping over a field, the two-hundred-fifty-foot-long submarine rose off the bottom of the tunnel and climbed the sloped side of the hill, her keel never more than ten feet from its irregular surface. At thirty meters, the U-boat cleared the top of the mound with the ceiling of the tunnel now only forty feet above her ruined conning tower.

Level once again and her screws churned with every remaining amp in her batteries. From here it was a race to the open sea. Mercer's gamble had saved them nearly eight minutes.

"When we surface," Ira said and took another draw from his breathing tube, "I'm going to blow compressed air through the boat to vent the gas. Be prepared for a pressure change."

Once he was satisfied they had cleared the tunnel and entered the fjord, Mercer ordered Ira to blow the tanks. The climb from a hundred feet seemed to take forever. His air supply was about exhausted, and each breath was a supreme effort that left his chest aching. Anika and Ira were in even worse shape.

Come on, damm it. We are so close. He gave Anika a draw off his supply and she sucked at it greedily. *Hers must be empty,* he thought. Passing through twenty meters, Mercer felt his vision begin to close in on him and he took the breathing tube back for a moment. He could taste Anika on the mouthpiece.

Somehow, Erwin found the strength to climb the ladder to the escape hatch. He wasn't going to remain on the U-boat one second longer than necessary, pushed more by fear of confinement than of the gas.

The sub emerged from the sea bow first, lifting forty feet from the water before slamming back again, blowing off sheets of frothing water. Protected from the waves of the Denmark Strait by the fjord's towering mountains, the cauldron of turgid water around the sub was the only mark on the otherwise calm bay. She rolled for a moment as Ira pumped up the air pressure in an effort to vent the poison gas.

As soon as the ex-Navy man nodded to Erwin, he undogged the hatch. Air pressure blew the hatch outward, sucking out a majority of the gas. Icy water from the flooded attack room rained into the control space, showering the crew. Erwin scrambled up the ladder, twisting around the bent remains of the two scopes to reach the next ladder. The outer hatch spun freely and he threw it open, reveling in their first sight of daylight in a week, Hilda and Anika at his heels. He clambered the rest of the way out of the sub and stood fully upright, facing eastward to the open end of the fjord several miles away.

No one heard the shots hammering the conning tower, but the metallic twang of ricochets sounded clearly, lead and fractured steel exploding in all directions.

Erwin felt a twin sting as his brain registered what was happening and he went limp, allowing himself to fall back into the attack center. His blood stained the pooled water pink. Hilda screamed. Even as the barrage continued against the U-boat's steel hull, Anika began to check his injuries.

Like her, Mercer didn't hesitate. It was as if he'd expected such an ending to this hellish trek. He raced back to his cabin and reemerged with a machine pistol in each fist, spare clips tucked into the pocket of his snow pants. Wordlessly, he tossed one MP-40 to Ira, racked back the cocking handle on his own, and climbed for the bridge.

The Geo-Research Bell Jetranger 414 flared into a maelstrom of ice and snow that its rotors had just kicked up. The impenetrable fog settled only after the blades began to slow, dusting the two idling Sno-Cats, a dozen men, and a cargo sledge stacked with the recovered Pandora boxes. The smaller box, found in the antechamber at the top of the air vent, was kept separate. The snow around the vent had been trampled flat by the frantic work to recover the golden chests. Nothing remained of the tunnel itself but a stain of dust that had belched from it when it had been dynamited. The men who had completed the work waited for the rotor-stat to come and carry the boxes away.

Klaus Raeder was sitting in the insulated Sno-Cat and hadn't heard the chopper's approach until it was nearly upon them. The flash of anger that jolted his body gave way to an eerie calm. There was no need for the chopper here. That meant Rath was about to make his play for the deadly hoard. For the tenth time in the past hour, he glanced into the cargo area behind the 'Cat's rear seat. The two assault rifles used to sink the fuel drums in the cavern were safely locked into an integrated rack. Raeder stripped off his heavy glove and jammed his right hand into his snowsuit pocket, where he had the loaded automatic pistol he'd taken from his office. He'd had no problem sneaking the weapon out of Germany. Customs paid little attention to corporate jets.

He opened the vehicle's door and stepped out. There was little wind, but the air was as clear and cold as crystal. Gunther Rath stood a short way off with Greta and the professional driver, Dieter. Before Raeder took two paces, a shadow passed overhead. He looked up. The rotor-stat had come over the crest of the mountains that divided the ice sheet from the sea, its bulk eclipsing the weak sun for a moment. It was an otherworldly sight, more befitting Titans than men. The four engine pods mounted on the side of her great white hull were larger than the Jetranger helicopter sitting insectlike in the snow.

The pitch of its airship's engines changed as it began to slowly settle toward earth.

Raeder approached Rath. "What is the helicopter doing here?"

"The rotor-stat won't be able to land out here without a mooring mast. We'll attach her lifting cables to the cargo and then follow in the chopper as she heads out to sea to drop the boxes."

"No." Raeder wouldn't pretend to go along with this charade. "I'm not going to let the Pandora boxes out of my control until I know they will be dumped. We are getting on the rotor-stat."

"Klaus, she can't pick us up without a mooring mast," Rath said placidly. "We can watch from the chopper."

The noise of the descending airship increased as she fell below the tops of the mountains, the drone of her power plants echoing off the rock. The downdraft from her rotors began to stir the surface snow.

Rath's logic was reasonable. It was always reasonable, Klaus reflected. His special-projects director could find excuses for murder and torture and make it sound sensible, as if there was no other way. But there were always other ways—only it had been easier for Raeder to let Rath give in to his brutality. No more. Raeder had just a few minutes left. The boxes would slip from his grasp if the dirigible took off without him. "This is as far as I'm going to let you go, Gunther. Tell the airship pilot to pick us up."

Raeder's pistol came out in an easy maneuver, unwavering and deadly.

And then the gun was lying in the snow ten feet away and Klaus Raeder's arm was numb from fingertips to elbow.

Klaus Raeder looked first at his limp hand and then at the gun and finally at Gunther Rath. Expecting the pistol to paralyze Rath, Raeder had not anticipated the lightning kick that sent the automatic flying. Rath stood implacably, a trace of a smile on his face as if inviting Raeder to dive for the weapon. He was closer by ten feet, but when he peered beyond Greta and Rath, Raeder saw that the workers who'd emptied the Pandora cavern had watched the one-sided confrontation. And each man was armed with either an assault rifle or a pistol. The guns in the back of the Sno-Cat weren't the only ones Rath had brought to the area. Raeder realized too that he didn't have the men's loyalty. They were Rath's.

"Klaus, I don't blame you for trying to stop me. I think I would have been disappointed if you hadn't." Gunther picked up the fallen pistol and handed it to Greta.

Knowing he had been outmaneuvered, Raeder accepted temporary defeat. "What do you plan to do with them? No one will ever be able to build a bomb with the meteor fragments."

"They don't need a chain reaction, Klaus. Hitler's plan was to load bits of it into V-2 rockets at Peenemunde and launch them at London. They were designed to explode a thousand feet above the ground and spread their radioactive payload over a tremendous area. Since much of London was rubble, the Pandora dust would have lain there undetected with all the other debris, silently poisoning an entire population. It was estimated that just six warheads would have killed every living thing in London within two months.

"It seems, though, that the U-boat used to transport the fragments must have been lost during the mining operation and an accident in the cavern killed everyone else. I assume *Der Führer* lost interest in the project then.

"However, in today's world, the Pandora fragments have a certain value as a terrorist weapon. It's less random than a chemical weapon, easier to maintain than a biologic one and unlike other radiation sources, it is completely untraceable. Just a few grams placed in, say, a busy subway station would consign every person walking by to a lingering death. As it decays, it creates its own shielding and can be removed safely. I can't think of a better weapon for terrorism, can you?"

"You're going to sell them?"

Rath looked pleased with himself as he replied, "I had three different bids to choose from. North Korea offered the most money, but I can't see exiling myself to Pyongyang. Ditto goes for Iraq. I ended up accepting the Libyan offer since it's close enough to Europe to sneak over occasionally."

"What about your precious Nazi Party now? Are you abandoning them?"

"Who do you think gets most of the hundred million dollars?"

Thirty minutes later, the cargo pallet laden with the boxes was secured to the airship's lifting cables. Raeder, Rath, and Greta Schmidt were in the back of the stripped-down Bell helicopter. The workers were already aboard the two Sno-Cats and on their way back to the temporary northern camp, where they would disassemble everything for the return to Camp Decade. Because the weight of the cargo approached her maximum limit, the rotor-stat had to first fly out over the ice sheet to build up aerodynamic lift before turning back for the coast. It took the dirigible twenty minutes to gain the thousand feet of altitude she needed to clear the mountains. Only then did the Jetranger take off with the smallest Pandora box resting between Rath and Raeder. Greta sat next to her lover, the confiscated pistol clutched on her lap.

Klaus Raeder twisted in his window seat to get a glimpse of the rotor-stat trailing the helicopter. The airship was sailing a half mile behind them and yet seemed ready to swallow the chopper. After being airborne for ten minutes, they were still over Greenland's jagged coast of bays, inlets, and fjords. That was when Raeder saw the research ship *Njoerd* in a narrow bay two thousand feet below them.

He realized that the cargo would be transferred to the ship but didn't understand why. He asked Rath.

"For one, we need the rotor-stat to return the Sno-Cats to Camp Decade. Also the airship tends to advertise her presence wherever she is. My plan is for the *Njoerd* to take the boxes to Tripoli while the rotor-stat returns to Europe for the completion of her test flights."

A large area of deck behind the *Njoerd*'s superstructure had been cleared to receive the cargo of golden crates, and workers were preparing to guide the nets into position. The chopper swung wide to leave plenty of room for the ponderous dirigible as it descended toward the ship. Hovering a quarter mile astern and five hundred feet up, the pilot spun so that his passengers could watch the delicate placement of the cargo.

Suddenly, a portion of sea just fifty yards from the research ship came alive, as if the water was being boiled. Like Leviathan rising, a gray torpedo shape emerged from the swelling waves, rising into the air until a quarter of the vessel's length was exposed. *"Mein Gott!"* Rath, Raeder, and Schmidt said at once. They recognized the antique U-boat at the same time and knew where it had come from.

Still bobbing on the swells of its own creation, the conning tower hatch crashed open and a figure emerged. Rath ordered the pilot in for a closer look, hoping it was Mercer who had exited the submarine first because some of his guards were already at the rail of the *Njoerd* armed with assault rifles.

Before Rath could discern the man's features, winking lights shot from the weapons and the man vanished in a red mist. "Patch me through to the rotor-stat," Rath ordered.

A moment later the airship's pilot came over the radio. "What do you want me to do?"

"Abort the cargo transfer until we take care of the submarine."

"I don't know if I can. The engines are straining just to slow our vertical descent."

The airship's four rotors whipped the air so strongly, they rippled her Kevlar skin. The dirigible would need to build up forward speed so her airfoil shape gave her additional lift. The cargo nets dangled only fifty feet from the surface of the bay. Her heavy mooring lines already trailed in the water. Rath looked back to the sub just as another person gained access to her protected bridge. It was Mercer, and he remained huddled out of sight from the *Njoerd*. His attention was on the airship, so he didn't notice the helicopter hovering behind him.

Making sure his seat belt was tight and Greta had Klaus covered, Gunther Rath opened the Jetranger's side door. Arctic air blasted him like a hurricane and numbed his face and hands. He couldn't wear his gloves and fire accurately, so he left them off when he drew his pistol. He activated the weapon's specially mounted laser sight. With the sub rolling and the chopper bouncing, he doubted he could get off an accurate shot, but all he wanted was Mercer's attention until the rotor-stat could bull its way out of the fjord. The red dot of light wavered all over the top of the conning tower until it streaked across Mercer's stooped form. Rath began firing.

From his vantage, Mercer couldn't see the rotor-stat. He could only hear it thundering above him. Its noise drowned out everything. Figuring they couldn't see him, he chanced a look over the lip of the bridge's coaming. That was when he spotted the *Njoerd* and the men lined at her side with weapons trained at him. He ducked again as fire raked the conning tower.

When Erwin had fallen back into the sub and he'd heard the dirigible, Mercer had assumed the shots had come from above. Now he knew who had fired the scathing fusillade. They'd surfaced right in the middle of the cargo transfer.

"If it weren't for bad luck . . ." he whispered. Ira's head appeared through the hatch. "How's Erwin?"

"Anika's working on him now. I don't think it's too bad. What happened?"

"The *Njoerd* is about fifty yards off the port side, and the rotor-stat's hovering just beyond her. She's coming this way. Get back below and crank up the compressors. Fill the ballast tanks with air and prepare to dive. Leave your gun. I have an idea."

"I don't like it when you say that," Ira remarked and disappeared below.

Mercer was preparing to take another look at the airship when a shard of white-hot steel ricocheted inside the bridge and buried itself in his thigh. He fell heavily, clamping a hand over the burning wound, and looked up. A big Bell helicopter hung in the sky behind him with its side door opened. He could clearly see the pistol in Gunther Rath's hand and the sick smile on his face. Fluidly, Mercer pulled the MP-40 from under him and squeezed the trigger. The heavy machine pistol bucked like he was holding a live wire and jammed after half its thirty-two-round magazine emptied. As he recocked to clear the fouled breach, the chopper twisted out of range.

He next aimed blindly toward the *Njoerd* and pulled the trigger again, raising himself as the barrage scattered the gunmen at the vessel's rail. In the moment's reprieve before they regrouped, he slammed home a fresh magazine. He yelled down the hatch, "Marty, I need help!"

"Screw this. Let's get out of here."

Though angered, Mercer couldn't bring himself to blame Martin Bishop. Sealing the hatch and motoring away would be the smart thing to do. But Mercer wouldn't let that happen. Not when he had a chance to end this once and for all. The Pandora boxes were vulnerable, and judging by the width of the fjord and the height of the mountains, the bay was a thousand feet deep. More than enough.

"Goddamn it, Marty, get your ass up here." The rotor-stat was struggling over the *Njoerd*'s deck, slowly building speed that would become altitude in a few moments. While the cargo nets were out of range, the airship's mooring lines made parallel V's as they were dragged through the calm water. They would sweep across the U-boat's forward deck in twenty seconds or less. The monstrous gas bag blotted out the sun as it came toward him, its shadow spreading across the bay like a malignancy. Prop wash stirred the water behind her.

"What do you need?" Marty appeared at the hatch, his firm voice in opposition to his frantic eyes.

"Take this." Mercer handed him Ira's MP-40. "Point it at the helicopter if it gets too close or at the *Njoerd* if those men get organized again."

"I've never fired a gun in my life. What if I need to change the clip?"

"If you need that much ammo, I'll probably be dead."

In his nervousness, Mercer cocked his gun again by mistake and ejected an unused round. The chopper was a quarter mile away, watching from a safe distance. Rath's pistol was no match for a submachine gun. The men who'd been at the *Njoerd*'s rail had found cover behind her gunwale or pieces of equipment. They darted looks at the stationary submarine and fired occasional rounds to keep Mercer pinned. They seemed content with the stalemate because it allowed the rotor-stat the time it needed to get clear.

"Screw that," Mercer said and unleashed a burst at the research vessel, satisfied by the angry sparks of lead meeting steel. He vaulted over the bridge rail on the opposite side of the conning tower and landed on the deck in a heap. Rath's chopper roared at him, but when he raised his weapon it banked away again. Rath took a snap shot as it pirouetted and hit nothing.

The dirigible was directly overhead, looming like a forty-story building. Emptying a clip into its belly would have had the same effect as spitballs against an elephant, so Mercer ignored it. The mooring lines were what he wanted. They dangled from her bow to the sea, crossing over the sub's hull in the center of the U-boat's forward deck. In seconds, the fleeing airship would draw them out of reach. Mercer would need to cross thirty feet of metal no-man's-land with an unknown number of gunmen holding him in their sights. His mouth was dry and his leg strobed with pain in time with his heart. Now or never.

"Cover me, Marty!" He couldn't be sure he had been heard over the airship's quad rotors, but he launched himself anyway.

The firing began at once and was met by a burst from the conning tower. Mercer ran on, weaving along the deck until his foot caught against a hatch and he sprawled. Bullets searched him out and he scrambled to his feet, firing to his left as he cradled the MP-40. The mooring ropes were manila, at least three inches around, permanently attached to the airship's internal structure and strong enough for ground handlers to haul the rotor-stat against a stiff breeze. As one oozed across the deck like a fleeing snake, Mercer dropped to his knees, fired the last of his clip at the *Njoerd*, and tossed aside his weapon. He needed both hands to lift the line. It was slick with seawater and doubly heavy. He ran back to the conning tower, Marty's wild bursts keeping the gunmen at bay for precious seconds. The rough line smeared skin off his hands as the rotor-stat towed it past the U-boat. By the time he reached cover, only fifty feet remained before the end would slither through his grasp.

He looked up to see the chopper returning. Rath must have realized what he was attempting and was coming in to stop him. Rath's clothes whipped in the downbeat of the helo's rotor. The noise drowned the report but Mercer knew the German had fired from the recoil of his gun arm. He wrapped a loop of the mooring rope around a railing stanchion so it wouldn't be dragged back forward.

A shouted warning to Marty was muffled by the rotor-stat, so all Mercer could do was pray as he threw himself off the side of the sub, more shots pinging against the U-boat's metal hide.

The frigid water sucked his breath out the instant it reached his skin. The cold was solid, like ice, but much, much worse. It pounded against his skull and lanced into his joints. The wound in his leg went numb. Mercer's clothes quickly became saturated, and he felt himself being dragged under the surface. Kicking first one foot and then the other, he managed to remove his moon boots, saving himself several pounds, but the swim back up was agonizingly slow.

His head broke the surface. He reached for and grabbed one of the many slits in the sub's outer hull. The Bell Jetranger was showing her tail as she moved out of range again. Marty must have chased him off. Mercer struggled to climb the side of the boat, the rough edges in the slits digging into his stocking feet like razor blades.

A hand touched his arm and he saw Anika Klein reaching for him. She must have joined Marty on the bridge and jumped to the deck when she saw Mercer dive into the water.

"Tie off the landing line!" The shout sounded distant in Mercer's frozen brain.

"Marty's doing it." She got a grip on Mercer's forearm and heaved him up to the deck. A couple of feet away Marty worked knots into what little remained of the disappearing landing rope, threading the line through a number of larger hull slits.

It came taut just as he got the line secured to the sub. He looked up to see the rotor-stat come up short against its leash. Straining, the huge dirigible pivoted around its bow, losing altitude until her deadly cargo dipped into the ocean for a moment. Her engines screamed. "Got you, you son of a bitch," Marty shouted.

"Let's finish this." Mercer stood. Above them the *Schmeisser* rippled again, and Hilda Brandt motioned them to hurry, the black gun smoking in her beefy hands.

Like a fish struggling for its life, the airship whipped back and forth on the end of its tether, straining to break free from the U-boat. Rath must have radioed the pilots and told them that if they released the Pandora boxes their survival would be short-lived.

Mercer's hands were frozen claws as he climbed the ladder to the bridge under Hilda's covering fire. Anika's shoulder was under his backside as she headed to the top of the conning tower. Once they were safely on the bridge, Hilda directed them to get below. She would keep up a steady barrage to prevent anyone from the *Njoerd* launching a boat and cutting the line.

As he reached the control room, Mercer saw Erwin Puhl propped against the chart table. His shirt was off, and seeping bandages covered his shoulder and wrapped under his arm. The meteorologist was ashen, his lips pressed tight in pain.

"Are you okay?" Mercer asked through chattering teeth.

"Anika said I am. The first bullet went in and out under my arm. The other was a ricochet buried in my shoulder. It hurts but . . ."

"Ira," Mercer gasped as he started stripping off his wet clothes. "Are you ready?"

"Say the word."

"Close the hatch, Marty, and get down here."

Anika helped Mercer remove the remainder of his clothes. He stood naked and dripping watery blood, his skin blue and puckered. "Don't judge me in this condition," he said when she glanced at his groin. She threw blankets over him as Hilda and Marty descended into the sub.

"Dive!" The ballast tanks gurgled as they filled with water, and the boat slowly began to sink.

Above them, the rotor-stat pilot saw the swirl of air bubbles around the antique sub and knew what was going to happen next. His loyalty to Rath ended at that instant, and he nodded to his copilot. "Don't do it," he heard Rath screaming over the headset. "The *Njoerd* is sending out a boat to cut the mooring line. You can hold on."

"Dump it," the pilot said. The copilot hit a switch that severed the cables securing the cargo nets to the airship. Thirty tons of gold plundered by the Nazis and a ton of the deadliest element on the planet fell away from the dirigible. It splashed into the sea and vanished.

The rotor-stat rose like a child's balloon until it once again came up against the rope. Nose down and engines straining, she fought a tug-of-war against the sinking U-boat trying to pull her into the ocean. They would be free if they could hold out long enough for men from the *Njoerd* to cut the rope. The entire craft shuddered with the power of her four engines and massive rotors.

The pilot jettisoned fuel in an attempt to lighten his ship further, but it made no difference as the altimeter unwound slowly. He didn't need to look out the cockpit window to know it wouldn't even be close.

"What are we going to do?" his copilot asked.

Finally glancing out and seeing the smooth bay rising to meet them, the pilot's answer was just one word. "Die."

The bow of the airship struck in a colossal explosion of spray, and her remorseless downward plunge was checked. She continued to hang there, her nose like a dimple in the sea.

On the U-boat, they all felt the hull lurch when the rotor-stat hit the surface. Even with the ballast tanks full, the sub couldn't overcome the buoyancy of 1.2 million cubic feet of helium. The tug-of-war had come to a standstill.

"What's our depth?" Mercer gasped as he drew a mouthful of brandy to warm his insides.

"Forty meters and holding. We can't pull her under."

"We don't need to." Mercer's expression was savage. "Blow the tanks and surface."

Not fully understanding Mercer's plan, Ira blew compressed air back into the ballast tanks and watched the fathometer as the sub ascended once again.

Because of the airship's near-vertical position, the rotors were no longer adding lift, so when the sub rose and tension was released off the bow line, her tail dropped before the pilots could compensate. The massive underfin sliced into the water like a knife blade as she belly flopped and then she began a roll onto her side. Powered by jet turbines, the rotors sliced air in a blur, but when they came in contact with the water, the Teflon blades came apart like scythes. Hundred-foot slashes appeared in her skin and helium burst from the envelope in a screaming torrent. It was her death cry.

Half deflated and waterlogged, the airship settled into the water and began to sink, internal pressure pooling her lifting gas into pockets within her envelope that ruptured like boils. Part of her envelope fell across the stern of the *Njoerd,* Kevlar fabric tangling and snaring on her deck cranes. Men scrambled to cut away the entanglements before the huge weight capsized the ship. The airship's other engine pods struck the ocean, and more pieces of blade ravaged the gas bag and the *Njoerd.*

A hundred feet from the dirigible's limp bows, the U-boat appeared once again as plucky as a bathtub toy.

Gunther Rath had watched the destruction from a safe distance and when he saw the sub, he went berserk. "Get closer," he shouted at the pilot, loading a fresh magazine into his Glock.

He could see movement in the conning tower as two people came out on the deck. One held an ax while the other had a *Schmeisser.*

"There's nothing we can do," the pilot said.

"Get me down there!" Rath screwed the gun's muzzle into the pilot's ear.

The chopper came at the sub like a hawk in a stoop and raced into a burst of 9mm rounds from the MP-40. Rath got off only one shot of his own before the charge carried him out of range. In the moments it took the pilot to swing around for another pass, one of the men had leapt to the deck and was hacking at the rope with the ax. It parted at the third swing.

"I'll kill you!" Gunther Rath raged.

"I doubt it." Klaus Raeder laughed over the wind swirling through the helicopter's cabin. "You'll get one more shot off while they pump a dozen rounds into us. And then they'll close the hatch and there won't be a thing you can do."

"Darling, he's right," Greta said. "The boxes are gone, but we still have this one." She nudged the golden chest at her feet. "We can land on the *Njoerd* and be far away by the time they reach civilization."

For a second she thought he was going to shoot her for suggesting it. Instead, Rath reholstered his pistol and turned his gaze out to the ruined airship draped across the stern of the *Njoerd*. Greta wasn't going to risk asking him to close the door, so she hunkered deeper into her parka. Rath looked across to Klaus Raeder, sizing him up as if he were a commodity. He said nothing, but Raeder recognized the feral look of a cornered animal.

Rath was about to lash out. The emotion was there, just at the surface and ready to explode. Gunther reached into his coat again and withdrew the Glock. With a casual flick he tossed it out the door.

"I would have killed you if I hadn't," he explained. "By the time they get *Njoerd*'s deck cleared enough to get under way, Mercer will be halfway to Kulusuk. We'll never be able to catch him, so we're altering our plans. We're going someplace where I'm going to need you."

It took twenty frustrating minutes for the helipad on

the *Njoerd* to be cleared of debris from the destroyed airship. Once they were down, Rath learned that there wasn't enough aviation fuel on the ship to use the chopper for the next leg of their journey. They unlashed one of the powerful boats stored on the research vessel. By then the U-boat was long gone. An hour later, Gunther Rath, Greta Schmidt, and four of Rath's best security men were aboard the sleek, oceangoing boat. Klaus Raeder was trussed in the hold with the last box of meteorite fragments.

At thirty knots, the boat had a range of three hundred miles. They would make their destination shortly before nightfall.

Oily smoke billowed from the port diesel and poisonous vapor rose from the battery compartment, forcing the crew to leave all the sub's hatches open. Ira futilely waved a rag above the clattering forest of con-rods, cams, and lifters, trying to see what was fuming so badly. The noise of the faltering motor absorbed his string of curses.

"How's it look?" Mercer shouted over the din.

Lasko wiped grease from his face. "Like we aren't going to make it to Iceland, Kulusuk, or anywhere else." He spat a black glob onto the deck. "Piston rings are shot in at least two cylinders, gaskets are failing all over the place, and if it weren't for the oil I salvaged from the starboard engine, this pig would be dead in about an hour."

"What can you give us?"

Ira scratched the stubble now fringing his otherwise bald head. "Four hours, maybe five. We can return to the Greenland coast, but we'll be right back where we started from."

"So we've got a decision to make."

"Yup. Talk to the others. I'll go along with whatever you decide. I have to stay here and coax her along."

Mercer carefully backed out the narrow alley between the engines and ducked through two watertight hatches to reach the control room. He yelled up to the bridge at the top of the conning tower, where Marty was acting as lookout. Hilda Brandt sat at the helmsman's station, making sure the boat stayed on course. Anika had just come back to the control room after checking on Erwin, who was resting in his bunk.

Marty clambered down the ladder and moved to Anika's side.

"What's Erwin's condition, Doctor?" he asked her.

"He's fine. I've got antibiotics keeping infection at bay and he didn't lose enough blood for shock to be a concern. The bullet fragment in his shoulder should come out, but isn't doing much harm in the short term. The one that passed through under his arm didn't hit any major blood vessels or bone. I just wish there was something I could do for his pain."

"Erwin's a lot tougher than he looks," Marty opined.

"That's for sure."

"Okay, folks," Mercer began. "The good news is, we have enough brandy for an impromptu party. The bad news is, we can't invite guests since it appears we won't make it to civilization." His tone then became serious. "Ira says the engine won't last for more than five hours, meaning that if we continue east we'll stop long before Iceland, and if we turn south we won't reach Kulusuk either."

"What are our options?" Anika asked, confident by now that Mercer would find a way.

"A: we don't reach Kulusuk. And B: we don't reach Iceland. That's about it."

"Can we return to the coast of Greenland to wait for rescue?" Marty asked.

Mercer shook his head. "I doubt anyone will find us. Remember, this is one of the most remote places on earth. Providing we find a suitable place to beach, our food's just about gone, and without communications gear we'll be marooned again."

"We have guns. We can hunt seals," Marty said reasonably.

"Once Rath gets the *Njoerd* under way, he'll scour the coast looking for us. He'll spot the sub from his helicopter on the first pass. If you think we can submerge until he flies away, you can forget about it.

Because we know about the Pandora boxes, Rath won't leave until he's certain we're dead."

No one spoke for a minute because none could think of an argument. Their fear further chilled the control room.

"We have a third option." It was Erwin Puhl. He stood at the hatchway connecting the crew's quarters to the control room. His upper body was swathed in bandages. A wad of surgical tape at the bridge of his nose held the broken halves of his glasses together. "I heard you talking."

Anika crossed to him in three strides, bracing his shoulder with hers. She led him to the seat behind the plotting table. Her expression was a mix of concern and annoyance. She didn't want him out of bed, but the determination on his face led her to believe that any admonishments would be wasted. By the time she eased him into the chair, Erwin was trembling. In the dim light of the control room, his skin had become gray. A map of the Denmark Strait was flattened against the plotting table with the broom-handle Mauser pistol and the captain's log. "Where are we exactly?" he wheezed.

Mercer indicated a spot about eighty miles off the coast of Greenland, a bit south of the fjord they had just escaped.

"And today's date is the fifteenth, right? There is a ship coming through the strait tonight that will be about here in five hours. Well within our range."

"There isn't much shipping through these waters," Mercer said. "How do you know?"

"Because another member of the Brotherhood of Satan's Fist is on her to take possession of the last remaining icon that Rasputin commissioned—the one Leonid Kulik never destroyed."

Realization struck like a punch. "The Universal Convocation aboard the *Sea Empress*?"

"Yes. The pope is returning the icon to the Russian Orthodox Church, and Brother Anatoly Vatutin is there to receive it."

Mercer was silent for a second, thinking. "I remember when we first met you mentioned the *Empress* would be coming through the strait. I thought it was strange that you knew her route, considering it was supposed to be secret. Your colleague on the ship told you the sailing schedule."

"That's right," Erwin agreed.

"Why is the ship this far north?" asked Anika.

"To take advantage of the spectacular aurora borealis created by the solar-max effect."

Mercer didn't like coincidences and he was suspicious about this one. He thought there could be another reason the *Sea Empress* happened to be in these waters, but he kept it to himself. "How sure are you of this information?" he asked Erwin.

The scientist's voice firmed. "Positive. The top delegates had to approve the route long before they sailed. Brother Anatoly stole the schedule from Bishop Olkranszy, his superior at the convocation."

After Anika translated the conversation for Hilda's benefit, Mercer could see that the group was evenly mixed about their options and decided that this wasn't the time for a vote. It would be smarter just to make the decision himself.

He had gambled many lives over the years, his own the most often, and the burden never got lighter. The five other survivors had put their trust in him and as their leader Mercer had to do what he felt was necessary. Life, he'd learned, wasn't about making the most right decisions. That was simple. The true test was being able to minimize the effects of the wrong ones. And he felt he'd made so many of the latter in the past weeks that just one chance remained to put everything right again.

He carefully worked out the vector on the chart. "Anika, have Hilda steer one hundred and four degrees. Marty, run back to the engine room and tell Ira to open her up as much as he dares."

His orders were carried out instantly. "I'll be topside," he said, his voice suddenly becoming thick in his throat. "I need some air."

Like the night the *Titanic* sank a thousand miles south of their position, the ocean was as calm as a millpond. Darkness was creeping across the cloudless skies and already faint waves of light were appearing high in the heavens. The aurora was going to be breathtaking. Its added illumination would also reveal any drifting icebergs in plenty of time to maneuver around them. Mercer tightened the hood of his parka, jamming his fists into his pocket.

He was left alone on the bridge for a half hour until Anika bobbed up through the hatch. Wordlessly, she handed him two protein bars for dinner. They munched in silence. The cup of water had a skin of ice when she took a sip. Her eyes rarely left Mercer's face. "*Pfennig* for your thoughts."

"With the exchange rate, that's about half a cent," he said darkly. "Sounds like you're overpaying." His words stung her. "Sorry. I'd like to be alone right now."

"So you can brood?" she challenged.

"So I can think."

"For you, I believe it is the same thing. Why do you continue to blame yourself? Without you, we'd all have been dead on the plane from Camp Decade. Because I interviewed Otto Schroeder, if anyone is to blame it is me."

"No. It's Gunther Rath."

Mercer had fallen for her trap. Anika smiled, a kaleidoscope of color from the aurora shimmering off her jet hair. "See, you know the truth and yet you beat yourself up as if everything is your fault. That is foolish."

"For me, it's inevitable."

"Because you let it."

Mercer couldn't respond and they lapsed into silence again.

Anika fidgeted as if she had something she wanted to say and didn't know how. When she finally spoke, her voice faltered. "Back in the fjord, I should have stayed below to tend to Erwin. I am a doctor and my duty was to my patient. Instead I went up to the conning tower. I thought I just wanted to help. Now I realize what I really wanted was to take the gun from Hilda and shoot those men on the *Njoerd*. I've trained my entire life to ease suffering and all I could think about was killing them for being part of the same evil that murdered all those people in the cavern sixty years ago. I have never wanted to kill before." The admission cost her.

"But you didn't. Wanting to do something isn't a crime, Anika. I want to cheat on my taxes every year. That doesn't make me a criminal."

"Yes, but you haven't taken an oath to pay your taxes the way I have to heal people. My place was with Erwin, not indulging in my desire for revenge." She paused. "You've . . . you've killed people before, haven't you?"

"Yes. The crew on the blimp being the most recent."

"How do you, you know, handle it?"

I don't. I justify it by telling myself that they would have killed me if I hadn't acted first. Then I bury the guilt as deep as I can, praying that one day the nightmares go away. But Mercer didn't say it, afraid that voicing the truth would somehow crack the barricade he'd built around those emotions. "The same way you deal with the trauma patients you lose. You concentrate on those you did help."

Anika searched his eyes and saw the lie. She let it pass because the joyrider who'd died in the ER before she came to Greenland was the fifty-seventh patient she'd lost and she had no idea how many she'd saved. "I shouldn't have asked. I'm sorry. How's your leg?"

"It hurts a bit but the stitches you laid feel fine, thanks." Mercer recognized that she'd let him off the hook. "I should make you my full-time doctor."

"After the helicopter and the DC-3, I'm never get-

ting on a plane again. Don't expect me to come to
the States for a house call."

Mercer smiled. "I'll only get hurt in Europe."

They talked easily for the next couple of hours, not
about anything in particular, just enjoying the sound
of each other's voice. The cold finally forced Anika
below again. She paused at the hatch, unable to resist
returning to the subject they had left behind. "If you
ever want to compare nightmares," she said, "I'll be
there for you."

She ducked out of sight before Mercer could
respond.

Ira Lasko came up the hatch a moment later and
found Mercer laughing to himself. "What's the joke?"

"Me. I'm learning that I'm a lot more transparent
than I thought. How you doing down there?"

"My head's about ready to explode from fumes, but
I'm hanging in. We should be about an hour from the
Sea Empress. I think the engine's going to make it.
I've even managed to cobble together enough good
batteries to give us some electrical power to maneuver
once the diesel kicks out."

"Great job."

"You think we'll find the cruise ship?"

"She'll be lit up like a carnival, and the weather's
cooperating for once. I think we'll spot her." Mercer
moved to the hatch. "I might as well let a couple of
the others stand watch. I'm freezing my ass off."

Marty took over on the conning tower while Mercer
spent a few minutes in the engine room, soaking up
heat from the big diesel. He was back in the control
room when, with a grinding crash, the port engine
seized. The thrashing propeller stopped so suddenly
that the entire boat torqued over. The eerie silence
seemed unnatural after so many hours of clanking
noise.

"You goddamned whore!" Ira was heard shouting.
"You filthy piece of shit! You can do better than this."

"Chief, you're supposed to whisper sweet nothings
to machinery," Mercer yelled back.

"This is a German engine. They like the rough stuff." He came forward. "Sorry, folks. The bus stops here. We've got about twenty minutes of juice in the batteries if we just creep along."

Mercer double-checked the chart and his position estimates. "We should be right in front of the *Sea Empress* when she comes through. With any luck we won't need that much from the batteries."

"Have you thought of how we're going to board her? With antiradar coating on the conning tower, she'll never see us and if we do appear on her scopes we're going to look like a tiny iceberg that she can plow right over."

"That's what I'm hoping for," Mercer answered. "You've never seen a picture of the *Sea Empress,* have you? She's a huge catamaran capable of launching boats from between her hulls. We just line up in the gap and let her come right over us. Once abeam of her integrated marina, we jump aboard."

"I'll be damned." Ira nodded in admiration. "Teachers must have hated you in school."

"Why's that?"

"Because you have an answer for everything."

After half an hour of waiting on the still waters, Marty shouted to the control room, "Mercer, I see her. She looks like she'll pass to our starboard."

Mercer joined him on the icy bridge to judge for himself. He took a pair of binoculars from Bishop. As he'd predicted, the *Sea Empress* blazed like a small city under the wavering curtains of the northern lights. She looked beautiful. And she looked like she would indeed pass them to starboard. "Okay, get below and prepare to move the sub."

As the cruise ship drew nearer, Mercer could better judge her speed and direction and ordered the U-boat positioned accordingly. The sub crept forward at a fraction of her normal power and barely made a ripple as she came about. Ira had been generous saying they had twenty minutes of juice remaining. They'd be lucky to maneuver into the path of the fast-approaching hundred-and-fifty-thousand-ton monster.

They got the stern of the sub pointed directly at the *Sea Empress.* "All right. Hold us here. Anika, you and Hilda get Erwin up to the front deck."

Through the binoculars Mercer could clearly see her twin hulls and the yawning channel between them. He continued to order small bearing corrections, making sure the U-boat was properly aligned with the *Sea Empress.* She was now close enough for him to see individual windows along the front of her wide super-structure. If he stood perfectly still he could feel the power of her whirling props through the water.

"Jesus, she's huge," he said to himself as the ship continued to widen as she closed, eating further and further into his range of view. They had to pass between her hulls at the exact center to avoid being slammed against one side or the other. Even a glancing blow would capsize the U-boat. "Ira," he yelled down, "when I give the order, give her everything she's got. Marty, you'll need to move the boat a little to port or starboard to get close to the dock. I won't know which way until we're between the hulls."

"Aye, aye."

He watched as it came at them, the sub in position. Bow waves peeling off the hulls reached the U-boat before she entered the gap, rocking her violently before she could find her center. The wide span of the superstructure didn't begin until fifty feet back from the prow of each hull, so for a moment it felt like they were motoring between two stationary ships. The water pulsed.

Then they were under the main part of the vessel and their perception of motion changed. Instantly, they could all see just how fast the *Sea Empress* was cutting through the water around them. The underside of the superstructure towered thirty feet above the surface of the ocean, creating an echoing tunnel between the hulls. There was enough light from the inside portholes to see a mural painted on the ceiling scroll past in a murky blur.

Mercer was as awed as the rest but snapped himself out of it quickly. "Ira, full ahead and flood the tanks." He studied the sides of the twin hulls, and spotted an alcovelike pier on the left side near the stern. Beyond the marina were tall garage-type doors for launching larger boats. "Marty, give me ten degrees to port and get up here."

Marty and Ira scrambled up the ladder as the U-boat accelerated and heeled over to the left. Their increased speed was far slower than that of the cruise ship, but it would give them a margin of safety when they leapt for the built-in landing. They assembled on the forward deck. Marty carried a knapsack full of documents from the cavern as well as the sub's log book. Mercer had the *Schmeisser* and the broom-handle Mauser. Ira had swiped the Enigma decoding machine from the U-boat's radio room as a souvenir.

"Nice touch," Mercer said.

"Almost as good as you writing 'Kilroy was here' on the side of the bridge."

"Just messing with a future marine archaeologist."

Air bubbled around the U-boat as her tanks filled with seawater and she continued to angle toward the marina. The dock was nothing more than a long fiberglass ledge cut into the hull. It was accessible from the interior of the ship through a standard hatchway placed next to two garage doors for launching personal watercraft. Farther aft were the bigger doors that shielded the storage area for the *Empress*'s larger excursion boats.

Although the portholes along the hull were small, they got an occasional glimpse of people in their cabins and once a face appeared at eye level across just a few feet of frothing water. Everyone waved cheerily. The startled person, an elderly priest, blinked hard, and when he looked again they had passed out of his view.

"That'll make him lay off the sacramental wine."

The force of water hissing along the *Sea Empress*'s hull created a cushion between her and the U-boat, a gap of about two feet that widened as the sub slowed due to the weight of her filling tanks.

Frigid water began to wash along the deck plates. "Shit, I opened 'em too wide," Ira cursed.

"Get to the stern of the sub." Mercer prodded Anika and Hilda, then helped Erwin. He began to run, kicking up spray as the ocean reached his ankles. "It'll reach the landing first."

With every step the water rose higher. It was at Mercer's calves by the time they reached the back of the U-boat. The dock was still twenty feet too far. Slowed by the added drag, the sub continued to sheer away from the towering side of the *Sea Empress*. As the cruise liner overtook the U-boat, the landing drew abreast of the floundering submarine. Mercer took two sloshing steps and launched himself across the four-foot gulf, calling back as soon as he landed, "Do it!"

They had five seconds at most before the U-boat was no longer alongside the dock. Erwin's struggling leap would have dumped him in the sea had Mercer not grabbed his good arm. He cried out and slumped to the deck. Anika came across like a bounding gazelle. Marty and Ira leapt with less grace but equal results.

"Hilda, you can make it," Anika cried. Water surged past the cook's thighs. Hilda rushed like a charging hippopotamus but couldn't make herself leap the widening gap. The water flooding across the sub's deck was too deep.

Frantic, Mercer spied a life ring mounted on the wall. He coiled the end of the rope around his wrist and tossed it to the stricken woman just as she floated free from the sinking U-boat. He wasn't sure she'd caught the life ring until the drag of her body against the cruise ship's fifteen-knot headway yanked him off his feet. It would have hauled him into the water if he hadn't braced his legs against a bollard.

The effect of water pulling against her body meant

Mercer had a five-hundred-pound weight at the other end of the line. His wrist was about to snap. "Help!" he cried. It came out as a strangled croak.

The others grabbed the line, taking up the strain, and like dragging an anchor up a raging stream, hauled Hilda Brandt back to the marina.

"Anika," Mercer gasped when Hilda clawed her way onto the dock. "Tell her she's the most beautiful mermaid I've ever caught."

Panting from the exertion, Ira helped Mercer to his feet. "Now that we're here, O great cruise director, and finished with our north Atlantic tug-of-war, what's the next shipboard activity?"

"Foraging for a cabin, food, and booze—in whatever order you'd like. Shuffleboard's at ten. Me, I'm going for the bar first." The next joke died on Mercer's lips. In the rush to save them, he'd forgotten that the ship's being here might not be as coincidental as they'd thought.

Anika was the first to notice the change in him. "What's wrong?"

Mercer didn't reply. Behind them was the watertight door leading into the ship. It opened into the Jet Ski garage. In the glow of a couple of night-lights, dozens of the personal watercraft sat on AstroTurf pads next to racks of scuba gear and other aquatic toys. Also in the garage were two mahogany-decked thirty-foot Aquariva speedboats. A sophisticated track crane mounted to the ceiling could launch any of the small vessels.

There was a glass-sided office at the far side of the garage for the boat attendants to handle the paperwork of their job. Mercer crossed to it and found the door locked. He used the machine pistol to smash the pane of glass in the door and let himself in. Switching on a desk lamp, he spotted what he was looking for: an invoice pad for passengers to charge a Jet Ski rental to their cabin. The ship's letterhead was on the top of the pages in bold script. At the bottom he found the name of the vessel's owners.

"Son of a bitch."

"What is it?" The group had gathered behind him after helping themselves to handfuls of fluffy towels.

"This ship's owned by a company called Rhine-marine."

"So?"

"It's a division of Kohl AG."

"I guess this ship being here wasn't such a coincidence, after all." Erwin Puhl's voice quavered. He'd never considered that the forces the Brotherhood were fighting could be so prepared.

"This is either Rath's fallback position," Mercer agreed, "or he planned to transfer the Pandora boxes here all along. Considering the ship's distinguished passenger list, I doubt customs is going to pay much attention to what's in her holds."

"You're not surprised, are you?" Marty snapped, more accusation than question.

Mercer matched his anger. "After what we've been through, I wouldn't be surprised if Gunther Rath is already on this tub. He can't risk sticking by the *Njoerd* in case we made it to Kulusuk and contacted the authorities."

"Doesn't matter who's surprised," Ira soothed. "We need to figure out our next move. Erwin, do you know what cabin your friend is in?"

"I don't know. It was assigned when he boarded."

"Then we have to go look for him."

"How do you propose to do that?" Marty's fury had not abated. "We look like a bunch of refugees."

"There must be some cabins close by," Mercer said, grateful for Ira's role as peacemaker. "We'll help ourselves to some new clothes."

After knocking to make sure the cabin nearest the marina was empty, Mercer splintered the lock with one kick. He motioned to his people, and they raced across the corridor and into the small room. It was barely big enough for the three beds, closet, and tiny

bathroom. There was no porthole. Mercer went
straight to the telephone hanging on the wall near one
bed. Next to it was a list of numbers. He dialed the
one for a ship-to-shore connection. After a single ring,
a recording answered, "Due to the solar-max effect,
all ship-to-shore telephone calls have been suspended.
If this is an emergency, please come to either of the
pursers' offices located on the entrance deck of each
hull. We are sorry for the inconvenience."

Mercer fingered the disconnect button. "Outside
communications are out. They claim it's the solar max,
but I bet Rath's already here and has isolated the
ship."

"I would if I were him," Ira said. "Who were you
going to call?"

"I wanted to reach Dick Henna, the head of the
FBI. We've been friends for years."

"No kidding?"

"It's a long story." Next, Mercer phoned the purser's office and asked to be connected to Father Anatoly Vatutin's room. A moment later, a shipboard
operator said that no one was answering. "Could you
give me his room number? It's important that I find
him."

"I'm sorry, sir," the tired operator said. "We aren't
allowed to give out cabin numbers. It's company
policy."

Mercer hung up the phone. "Damn it. They won't
give me Vatutin's room number either." He crossed
to the closet and opened the door. Hanging inside
were three saffron robes of Buddhist monks and rat-
tan sandals. The idea that flashed in Mercer's head
was a desperate one. He called to Anika, who was in
the bathroom. "Are there any razors in there?"

"A couple of them."

Mercer snapped open the longest blade on his
pocket knife.

"You're not thinking what I think you're thinking?"

"You know any monks with hair, Ira? Besides, what do you care? You're already bald."

"What are you doing?" Marty asked.

"We can't stay here because the monks will eventually return, and as you pointed out we can't walk around the ship dressed as refugees. So a couple of us are converting to Buddhism. One of the men will have to remain hidden in the boat garage with the women."

"I'll stay with them," Marty volunteered quickly and then added to defuse the tension he'd caused unnecessarily, "At my age, I can't risk cutting off all my hair. It may not come back."

"Okay." Mercer began hacking at his hair with the knife. "If you're up to this, Erwin, you're next."

"I'll be okay." He fingered the fringes around his head. "And like Ira, I won't be losing much."

Twenty minutes later, Ira, Mercer, and Erwin Puhl had the robes draped over their regular clothes, sleeves hiked to their elbows and pants carefully folded so their bare legs and sandled feet were exposed. Each was freshly shaved and their bald heads gleamed.

"I look like an orange bowling pin," Mercer told his reflection in the bathroom.

"I think you look handsome," Anika said. "Like Yul Brynner in *The King and I*."

Ira rubbed Mercer's naked skull. "If I was a phrenologist, I'd say you thrive on danger and alcohol, have impure thoughts about farm animals, and probably wet the bed."

Mercer chuckled. "Remember, my hair will come back."

"Touché."

Back in the little office in the garage, Mercer handed the *Schmeisser* to Marty, keeping the broomhandle Mauser for himself. "Don't use it unless you absolutely have to. If you get caught, Rath won't execute you until he has all of us. He'll lock you up instead and we'll find you."

"I understand." Bishop took the weapon. "Sorry about what I said earlier. It's just that I, ah, I'm . . ."

"Don't worry about it. I'm scared too. Once we link up with Vatutin, we'll be safe in his cabin until we can figure out what to do next."

"Before you guys go out, I have something for you." Anika removed a tube of lotion from the sundries rack near the office counter. "Suntan lotion with bronzer. It'll darken your complexion a bit. Make you look more . . . I don't know . . . Tibetan."

They smeared their hands, faces, and heads with the darkening cream. All things considered, their disguises weren't too bad.

"We should be back in a half hour."

"This ship is enormous. How are you going to find Vatutin so quickly?"

"It's nearly twelve," Mercer replied. "Cruise-ship tradition is the midnight buffet. Where else could he be? We'll even bring back some food."

In a tight bunch, the three men left the boat garage and started down the carpeted corridor. At a bank of elevators, their costumes were given their first scrutiny by a pair of French-speaking priests. The clerics eyed the makeshift sling Anika had made for Erwin but otherwise ignored the fake monks. Mercer exchanged relieved glances with Ira and Erwin. They rose seven decks in silence, following the priests when they exited. Eavesdropping on their conversation, Mercer understood they were headed for the buffet in the main dining room. He walked slowly, letting the Frenchmen draw out of earshot. "So far so good."

"What happens when we run into some real Buddhists?"

"Pray they think we've taken vows of silence."

They reached one of the ship's two cavernous atriums and crossed on a bridge next to a waterfall, glancing down to see a group of rabbis chatting in a piano bar surrounded by a riot of jungle vegetation. Above them, the aurora borealis washed through the skylights and cast wavering slashes of color on every surface it

touched. Particularly brilliant flashes brought appropriate gasps from the people loitering at the railings
of the multilevel atrium.

The crowds thickened as Mercer and the others approached the dining room in the center part of the
Sea Empress. The noise of conversations grew. Most
people ignored them, but a pair of sharp-eyed Sikhs
stared as they walked into the huge room. Mercer
didn't know if it was cultural animosity or if their disguises didn't fool the turbaned men. He submissively
bowed his head as he shuffled past. And stumbled into
a man dressed in black, like a priest.

The man turned and snapped something in angry
German.

Falling back into Ira, Mercer couldn't suppress the
recognition. The German was from Geo-Research! He
wasn't wearing a priestly suit. He wore a uniform. The
man said something again, jabbing a finger into Mercer's chest.

"Ungalabu," Mercer said quickly, casting his eyes
down in apology. *"Ee ala haboba."*

Rath's guard continued to glare, but Mercer refused
to meet his eyes. A trickle of sweat ran like a finger
down his ribs. Sneering, the German turned to his
compatriot next to him, said something derogatory,
and laughed. He hadn't recognized Mercer with his
orange robes and shorn pate.

Before joining the buffet line, they waited until the
guards were a dozen places in front of them. "How
do you know Tibetan?" Ira whispered.

"I don't." Mercer grinned. "And neither did he.
We'll get a table near them so Erwin can listen to
their conversation."

"I don't see Vatutin anywhere," Erwin said after a
quick search of the room.

"When we grab a seat, you walk around and look
more carefully. If he's not here we can maybe try out
on deck."

With his stomach straining to get at the magnificent
displays of food ringing the room, Mercer placed just

a few vegetables and some rice on his plate in keeping
with Buddhist practice. Yet when he reached the deli
station, he made two foot-long sandwiches and slid
them into the pockets of the robe. The chef shot him
an odd look, but he had seen a number of dietary
taboos broken on this trip.

There were only two people at the ten-place table
closest to where the Germans sat: a man and a woman
unlike any Mercer had seen outside of a Hollywood
stereotype. The man sported a shimmering blue shark-
skin suit with a shirt and tie of the same color. His
toupee looked like a dead animal perched on his head.
The woman had poured herself into a silver dress that
showed silicone cleavage to an inch above her nipples.
Her big hair was bottle blond and styled into a towering cone. Her makeup would have been comical if
it wasn't so appropriate to her overlifted face. Each
individual eyelash seemed as long and thick as a
baby's pinky.

With his eyes, Mercer asked permission to sit.

"Absolutely," the man slurred. In front of him were
three empty glasses and a full one. "I'm Tommy Joe
Farquar and this is my wife, Lorna. We're from the
U.S. of A."

"Gosh," Lorna squeaked in a voice shrill enough to
shatter crystal. "It's good to have some company. For
some reason no one wants to sit with us no more."

Mercer made a sympathetic gesture and shoveled
rice into his mouth to keep from laughing.

Tommy Joe leaned his elbows on the table and, in
an earnestness honed during his years of selling used
cars, asked, "Have you gentlemen accepted Jesus as
your personal savior?"

Another mouthful of food went in before Mercer
could swallow the first.

"I suspect you haven't, 'cause of the crazy getups
you're wearing. Now, I know it's not your fault, so
I don't blame you none. But I think it's time you
reconsidered the path you've chosen. It's never too
late to find Christ, our Lord."

"Tommy Joe knows what he's talking about," Lorna cooed. "He's on television."

Mercer jumped when he felt pressure against his crotch. Carefully, he reached under the table and grabbed at what he feared was Lorna Farquar's hand. His fingers sank into something warm and furry, and before he knew what he'd touched, tiny needle teeth sank into his thumb. He pulled his hand away with a gasp and flung the Farquar's Pekingese onto an adjoining table. The dog had been snuffling into Mercer's pocket for the sandwiches.

"Pookie, you bad boy. Get back into your bag." Ignoring the repulsed diners, the dog defiantly lifted its leg against the flowered centerpiece. After emitting a single drop, the Pekingese trotted through plates, jumped to the floor, and curled up in the carpetbag Lorna carried for him. "Good boy."

The other table cleared.

"Unless you accept Christ into your heart," Tommy Joe continued drunkenly, "you'll never find salvation in the hereafter. You'll be denied His everlasting love in Heaven and be cast into the Pit. I can imagine all the pagan things you've done and don't you worry. I have a special program in my ministry to help all sorts of people find His light, including"—he lowered his voice to a conspiratorial whisper—"homo-sexuals. If Jesus can forgive them, you can believe you'll be forgiven for praying to cows and false idols and such."

"Honey, I don't think they understand you none," Lorna said into the first silence since Mercer and Ira had sat down. "Do you speak American?"

Mercer shrugged. To keep from laughing out loud, he had to remind himself that Rath's men were right behind him.

Tommy Joe dropped his public persona. "Godless heathens."

"I think the younger one's kinda cute." Lorna batted her eyes at Mercer.

"You think anything in pants is kinda cute."

Tommy Joe pushed back his overflowing plate and gulped the last of his triple scotch.

"Ha! They're not wearing pants," Lorna snapped with a child's logic and obstinacy.

"Shut up." Farquar lumbered to his feet. "Let's go find a bar."

"I want to talk with these two some more."

"Lorna, you'd be the one doing all the talking. They can't understand you." He stalked off. She considered remaining but gave Mercer and Ira a quick smile and wiggled after her husband.

The ex-Navy man leaned into Mercer's ear. "Remind me to renounce my U.S. citizenship when we get home."

Mercer looked around the room and spotted Erwin Puhl weaving his way around tables toward them. His dark expression told Mercer that he hadn't found Father Vatutin. He sat and mechanically ate his bland food, leaning back far enough to overhear the conversation behind him. Rath's two men had been eating like wolves and finished a few minutes later. They left their plates and strode away.

"Anything?" Mercer asked when they were gone.

"I think they brought one of the boxes!" Erwin said in a rush.

Mercer's expression turned frigid. "Are you sure?"

"Not positive, but I think so. They talked about cargo transferred from Rath's chopper to the boat they used to get here."

"Goddamn it! Our status just went from fugitive to hostage."

That single box of meteor fragments meant Rath had complete control of the *Sea Empress*. He could open it at any time and resign some of the greatest leaders on the planet to an unspeakable death. Mercer closed his eyes, trying to block out the image of the *Sea Empress* becoming a coffin ship, doomed to forever sail the seas with her decks covered by thousands of radioactive corpses, a modern, horrific *Mary Celeste*.

His goal to save the survivors was no longer enough. They couldn't hide out when there was another Pandora box loose. He had to stop Rath himself. If just that single box got off the vessel, the whole world was at risk.

"They also mentioned they had a prisoner with them," Erwin continued. "Someone who could get them onto the *Sea Empress* without raising suspicion."

"Who the hell would Rath need?" Ira asked. "He's got to be high up in Kohl Industries."

"Apparently not high enough," Mercer mused. "No sign of your priest friend?"

"I didn't see Anatoly anywhere. We should try calling his cabin again from the phone in the corridor."

Mercer shot to his feet and handed the two sandwiches to Ira. "You two make the call and get back to the boat garage."

"Where are you going?"

"I'm going to the radio room to call Dick Henna. Rath may prevent passengers from calling from their rooms, but I can't believe communications are really out. No matter what happens to us, we have to get the word out about the box."

In the corridor, Mercer checked his watch. The half hour he'd promised Anika was gone. He looked around and spotted the two Germans walking across the catwalk spanning the atrium. If Rath needed leverage to get him on the cruise liner, Mercer would need their prisoner to get into the radio room. He began to follow the Germans.

The guards turned along one of the hanging promenades, passing darkened storefronts that read like a one-block section of Rodeo Drive—Gucci, Movado, Armani, Chanel, Godiva. Mercer stayed well back, partially to find cover in the thinning crowds, partially because he couldn't match their pace wearing ill-fitting sandals. The Mauser was tucked into his waistband, and he cleared away a fold in his robe so he could reach it easier.

The two Germans wound through a couple of corridors and stopped at an elevator. When the car arrived, they stepped inside. Mercer ran down the hall when the doors closed. Above the elevator was a digital counter indicating the floor the car was on. He watched it descend to one deck below where the marina was located.

He charged through the staircase fire door behind him. Pounding down two steps at a time, his feet hurting with every impact, Mercer paused after descending three flights when he thought he heard a door open above him. He captured his breath in his mouth but could hear nothing over the blood thumping in his ears. He continued downward.

One flight above his destination a STAFF ONLY door blocked his path. He stopped to listen again and then swung open the unlocked door. Gone were the rich carpets, subtle lighting, and wood paneling. This was the crew's area of the vessel. It was as utilitarian as a battleship and painted the same institutional gray.

He paused for a minute, his head held at an angle to see if anyone had followed him. The pistol grip became sweaty. Nothing. Dressed like a passenger, he knew he couldn't spend any length of time in the bowels of the ship without catching the attention of a crew member. Still, he needed to find Rath's prisoner.

Edging down a companionway so long he couldn't see the other end, he kept his back pressed against one wall. There were countless doors lining the corridor and every thirty feet or so another hall ran off at a right angle. The ship was a maze. The linoleum was so new he could see individual scuff marks and amid the subtle abrasions of waiters' loafers he recognized the heavy black smears left by rubber-soled combat boots. Rath's men.

He followed the trail like a bloodhound, twisting through the labyrinth while a subconscious part of his brain mapped his route of retreat. A door opened just as Mercer passed, and without breaking stride, he threw himself into the handsome, twenty-something man who had come out wearing a purple robe. They crashed into the bunk beds on the far wall of the cabin, the young man yelping in pain. Mercer closed the door with his foot.

"Don't hurt me please!" the blond boy said. He was English, delicate as a girl. A waiter, Mercer guessed.

"I won't." Mercer kept menace in his voice. "What size shoes do you wear?"

The boy's eyes widened. "What?"

"Shoes? What size shoes?"

"Twelve."

"Got any sneakers?" Mercer hoped the American and English sizes were the same, or at least close. The boy nodded. "Give them to me."

Mercer let the waiter back to his feet and stripped off his monk's robe. The boy blubbered when he saw the handle of the Mauser. "Give me the shoes and keep your mouth shut, and I'll leave you alone."

The young Englishman opened a closet and rummaged through the detritus at the bottom for his sneakers. "Here, here you are. You won't hurt me?"

"I promise. Now turn around and put your hands behind your back." Mercer used a tie from the closet to bind the waiter's hands to the metal bed frame. The ball of socks he found was still warm and damp from the day's use. Mercer jammed the socks in the youth's mouth.

Gagging at first, the young waiter calmed enough to start drawing even breaths. Mercer put on the shoes, pleased that they fit. "When your roommate unties you and you go to the security office, you might want to come up with a better story than a deranged terrorist stealing shoes."

The boy mumbled into his gag and Mercer laughed. "Don't worry, kid. Believe it or not, your sneakers might save everyone on this ship."

Back in the hallway, Mercer took up the trail again. The scuff marks led him to a watertight door much thicker than any he'd seen in the below decks area. It was marked ENGINEERING STAFF ONLY. The floor thrummed with the force of the ship's mighty power plants. He decided that he'd come as far as he should. Fumbling around down here was wasting time he didn't have. He'd take his chances getting into the communications room without Rath's prisoner. He had the Mauser and the element of surprise.

Backtracking, he passed the waiter's cabin again. He couldn't hear anything from within. Satisfied, Mercer rounded a series of corners, brushing past a few off-duty crewmen who shot him queer looks but said nothing. As he turned one more corner, he had just enough time to recognize a mass of blond hair before his crotch exploded in agony. Mercer dropped to his knees and through tear-streaked eyes saw a knee coming at his face. He could do nothing. His world had gone black by the time his head hit the deck.

Fighting the urge to retch, Mercer came awake in slow increments. His lower body felt distant, like the pain belonged to someone else. But as he became more aware, he knew the agony was his alone. The pulsing waves radiated from his genitals and settled in his lower belly like molten lead. To distract himself, he concentrated on the sharper pain in his face. Experimentally he traced his tongue across his teeth and was relieved they were all there. He tasted blood. Opening his eyes sent bolts of electricity to his battered nose. He spat.

"Who are you?" The question came from beyond Mercer's gray vision.

"An idiot." Mercer's voice was pinched by clotted blood in his nose. He braced himself for what was about to come and sharply exhaled twin jets of red mist. After a surreal moment where his head felt like it had shattered, he peered around the spiky pinwheels of pain. It took him a minute to realize where he was—a crawl space below some kind of engineering room tangled with piping—and who had spoken—the blond man he'd first spotted talking to Gunther Rath in the Pandora cavern.

"I promised myself when I saw you again I'd kill you." Mercer pulled his hands against the plastic strip ties binding his wrists over an insulated pipe above him. The man was similarly shackled. "You're Rath's boss, aren't you?"

"Klaus Raeder." They were both on their knees under a steel catwalk. Even if they could stand, there was barely enough room. Lamps in the room above them made the floor under the grated catwalk look like bricks of light mortared with shadow. The ties were threaded over a pipe suspended from the metal grid. Mercer pulled until the plastic ripped his flesh.

"I've tried that," Raeder said. "You won't be able to do it." He paused. "I recognize you now from your Surveyor's Society picture. You're Philip Mercer."

Mercer was unwilling to give Raeder the satisfaction of being right. He'd already guessed that Rath had somehow double-crossed his superior to steal the last Pandora box. "Why did he lock you up?"

"He needed me to get aboard the *Sea Empress*. We came on the boat stored on the *Njoerd*. The captain wouldn't have given him permission if I wasn't forced to order him to."

"And when you got to the ship, you were put in here in case Rath needed you again?" Raeder nodded. "What's Rath's plan with the last box?"

"I was going to dump them in the sea," Raeder boasted. "No one was supposed to know about it and no one was supposed to get hurt."

"You think I care about your intentions?" Mercer couldn't believe the German's self-righteousness and lack of shame. "Your hopes don't amount to shit and never have, considering how easily Rath managed to hijack your plans. Someday I'd like to know how you thought you could sweep something like the Pandora Project under the rug. For now I have to worry about stopping Rath."

"It was an economic decision." Raeder feebly clung to his original justification. "I was trying to save my shareholders from paying hundreds of millions of dollars for something none of us are responsible for."

"Your company profited from the thousand dead slaves in that cavern and you're telling me you're not responsible?" Mercer couldn't believe what he was hearing. "Hate to tell you this, Raeder, but you are. There's no statute of limitations on murder. Just because you didn't pull any triggers doesn't mean you can duck the culpability of the company you represent."

"I thought I could get away with it." Raeder's voice was nearly drowned by the sound of pumps and other machinery. The air was stifling hot.

"No one can walk away from their past." Mercer began looking around for something sharp to cut his bonds. "And that includes a company like Kohl. Now your company is going to lose a lot more than the money it rightly owed and you are going to pay with your life."

"Do you think you're immune? Your life is as forfeit as mine. No one can stop Rath. He controls the box—and me—which means he controls everything. He's invincible."

There were no tools within reach, but Mercer's tone was still defiant. "You sound like you want him to win."

"No. I just know he will. It's hopeless."

"Because he beat you?" Mercer scoffed. "Arrogance and gullibility are a dangerous mix. And Rath will be stopped. There are five other people from the U-boat with me, and we have a contact on the ship. They'll get the alarm out."

"Sorry to tell you this, but when they brought you down here, Greta Schmidt was talking with another of Rath's people about a report of stolen clothing near the ship's marina. I suspect that was your doing. She was on her way there to investigate."

A door above them crashed open and Mercer heard a babble of voices he recognized: a snarling curse from Ira, Hilda's quiet sobs, and Anika's attempts to comfort her. Greta Schmidt's clear laughter sounded, and again Mercer strained at his bonds. The effort left him panting. A guard lifted a section of the catwalk directly above him and let it fall back on its hinges. His partner kept Mercer and Klaus Raeder covered with a submachine gun as he came down the steps to the low crawl space.

"How are your balls?" Greta smirked from the catwalk above.

"Sweaty. Want a taste?"

In a fury, she slammed her boot onto his exposed hands and would have broken Mercer's wrists if he hadn't laid them flat together. Gritting his teeth against the pain did little. "When Gunther is finished on the bridge, you are going to be the first to die."

The guards led Mercer's party into the cramped space and tied them to other lengths of pipe, far enough apart so they could not help one another escape. Hilda was in tears, and despite the bravado he was trying to show in front of the women, Marty Bishop's cheeks were also wet. Erwin was nearly catatonic. Only Ira and Anika had embers of the fire that had carried them so far. Anika even managed to throw Mercer a smile just before her plastic cuffs were wrenched tight. Her body rippled with pain.

Ira waited until Greta finished speaking with one of the guards before he said, "Mercer, don't worry. We made the call to your FBI buddy Henna on the satphone. By now he's alerted our Navy as well as Iceland's."

"So the solar max abated enough for us to use it." Mercer smiled. "About damn time. I was tired of playing staked goat until you could use it."

Greta looked from one man to the other, dismayed that she couldn't detect fear in their voices. "You have no satellite phone," she said at last.

Ira gave her the withering look he'd used on a generation of naval cadets. "I tossed it just before you captured us. Why do you think we didn't put up a fight? We've won already—only you don't know it."

"This is not true." There was doubt in her eyes.

"You go right ahead and believe that, you sick bitch," Anika Klein blazed. "The truth should be here in about an hour aboard a dozen American helicopters."

Greta crossed over to where Anika was tied to a heat exchanger. "And I will tear out your ovaries long before they get here."

She considered slapping Anika's face, thought better of it, and climbed the seven steps back to the catwalk. A guard closed the hatch grate, and the outer door slammed with a metallic bang.

From his position, Mercer couldn't see where Ira Lasko had been secured, but he thought it was someplace behind him and around a piece of equipment. "You were trying to tell me that you found Erwin's friend and he had a sat-phone, right?"

"Ah, no. That was all bullshit. We called his cabin again, but he wasn't there. Greta found us about five seconds after Erwin and I got back from the dining room. Seems we robbed the only Buddhist monks who actually care about their property. They had gone to the ship's security office and Rath was alerted. Greta and a couple of his boys ferreted us out. Considering their firepower, we figured surrender was a better idea than suicide."

"We thought you were still free," Anika added.

"I went to find Rath's prisoner. That's him over in the corner. Klaus Raeder's his name. He's the head of Kohl."

"Hi, hope you burn in hell," Ira called as a greeting.

Perhaps he'd survived one narrow escape too many or perhaps because with all of them together and under Rath's control they were as good as dead—either way, Mercer finally lost control. This was as far as he could go. There were no other options. There was no hope.

He began to laugh. The deep anomalous sound crashed against the steel confines of the machinery room, lashed everyone and echoed back, hammering.

It was manic, frightening. When he caught his breath again, silence hung as heavy as steam.

"I figured out the paradox to the mythological story of Pandora," he said, in control of his voice if nothing more.

"What paradox?" Anika asked. "She opened a box that Zeus gave to Epimetheus and accidentally released all the ills on the world. But when everything like greed and envy and disease had escaped, she found that hope was still in the box. It's a beautiful story that means despite everything that may happen to you, hope always remains."

"That's the lesson people get from it," Mercer agreed bitterly. "That's not what I'm talking about. Hasn't anyone ever wondered why hope was in the box to begin with? Why was it in there with disease and hate and lust? Because hope's as destructive as any of those, maybe worse. It was never meant to be a gift from the gods. It was punishment. Hope gives you strength when you have a chance. When the situation's impossible, it becomes a torture."

The pain in his voice stunned everyone, especially Anika. "Are you really that cynical?"

Mercer didn't answer. Despite his words, he pulled against his shackles with every fiber of his being, his eyes closed so tightly they felt crushed into his skull. He bellowed in rage and frustration and . . . hopelessness. And with a metallic snap the thick plastic cuffs parted and his hands were free.

For a moment he stared at the cleanly severed ends dangling from his wrists. It wasn't humanly possible to break these cuffs yet the evidence was right in front of him. How? A miracle? The divine intervention of the gods telling him he'd missed the point of the Pandora myth?

Klaus Raeder was the only person who could see what Mercer had done and he gaped. "How did you do that?"

Mercer looked upward in an age-old glance of reverence to a higher power. That's how he spotted a spectral figure standing on the grating above him with a fire ax in his hands. He was dressed in black with silver hair and a beard that approached his waist. Understanding dawned immediately. "Father Vatutin?"

"Da." Vatutin lifted the hatch and moved down the steps. The others began to cheer when they heard what was happening.

Mercer massaged his wrists. "I'm not complaining, but how did you know?"

"I see a Buddhist monk near dining room when I go in for supper." Vatutin's English was terrible. "I see him check expensive Swiss watch that no monk can own. I look more closely. Not monk but man made to look like monk. I follow. You knocked out by blond woman and brought here. I hide. Then more people brought here and I see Erwin. I wait until guard posted at door turns away and use blunt edge of ax."

Mercer got to his feet and shook the Orthodox priest's hand. "You have no idea what I was thinking when the cuffs broke."

Vatutin touched the heavy cross resting on his chest. "I know what you think."

The two began to release the others. Anika smiled when Mercer reached her. "I told you that there's always hope."

"Thanks for the reminder." Mercer was chagrined.

Vatutin and Erwin Puhl embraced for a long time after the priest learned Igor Bulgarin was dead.

"I'm gonna start calling you Pessimism Man from now on," Ira Lasko said to Mercer when he was freed. "That thing about hope being in the box was a good point. Just promise me it's your last death-row revelation."

"I promise." Mercer took the weapons Vatutin had liberated from the guard: a silenced H&K P9S automatic pistol and a compact MP-5 submachine gun also fitted with a long silencer. "Now it's time to put an end to this nightmare."

"Any ideas?" Marty asked.

"That all depends on Herr Raeder." Mercer looked down at him since they had yet to cut his bonds. "How about it? You willing to help?"

"I told you earlier that I wanted to destroy the boxes. It is Rath who wants to sell them."

"Does he have a buyer?"

"Libya."

Shit! "And when this is over you're going to make full restitution?"

"Yes."

Mercer had a hard time believing such a quick answer. "Because you got caught?"

"Because I was wrong," Raeder countered. "Think what you like of me, Dr. Mercer, but I am not a monster. I am a businessman. A capitalist. Being an American, you should understand. My personal beliefs had nothing to do with my decision to conceal Kohl's past. And no matter how much my company pays, I don't believe full restitution can ever be paid to the victims of the Holocaust."

"I don't trust you but I also don't have a choice," Mercer hissed. An ax stroke severed Raeder's plastic cuffs. "What are the security arrangements on this ship?"

"The pope's Swiss Guards are in charge of the Convocation's delegates and the *Sea Empress* has personnel of her own. About twenty, I think. I recognized several of them as part of Gunther Rath's special-projects department. They're his people, like those at the Greenland base. They won't listen to me."

"Who did you speak to when Rath needed permission to board?"

"The captain," Raeder answered at once. "He wouldn't let Rath approach the ship until he heard I was on the boat from the *Njoerd.* He doesn't know that I am Rath's prisoner. No one does."

"So he'll listen to you?"

"Absolutely."

"Once we reach the captain, will Rath make a stand or try to run?" Mercer said, thinking aloud.

"Neither option's too good," Ira said. "The world's religious leaders are on this ship. If Rath opens that box the repercussions are going to be bloody. Every fanatic in the planet would use their deaths as an excuse for holy war."

"But who will die if we let him run with the box and can't catch him again?"

"We'll get him." Ira Lasko considered leaving it at that, but he continued, his voice tinged with guilt. He edged Mercer away from the others for privacy. "Get me to a working phone and I guarantee that Rath won't make it fifty miles from the *Sea Empress.*"

The confidence in Ira's statement made everything suddenly clear to Mercer. The fury was like an explosion ten times more powerful than Greta Schmidt's knee to the crotch. "You're working with the goddamned CIA, aren't you?"

Ira nodded. "I'm sorry, Mercer," he said, meaning it.

"That fucker Charlie Bryce set me up."

"You were my backup in case something went really wrong."

"I can't believe this!" And then Mercer thought it through and he could believe it. Who better to back up an agent on a scientific expedition than a scientist? His name wasn't unknown in various government circles, including the CIA. It all made perfect sense in a compartmentalized, need-to-know sort of way. "You were after the boxes for our military."

"Failing that, I was to make sure no one else got them. Personally, I was more than happy to see them sunk when the rotor-stat went down. Listen, I am really sorry about this. I would have told you if I could, but I was briefed personally by Director Barnes himself."

"Christ," Mercer spat. He'd met Paul Barnes a few times before and thought the CIA director was an ass. He tried to run his hands through his hair, and his fingers met naked skin. This only fueled his anger.

"How the hell did the government know about the boxes and why didn't you go after them years ago?"

"We didn't know where the cavern was other than Greenland. That information came from documents brought to the States in the 1940s by German rocket scientists stationed at Peenemunde with Werner Von Braun. They'd been working on a Nazi plan to load V-2s with meteorite fragments and irradiate London. The scientists only knew that the meteor would be coming directly from Greenland's east coast aboard a submarine."

"Of course the sub never arrived and the Germans shelved the Pandora Project."

"Right," Ira said. "After the war, our Air Force learned about it from the Operation Paperclip scientists we were using for our early rocket program. They considered the Pandora radiation as a potential American weapon and established Camp Decade, in part, as a base to search for the cavern. After a few years of searching—too far south it turns out—the brass gave up, stating that the whole thing had been a pipe dream of Hitler's and wasn't true."

Mercer recalled his conversation with Elisebet Rosmunder and how she'd asked if he knew why the U.S. government wanted to build an under-ice city like Camp Decade. Now he knew the answer. He let the anger wash out of him so he could concentrate on what Ira was saying.

"Shoot ahead sixty years, and all of a sudden, Kohl Industries is buying Geo-Research and planning to establish an Arctic research base close to where the cavern was supposed to be. The old documents hinted that Kohl was involved with the Pandora Project in some capacity, though there was nothing definitive, nothing we could use in a courtroom. Unwilling to take the chance that they knew something we didn't, the CIA scrambled to have their base moved to our old site to throw them off."

"That whole thing with the Danish government that

Charlie Bryce told me the Surveyor's Society engineered?"

"Was actually a CIA operation to get me to Greenland," Ira said. "I was brought in to keep an eye on Geo-Research in case the cavern turned out to be real and they tried to find it. There's a military strike team waiting in Iceland in case we needed them to stop Kohl."

"So you weren't a chief in the Navy?"

"My naval experience was why I was sent."

"Of course!" Mercer exclaimed. "They knew a submarine was involved and wanted a man who had the proper background. That's how you're such an expert on the type VII U-boat."

"Before leaving for Greenland, I spent two weeks at the Chicago Museum of Science and Industry going over the U-505 they have on display. As to being a chief, well, I used to work on subs, but then switched to intelligence work. I retired as deputy chief of Naval Intelligence. My rank was admiral."

"And the bit about owning a truck stop in Connecticut?"

"My father's place. I grew up working there. My brother runs it now. In reality, I live about twenty miles from your brownstone and work in the White House for the president's national security advisor."

A piece of the puzzle was still missing. "I assume you had Marty's military friend called away for active duty, but what the hell did you need me for?"

"Jim Kneeland, yes," Ira answered. "We felt the fewer people at Camp Decade the better. We would have excluded Marty too if we could have come up with a better cover story to get me close to Geo-Research. Bringing you in was Director Barnes's idea. While I have a background in subs and intelligence, he wanted someone who knew science but not one of the pencil necks from Langley's technical-support division. When he showed me your dossier and I read that article about you in *Time* magazine, I knew you'd be perfect."

"So I have you to thank?"

"No need to show your gratitude with a gift or anything. A card will be fine."

They drifted back toward the others. "When we get out of this, you're going to get a pounding," Mercer said but already his anger toward Ira was abating. Paul Barnes, on the other hand, was going to pay. "Well, Agent Lasko, what do you propose?"

Ira turned deadly serious. "We have Rath contained on the *Sea Empress,* but we can't risk him nuking these people."

Mercer agreed. The Universal Convocation had to be protected at all costs. The men and women on this ship represented the hopes and dreams of billions of people. "We have to flush him out so we can take him at sea."

"How? All Rath has to do is threaten to open the box and everyone on the ship is his hostage."

Mercer shook his head. "He knows that he can't win a hostage situation. No one ever does."

"So what do you suggest? We'd be in for one hell of a mess if we alert the Swiss Guards. They'd probably make the situation worse in their zeal to protect the pope."

"You're right about the Guards not being an option, which means we're on our own. Remember that Raeder said the ship's security men are in Rath's pocket. We have to get him to escape from the *Sea Empress* the way he came."

"His boat is with the larger launches next to the marina I think you were hiding in," Klaus Raeder offered.

"And Greta said Rath's on the bridge," Anika added.

Mercer had gone quiet, his eyes out of focus. Suddenly his features sharpened and he grinned wickedly. "I can think of only one way to get Rath to leave the ship without him feeling directly threatened. Actually, I can think of another way, but I doubt the seven of us could get the ship to start sinking."

Anika and Ira exchanged startled looks and regarded Mercer as if he'd lost his mind. "Thank God you're not thinking that," she said. "So what is your idea?"

"Simple. We hijack the *Sea Empress* ourselves."

Before Mercer launched into his explanation, Ira suggested that Anatoly Vatutin's cabin would be a better place to talk. Mercer gave him the MP-5 to tuck under his robes. He took point when they exited the machinery room, the pistol held behind his back with a round in the chamber. They left the guard Vatutin had dispatched behind a large hydro pump. Ira walked the drag slot, moving backward so they couldn't get jumped. Because it was so late at night, the *Sea Empress* was running with just a skeleton crew on the bridge and fortunately no one in the engineering spaces. Mercer found an elevator after a few minutes, and they ascended to Vatutin's deck. Moments later, they piled into the priest's room.

"So far so good." Anika smiled with relief.

"Hear out my plan before you have me committed," Mercer said when they were settled. He ticked his fingers as he counted their options. "We can't stay here until the ship docks because Rath will organize a room-to-room search once he realizes we've escaped. Even with Raeder's help, we can't approach the captain because Rath's people are likely watching him. The Swiss Guards are out because they'll probably turn us over to ship's security, i.e., Rath. We could try to find a satellite phone belonging to one of the reporters covering the Convocation, but there are two thousand cabins to check and we'd be stopped long before we found one. And finally we can't risk a direct confrontation with Rath in case he opens the box.

"Does everyone agree so far?" Mute nods. "Okay, to get Rath off the ship we have to make him think escaping is a better option than remaining on board. To do that we either sink the *Sea Empress* or create a situation where he feels just threatened enough to want to leave. That's where we come in."

"By pretending to be hijackers?"

"It's going to put the Swiss Guards on full alert and distract some of Rath's people. Rath will figure out what's going on but he can't say anything without compromising himself. It would be easier for him to cut his losses rather than fight us. He'll let the Swiss Guards and the ship's regular security detail handle that."

"Why wouldn't he just hang around until his goons kill us all?" Marty asked.

"Rath can pretend the solar max has shut down the ship's communications but when we fire the first shot every reporter with an independent satellite uplink will be calling in the scoop. In hours, the *Empress* will be swarming with choppers and motor launches from Iceland. Rath would be trapped."

"Once he's gone," Anika interrupted, "we give ourselves up, bring Raeder to the captain, and alert the authorities about Rath's escaping with the Pandora box."

"You got it."

"Once he's flushed out, why don't we ambush him when he's trying to launch his boat?" Erwin's suggestion had merit, and a fatal flaw.

"He may have fifteen or twenty men with him. If we can't guarantee a clean kill, he could open the box." Mercer saw Ira's skeptical look, and added, "All we need to do is fire off a few rounds, terrorize some passengers, and let panic do the rest. As long as we don't get caught before Rath leaves, we've got nothing to worry about."

"Except Swiss Guards are not wearing blue-and-gold uniforms and carrying medieval weapons," Anatoly Vatutin said. "They have combat armor and machine pistols, and they will shoot to kill."

"This isn't without risks," Mercer answered solemnly, looking each person in the eye.

Ira Lasko didn't hesitate. "Tell me how you want to do this."

Mercer spent ten minutes outlining his plan and refining it with suggestions from the others. The key was to protect Klaus Raeder until after Rath left the vessel. Mercer estimated that would be about twenty minutes after the first firefight.

Because of his injuries, Erwin would wait with the industrialist in Vatutin's cabin. Mercer wanted the others to stay with them. Martin Bishop agreed. However, Vatutin categorically refused. He reminded Mercer that he'd been fighting for this for his entire life and wouldn't back out at the end. And once Anika translated their plan to Hilda, the chef too wanted to help. She had military training, she stated, and could handle a gun. Mercer's eyes asked Anika her intentions.

She looked at Erwin.

"I can hold out for a while longer," Puhl said as if reading her mind. "The pain's worse and my arm's numb to my fingers, but once Raeder talks to the captain, I'm going to the ship's doctor."

Without a professional excuse to remain behind, Anika Klein tried to find a personal one. And couldn't. The others were risking their lives for something much bigger than they were and she couldn't let them go alone. "I'm in."

Moments later, the ersatz terrorists left the cabin.

Finding additional weapons for the teams was easier than they thought. In the elevator headed up to the main deck, the car stopped a few floors short of their destination and two Swiss Guards stepped in, barely giving Mercer and his band a passing inspection. Both uniformed men carried Beretta Model 12 submachine guns on slings. As soon as the doors swept closed, Mercer clubbed one with the butt of the H&K at the same time Ira laid open the other's scalp with his machine pistol. A minute later, the Swiss were bound and gagged, and their weapons, including concealed pistols, were distributed.

"You promise we're not going to kill anyone?" Anika asked when Mercer handed her his H&K in favor for the Model 12. He'd unscrewed the German pistol's silencer.

"We'll be shooting for effect," Mercer reassured. "If it comes to a real firefight, aim for people's legs."

"That still goes against the Hippocratic oath." Despite her protest, Anika tightened her grip on the big handgun. She'd do what was necessary.

"This is where we split into two teams." Mercer's voice was harder than he'd intended. "Ira, take Hilda and Father Vatutin and find the biggest group of people you can, maybe in the theater. I saw a bulletin for a midnight showing of *The Agony and the Ecstasy*. Take them hostage, scare the hell out of them, and get out again. Stay loose and mobile. Don't remain in one location for any length of time, and make sure when you escape no one follows. We meet back at Father Vatutin's cabin in thirty minutes to wait for Erwin's all-clear from the bridge."

The doors opened before anyone could acknowledge his final instructions, and they scattered without a word. Because the majority of the passengers were men, Mercer and Anika used a ladies' rest room to give the others time to get into position. They both even managed a nervous pee.

They reemerged from the tiled bathroom after five minutes. Casually Mercer walked across the corridor near the main atrium and yanked the handle for the fire alarm. Nothing happened for a second, and he feared the system remained silent until an actual fire was confirmed. Then the electronic horns began to cry, wailing like a colicky infant drawing breath. They kept their weapons out of view as a few late-night strollers looked around anxiously.

It took about three minutes for an emergency crew to be dispatched to the pull station. When they rounded the corner from a stairwell, Mercer drew his weapon and fired a tight burst over their heads, shredding the acoustical material in the ceiling. A light fixture exploded, and the screams of passengers reached an instant fever pitch.

The battle for the *Sea Empress* had begun.

Usually when he was inside Greta Schmidt, Gunther Rath delighted in making her bleed. He had to make up for his small size by the punishing savagery of his strokes, making their sex more akin to rape than a display of intimacy. This time, however, he made love with a grateful tenderness unlike anything he'd ever shown before.

Rath had been in the cabin he'd commandeered from the *Sea Empress*'s second officer when she'd come to him, her expression a mix of smug pride and feverish anticipation. She whispered she had a secret for him but wouldn't reveal it until they'd made love. Rath wasn't in the mood for one of her games and would have struck her if she'd been within range of the chair he occupied, a glass of vodka in his hand. Instead, he simply ignored her. Seeing that she wasn't going to get what she wanted, Greta doled out a little more information.

"In fact, I have six secrets for you."

"What are you talking about?"

"Get into bed and I'll tell you."

"Tell me now or I'll beat it out of you." His threat was more habit than menace.

"I went below to check on Raeder and guess who I ran into?" Rath didn't ask. "Philip Mercer."

"What?"

"And what's more, when I had him tied up with Raeder, a break-in was reported on a lower deck near the marina. I went with a couple of the ship's security people and found the other five survivors." She loved that her gift lifted his spirits. "They actually did try for Iceland in that antique sub but made it only as far as the *Sea Empress*."

From the moment he'd lost the boxes, Rath had

been scrambling to minimize the damage. The Libyans were waiting for the *Njoerd*'s precious cargo, and he had to get the one remaining box to them until a salvage operation could be mounted to raise the rest. He also needed to track down and kill Mercer and the others. It was clear they had been in the cavern and doubtlessly watched Rath empty the chamber through the submerged U-boat's periscope. If Mercer managed to raise an alarm, Rath could forget any attempt at recovering the sunken boxes.

He laughed. "Mercer's audacity is going to cost him his life. I wonder if he knew we were going to use the *Sea Empress* as a refueling stop on our trip to Iceland?"

"How could he? We didn't know we'd need to come here until the rotor-stat went down. I'm just grateful it was here at all."

Far from a lucky break, the *Empress*'s presence in the Denmark Strait had been the result of careful planning and timing. Greta had been the one to suggest it as fallback position months ago when Klaus Raeder was in discussions with the Vatican over the ship's lease. Needing the cruise liner as a contingency had seemed unlikely, but Greta had insisted that, with so much money on the line, it would be foolish to rely solely on the *Njoerd* as transport. Raeder had had no idea of Rath's ulterior motives when he passed along the suggestion to Cardinal Peretti, the pope's secretary of state. The priest had thought cruising under the northern lights was a wonderful idea and successfully lobbied the other delegates to accept.

Greta pulled her shirt over her head, her breasts still red from earlier rough treatment. "Is my surprise worth a lay?"

"That and much more," Rath said, launching himself from his chair and sweeping her into his arms. He laid her on the bed. "From triumph to disaster back to triumph, and I couldn't have done it without you."

His lips never left hers the whole time they were joined.

Rath was in a self-satisfied sleep when the call came from young Bern Hoffmann, who'd been detailed to relieve the guard they'd posted at the auxiliary pump room door. The prisoners had escaped! Rath slammed down the phone and tossed Greta aside.

"What is it?" She wiped sleep from her eyes, her body sticky with dried sweat from their lovemaking.

Rath was already in his pants. "Mercer escaped."

She came more awake. "He couldn't have. We've accounted for everyone on the DC-3, those killed in the crash, and the body we found after the *pitaraq* storm. There's no one left to help him."

"The guard they knocked out recalls a priest approaching him before he was struck." Rath wanted to shower her scent from his skin but didn't have time. "Somehow, Mercer has a contact on the ship we didn't know about, maybe another member of the Brotherhood of Satan's Fist. I should have killed Mercer's group when you told me you'd captured them."

"He can't go anywhere." Greta legged into her panties. "The marina garage doors are rigged to an alarm on the bridge, and he can't launch a lifeboat for the same reason. There's no sign of the U-boat, so they're trapped. Mercer can't go to the ship's security people because Raeder must have told him they are loyal to you and the Swiss Guards would lock them up as stowaways."

"I know the options he won't choose," Rath snapped. "I don't know the one he will. He's unpredictable."

At that exact moment the fire alarm went off. Rath actually smiled. "You clever son of a bitch."

"What's clever about pulling the alarm? It's a pathetic attempt to distract us so Mercer can escape."

"But it alerts everyone on the ship to danger, and it won't end with that single alarm." Before Rath finished dressing and checking his personal weapons, the phone rang again. "What is it?"

"Herr Rath, it's Dieter. I'm in the security office.

We're getting reports of gunfire in the port-side atrium."

"Against our people?"

"No," the rally driver said. "Someone shot at the damage-control team checking the fire pull station that just went active."

"Mercer's trying to make the Swiss Guards think the Convocation's delegates aren't safe."

"It's working. The captain of the Guards is screaming for an immediate SOS to bring reinforcements from the Italian warship shadowing the *Empress*."

Rath made his decisions quickly. "Have everyone meet at the launch. We'll let the Swiss Guards fight Mercer and leave the ship during the confusion."

"Why leave?" she persisted. "We control the ship."

"Not after Raeder contacts the captain and he turns to the Swiss Guards. We don't have enough people to fight them."

"But we'll never be able to get the rest of the boxes!"

"Calm down. We can charter a helicopter in Iceland and return to the *Njoerd*. She has the right gear to mount a quick salvage job. We won't recover all of them, but we'll get enough to satisfy the Libyans." Rath turned his attention back to the phone. "Dieter, I have an idea to buy us a little insurance. Have some men meet me on A deck."

"I'll join you myself."

Rath turned to Greta, who had been dressing. "Once we get away from the ship, no one will touch us."

"And if they try to follow?"

"Good point." Rath used his walkie-talkie to contact the men converging on the marina and ordered them to disable all the large boats stored there. "That'll buy us enough time to reach Reykjavik and take off again for the *Njoerd*."

"What's this insurance you mentioned?"

"We're taking a few guests with us."

*   *   *

They raced into the atrium from the corridor where the damage crew was cowering. Mercer unleashed another barrage into the skylight above, dodging a rain of glass shards. "We are the Action Front for Liberation," he roared at the few men on the bridge with them. He menaced them with his gun and they dropped to the carpet. "End tyranny now!"

Leading Anika across the bridge, he dashed through a fire door and collided with a pair of Rath's men coming up the echoing stairwell. Mercer's momentum knocked one down the half flight of steps, and the other was a fraction too slow recovering from the unexpected collision. Mercer smashed him in the forehead with the side of the Model 12 and spun to target the guard on the landing. Recognition flared. It was Bern Hoffmann, the young German Mercer had saved from carbon-monoxide poisoning in Camp Decade.

In the moment of hesitation before Hoffmann reached for his holstered pistol, Mercer jumped the eight steps to the landing, dropping so his foot broke the young man's wrist. Hoffmann cried out, but was silenced by a well-executed pistol-whip to the jaw. Mercer removed the pistol from Hoffmann's limp hand and recovered a matching weapon from the unconscious man at the head of the stairs.

"Anika, let's go. They'll be fine."

Her face was a mask of shock and revulsion. Mercer's quick savagery had stunned her. "I can't. I just . . ."

"Then give me your gun and hide yourself. We don't have time to argue."

She snapped out of her panic and came down the steps. She couldn't tear her eyes away from the broken figure of Bern Hoffmann. "I'm sorry," she said. Mercer didn't know if she was speaking to him or the unconscious man.

"Come on." He took her by the hand, and they continued their descent. The sound of the fire alarm was diminished in the stairwell but came back when they emerged a few decks down. They were near one of the spas. Through a glass wall Mercer could see an elaborate gymnasium and an Olympic-sized swimming pool. A fire pull station was across the hallway and he yanked the handle. The other team would be doing the same at any pull station they happened across. The alarm panel on the bridge should be lighting up like a Christmas tree.

Through a set of double doors, Mercer and Anika came upon a number of Convocation delegates milling in a hallway, muttering unanswerable questions to each other about the situation. He kept his weapons from view as they walked down the corridor. He stopped when they reached the far end. There were a number of escape routes in view. He fired the remainder of the thirty-round magazine into the floor. The companionway emptied except for the cordite stench and smoking brass.

He fitted another clip and racked the slide. They ran for an outside door and emerged on a wooden-floor promenade deck. The cold tang of the sea caressed their skin. In the distance hulked the dark silhouettes of lifeboats on their davits. A number of ship's officers were checking them in case this turned out to be a catastrophic fire rather than a false alarm. They hadn't heard the gunfire.

Running in the opposite direction, Mercer and Anika made their way toward a flight of stairs leading to one of the vessel's many outdoor cafes. Mercer took the H&K from Anika and refitted the silencer. Two quick shots destroyed the lock on the sliding glass doors and they were back in the ship.

The hallway beyond the café's entrance was deserted. Moving carefully because they were exposed, they passed a number of shops and another bar that overlooked an outdoor pool. Across the smooth water they could see a towering funnel lit with floodlights. Neither saw the two figures crossing the pool area en route to an entry door until the door was heaved open.

The figures, dressed in black and carrying MP-5s

with probing laser sights, swept the corridor to their right and turned to look behind them. Mercer and Anika stood just ten yards away. He pushed her down and dove across the hallway as the laser cut the air above him. Mercer rolled onto his knee and fired, a tongue of flame shooting from the Model 12. The fusillade caught the security personnel across the chests, tossing one back onto the patio and standing the other against a wall, his body jerking like a puppet.

"You said you weren't going to kill anyone!" Anika shrieked.

"They were Rath's men," Mercer shouted above her screams. "They were carrying German machine pistols, not the Italian ones the Swiss Guards have."

She edged closer and recognized the corpse in the hall from the Geo-Research station in Greenland. She couldn't believe the speed of Mercer's reaction.

"I didn't have a choice," Mercer added and led her away.

He pulled another fire alarm as they entered a long corridor lined with cabins. As before, a few passengers were in the hallway but not many because rumors of a terrorist attack were already spreading. Mercer glanced at his watch, assuming that the twenty-minute time line had passed. He was stunned to find less than half that had elapsed. Like all combat, time had telescoped into a weird distortion where seconds took hours and hours could vanish in a blink.

They reached the double doors at the end of the hall just as Swiss Guards poured onto the companionway. Mercer fired a snap burst from his submachine gun, praying he didn't hit anyone. Pounding the doors against their stops, Mercer pushed Anika ahead of him, taking up a defensive crouch when he found cover behind a large planter overflowing like a jungle. A few seconds later, a pair of Swiss Guards came racing after them. He used the H&K pistol he'd taken from Hoffmann and placed rounds in each of the Guards' thighs, far enough from the femoral artery so they wouldn't bleed out.

"Let's go." He'd bought a few more seconds.

They burst into an empty ballroom. The ornate chamber echoed as they ran toward the glowing EXIT signs on the opposite wall. At the far side, Anika collapsed onto a sofa, her chest heaving to get enough air into her body. Mercer too was winded, but they couldn't rest here.

"You're doing great," he panted. "Just a little while longer."

They checked the antechamber beyond the ballroom and began walking more normally, their weapons hidden from the two Muslim clerics arguing in Arabic despite the wailing fire alarms.

They moved through several more passages, firing indiscriminately at walls and ceilings, spreading fear wherever they went. At one point Mercer found a stack of the ship's newspaper awaiting delivery to the cabins. He stuffed handfuls of them into a ventilation grate and set them on fire. Considering the size of the vessel, it would take many minutes for the smoke to be detected, but he hoped by then it would have diffused all over the ship. More confusion. More panic. They dodged in and out of two more firefights with roaming Guards, each time escaping to a lower deck and blending with frightened passengers until they were safe.

By now Mercer was thoroughly lost, but he guessed that all passages on the each half of the catamaran eventually led to one of the atriums. As they walked down a hall, keeping watch for pursuing Guards, Mercer spotted a sign indicating the atrium was just ahead. He broke into a jog, with Anika beside him. She'd emptied all her clips but continued to carry the silenced H&K.

They entered the atrium one level below the dining room where Mercer had met the televangelist and his wife. The cavernous space was deserted. Hunched to minimize his size, he led Anika to one of the bridges to get to the center of the ship so they could then lose themselves in the starboard hull, an area they hadn't been to yet.

A piece of the bridge's brass railing exploded the same time Mercer heard the whip crack of a pistol shot. He pushed Anika to the carpet and covered her with his body. It felt like the shot had come from across the mall-like atrium and one level up. He chanced a look and saw a dozen Swiss Guards lining the upper railings. Some of them were headed to the escalators. The Guards would reach the ends of Mercer's bridge long before he and Anika could escape.

"Drop your gun," Mercer whispered to her, visually checking distances in the opposite direction of the group of Guards.

"Why?"

"I'm saving your life," Mercer said. "Do it."

"What are you going to do?"

"You don't want to know." Mercer's grim tone sounded like a final good-bye.

As soon as Anika laid the pistol on the floor, he grabbed her by her collar and hauled her to her feet. Making sure the Model 12 was on safe, he put her in a hammerlock and jammed the weapon into the side of her head. Her scream was no act.

"One step closer and I kill her." Mercer's shouted warning stopped the approaching men dead. He kept twisting in place so no one could get an accurate shot. Because Anika was so short, using her as a shield was a lot harder than he'd envisioned. "All of you drop your guns and back up."

A few guards pulled their aim high, but none of them relinquished their grips. The men coming down the escalator took up firing stances. Had any of them had laser sights like Rath's troops, they would have taken a shot. Still, Mercer's weaving form danced in and out of the crosshairs of eight different shooters.

"Let her go," a Guard officer shouted in rough English. "We will not fire."

"Drop your weapons." While Mercer wanted them to think he was unstable, the anxiety straining his voice was very real. This situation went far beyond anything he'd ever experienced. One twitchy finger and he and Anika would be shredded. "I'll kill her, I swear to God."

Come on, keep me talking, keep up the dialogue. I need a minute more. The way he was holding Anika allowed him to see his watch. His twenty-minute deadline was up in forty-five seconds. After that, he didn't care what happened. Ira and Erwin were more than capable of alerting the CIA about Gunther Rath.

"You don't want to do this," the Guard captain called down in a soothing voice. "We can talk about it."

"No!" Mercer shrieked, allowing his voice to become hysterical. He wanted the Swiss edgy and nervous. It would throw off their aim. "Lorna Farquar's dog bit me, and I will hold this woman until she apologizes."

The absurdity of Mercer's demand had the desired effect. For a fraction of a second the Guards' concentration wavered. He whispered, "See you later," in Anika's ear, pushed her to the floor once again, and threw himself backward, blindly vaulting over the railing behind him.

The rush of the free fall left his heart in his throat and the sound of Anika's cry fading like a distant whistle. Mercer wouldn't know if his leap had been accurate until he hit. He could only see the waterfall looming over him if he tipped his head back. The falls seemed to have come to a standstill as he plummeted at the same speed as the water. The drop was twenty feet and took more than a second—more than enough time for the quicker of the Guards to react. Automatic weapons opened up like chainsaws. Spray from rounds hitting the falls landed on Mercer and then he himself landed. Flat on his back. In the pool at the base of the falls.

He went deep and slapped against the concrete bottom of the four-foot-deep faux lagoon. The water crashed back over him, swirling with bubbles from the air forced from his lungs. He lay at the bottom of the pool, his entire body aching until he opened his eyes and saw streaks of silver slashing the water. The Guards were firing down at him.

With no breath to hold, Mercer swam under the falls and emerged in a hollowed space that housed the pumps needed to create the aquatic effect. Beyond was an access hatch so workers didn't have to wade through the pool to service the machinery. Soaked and struggling to refill his lungs, Mercer kicked open the hatch and emerged in a utility corridor.

It wouldn't take long for the Swiss Guards to figure out where he went. Anika, he felt, would be treated well by the Swiss. They knew her as a hostage, not an accomplice. It would be hours before they discovered she wasn't part of the Convocation, and by then Mercer hoped to have the whole situation wrapped up.

Once he got his bearings, he descended several decks, explaining to a few crew members he passed that he'd been doused fighting a kitchen fire. It took about five minutes to navigate to his destination, and once he was there, he found the door locked. Nonessential crew must have been ordered to their cabins until the nature of the emergency could be determined, he realized.

He knocked and a second later the English youth who'd already lost a pair of sneakers opened the door. "Hi." Mercer grinned. "Remember me?" He showed the submachine gun, and with wordless resignation, the boy let him into the room. His roommate stared wide-eyed from his bunk. Mercer didn't bother tying them this time. He just "borrowed" another pair of shoes, jeans, a Manchester United sweatshirt, and a long-billed Benetton cap that slid on his bald head.

As he closed the door he heard the Englishman say to his roommate, "I told you I wasn't playing kinky games with that guy from housekeeping."

Mercer tossed his weapons into a laundry cart. With a spare key card to Vatutin's room, he could only pass as a panicked passenger if he wasn't armed to the teeth. If everything had gone according to plan, Gunther Rath should be on his high-speed motor launch with Greta Schmidt and the Pandora box while Erwin and Klaus Raeder were speaking with the *Sea Empress*'s captain about stopping him. In all, Mercer felt pretty damned pleased with himself, even if he walked like he had a massive sunburn on his back. Every square inch of skin stung, and he knew he'd be black-and-blue for weeks.

He took an elevator back to the passenger area and a minute later fitted the magnetic card into the lock and fell into Vatutin's room. The Orthodox priest and Hilda Brandt were already back from their excursion. The large woman looked stricken when she saw that he was alone. *"Wo ist Anika?"*

Mercer lowered himself into a chair and closed his eyes, letting the fear and tension wash out of his body. "She's fine. The Swiss who have her think I took her hostage. They don't know she was with us."

Hilda looked to Vatutin and the Russian translated the answer as best he could. *"Sehr gut,"* she said.

"You guys have any trouble?"

"Nyet," Vatutin said. "We separate from Mr. Lasko after theater, then come back here five minutes ago."

There was a knock on the door, shave and a haircut but only one bit. It was Ira's signal and Mercer reached behind him to flick open the handle. "God-damn, that was fun," Ira said, crashing onto the bunk. "But if I were the pope, I'd reconsider my security arrangements. Those Swiss Guards never got close."

A few minutes later, the fire alarm cut off at the same time Vatutin's phone rang. Hilda picked it up and handed it to Mercer. "I can tell by the silence," he answered, "that you've succeeded."

"Yes and no," Erwin Puhl said from the bridge. He sounded sick.

"What happened?" Mercer sat forward in his chair, suddenly tense again.

"Raeder explained to the captain what was going on, how we aren't really terrorists and that Gunther

Rath was the true threat. The captain said that, fifteen minutes ago, the ship's computer reported the marina doors had been opened. He dispatched two officers to see what was happening, and they reported back that Rath's boat was gone. We've tried to raise Rath in the cabin he commandeered, but no one's answering."

"What's the problem? Sounds to me like everything went exactly as planned. Ira can now call Director Barnes at the CIA and have Rath intercepted. We won, Erwin. Relax."

"We didn't win, Mercer. Remember when you tried to reach your FBI friend and were told communications were out because of the solar max?"

"Yeah, we figured it was Rath blocking outgoing signals."

"It wasn't. The solar max *has* killed all radios and satellite phones on the ship. Ira can't call anybody. Nobody can. We're cut off."

Conversation outside the launch's cockpit was impossible with her twin Saab turbo-diesels at full throttle. The sea was calmer than could be expected, so the forty-foot craft once stowed aboard the *Njoerd* shot across the low waves like a thoroughbred. Gunther Rath was in the throttleman's seat while Dieter, the professional car racer, manned the helm. Greta Schmidt and two of Rath's security people were strapped against the bench seat behind them. Because of the boat's offshore capabilities, no one actually sat. Rather, they leaned into specially designed C-shaped cushions that allowed them to use their knees to absorb impacts.

Everyone was armed. Everyone was tense.

The Pandora box was secured in the forward cabin accessible through the low door between the drivers' positions. With it were four "guests."

Thanks to the confusion Mercer created, their escape from the *Sea Empress* had been relatively simple. Soon after the initial burst of automatic fire at the atrium, Rath understood Mercer's intentions weren't to kill, merely to spread enough panic to ensure he left the ship. The German knew he was being manipulated, hated it, but had little choice. Raeder would need just a moment alone with the cruise ship's captain and Rath's plans were finished. Once he'd taken his hostages, he and Greta raced for the marina, avoiding any area where gunfire was reported. After making certain the *Njoerd*'s launch was fueled and ready, they wrecked the eight large shuttle boats

stored in the garage by smashing holes in their fiberglass hulls with sledgehammers.

From the radar repeater on the *Empress*'s bridge,
Rath knew the Italian destroyer was eight miles south
of the luxury liner, protecting her seaward flank, and
would be unable to pursue the launch once they swung
north toward Iceland, ninety miles away. With the
solar max at its zenith and even the most powerful
marine radios hampered to a few miles' range, the
Italians were deaf and mute.

Rath was making the best of the disasters that had
befallen him and maintained optimism that they would
be able to recover the sunken Pandora boxes and turn
them over to Libya. If he couldn't, he was confident
that the single box in his possession would guarantee
a financially secure future for him and Greta.

He figured he only needed a two-hour head start to
escape Iceland once they reached its shores. It would
take twice that time just for the *Empress* to get close
enough to the island to report what had happened. By
then Rath would have sent a chopper to the *Njoerd*,
and he and Greta would be on a leased jet for a hop
to Tripoli. He looked over his shoulder to where she
huddled in her parka and offered her a reassuring
smile. They'd be okay.

Mercer would have slammed down the phone if
Rath's unimpeded escape hadn't been entirely his
fault. It didn't matter that the rest of his team had
agreed with his assessment about the communications
from the *Empress*. He'd made the call to let Rath
go and radio the authorities afterward. And now the
German was miles away with one of the boxes and
there was nothing he could do to stop him.

Like hell there wasn't. The idea came to him in a
moment of clarity that overwhelmed his swelling feelings of defeat. "Erwin, put Raeder on the phone."

"You're on a speaker phone here in the bridge,"
the president of Kohl said at once. "What do you want
me to do?"

"Rath will be heading to Iceland. Turn the *Empress* northward and tell the captain to push the engines as far as they will go."

"Herr Mercer, this is Captain Heinz-Harold Nehring." The voice was accented but commanding. Mercer imagined a ramrod-straight veteran who'd seen and done it all. "The *Sea Empress* is capable of twenty-eight knots. We will never catch Rath. His boat is too fast. I recommend we alert the destroyer *Intrepido* with signal flares and, once we are close enough for voice contact, have them take up the hunt."

"Where is she?"

"About eight miles south of us," the captain admitted.

"It'll take too long." Mercer fought to keep frustration from his voice. "Every second we waste gives Rath that much more of a lead. We have the capability to go after him ourselves. Turn us to Iceland and start firing those flares. The *Intrepido* can catch up and you can tell them what's happening en route. Does she have a chopper?"

"Yes, but it is down right now for a transmission problem."

"Doesn't matter. I can catch Rath."

"How?"

"Turn the ship and let me worry about it." Mercer looked at Ira Lasko. "How many guns do you have?"

"I dumped them all."

"Father Vatutin?"

"So did I."

Hilda had also returned to the cabin without her gun. "Erwin," Mercer said into the phone, "get some weapons, MP-5s and pistols. Also a cell phone and a sat-phone. It may work when we're closer to Iceland. Meet me in the marina where we first came aboard."

"What are you doing?" Ira asked when Mercer cut the connection.

"Remember the Riva speedboats next to the Jet Skis? They're ten or fifteen miles an hour faster than

Rath's boat. Rath's going to beat us to the coast, but we'll be right on his heels."

Lasko made a sour face. "Those boats are thirty feet long," he said doubtfully. "We must be a hundred miles from Iceland. They'll never survive a race across the open ocean."

Mercer was already at the door, forcing the others in the cabin to follow. "The boat will be fine. It's *us* who may not survive."

Ira got a sudden idea. "Wet suits?"

"Now we're on the same page. They're right next to the Aquarivas."

Like a squad of soldiers bent on a one-way mission, they descended to the marina, grim faced and silent. While the alarms had been canceled, the public-address system repeated a call for all passengers to report to their rooms for a head count. The hallways were deserted.

Mercer's body vibrated with tension, but his senses were on the hyperacuity he experienced whenever he faced danger. He felt he could almost hear the second hand of his watch.

He crashed through the doors to the marina and snapped on the overhead lights. The two Rivas were along the left wall, their polished forward decks gleaming under the fluorescents. The long stern decks hid a pair of 315 horsepower Mercruiser engines. Each had a leather-trimmed open cockpit behind a windshield that was more decorative than functional. They were expensive toys designed for running around secluded tropical coves, and he was about to take one out in the open north Atlantic on a chase her builders had never imagined.

He moved to the crane controls next to the glass office where Greta Schmidt had captured the others. "Ira, check the fuel status of the boat closest to the exit doors. If she's full, dump out half the gas. We need speed, not range."

"I'm on it." He was already unclamping the rear hatch to get at the engines.

Mercer pulled an oversize wet suit over his stolen clothes. The garment was stiff and new, cutting his mobility, but he'd need it when the Riva approached Iceland's wave-lashed coast. He and Ira were in for a wet, freezing ride. The boots had no treads, so he was forced to keep on his sneakers. The smell of spilled gas began to envelop the space. "Good job. Father Vatutin, monitor the gauges so Ira can change."

Erwin was not alone when he came in to the marina a moment later. Marty, Anika, and Klaus Raeder were with him. Mercer allowed himself a second of relief that she was all right and turned his concentration back to what he was about to attempt.

"Give the weapons to Hilda to check over." She had proved her weapons training equaled her cooking skills. "What's the status on that fuel?"

"Almost there."

"Anika, go open the outer doors," Mercer said, paying no attention to her expression.

She ignored his order and crossed to him. Mercer was bent over, tying his shoe, and didn't know she was there until he straightened. She slapped him across the face harder than any woman had ever struck him. He reeled against the rack of wet suits, his cheek numbed.

"That was for sticking a gun to my head." Fury thickened her accent and made her eyes burn. "And I'd hit you again for jumping off the bridge. You didn't need to do that. You could have given up right then. We had already won. It was a stupid stunt. You just wanted to see if you could do it, didn't you? God-damned men and their egos. You remind me of a climber I knew who attempted an impossible ascent but was willing to die trying. Which he did."

She turned away, but Mercer placed a hand on her shoulder. She shook herself free. "Don't touch me."

Behind her anger, Mercer saw fear. For herself mostly, but a little for him too. "If you want to pigeonhole me with suicidal rock climbers I can't stop you." He showed no anger because he couldn't blame her. "But I think you're wrong. Am I reckless? When I have to be. Do I take chances no sane person would? Yes, but not because I want to. I do it because I have to."

"And you *have* to chase Rath in a boat that will sink after the first mile?" Concern dampened her rage and her true feelings welled into her voice.

"Yes. Because he has to be stopped. I didn't choose to be here, Anika. Nor did I choose to be on that walkway with a dozen guns pointed at me. In case you hadn't noticed, I react to situations. I don't go looking for them. If you think of me as some clichéd macho guy driven to danger that's fine. But I don't think you know me well enough for that kind of judgment." Mercer became more conciliatory. "I'm sorry I scared you."

He broke eye contact. Then noticed that Klaus Raeder was pulling on a wet suit. "What the hell are you doing?"

"Coming with you," the industrialist said. "None of this would have happened if I'd faced my accountability rather than trying to buy it off. I'm not going to let you clean up my mistake."

Mercer considered denying Raeder his opportunity for repentance, but he sensed the German's sincerity. Raeder wanted Rath dead more than he did. Mercer understood why. "Know how to handle a weapon?"

Raeder nodded, then boasted, "I'm also a black belt in judo."

"Good for you." Mercer was unimpressed. "I intend to shoot Rath from as far away as I can. If you want to go beat up his corpse afterward, be my guest."

Erwin Puhl had opened the outer doors, and frigid sea air swept the gasoline fumes from the garage. While Ira Lasko slid his thin frame into a wet suit, Marty attached the lifting lines from the overhead crane to hard points on the speedboat. Retractable rails would move the Riva out of the garage and lower it to the ocean between the *Empress*'s twin hulls.

"Let's saddle up," Ira said when he was dressed.

Just before Mercer fired the Mercruisers, a ship's

officer burst into the marina. Erwin and Raeder recognized him. Captain Nehring. No one paid attention to the elderly figure behind him wearing black slacks and a gray sweatshirt.

Nehring was white haired and commanding as Mercer had imagined, but also physically and emotionally exhausted. "I've had stewards going over the ship to take a count of our passengers." He panted from the run from the bridge. "We just discovered that Gunther Rath has taken hostages."

"Damn it!" Mercer hadn't anticipated this possibility. "Who?"

The gentleman behind him stepped forward. Not until Mercer looked closely, seeing past the casual clothes, did he recognize Pope Leo XIV. In the hallway he caught the shadows of several Swiss Guards. Stunned, Mercer spoke before thinking. "Holy shit."

"The pope informed me that his secretary of state, Cardinal Peretti, is missing, and we've been unable to locate an American televangelist and his wife."

"Tommy Joe and Lorna Farquar?" Ira recalled the flashy minister and his ditzy wife.

"Possibly a target of opportunity he grabbed in a hallway," Captain Nehring said, then added somberly, "Rath also kidnapped the Dalai Lama."

Everyone exchanged frightened looks.

Rath couldn't have chosen a more emotionally evocative hostage if he'd tried. The Dalai Lama's influence beyond his six million Tibetan followers was incalculable. After the pope, the Nobel Peace Prize winner was the most recognized religious figure in the world, seen as a sage statesman and the voice of the oppressed all over the globe.

"The captain has told me you are going after the kidnappers." The pope's English was accented yet musical. "I understand why you want to do this thing, but I can't allow you to sacrifice your lives for the hostages. I have known the Dalai Lama for several years. He would not wish you to trade your life for his. Neither would Dominic Peretti. And in his own way Minister Farquar worships the same God as I do, and my heart tells me that he too would not want you to die to save him."

Who had been taken hostage meant nothing to Mercer. To him, it didn't matter if one of them was the Dalai Lama or the guy that fetched the Lama's morning tea. This wasn't about hostages or even revenge. It was about preventing the Pandora box from spreading death.

"I understand what you're saying, Your"—*Worship? Holiness? Grace?* Mercer didn't know what title was appropriate—"sir. And I appreciate your concern. But we're not going to rescue the four hostages. We're going because Gunther Rath possesses something that threatens every living thing on the planet." Not knowing if he'd offended the pontiff, Mercer pointed to Anatoly Vatutin. "Father Vatutin can tell you what I'm talking about."

The pope looked like he was going to ask another question but stopped himself. The determination in Mercer's eyes and voice was enough to convince him that the men on the speedboat had no intention of martyring themselves. "Go with God and my blessing."

Mercer felt the power of a billion Catholics behind that simple sentence. "Thank you." He refocused on Captain Nehring. "Keep trying those radios. Alert the American base at Keflavik as soon as you can. If the Italians get their chopper in the air, send it after us."

He keyed the Riva's ignition, and the roar of the engines drowned out any other attempt at conversation. Raeder and Ira hung on tightly as Marty used the crane to lift the boat off its cradle and maneuver it to the launching rails. Mercer took a second to look at Anika. She was at the door of the marina, her arms crossed over her chest, her expression unreadable. Against his better judgment, he gave her a wink and thought he detected a small crack in her resolve, a tiny lifting at the corners of her mouth. It could have been his imagination.

The canal between the hulls streamed like a swift-flowing river. Marty's hands were unsure on the crane controls, so when he lowered the Riva, it hit with a powerful splash and immediately bucked against the ropes. Mercer advanced the throttles to the same speed as the *Sea Empress* and their ride stabilized enough for Ira to cast off the lines.

Like the other extravagant marques Italy is famous for—Masarati, Ferrari, Lamborghini—the Riva came alive when Mercer gave it her head, firewalling the engine controls as soon as she was free. She came on plane and shot from the canyon-like channel, rounding the bow of the *Sea Empress*. The three men settled dive masks over their faces to protect themselves from the stinging wind and the spray whipped up when she cut through the swells. They wore throat-to-ankle two-piece suits, dive gloves, and hoods, and the goggles covered the last area of exposed skin. As long as the speedboat didn't encounter seas she couldn't handle, they would be safe from hypothermia. If she did hit a wave and capsize, the suits would buy them another few minutes in the water, which hovered just a few degrees above freezing.

The night dazzled with swaying tides of auroral light intense enough to hide all but the brightest stars. None bothered to notice. At the helm, Mercer kept his eyes focused to where he thought the horizon line divided sky from sea while Ira watched the compass to make sure they stayed on course. Klaus Raeder hunkered behind them on the bench seat designed for cocktail parties and relaxing soirees. The guns were at his feet. Without wind to roil its surface, the north Atlantic remained calm enough for them to maintain maximum speed.

With the air whipping past them at fifty miles per hour, speaking was out of the question. Instead, the three men were left with their nagging fears, constantly aware that a rogue wave could rear up without warning and end their desperate race. If by some miracle they survived the sea when it shelved against Iceland's jagged shore, they still had to deal with a determined, and dangerous, Gunther Rath.

Mercer calculated that, with Rath's one-hour head start, the two boats would reach the coast at about the same time, provided he could maintain their current speed.

That likelihood vanished as the sea grew restless.

It was barely noticeable at first, just a slow undulation like gently rolling hills, but after they were out in the open for an hour, the waves grew until the white slashes of foam topped all but a few of them. The Riva began to rock. Mercer was forced to nose the boat into the waves, pulling them off course so they didn't take the swells broadside. Even with the Riva throttled back to thirty-five knots, the ride was punishing. The sleek craft became airborne off the larger waves, skipping across swells so that her props thrashed water and air in equal measure. Explosions of black water doused the men as they rode the turgid sea. Punished by their safety straps and lashed by an icy wind from the west, they held tight.

Ira placed his lips to Mercer ear and screamed, "You think Rath will have to slow too?"

Mercer shook his head no. It was too loud to explain that Rath's larger boat was designed for these kinds of open-water waves. They had been lucky to make up nearly three-quarters of Rath's lead and could only hope not to lose any ground as they powered northward.

The sea grew rougher still, and with the first blush of dawn smearing the eastern horizon, the wind kicked up. Mercer's knees burned from the constant flexing and his hands ached from maintaining a white-knuckled grip on the wheel. His feet were soaked from water sloshing around the cockpit and a numbness was creeping up his calves. Through the salt-streaked face mask, he continuously scanned the sea for a glimpse of a wake or a running light. So far nothing.

Behind him, Klaus Raeder threw up.

Mercer spotted a wave twice the size of anything

they'd encountered just before it hit. He whipped the
wheel into the surging wall of water and the Riva
rocketed up its face in a gut-churning swoop.
Launched from the crest in a corkscrew flight, the boat
landed with her gunwale almost awash and she would
have capsized if Mercer hadn't jerked the wheel in the
opposite direction and slammed the throttles to their
stops. Before he could fully recover, the next monster
wave hit them broadside and water poured into the
cockpit. This time there was nothing he could do but
pray the wave passed under them before the Riva
floundered.

The speedboat tumbled into the trough and Mercer
had enough time to kick her around again so they
sluiced through the third large wave in the set. It was
a masterful demonstration of driving and Ira gave him
a wide-eyed stare of disbelief. Mercer's matching incredulity showed it had been luck and not skill.

The Riva's bilge pumps cranked overtime.

With no idea when the next big series would hit,
Mercer pointed to the west to tell Raeder to keep
watch. The German tapped him on the shoulder in
acknowledgment. Settled again on their northerly direction, Mercer throttled back slightly for better control and continued their pursuit.

Five more times they hit high rolling sets of waves,
and each time Raeder gave Mercer enough warning
for him to steer into them. The ranks of swells between the big ones were still large enough to sink the
boat, but Mercer had found their rhythm and kept
them safe.

After another hour, what appeared at first to be a
pinprick of light ahead and slightly to their left slowly
revealed itself as a lighthouse. They were approaching
the eastern side of the Reykjanes Peninsula, very close
to where Iceland's Keflavik Airport was located. Mercer racked his brain to remember the geography of
the area. As he recalled, the only accessible village on
this part of the peninsula was the small fishing commu-

nity of Grindavik, about ten miles farther along the coast.

Assuming Rath would follow the most direct course to Iceland and would need to steal a truck to complete his escape, he edged the Riva to starboard and increased their speed when they entered the coastline's protective cover. The twin engines sang.

The dawn grew to a white-and-gold ribbon, and the nature of the coast became more clear, forlorn, and tortured by its volcanic creation. Mercer could see the outline of a couple of volcanoes like elongated triangles on the flat plain beyond.

Also revealed in the growing light was a distant speck of white on the water: the wake of a boat running hard. When the others spotted it too, Raeder passed a machine pistol to Ira Lasko and kept one for himself. The cold and misery of their trip was lost in the desire to see it through.

The *Njoerd*'s launch seemed to grow in size as they approached. The little town of Grindavik was still dark but visible, and they would be abeam of Rath's boat at least a mile before they reached it. Swaying in time with the boat's motion, Ira jacked a round into the chamber of his MP-5.

Mercer steered for the stern of the offshore launch, masking the sound of his approach with the other powerboat's thundering diesels. They needed only a few seconds in range to disable the steel-hulled craft, and as long as Rath and his crew kept their focus on the town they would never know they'd been spotted. Mercer slowed the Riva, matching the launch's speed when it was just twenty yards ahead. He could see the name *Njoerd* painted on her flat transom. Beyond, he saw four heads, one of them with streaming blond hair.

Just as Ira raised the H&K to his shoulder, some instinct made Greta Schmidt look behind her. Mercer couldn't hear her shouted warning, but her mouth moved in frantic command. Ira squeezed the trigger, and a flat spray of bullets kicked up spray at the spot the launch had been an instant before. Dieter had reacted to Greta's screams with the exceptional reflexes that made him such a skilled racer. He began slewing the larger boat in a random slalom that was impossible to accurately track with a submachine gun. Ira couldn't risk randomly firing at Rath's boat in case he hit one of the hostages. Mercer backed off the throttles, not wanting to overtake the swishing launch. The race would only end when they reached shore.

Greta had disappeared from their view for a moment. When she emerged from the forward part of the launch, she had a pistol in one hand and a hostage in the other. Her greater size and strength all but smothered the struggles of her victim, the scantily dressed Lorna Farquar.

While his life had hardened Mercer to violence, he was not immune to it. There was no way he could brace himself to what he knew was about to happen. Lorna must have realized her fate too because her writhing became desperate. Greta's expression didn't change as she clubbed the woman behind the ear with the pistol and shoved her limp form off the back of the boat.

Instinct told Mercer to ignore the motionless body that bobbed in the launch's wake and concentrate on Gunther Rath and the last Pandora box. That was what was important. Yet his humanity was a much stronger drive than any personal desire for justice.

There was no hesitation.

He chopped the throttles, holding fast against the steering wheel as the Riva dropped from plane like a head-on collision. Rath's boat thundered away while Mercer swept the Riva in a tight circle to recover the evangelist's wife. She lay facedown, her skimpy dress peeled from her body by the impact with the water. Her flesh was white against her translucent panties, already looking lifeless. With the Riva's Mercruisers burbling, Mercer drew up next to her, edging wheel and throttle so the speedboat pirouetted and Klaus

Raeder could grab her. He heaved her across the gunwale.

As soon as her feet cleared the frigid water, Mercer opened the throttles again. He looked over his shoulder in time to see clear water erupt from Lorna's mouth and her body convulse in a coughing fit that sounded over the throb of the engines. She curled into a ball and retched again. She'd be shivering for the next couple of hours and her head would ache, but she'd be all right.

Rath was a quarter mile ahead, angling in toward the wooden jetties fronting Grindavik. His launch didn't slow until the last second, its wake slamming fishing boats into each other and the floating docks. The one permanent pier thrusting out in the water was a concrete structure with a high-bowed purse seiner snugged against one side. A battered van was parked on the dock, and five early-morning fishermen talked amiably as they prepared the boat's lines. Rath ordered Dieter to the other side of the pier, and the driver deftly coasted the last few yards. One of the security men leapt from the launch to secure a rope to the rusted cleats. Another man followed him, his attention on the fishermen, theirs on his gun.

As Mercer brought the Riva in toward the town, two other gunmen appeared at the big launch's transom and unleashed matching sprays of automatic fire. The range was extreme, and yet Mercer had to sheer away from the stream of bullets, cutting a deep crescent in the sea. Like a shark kept at bay, he cruised just beyond the limit of the weapons, patrolling back and forth restlessly, seeking an opening that would never come. Rath held the superior position, and until he'd loaded his hostages and the Pandora box into the truck, Mercer, Ira, and Raeder could do nothing but wait.

"Get Mrs. Farquar below and wrap her in as many blankets as you can find," Mercer ordered. "There should be heating vents mounted on the ceiling of the cuddy cabin. Open them wide."

As Raeder maneuvered the woman into the cabin and Mercer watched the frenzied activity on the dock, Ira Lasko got an inspiration. He flicked on the sat-phone he'd carried and tried to get a signal through. "Damn it! Nothing."

"What about the cell phone? It doesn't rely on a satellite. Its signal only has to reach the closest tower, and I think I can see one just inland of the town."

"Good idea." He tossed the sat-phone aside and snapped open another telephone no bigger than a wallet. "I've got a signal!"

"Call Paul Barnes and get us some help." Mercer could see that three of the fishermen were being pressed into service to carry the golden box from the launch to the rear of their van. As Rath directed the transfer, Greta Schmidt covered a rubbery Tommy Joe Farquar, the squat Dalai Lama, and Cardinal Peretti. Farquar still had on his shiny suit while Peretti wore black pants and shirt. The Lama suffered in the cold, wearing nothing more than a red robe and sandals. His eyebrows looked like dark smudges on his nearly bald head.

Ira worked the phone for a minute, speaking in non-sequitur codes until he finally reached his case officer. "Rudy, Ira Lasko . . . shut up and listen. It's all true . . . yes, the meteorite fragments and Kohl industries and every other damned thing. Klaus Raeder isn't the man we want. It's his special-projects director, Gunther Rath. Now listen to me. Rath has a box loaded with an unknown amount of the meteor as well as three hostages, including the Dalai Lama and the number two man at the Vatican. We're off the coast of Iceland near a town called Grindavik. . . . It doesn't matter how we got here. We're here and we need some serious fucking help. Get on the horn and get us a chopper from the Keflavik airbase. Rath's in a white stretch van and will probably be heading across the peninsula toward the Reykjavik road. I think it's Route 41."

Mercer interrupted. "Have him tell the pilot they'll

be on the access road to the Blue Lagoon thermal spa."

Ira passed on the information, adding, "We're going to try to get ground transportation and maintain pursuit. Rath has four or five men armed with pistols and subguns. He will not hesitate to fire . . . No! Don't take the van from the air unless absolutely necessary. He's got hostages, for Christ's sake. You've got a trace on this line, so call me back at this number when you have Air Force cooperation." He snapped off the cell phone. "He had a million questions that don't need to be answered until this shit's over."

"How long to get a chopper?" They couldn't afford a delay. Rath would be miles ahead by the time they stole a vehicle of their own and took up the chase again.

"Only fifteen minutes. Military's been on alert since I stopped checking in."

Klaus Raeder clambered up the steep steps from the Riva's cabin. "She should be fine. The knot on her head is bleeding a bit, but I don't think her skull is cracked."

Every time the speedboat drifted toward shore with the rising tide, a burst of machine gun fire erupted from the dock and Mercer jammed the boat into reverse and hauled them out of range again. They used the time to strip out of the restricting wet suits. Wind cut through the clothing but adrenaline insulated them from the chilling effects. Had Grindavik been more than a clutch of white clapboard structures, he would have beached the Riva farther away and tried to flank the fugitives. But there was nothing on either side of the village except miles of barren desolation.

On the dock, Gunther Rath raged at his men. He'd been ensured that there was no way anyone could follow them from the *Sea Empress* and yet evidence to the contrary lurked a few hundred yards off shore. Granted, even he couldn't have predicted Mercer would attempt the dangerous open-ocean crossing in such a small boat, but if he'd known about the Riva speedboats in the Jet Ski garage he would have ordered their hulls smashed too.

The petrified fishermen had almost maneuvered the two-hundred-pound golden box into the back of the van. Once it was secure, Rath planned to leave one gunman on the dock to hold Mercer at bay while they made their escape. He needed a half hour to reach Keflavik Airport, where they could trade the hostages for a jet to get away from Iceland.

"Come on!" he shouted and cuffed one of the fishermen. The man staggered and the box fell heavily into the cargo area of the van, rocking its suspension.

Without thought or mercy, Rath pulled his automatic pistol from where it was jammed into his belt and shot two of the fishermen. Two others leapt onto their boat and hid from view and the fifth jumped into the water. "Load up," he snarled, gesturing at the three hostages with the smoking gun. Mutely, they climbed into the van, the Dalai Lama giving him a look as if he understood what demons drove Rath to murder so callously. Tommy Joe Farquar, while sobered by the long boat ride, simply allowed himself to be maneuvered, too stunned by what happened to his wife to offer any kind of resistance. Cardinal Peretti did nothing to hide his contempt.

"Willie, I want you to stay on the dock," Rath ordered the youngest of his men. "Keep that boat from landing as long as you can. Buy us thirty minutes and get yourself out of here. Stay away from the Geo-Research office in Reykjavik and get word to the Party's office in Hamburg. They'll know how to contact me and we'll extract you in a couple of days."

"*Ja wohl!*" the young neo-Nazi replied, proud to be able to serve his cause.

Greta kept her pistol on the hostages as she entered the van through the side door, reveling in the smell of testosterone and fear filling the cab. She was near a sexual peak and the pressure of her clothing against her breasts sent ripples of energy through her body.

Her faith in Gunther was so absolute that she knew they would make it away.

With Dieter behind the wheel and Rath in the passenger seat, the van started rolling down the dock. Once it was on the road, they accelerated quickly. The airport was just thirty miles away.

Frustration filled Mercer as the hostages boarded the van for a ride he doubted any would survive. As soon as the vehicle disappeared into the quiet town, he started for the dock and only realized Rath had left behind a picket when the water around the Riva exploded and bits of her forward deck blew away in bright slivers of precious wood. He cranked the wheel while Ira and Raeder returned fire. The gunman on the dock had cover behind a stack of heavy steel fish traps, and nothing short of a missile would dislodge him.

"I'm going to beach down the coast and we'll run back to town to find a car," he shouted over the engines.

Before he could execute his plan, the gunman suddenly staggered out from his hide, his hands smeared red where they clutched his stomach. The sound of a rifle reached the men on the water a second later, and they all saw a puff of smoke blow from the bridge of the fishing boat tied to the dock. The neo-Nazi looked up to where the shot had come from, and the back of his head erupted as the rifle the fishermen used for sharks blew his brains all over the dock.

Mercer didn't waste a second. He took them in under nearly full power, not caring that he scrubbed off speed using the side of the $300,000 Riva against the dock. Ira vaulted up to the concrete quay with a line and cinched it tight. Raeder came next and then Mercer, now holding a submachine gun and a Beretta pistol. Two Icelanders stood on the bridge of the boat, their deeply weathered faces and suspicious eyes never leaving the three men. The third survivor of the group had just reached the rocky beach and began walking back to the dock.

"There's a woman in the cabin." Mercer pointed at the Riva, hoping that these men spoke English like most Icelanders. "She's near hypothermic and needs a doctor for a concussion." The fishermen said nothing. The old bolt-action rifle was leveled at Mercer's head. "The men who killed your friends dumped her in the sea. We need a car to go after them."

The wind whistled through the fishing boat's rigging.

"If you won't help us, at least don't stop us," Mercer pleaded.

The man holding the shark rifle let the barrel fall until it was pointed at the deck of his boat. "How long the woman in the water?"

"Five minutes, maybe eight."

Gunfights and cold murder were beyond what these men knew. A person sacrificed to the sea was a danger they could understand. "The two men they kill. My cousins," the captain of the boat said and reached into his pocket. He tossed a wad of keys onto the dock at Mercer's feet. "You know killing. You kill them. I know sea. I will help woman." He raised his hand toward the town. "Blue Volvo in front of Vsjomannas-tofan Restaurant."

Mercer didn't thank them. They wouldn't expect it and he didn't have the time. He scooped up the keys and raced off the dock, confident that Ira and Klaus would keep up. He was stopping for nothing until Rath was dead.

The Volvo was a beaten four door, rust smeared and so often repaired that little of its original paint remained. The interior reeked of pipe smoke and the seat covers were so shredded they showed more foam padding than black vinyl. The engine belched and snorted and barely settled down when he forced the transmission into first gear with a painful grind. Mercer's Heckler & Koch was across his lap. Ira's window refused to roll down, so he smashed it out with his machine pistol.

The road twisted out of town, following the vagaries of the volcanic terrain. As their speed approached sixty, the bald tires and mist-slick macadam tried to throw them in the ditches bordering each curve. Mercer wished he had his Jag right now. They'd be doing a hundred without a chirp from the wheels. Still, he pushed the old Volvo harder, drifting through corners with quick touches of brake and gas, his hand working the stick without regard to the gears' worthless synchronizers.

In the distance, he could see steam plumes from the Svartsengi power plant rising into the gray dawn like clouds struggling from the black landscape. What he couldn't see was a white van driving as recklessly as he was. At the end of this road was a branch east to Reykjavik or west to the international airport and Keflavik. Each route held promise for fugitives, and Mercer needed to be close enough to see where Rath was heading.

"Any sign of that chopper?" he asked. The Volvo briefly lifted on two wheels as its tires screamed through a tight bend.

"Ceiling's only about five hundred feet," Ira said, referring to the low cloud cover that hung from the tallest peaks like muslin. "We won't see it until we pass under it."

The road leveled out and straightened as they neared the geothermal generating station and the adjacent Blue Lagoon spa. A trio of hundred-foot cooling towers rose from the lava field like slender rockets on a moonscape, their tops wreathed in steam. The rest of the sprawling facility was hidden in a dip in the topography. A half mile ahead was the turn for the plant and spa—and just beyond that was the van. Mercer's jaw tightened. Then he realized something was wrong. The van wasn't in his lane, it was in the opposite. It wasn't heading away from them. It was coming closer!

Like an enraged insect, a Hughes 500 helicopter painted olive drab hovered above the hurtling van, its

skids no more than fifty feet from the vehicle's roof.
A sniper with a Barrett .50 caliber rifle sat in the open
door, his clothes rippled by the wind, his eye screwed
to the weapon's enormous scope.

Mercer slammed on the Volvo's emergency brake
and slipped the car into a skid that completely blocked
the two-lane road. Even the sturdiest four-wheel-drive
SUV couldn't penetrate more than five feet into the
moss-covered lava fields. Rath was caught between the
helo and the car. Throwing open his door, Mercer
pulled the H&K and watched the van approach over
the sights. He pulled the trigger, intentionally aiming
low. He couldn't risk the driver or a stray shot ricocheting in the cab.

It was one thing for Dieter to risk his life on a race
track, another thing entirely facing the winking eye of
an automatic 9mm. It was a game of chicken that he
wouldn't play. Braking so the van's back end broke
loose, he spun into the driveway of the generating
plant and accelerated away.

Mercer knew from his tour of the facility a couple
years ago that this was the only way in or out of the
complex. As long as he could disable the van, the
Pandora box was trapped. He dove back into the
Volvo, willed the transmission into gear and tore after
the fleeing vehicle. Ira jammed a fresh magazine into
Mercer's MP-5. The van continued past the turnoff for
the power station and drove toward the newly constructed Blue Lagoon spa. The Hughs 500 flashed over
the car, nose down and menacing.

The spa's modern glass-and-steel building was set
back from the empty parking lot. It was reached by a
meandering foot path cut into the lava, a narrow trail
flanked by ten-foot walls of tortured stone. Dieter careened through the lot and shot down the footpath,
sparks flying whenever the fenders scraped rock. With
Mercer still several hundred yards behind them and
unable to communicate with the chopper, the maneuver bought them a few minutes to hustle their hostages

from the van. They had no choice but to leave the golden box in the rear.

One of Rath's gunmen waited in the van, his machine pistol able to cover the entire trail. When they followed, Mercer and his men would run headlong into a scathing ambush.

Rath blew apart one of the spa's glass doors with his pistol and rushed in, confident that his men had Peretti, Farquar, and the Dalai Lama well covered. Ahead was a cavernous room bisected by a reception counter. Beyond was a waiting area with a twenty-foot glass wall overlooking the steaming waters of the artificial lagoon. In the weak light of the encroaching dawn, the water had a peculiar shade of milky blue, a combination of silica and bacteria that gave it curative powers and the unholy stench of sulfur.

With an eye for urban street fighting, Rath positioned his men to best cover the entrance in case Mercer's team made it past the gunner in the van. He also scouted out his escape route for when Mercer was dead. The building echoed with the reverberations of chopper blades just a few feet above the roof.

When he reached the parking lot and saw the spa's canyon-like entry path, Mercer instinctively knew where Rath had gone. He braked hard at the beginning of the trail, blocking it with the body of the Volvo to trap the van. Hyped on adrenaline until his veins burned, he never considered waiting for reinforcements from the military base at Keflavik.

"They'll be waiting for us to follow," Ira said.

"We'll flank 'em," Mercer grunted. "You two climb up the left side of the path, and I'll go right. We'll stop when we're above the van."

The lava on this part of the Reykjanes Peninsula had been laid down in A.D. 1226, and despite Iceland's scouring winds it had not yet succumbed to the polishing effects of erosion. Clambering up the wall on one side of the path was like climbing a mound of broken glass. A mistimed lunge for a knuckle of stone resulted in a bleeding gash on Mercer's knee and what felt like four fingerprints being abraded off his left hand. Slowed by his injuries, he made his ascent and started off for the building he could see nestled in an excavated bowl of rock. The lagoon behind it simmered like an aquamarine cauldron. Watching for a guard atop the lava and keeping one eye out for anyone lurking in the shadowy trail below, Mercer scrambled along the rim of the path until the van was directly below him. He looked through the multiple windows fronting the spa but saw nothing in the darkness within. The helicopter's downblast blew a freezing gale across his naked scalp.

Once Ira and Raeder were across from him and had the building covered, Mercer raised himself slightly to zero in on the rear of the white van and gave the H&K's trigger a long squeeze. He emptied a clip, careful to direct his fire away from where he thought the van's fuel tank would be. The crashing shots deafened him, so he didn't hear the rear door unlatch, but he saw it swing outward. A man in a black Geo-Research jumpsuit oozed slowly to the ground, small eruptions in his uniform leaking blood.

Gunfire burst from one of the windows a story above his position. Ira and Raeder's returned fire had no effect on the sniper. A steady stream of rounds continued to explode around Mercer. He had a small measure of shelter behind an outcropping of lava, but the 9mm rounds were quickly eating away at the volcanic stone. He slapped in another clip. Then, rather than run away, as the gunman anticipated, Mercer charged the spa, firing a short burst.

The gap between Mercer's hill and the building's second story was eight feet across, and in the instant before he jumped down, he saw another gunman lurking below him. Unable to stop, Mercer angled slightly and leapt instead for an office window, snapping off a couple rounds at the black glass as he flew. The window was just starting to come apart as he burst through in a shower of glass. He landed atop a cluttered desk, scattering papers and knocking a computer to the floor. He levered himself back to the window, ready to fire at the guard he'd glimpsed below, but the man had vanished.

He saw Ira and Raeder moving out to find their own access to the building. Mercer took a deep breath, prepared for the lancing pain of a broken rib or two, but other than the dull ache from his impact with the desk, he was all right. He eased out of the office after recharging his half-depleted clip with bullets from a pair of pistol magazines. The interior of the spa was murky and indistinct, filled with shadows that shifted as the sun rose higher.

At the end of the corridor was a bridge that overlooked the entry foyer and waiting area. Dozens of chairs and tables had been hastily stacked in one corner about halfway across the room. A shape moved behind them. Mercer sighted in and fired off a three-round burst. A hail of return fire pinned him to the bridge. Its glass railings disintegrated in a rain of shards. He had a sudden inspiration. When the autofire ceased, he rolled and fired above the hidden gunman's redoubt. The twenty-foot wall of glass was divided into huge sections by a steel lattice. He concentrated his aim on the top section above the neo-Nazi and held steady. The inch-thick plate splintered and came crashing down, hundreds of pounds of glass falling to the stone floor, the table, and the gunman. It was Dieter. Caught in the avalanche he had just started to dive out from under the onslaught when a fifty-pound piece of window caught him on the shoulder and severed his arm from his body. Mercer cut off his scream with a shot to the head.

Movement caught his attention, and he raised his weapon, holding his fire when he recognized Ira and Raeder approaching from the other side of the bridge.

"Stay down!" Mercer shouted too late.

The shots came from behind and below them, near the spa's gift shop. Ira's quick dive wasn't enough. His body jerked as two bullets found their mark. The remainder of the short blast pinged off the structural steel in the ceiling. As Raeder provided cover fire, Mercer grabbed Ira's collar and dragged him to the safety of the corridor. A snaking trail of blood was smeared into the carpet behind him. Mercer rolled him on his back and Ira's brow beaded with sweat. He'd gone completely white and his breath came in short, choppy slurps. Blood bloomed across his abdomen and looked like a black slick on the inside of one thigh.

"How bad?" Mercer asked, gently pulling up Ira's shirt.

"How the hell should I know?" the agent gasped. "I'm not a doctor."

Mercer used his sleeve to clear away blood and laughed. The bullet pierced the small flap of skin on Ira's waist, a clean in and out that left puckered holes but no lasting damage. "Had your wife been a better cook, it would have been worse."

The wound in the leg was much more serious. It hadn't cut the femoral artery, but the gushes of blood that poured from it indicated some other major vessels had been torn. Klaus exchanged more shots with the gunman in the gift shop.

Mercer used his belt as a crude tourniquet, cinching it as tight as he dared. It would have to be released every twenty minutes or Ira would risk gangrene. If he couldn't remain conscious to do it, Raeder would have to stay with him.

"Is he okay?" Raeder asked.

"Yeah." Mercer brushed glass from his shoulders. With two guards down, there were two left in addition to Greta and Gunther. The odds had been evening out, but without Ira, Mercer would have to go after them alone. And as long as the Germans had the hostages, he was fighting from an even more severe disadvantage. "I think the two gunmen are going to try to pin us here while the others escape over to the power plant where they can steal a vehicle."

"What about the sniper in the helicopter?" Raeder asked as he gathered Ira's spare clips.

"Unless they set down, they'll never risk a shot. The chopper's too unsteady. Ira, can you handle your own tourniquet?"

"I can for a while." He licked his lips. "What's your plan?"

"No idea." Mercer looked around, a haze of gunpowder smoke stinging his nostrils. He could almost feel the two armed men lurking someplace in the elegant building. He finally looked back to Ira. "How about contacting your case officer again? Have him phone Keflavik base so we can get the helicopter down. You need immediate evac and we need some men to secure the Pandora box. Klaus will stay with you until they land and then he can follow me."

"Where're you going?"

"After Rath."

"That isn't the smartest idea you've ever had."

Mercer laughed. "This coming from a man who just let himself get shot?" His next teasing comment died on his lips. A pistol shot had sounded somewhere below, near where he had seen the signs for the bather's changing rooms. There was only one reason for a single shot in this kind of situation. For some reason Rath had just put down one of his hostages. Mercer looked first at Ira and then at Klaus Raeder. They too knew what had happened.

"I'll be okay," Ira said, clasping Mercer's arm. He had a pistol at his side. "Move me into an office and go kill that sick son of a bitch."

"Make sure that chopper pilot knows which side we're on when we get outside," Mercer said once Ira was safely hidden behind a desk.

He grabbed up his H&K and took off down the hallway with Klaus Raeder. Several office doors were open, and their windows had a view of the lava-rimmed pool area. From this vantage point they saw figures moving through the swirling mist, dark furtive shapes that lurched from cover to cover. It was obvious that two were going against their will but was impossible to tell which one—the Dalai Lama,

Cardinal Peretti, or Tommy Joe Farquar—had been shot in the dressing room. It was also clear that the two remaining gunmen in Rath's command were with them. The Blue Lagoon spa was clear.

"There are stairs at the end of the corridor," Raeder said.

"Let's do it."

They went down and came out into another hallway. The men's changing room was behind them and Mercer entered first, his hands tight on the small machine pistol. His ragged breathing reverberated off the tile walls. He swept the dimly lit room quickly, checking behind islands of lockers, before swinging into the adjoining showers and rest room. A body lay against one wall.

Tommy Joe Farquar's toupee was missing and his suit had lost its luster, but he was alive, frightened and in pain from the bullet through his shoulder. He screamed when he saw Mercer with the gun, doubtlessly assuming he was with the men who'd kidnapped him and dumped his wife into the sea. Suddenly he choked off his own shouts and stared defiantly. "Philistine! God will smite you down with a vengeance only He can conjure," he raged in his best preacher's voice. "You will burn in an unspeakable pit for all eternity, your soul to become food for Satan's hell hounds."

"That's probably true, Mr. Farquar," Mercer agreed. "But we're not with your kidnappers. In fact, we're the ones who saved your wife."

"Lorna?"

"Is back in Grindavik, where you first made landfall. She's going to be fine."

"Oh, praise sweet Je-sus." He tried to raise his arms in supplication, but his wound quickly brought his hands back to his side. He shrieked and turned ashen.

"Why'd they shoot you?" Mercer asked.

"I tried to run away."

"It doesn't matter," Raeder snapped impatiently. "We have to go after Gunther."

"Mr. Farquar, medical help is on the way. If you can, try to crawl out to the hallway so someone spots you."

"You can't leave me." Tommy Joe raised his good arm. "They may come back."

"Not if I can help it."

They left him without another word, passing out of the building and onto the wooden deck surrounding part of the sulfurous pool. Heat radiated from the surface of the oddly colored water. Raeder followed Mercer around the lagoon, tracking across the deck in the same direction they'd seen Rath lead his prisoners. The uneven terrain separating the spa from the power plant offered a million places for the Germans to lay an ambush. Wary, Mercer stepped off the deck and onto the moonscape, an ounce more pressure on his index finger ready to unleash thirty rounds.

Fifty yards into the lava field, he burst out from the densest of the steam. The Hughes 500 swept across the plain at him, its rotors beating like thunder, forcing him and Raeder to dive into a craggy hollow. The industrialist landed on Mercer's back, pressing his face against a knife edge of stone that opened yet another gash, this one deep enough to leave a scar.

"What is he doing?" Raeder shouted, terrified.

"He thinks we're with Rath!"

The chopper came across again, this time standing off a hundred yards to give the sniper an open line of sight. The Barrett .50 caliber cracked once, and a chunk of rock the size of a basketball blew apart just a few feet from their position. Mercer and Raeder both lunged to their feet and began running, leaping from boulder to boulder, rising and falling with the wrinkled ground. The gun boomed again and this time the bullet passed close enough for Mercer to feel the shock wave.

"What can we do?"

"Keep running. Ira's got to get through to tell him who we are."

Another shot went wide as Mercer jinked like a

fleeing antelope. Then suddenly his leg folded under him and he fell hard. He heard more than felt something give way in his wrist as he tried to break the headlong tumble. The numbness that climbed his left arm became a stabbing sensation from hand to elbow. And then the pain behind his thigh hit, searing and hot. Yet he could move his foot, could see it rotate as he tested it. Something was wrong. A .50-caliber round should have crucified him to the ground and left him immobile, and yet he struggled to his feet, teetering as a wave of pain washed out of him. He felt for the wound. Amid the mass of blood he felt something gritty.

Jesus! His femur had been powdered by the shot. He was so deeply in shock he couldn't feel the full extent of the crippling injury. That was why he could stand. In a minute he knew he'd pass out. He could feel it coming.

But as he checked his blood-smeared hand, he saw particles of something black. It wasn't bone fragments. It was bits of rock. He'd been peppered by a ricochet of stone fragments from a round that had hit behind him. The wound was no more than being shot from a half dozen BB guns.

He sagged, but his relief was short-lived. He'd been concentrating on his wounds and not the chopper. Mercer had been standing motionless for fifteen seconds, long enough for a good sniper to shoot him many times over. He looked up and stared into the cockpit of the chopper hovering fifty yards away. The sniper had him zeroed.

At the instant the sniper eased the trigger, the pilot jerked the chopper. The bullet passed harmlessly over Mercer's head. The sniper glared at the pilot and shouted something, listened for a moment, and then looked over to where Mercer remained standing. He tossed a jaunty, apologetic wave, and the chopper heeled away, flying toward the spa's open parking lot.

"What happened?" Raeder emerged from a natural fortification of twisted rock.

"Ira must have gotten through," Mercer said, still amazed to be alive.

"Can you go on?"

The stinging in his leg was already subsiding as adrenaline overcame the pain. Mercer's answer came without thought. "Goddamned right I can."

They linked up with the pipeline that carried effluent from the generating plant to the spa's pool and began running. In the distance loomed one of the Svartsengi plant's many buildings, a two-story concrete structure with small windows that looked like portholes. From it ran countless other pipes in a tangled maze only an engineer could love. Steam drifted across the facility on the quirks of the wind. They raced past the turquoise pond that had been the old Blue Lagoon spa and now acted as the leach field for the mineral-laden water forced to the surface by earth's tremendous internal pressure.

Once at the plant, Mercer chanced a look down the central road that bisected the station. There were six principal buildings, and all but the administration center across the road were connected by pipes and conduits of various diameters. It reminded Mercer of a miniature oil refinery. Only this place was spotlessly clean as befitting its environmentally friendly power source. The air crackled with the generation of thirty-two megawatts of electricity, enough power for a town of thirty-two thousand people.

A flash of light, and bullets sprayed the corner of the building where Mercer and Raeder crouched. Raeder fired back, sparking rounds off pipes but hitting little else. Whoever had them zeroed was well protected by the steel forest. There were two cars parked in front of one of the administration building, most likely belonging to security guards since the regular work shift was hours away. As Raeder kept him covered, Mercer fired two quick bursts, blowing out the four tires he could see from his vantage. One way or the other it would end here.

They circled back around the building, taking a path

that ran alongside the lagoon of wastewater. At the next building, Mercer found an unlocked door and eased inside, his machine pistol held tight and ready. The interior space was well lit and futuristic, with cat-walks that ran along parallel rows of heat exchangers and turbines. The building hummed. Another door at the front of the building crashed open, and two figures stood silhouetted. Mercer was about to fire when he recognized the silver hair of Cardinal Peretti. Shielded behind him was one of Rath's men, a pistol held to the Catholic leader's head.

"Let him go," Mercer shouted over the whine of machinery.

The gunman jerked Peretti by the throat, ducking behind the cardinal as they moved into the building. "I see you make a move, he dies," the neo-Nazi shouted back in German. Mercer didn't need Raeder's whispered translation to get the gist of the remark.

"You can walk away," Raeder called out. "We only want Rath."

"Forget it, Herr Raeder. We all leave or we all die."

Mercer stood slowly so the gunman could see him, the MP-5 dangling from its strap. The man pulled his pistol from Peretti's skull and aimed it at him. "Now you die," the young fanatic shouted.

Dominic Peretti had been docile from the moment the gunmen had burst into his cabin aboard the *Sea Empress* because it was only his life he felt had been in danger. But seeing the stranger taking deliberate steps toward them, he couldn't allow such a sacrifice. Forty-five years before, he had been a star on his semi-nary school's basketball team because of a spin move some called divine.

He raised a hand to deflect the German's aim, planted a foot to throw off the man's weight and spun around him quicker than he'd been able to move in decades.

The gunman stood exposed for a fraction of a sec-ond. Mercer cleared the Beretta from his belt and triggered off three shots fast enough to sound automatic. The German was flung against the wall by the triple tap and crumpled to the steel flooring. Peretti dropped to a knee and felt for a pulse. He looked to Mercer with neither recrimination nor regret, then started last rites.

"Are you okay, Father?"

"I'm fine, my son," the Vatican's number two man said.

"Do you know where they have the Dalai Lama?"

"No. We split up when they took us here. The large man and the woman took the Lama with them. I believe they are in the administration building, but I'm not sure."

"Trying to call the Geo-Research office in Reykjavik?" Raeder suggested.

"Maybe," Mercer said. "Father, you have to hide yourself until this is over."

"I will in a moment," he said, continuing his prayers over the corpse. Only when he was done did he address Mercer again. "Can you do me a favor?"

"Ah, I don't really have the time," Mercer answered, not understanding what the priest could possibly want considering the circumstances.

"Ask for my forgiveness and say one Hail Mary." His eyes were alight. "Then sin no more after you send the others to hell, where they belong."

Mercer muttered the nearly forgotten prayer. Peretti made the sign of the cross over him and hid next to one of the massive conduits carrying superheated water through an exchanger, as safe a place as any at the site.

Glancing outside, Mercer saw no movement. The administration building's front doors didn't look damaged. He doubted that Rath had gotten that far yet.

"Klaus, keep that building covered. I'm going to check the next one." Mercer dashed from the doorway, using pipes as cover until he crashed against the base of the three towering smoke stacks, the metal still hot to the touch even after the steam venting up them had passed through numerous turbines and exchangers.

The walls of the building behind him were made of steel plate, like it had been armored. As Mercer reached a door he recalled why. This was Building #4 and it contained the secondary turbine loops that used waste steam to boil a petroleum derivative called isopentane. This liquid had been specially formulated to boil at a mere two hundred degrees Fahrenheit in order to extract the last bit of energy from the natural steam. He remembered the plant manager who'd given him the tour years ago also telling him that isopentane was highly explosive. Behind this building would be the outlets where the saline water driven from the earth's bowels was finally released back into nature after producing all the electricity and hot water needs of the citizens of the Reykjanes Peninsula. NO SMOKING signs were posted along Building #4's walls.

The knob had already been shot off a door, allowing Mercer to slip inside. Building #4 had a less modern, more industrial look than the others, with rows of long cylinders like rural propane tanks, but these held the isopentane in a closed-loop system of liquid and gas. Beside each set of tanks was a small steam-driven turbine. The floor was polished concrete.

Mercer was having difficulty keeping the MP-5 steady from the pain in his wrist. He had some motion in the joint and felt that some tendons had been torn. His left hand felt like a dead weight, and he steadied the machine pistol's foregrip on the crook of his elbow. With so much ambient noise in the powerhouse, he had to rely on his vision to scout the building.

Around one of the tanks he spotted a darkly dressed figure hunkered next to a turbine. Mercer recognized the gunman as a Geo-Research "technician." By his expression it was evident he recognized Mercer too. They fired at the same instant, both bursts going wild from the shock of discovery. Ducking around a turbine, Mercer was chased by more rounds, the sharp rip of a machine pistol tearing the air. An ember of steel burned his hand before he could brush it away.

He fired back. His adversary had moved, so the shots hit nothing but metal. *Okay, where the hell did he go?* Mercer moved to his left, sighted along an access walkway but saw nothing. He then went right. A burst of autofire raked the concrete at his heels as he dove under an isopentane cylinder. *Oh, that's where he went.*

He tried to get a bead on the assassin but there was too much machinery for a clean shot. He studied the tank above him. Ten different pipes, including a huge trunk line that brought steam from outside, linked the stacked vessels. Mercer had no idea which carried gas and which carried liquid but he could tell which were the most vulnerable. The trick would be to get the gunman into position. He switched to his pistol to conserve ammunition and began maneuvering around the plant, working the gunman like they were chess pieces, giving ground when he had to, but inexorably moving the man to where he wanted him.

Dashing across an open space, Mercer slid behind a support column. Shots ripped furrows from the floor behind him. Secure once again, his wounded leg all but dead now, Mercer felt he had the gunman. He steadied his grip on the pistol and cycled through the clip as fast as he could pull the trigger. The ricochets whined away as ten rounds slammed into the point where a pipe joined with the isopentane tank that shielded the assassin.

Even before he knew if he'd succeeded, Mercer began to run. Behind him, the German had flinched at the onslaught of bullets hitting steel so close to his head. He had a second to register the high-pitched hiss before the leaking isopentane ignited. Like a flamethrower, escaping gas blew out in a fifty-foot tongue of fire that mushroomed into an overwhelming inferno, eating everything it touched. Amid the blistering paint and melting wires, the assassin's body cooked like a joint of meat.

Blasted by the overpressure wave, Mercer was thrown into the side of the building hard enough to momentarily knock him out. When he came to, an alarm sensed the fire and shut down this portion of the facility. A Klaxon wailed and sprinklers began a rain that quickly turned into a torrent. He hauled himself from the floor, fingering the knot growing on his forehead. If none of the other tanks ruptured from the searing heat, the building wouldn't go up. If one did, they all would in a chain reaction that would likely wreck several square acres.

He fitted the last magazines into each of his weapons and ran for the next building. This structure was nearly identical to where he'd left Cardinal Peretti. Differently painted pipes and valves added the only color to the monochromatic steel interior. Doubled over and limping, his vision beginning to blur from a concussion, Mercer began a systematic sweep of the building. There were hundreds of crannies a person could hide in, miles of heavy pipes that could shield even the largest man and he wouldn't know they were there until he walked into their sights.

He jumped over a handrail to get off the exposed catwalk dividing the long room. At the end of the row of identical machines he thought he'd seen a shadow move. He hunkered down to look under the pipes blocking his view. There! Hiding behind the last turbine was a pair of legs. But as he watched, they vanished. The person was crawling on top of the boxy exchanger, getting the best location to cover the entire room.

Mercer stood, holding himself just out of the gunman's view. He had one chance to get this right. Not quite pistols at ten paces, this was more like automatic rifles at thirty. The assassin knew he was in here, had a good idea where he was hiding and would have the advantage of a secure firing platform. Mercer moved laterally, singeing his hands on a pipe but not making a sound as he crawled to a different position.

He brought the H&K to his shoulder and leapt up.

Through the sights he saw Greta Schmidt's head behind a small yellow-handled relief valve atop a thick pipe, her flaxen hair framing her beautiful/ugly face. Her expression approached sexual euphoria, eyes wide and dilated, her skin flushed.

She had her own machine pistol clamped at her side, but her aim was off by a few degrees of arc. She saw Mercer pop up from behind a piece of equipment and tried to adjust. A streaming hail of rounds followed her swing. Mercer fired once before the slide on his MP-5 racked back and jammed. The single bullet struck the valve and vectored harmlessly away.

After a second of silence that seemed to unroll in slow motion, the tremendous pressure of steam driven by the planet's molten center exploded through the damaged valve in a screaming eruption. In the fleeting moment before the jet of vapor obscured his view, Mercer saw Greta's face begin to dissolve. Her hair vanished first, burned away by the five-hundred-degree steam. Then the flesh began to melt away until patches of bone showed through. The steam turned red as it boiled the blood and tissue from her skull.

She vanished and Mercer choked on the acid that scoured the back of his throat. Hyperventilating, he cleared the jam, knowing that blind luck had saved him. He remained where he was while the mental image of Greta liquefying lost some of its vividness. His head pounded.

A scream galvanized him, a hoarse animal sound of primeval fury. Gunther Rath had entered the building from the opposite end and spotted what remained of his lover. "Mercer!" he roared. "I am going to kill you!"

"Better men than you have made that threat," Mercer shouted back.

Rath fired off a wild burst that rattled around the room, sparking off countless metal surfaces. "I still have the Dalai Lama."

Mercer almost made the mistake of telling him about Klaus Raeder in the next building. He was tired, hadn't slept in thirty-six hours, and his brain wasn't functioning anywhere near where it should. If it weren't for the adrenaline he would have collapsed hours ago. "Give it up, Rath. Even if you make it out of this plant alive, you'll never leave Iceland. You saw the helicopter. You know we've alerted the military. They'll quarantine this entire island if they have to."

"You think that matters now?" Rath challenged back. "Even if I do escape, the Libyans would have me killed for not delivering the Pandora boxes."

Shit! He's ready to die right here and he wants to take me with him. Mercer went from hunter to hunted in that one statement. He could leave now, slink away and wait for troops from Keflavik base to end this. Suddenly an image flashed into his brain of Elisebet Rosmunder feeding the ducks in Reykjavik.

"The Libyans won't get the chance," he yelled. He fired a quick burst and raced for one of the building's back doors. Bullets chased him, but none hit before he rolled onto the asphalt outside. He knew Rath would never let him escape. The man had nothing left to lose and only revenge to keep him going.

Mercer gave Building #4 a wide berth as he circled around it, limping across open pavement until he reached a rocky area along the shores of the man-made wastewater lagoon. The water shimmered with sunlight that had burst from over the horizon. As he stopped at another tangle of pipes, he saw Rath at the door he'd just passed through. He was holding the Lama by his collar.

The Dalai Lama had lost one of his sandals during his ordeal. One foot was a bloody mess from running across the lava rocks. He couldn't put any weight on it and his normally dusky complexion had paled from the pain. Yet his expression remained neutral, as if the agony wasn't his own. The strength he used to defy a nation as large and powerful as China extended to a will over his own body.

The burst of gunfire came from the far side of the complex. It hadn't been intentionally aimed to kill

Rath, but passed far over his head. Klaus Raeder walked down the road like a Western gunslinger, changing clips as he approached, his squint never leaving the man who had once been his most loyal assistant.

The Dalai Lama seemed to come alive when he interpreted Raeder's actions as a rescue attempt. He shifted his weight when Rath tried to return fire. The shots flew far wide as the Buddhist moved to smother his kidnapper in a bear hug. Mercer got ready for the moment the neo-Nazi let the Lama go. His machine pistol had become too heavy to hold, so he switched to the Beretta handgun. His grip was loose and shaky, his eyes barely able to focus. He squeezed his eyes shut to clear them and actually made his vision worse.

Fifty yards separated Rath and Raeder, hatred sparking between them like an electric arc. Frustrated that he couldn't hit his former boss because of the Lama's untutored struggles, Rath rammed the muzzle of his pistol to the Tibetan leader's head, drawing blood. Having drawn the danger back to himself, the Lama went still, more concerned with Raeder's safety than his own.

"No closer, Klaus," Rath said in German, in a voice that was unnaturally calm. He'd already made whatever mental adjustments were necessary to die.

Either Raeder didn't hear him or didn't care. He kept coming. Mercer wished he could understand what they were saying to each other.

"Kill him, Gunther. It doesn't matter," Raeder said calmly. "You will still die."

"I'll do it."

"I know you will." He'd closed to within thirty yards. "What's one more death to you, eh? I'd say it was one more soul on your conscience, but you don't have one. I thought I had been your teacher all these years. Now I see it is you who taught me. Your life and mine are meaningless."

"And his?" Rath forced the gun harder against the Lama's skull.

"He believes he'll be reincarnated on a higher plane. I'm sure he fears death even less than we do. Let him go and the two of us will end this together. Let's see how much you have taught me." Raeder dropped his MP-5 and threw aside the pistol in his belt. "One on one."

"I let him go and Mercer drops me where I stand."

Raeder flicked his eyes in Mercer's direction and switched to English. "Don't shoot. I am going to handle this."

"What the hell are you talking about?"

"Dr. Mercer, this is between Gunther and me. He is going to release the Lama if you don't interfere."

"Screw that."

"Please," Raeder begged. "I told you before that this is my mistake to fix. Allow me that. Afterward you can arrest me and throw me in jail. Let me end this my way."

Mercer blinked, seeing two of everybody now. "You know what you're doing?" he asked doubtfully. Raeder had boasted he was a martial arts expert, but Rath had forty pounds and four inches on him.

"Even if he wins, I guarantee he'll be in no condition to leave this place."

The inside of Mercer's sneaker was spongy with blood from the sniper ricochet. "You'd better be sure about that. I'm in rough shape." A wave of blackness swept across his vision, and he stumbled back, falling against an insulated outlet pipe that pulsed with the force of near-boiling water. He couldn't prevent his aim from dropping.

Rath tossed his automatic and gave the Dalai Lama a shove that sent him sprawling. His glasses shattered when he hit the pavement. Though he struggled to get between the two antagonists, his injured foot refused to support him. The Lama called out for them to stop, but neither German listened.

Rath and Raeder moved closer, circling warily. Raeder threw the first punch, a lightning strike that would have crushed the throat of a normal man. Rath easily caught his fist, twisted Raeder over and kicked him three times in the stomach before releasing the arm and letting Raeder fall to the ground.

"Klaus," he laughed. "Do you really think I taught you everything I know?"

Raeder lurched to his feet, clutching broken ribs. Mercer raised his pistol, but the two began circling again and he wasn't sure which of the figures he saw were real and which were chimeras. He threw up. His concussion from the explosion in Building #4 was far worse than he'd thought.

The two men exchanged flurries of blows, deflecting most, landing occasionally. Both knew this match would have only one outcome. Rath was stronger, fitter, and more skilled. He'd trained Raeder and for years had allowed his pupil to win bouts to keep him interested. At any time Rath could have killed him in the *dojos* where they sparred—one more of Rath's many deceptions that was turning out to be as deadly as the rest.

Soon Raeder's mouth bled from broken teeth and one eye was nearly closed. He limped from a kick aimed at his crotch he'd deflected into his thigh. And yet he fought on, giving ground whenever Rath came in on him, sacrificing his body as if the pain would somehow expunge his sins. Mercer had to drag himself to keep the combatants in view, crawling across the rocks at the edge of the lagoon as they battled. Heat radiating from the pool drew more sweat to his already soaked face.

He was too dulled to understand what Raeder was doing, and Rath was too intent on the kill. The water feeding the nearby spa was regulated to a constant temperature of 158 degrees, hot enough to scald but cooling when it mixed in the 45,000-square-foot pool. Here, there was no need to artificially cool the effluent, and it erupted from the outlet pipes at near-boiling temperatures. Steam rose as from a volcano's caldera.

Raeder absorbed a roundhouse kick to the head

that dropped him near the outlet, and when Rath allowed him to get to his feet, he swayed drunkenly, almost toppling. As Rath came in again, the industrialist showed that last bit of reserve he'd clutched, a flicker of hatred that drilled diamond hard through the pain. Clutching Rath's jacket, Raeder threw himself into the pool.

Mercer drew back as scorching water splashed his legs. The two men remained submerged for no more than a few seconds, and when they surfaced, Klaus Raeder had yet to relinquish his grip. Their faces and hands had turned bright red, and the water sluicing off them carried their topmost layers of skin. They were boiling alive. Writhing to break free, Rath lost his footing and sank under again, coming up when his boss no longer had the strength to hold him. It was far too late to save himself. The Nazi's eyelids were gone. Rath's scream was something Mercer would carry for the rest of his life. So too would he forever remember the look of triumph on Klaus Raeder's face as he collapsed back into the water, pressing his apprentice's body under the seething waves. Tendrils of flesh formed a sickening broth around the corpses.

A minute might have passed, maybe an hour. Mercer became aware of time again only when he felt a touch on his shoulder. He opened his eyes. It was the Dalai Lama. He had dragged himself over. Without his glasses, his eyes were squinted and watery.

"Where are you hurt?" he asked.

"Everywhere but my conscience." Mercer managed a tired smile. "Are you all right?"

"I believe so, yes," the Buddhist replied. "I wish I could have stopped them."

Mercer rolled his head to stare into the boiling pool. "The man who saved you had a karmic debt that only his death could pay. I think it's better you didn't."

Either the Lama agreed or was too played out to respond. Mercer wasn't sure. The silence between them, punctuated by the muffled alarms still sounding from the isopentane explosion, continued until battle-dressed soldiers appeared from the mist like wraiths. They swarmed over the facility in squads of four, barrels of their M-16A1s in constant sweeping motion. A trio of medics approached Mercer and the Lama. However, another figure beat them to the wounded pair. Anika Klein's expression showed a mix of concern and clinical professionalism. The soldiers must have already known her medical background because they deferred to her as she checked her patients.

"I thought you didn't make house calls," Mercer croaked.

"And I was going to give up flying too," she agreed, rolling him to examine the bloody wound in his leg, "but the Italian Navy got their helicopter running again and I knew you'd need a doctor."

"What about Ira and the hostages?"

"They're fine. Ira has already been airlifted to Reykjavik along with Mr. and Mrs. Farquar. Cardinal Peretti was unharmed. Stop worrying about the others." She used scissors from one of the medics' bags to cut away his pants while they concentrated on the Dalai Lama. Her fingers were sure and quick. "This isn't too bad. We found what's left of Greta and the other two Geo-Research guys. Where are Rath and Raeder?"

"Still fighting in hell, I would think," he slurred.

Anika flashed a penlight in his eyes. "Looks like you've got a slight concussion. I'm surprised, thick skull like yours." Her tone was teasing.

"You're losing points for bedside manner."

"How's this then?" And she leaned over to kiss him lightly.

"Does that mean I'm forgiven?"

"No, it means that I understand you a little better." Her eyes softened. As two stretcher bearers approached she whispered, "And I still like what I see."

EPILOGUE

The Secret Service agent examined Mercer's passport and the videocassette in the large envelope he carried before waving him toward the town house. The summer sun beat on the narrow Vienna street, gilding many of the architectural details of the Baroque and Rococo buildings. To Mercer the temperature felt like a sweet caress after so many freezing days. He climbed the couple of steps to the Institute of Applied Research, moving slowly because he'd abandoned his cane in Iceland. An elderly housekeeper opened the door before he knocked. She stepped aside wordlessly but her expression was one of displeasure. Knowing who was already here, Mercer couldn't blame her.

He paused in the entryway. The tumult of books hanging from every wall and teetering on every surface overloaded him like a child at Christmas. He loved books, collected them and treasured them the way others accumulated fine wine, or stamps, or antiques. His collection ran toward old texts on geology and the earth sciences and first editions written by the pioneers in those fields, but any old book gave him a sense of excitement. It was the thrill of knowing that within their covers was information he didn't have, a detail or an observation he'd never made. He loved their unique power to humble and enlighten at the same time.

Seeing the material Anika's grandfather had accumulated reminded him that in a few months he'd be in Paris for an auction of journals written by the French engineers who'd failed in their nineteenth-century attempt to cut a sea-level canal across Panama. He wanted the diary of Baron Godin de Lepinay, the first man to propose the lake-and-lock solution that was eventually built. Mercer had an eccentric friend who was convinced the journal contained the last clue to the whereabouts of a treasure stolen from the Spanish Main and was willing to pay for half the book just to make a copy.

Frau Goetz indicated that everyone was in a dining room at the back of the town house. He heard a pendulum clock chopping at time. Like the rest of the building, the dining room was lined with shelves, and the books once covering the wooden table had been stacked around the room's perimeter. With the door to the garden closed, everything smelled musty and accented with pipe tobacco. On the floor in front of the glass door was an apparatus for creating random sound vibrations to defeat laser microphones. And since the Director of the Central Intelligence Agency had brought a security contingent to this meeting, Mercer assumed the house had already been swept for other types of listening devices.

The DCI, Paul Barnes, was in his late fifties, with gray-streaked hair and a constant expression of irritation. His intense eyes weren't enough to draw attention from the bulbous mole that sat in the crease where his nose joined his face. The mole appeared raw from constant rubbing. Mercer knew Barnes to be a political infighter who spent a great deal of time on damage control in front of the congressional intelligence committees. Uniformly agreed to be the worst of the president's appointments, he didn't have the proper background to effectively head America's premier spy agency and fought tenaciously to maintain his position. Seeing Mercer, his eyes went tight. The animosity between them stemmed from Mercer's successful involvement with several recent crises that Barnes should have handled.

Anika Klein was sitting between two elderly gentlemen in somber ties and worn shirts. One he assumed was her grandfather, Jacob Eisenstadt, and the other his research partner, Theodor Weitzmann. Mercer grinned when he saw her. She leapt to her feet quicker than she'd intended, paused to smooth her black skirt, and crossed to plant a chaste kiss on his cheek. She wore no makeup and was dressed modestly out of respect for her grandfather, yet her attempt to stifle her sexuality only made Mercer more aware of it.

"I can't believe the doctors in Reykjavik released you." She regarded the bruising on Mercer's face and the sunken hollows that hid his eyes.

Only four days had passed since Gunther Rath's defeat. Mercer's left arm was in a sling for a sprained wrist, and he walked with a noticeable limp. "They didn't. I checked myself out as soon as you left Iceland."

"If I'd known you lacked the good sense to stay in the hospital, I wouldn't have come here." She introduced him to Eisenstadt and Weitzmann, who shook his hand in turn.

"It is good to meet you," Eisenstadt rumbled in his accented English. Mercer and he had spoken on the phone a few times when the details of this meeting had been hammered out.

"My pleasure, sir." The elderly researcher matched Mercer's impression. Solid and apparently humorless, he had a formal grace lost to younger generations and a sagacity that commanded instant respect.

Frau Goetz put coffee and a glass of water at a place open for Mercer. He caught her scrutiny and her approving nod to Anika. Anika shook her head slightly, then smiled before making a slight gesture with her hand as if to say maybe. She blushed when she noted that Mercer had seen the exchange.

Barnes sighed. "Since we're all here, we can get this over with." He'd made no gesture to greet Mercer properly.

Thanks to Ira Lasko's efforts from his hospital room in Reykjavik, Mercer had learned that Barnes had spent a very long afternoon in the White House. The chief executive was furious with Barnes for how he'd handled this affair, and Mercer understood that Barnes was under orders to make any concession necessary to set things right. He'd even been forced to Vienna to accommodate Eisenstadt and Weitzmann rather than hold this meeting in Washington.

Essentially, Barnes was here to agree to whatever Mercer asked for. Mercer would have flaunted his control over the DCI had he not gained some perspective in the past few days. Instead, he savored knowing he held all the cards and allowed Barnes a measure of dignity.

"Mr. Barnes, I want to thank you for agreeing to come here today," Mercer began, perpetuating the illusion that the DCI still had a choice, "and I especially want to acknowledge your efforts camouflaging what happened aboard the *Sea Empress*. I sense your hand in the cover story about a terrorist attack in which all the hijackers were killed by the ship's security personnel."

"It fit close enough to the facts to convince the media," Barnes acknowledged. If he was relieved that Mercer wasn't rubbing in his errand-boy status, he didn't show it. "We effectively blacked out information about the fighting at the Blue Lagoon and the Svartsengi power plant, saying it was a pressure explosion that rained debris on the adjoining spa."

"Your government will pay to repair the facilities?" Anika asked.

"Plus a little extra for the families of the fishermen murdered in Grindavik." Barnes nodded. "That's how we got the cooperation of the local authorities."

"That takes care of those on the periphery," Mercer said. "But there are a number of people more directly involved who can't be silenced so easily."

"That's why I'm here." Barnes folded his hands on the table, preparing himself for the negotiations. "To discuss the terms for your cooperation."

"This won't be a discussion, Mr. Barnes." Mercer's tone sharpened, reminding Barnes of his role. "A dozen innocent people are dead because of this, and you have an obligation to them and their survivors. I've compiled a list." He still suffered from the emotional hangover of writing the names, especially scarred by Elisebet Rosmunder's, who would have been alive if he hadn't spoken with her. "Before we get to specifics there are a few things I want to know first. Beginning with Charlie Bryce and the Surveyor's Society and their relationship to the CIA."

Barnes's eyes swept the others around the table. "This isn't the time or the place to talk about that. If there is a relationship, which I'm not saying there is, it would be classified."

Mercer ignored Barnes's security concerns. "Until we're all satisfied, there aren't going to be any secrets. Anika knows how I got involved in this expedition, so she's already drawn some inferences. I've also made Mr. Eisenstadt and Mr. Weitzmann aware that I was approached by the Society to help Ira Lasko, one of your agents. Do you want to leave us believing that the Surveyor's Society is a CIA front?"

Although this was a minor point, Barnes still resented sharing anything. "They aren't a front. The Surveyor's Society does"—he searched for the right word—"favors for us. You may recall Bryce's speech about the three kinds of explorers—real ones, armchair ones, and those who pay others to explore for them. Let's just say that the CIA falls into the latter category when we need certain deniable operations carried out."

"And you pay them?"

"Why do you think every school in the nation pays twice the normal subscription price for their magazine?"

"A black budget subsidy?"

"Exactly. By the way Ira doesn't work directly for the CIA. He was seconded to us for this mission from the White House."

"He already told me. In fact, he's trying to talk me into accepting a job there. Special science advisor to the president or something." Mercer wasn't sure if he'd accept, but he was honored.

"If it's any consolation," Barnes added, "Bryce wasn't too pleased when I had him recruit you."

"I'll deal with Charlie at another time," Mercer said. "We're here to discuss what to do about each other."

"And to handle the final disposition of the remaining Pandora box and an icon belonging to a Russian priest. They represent the last link to an unprecedented discovery. As a scientist, you must know the Pandora fragments could contain untold knowledge about our universe and its creation."

Barnes tried to press his point with a hard stare, but Mercer remained unfazed. "I doubt you believe in science for science's sake, Mr. Barnes."

"Where are the fragments?" Barnes leaned across the table in another effort to gain some psychological leverage. "When Ira Lasko was debriefed in the hospital he said he didn't know."

"He lied." Because of the prior arrangements, the old Nazi hunters had brought their small television and VCR into the dining room. Mercer slid the cassette into the tape slot and waited while Frau Goetz pressed the correct buttons to bring up the picture. "This footage was taken yesterday."

The image on the screen was bouncy and the audio was filled with a deep thrumming rattle. The watchers quickly realized that the video had been taken aboard a speeding helicopter. The chopper's side door was closed so the camera panned down through the scratchy window. A thousand feet below, the cold north Atlantic surged with its unending rhythm. They were high enough that the whitecaps looked like bits of string. The frame jumped and suddenly Mercer was shown sitting on the bench seat in the rear of the cargo chopper.

"Who took this?" Barnes asked sharply.

"Ira wanted to be with us but couldn't get out of the hospital. Father Anatoly Vatutin ran the camera,"

Mercer answered before the video image of himself bent forward to strip a tarp off a box sitting next to the door. A golden reflection filled the dim interior of the chopper. Resting on the only remaining Pandora box was another glittering relic, the last of Rasputin's icons.

Jacob Eisenstadt grunted when he saw the box. Although he'd already been warned what was on the tape, his eyes were wet, doubtlessly thinking about what the box represented—the origin of that gold and all those who'd died filling it.

Barnes sucked in a quick breath. He glanced at Mercer, trying to understand what was happening behind his gray eyes. Mercer gave a triumphant smile that told Barnes everything. "You didn't."

The tape made Mercer's answer unnecessary. Father Vatutin set aside the camera to open the cargo door and then refocused on Mercer as he kicked the heavy icon out the door. The camera image followed the antique as it pinwheeled toward the sea, swallowed by distance before it was swallowed by the water. Barnes went pale with impotant rage. Next, the tape showed Mercer bracing his legs against the seat supports and levering his back against the two-hundred-pound Pandora box.

Vatutin had tightened his focus on the swastika adorning the side of the Pandora box, tracking it as Mercer pushed it to the door. Pausing with the box on the edge of oblivion, Mercer addressed the camera, shouting over the wind and the rotor's steady beat.

"The problem with any scientific discovery is that, once something is known, it can't be unlearned. We can't forget how to make a nuclear bomb or poison gas, nor can we prevent the propagation of that knowledge. To use a cliché, once the genie's out of the bottle, it can't be put back. Well, this is one genie that I'm not going to let escape. The military applications of Pandora radiation far outweigh any potential scientific use. A Russian madman realized that a hundred years ago and hid the truth until a German madman nearly succeeded in unleashing Pandora's destructive potential one again. Now it's my turn to end this once and for all."

"What gives you the right?" Barnes shouted at Mercer.

"No one gave it to me." Mercer's voice was steel. "Thanks to what you've put me through in the past weeks, I've earned it."

Everyone's focus returned to the television as the chopper banked over, aiding Mercer's final effort to heave the Pandora box into the rolling swells far from where anyone would find it. Again Father Vatutin, one of the two remaining members of the Brotherhood of Satan's Fist, videotaped the object of his lifelong quest until it was gone. From the helicopter's altitude, the splash appeared puny, an anticlimactic end to such a malignant artifact. The screen turned to electronic snow as the drama came to an end.

Eisenstadt reached over to shut off the television. "Thank you, Dr. Mercer, for showing me that. And thank you for including me in your decision to destroy the last of the gold I had been searching for. Once Anatoly Vatutin explained that it was his group in Russia feeding Theodor and me information about the shipment and told me what the Nazis had used it for, there was no other alternative. The financial loss to living Jews is painful but unavoidable."

Mercer acknowledged the compliment but continued to study Barnes, sensing the machinations already churning in his head. "If you're thinking that you can return to the site where the rotor-stat went down and retrieve the rest of the boxes, forget it. I can't stop you from recovering them, but I know every top scientist you would use to analyze the meteorite fragments, including the people at Sandia and Livermore labs. The instant I find anyone is working on Pandora, I'm going to bury you."

"Is that the price of your silence?" Barnes knew the threat wasn't an idle one.

Nodding slowly, Mercer was too emotionally

drained to summon outrage at the DCI's intrinsic duplicity. He'd expected no less.

"And what about the others? What will their cooperation cost?"

Jacob Eisenstadt pointed a gnarled finger like an Old Testament prophet. "You must know that receiving our cooperation does not mean you also get our approval." His voice thundered. "However, if Kohl's entire board of directors is replaced and the company agrees to pay double what the Jewish reconciliation commission is asking for, Theodor and I will let this matter drop."

Barnes rocked back from the verbal broadside but answered quickly. "The German government has been cooperative so far. The *Njoerd* has been impounded and those crewmen loyal to Rath will be prosecuted. The innocent sailors, members of Geo-Research from before Kohl bought the company, are being released after signing secrecy agreements. In order to keep this as quiet as possible, I see no reason why they won't compel Kohl to agree to your request."

Though he'd received the answer he wanted, the old Nazi hunter didn't look happy. Mercer doubted he'd ever be truly at peace.

"Is that it?" Barnes prompted into the silence.

"Not quite." Mercer pulled a sheet of paper from his pocket. "Hilda Brandt wants enough money to start her own restaurant in Hamburg. Once he's recovered from his injuries, Erwin Puhl wants a permanent staff job at McMurdo Station in Antarctica to continue his weather research. Father Vatutin is asking for the funding to rebuild a particular church in St. Petersburg. Marty Bishop disappeared as soon as the *Sea Empress* put in to Reykjavik. His fight's with his father, not you, so I doubt he'll make any demands."

"What about you, Dr. Klein? What do you want?"

She gave Mercer a significant look. "I'm all set, thanks."

They spent a further twenty minutes hammering out details, Barnes capitulating on each and every point.

After Barnes left the Institute, Anika invited Mercer out for a drink, asking him to give her a moment to say good-bye to her grandfather. He was left waiting for fifteen minutes.

"Ready," she announced when she came out of the dining room, a large bag over her shoulder.

Outside, the afternoon light made her hair glisten like polished anthracite. She walked with an infectious bounce that Mercer wished he could keep up with. He was thinking that maybe he shouldn't have abandoned the cane given to him in Iceland.

"Seemed like a long time to say good-bye. We're only going to a bar, aren't we?"

She gave him a mocking look. "You're not very bright, are you?

"Not usually, no."

"I have to be back to work in a week and I won't have any vacations for a while."

"Rededicating yourself to medicine?"

"I've learned that playing at danger isn't the same as actually experiencing it. There will be no more rock-climbing expeditions. I'm returning to the hospital and kissing my boss's backside until my lips go numb. I've had all the excitement I want."

"My sentiments exactly. But what's that got to do with getting a drink?"

Anika stopped them on the street. He stood a head taller than her, but the force of her personality made the physical difference all but disappear. There was a mischievous gleam in her eyes. "I'm in the mood for wine, and a certain American geologist I know promised me a couple of days in the Loire Valley. I was saying good-bye to my grandfather because you're taking me to France."

"I am?" Mercer was both stunned and delighted. He had already booked an evening flight back to the States.

"You are." She started walking again, taking his hand and turning away so he couldn't see the flush rushing up her throat. "Do you remember how I told you I get drunk on a single glass of wine? I have to warn you that, when I'm tipsy, I usually get aroused too."

Mercer's heart tripped and suddenly his aches didn't bother him so much. When he found his voice, he stammered, "I consider myself warned."

They went off to restore each other's spirit so that at least this one episode wouldn't haunt their dreams. And after their first night together in a quaint guest house perfumed by vineyards, they knew it wouldn't.

Author's Notes

I've tried to blend a great deal of history into this story and have taken some license to make it work, but maybe not as much as you'd think. Project Iceworm was a real operation, but their Camp Century was built in 1960 about 150 miles from Thule on Greenland's west coast. The story Erwin Puhl tells about Hitler's operation on Rugen Island is true. The real U-1062 was a cargo sub that was sunk in the Atlantic after delivering a load of torpedoes to Indonesia for the Nazi's *Monsun* boats, their secret Indian Ocean Wolf Pack.

As for Rasputin and the truth behind the Tunguska explosion? The mystic had been exiled from St. Petersburg at the time I place him near the explosion site. Many eyewitnesses did report that a portion of the object that slammed into the Russian taiga continued on in a northwesterly direction. Leonid Kulik was the first scientist to study the area and he did die as a prisoner of war. To date, science has yet to come up with a full explanation of that mysterious cataclysm because no physical debris has ever been found. So who's to say what it was? Comet? Asteroid? Spaceship? Or the final misery to spill from Pandora's box?

Acknowledgments

Pandora's Curse wouldn't have been possible without the help of many people. First is Bob Diforio—agent, friend, and constant motivator. For research, I need to thank Thorsteinn Jonsson at the Svartsengi geothermal generating station and Magnea Gudmundsdottir at the Blue Lagoon Spa in Iceland as well as all those I met during my days in Greenland. Another thanks goes to Dr. Dennis Grusenmeyer; to Kim Haimann for help negotiating Munich's suburbs; and to Angelo and Remo Pizzagalli for sharing their stories of excavating one of the P-38 Lightnings from the "Lost Squadron" that crashed in Greenland in 1942.

At NAL, my special thanks goes to Doug Grad, my editor. Like a jeweler who can turn a lump of stone into a gem, Doug never fails to expertly polish a rough manuscript into a finished book.